The Heir to Rhodes Castle

PATRICK WETENHALL

authorHOUSE®

AuthorHouse™ UK
1663 Liberty Drive
Bloomington, IN 47403 USA
www.authorhouse.co.uk
Phone: 0800.197.4150

Published by AuthorHouse 05/12/2016

ISBN: 978-1-5049-9542-9 (sc)
ISBN: 978-1-5049-9543-6 (hc)
ISBN: 978-1-5049-9541-2 (e)

CHAPTER ONE

Eight months after his wedding Jim Sandy was finding, more or less, that marriage was indeed turning out to be the blissful experience that he had hoped it would be. There had, of course, been a few times when they had quarrelled, but these petty altercations had never amounted to anything of any significance.

On one very warm morning at the end of April he and Susan were setting out their deck chairs on the Private Lawn of Rhodes Castle. At breakfast that morning Jim had been reminded of something which had happened on their honeymoon in the Western Isles. He and Susan had both been delighted to find in the post a postcard showing a view over Stornoway Harbour; it was a place they remembered well from their voyage in Susan's yacht, Osprey. The card had been sent by their friends, Martin and Anne Himmel, who allowed Osprey to be berthed at their boathouse in Maryport in Cumbria. Jim had at once been reminded of Margaret MacAllen, Samantha's cousin, whom they had met at the Lewis Hotel in Stornoway. Jim did not want to be reminded of Margaret MacAllen. She was an attractive young woman; indeed she was far too attractive to Jim now that he was happily married to Susan. As they walked together across the Private Lawn towards the summer-house Jim was remembering that postcard, but suddenly an image of Margaret flashed momentarily in his mind' eye. Impatiently he dismissed it from his mind. He did not want to think about Margaret.

"Isn't this delightful?" said Susan, as she and Jim each took a deck chair from a pile of deck chairs inside the summer-house. "It's as warm as a good May day today!"

"And it *is* May Day tomorrow!" said Jim happily.

"As I was just going to say myself! Where shall we have our chairs, darling? Just here?"

"Here would be fine, I should think," said Jim. He sat down in his deck chair, having adjusted it to a good angle to lie back comfortably. "Yes, this is fine!"

"Mmmm...!" said Susan as she sank comfortably into her deck chair. "Doesn't that cherry blossom look simply gorgeous, seen against the sky, looking up like this?"

Jim, like Susan, was staring lazily up into the sky, where a diffuse cloud of white blossom contrasted with an almost mesmeric effect against the burning blue of the sky. "So blue, and so white!" he said dreamily.

"Positively Japanese!" murmured Susan.

Yes, it is like Japanese cherry blossom, thought Jim, knowing well what his wife was thinking. Now, however, his thoughts were moving in a different direction. He had all but forgotten about Margaret MacAllen, but now other memories, almost painfully sweet memories came flooding into his mind in a few minutes of silence in which the only sound to be heard was the buzzing of bees around the cherry blossom. He was remembering his last morning at Rhodes Castle before he had left to return home to Cockermouth, following his dismissal by Lord Dalmane, Susan's former husband. That morning had, in a way, been very like this morning. On that morning, three years ago, he and Susan had been sitting almost exactly where they were now sitting, in deck chairs just below the octagonal wooden summer-house in a corner of the Private Lawn. That other morning, too, had been beautifully warm and sunny, although it had been slightly earlier in the month. On that day, as on this day, they had been struck by the etherial beauty of the cherry blossom seen floating just above their heads against the background of the bright blue sky. The similarities between the two mornings were, in fact, so striking, as Jim now realized, that it was tempting to think that no time at all could have passed between them. The circumstances of the two mornings were uncannily alike - and yet they were completely different. The similarities were merely superficial, for everything had changed since that April morning of three years ago. Yes, Jim said to himself rather sadly, everything's changed now... and the magic of that day has gone! It's gone for ever; I can never get it back...

"Ah!" he sighed slowly, opening his eyes, which he had closed while he had been trying to recall his feelings on that momentous morning, the morning of his farewell to Susan.

"Darling?" said Susan, half turning her head to look round at him. She had been gazing up dreamily at the blossom. "Are you all right, darling? Not comfortable?"

"Oh, yes, very comfortable. But I was just thinking, Sue, darling... well, I was just remembering, actually."

"Ah!" said Susan. "I think I know what you were remembering!"

"Well?"

"Were you remembering how we sat down here that day when I had to leave you at lunch time, and then you had to leave us the next morning because John had had to dismiss you?"

"Yes, that was it; I was remembering that morning."

"It brings it all back, doesn't it?" said Susan dreamily. "You know, it was a morning just like this, wasn't it?"

"It was indeed!"

"You know, darling, we were both thinking at the time that there was something about that morning that was... well, very special - very precious. It was very precious because we had to say good-bye."

"Yes, and because we had so little time left that morning to be together, just the two of us, in this lovely garden!"

"So little time!" echoed Susan dreamily. "And then it was time for our parting... going our separate ways."

There was another little pause in their conversation, and then Jim spoke again.

"Yes, I was thinking about that time, actually."

"Time?" said Susan, glancing at her watch as she remembered something else. "How do you mean?"

"Well, I was thinking about this morning, and us being here just like we were on that other morning, and everything seeming to be so much the same today as it did that other time: the same sun, the same cherry blossom over our heads, and us sitting here like we did that other time, three years ago. And then I thought suddenly that it was rather as if no time at all had passed since that other morning."

"H'm... in a way, I suppose, it is like that - as if time had stopped - but a lot's changed since then, hasn't it? But do you know, darling, isn't it about time (talking about time) that Sam was out here with the coffee?"

"So it is!" said Jim, suddenly looking down towards the place where the little path from the footbridge over the brook emerged from the bushes. Was that a sound of footsteps somewhere down there?

I wonder where she's got to?"

"She's here!" called a voice, and at the same moment they saw Samantha emerge from the screening bushes, carrying a tray on which there were three cups and saucers, a coffee jug, a milk jug, and a plate of biscuits.

"Oh, bother!" said Susan. "We've forgotten to put out the table!"

"I'll get it!" said Jim, at once springing to his feet. A moment later he came out of the summer-house carrying a light-weight picnic table. It folded up when not in use, and stood on a tripod. He set it down on the lawn, opened out the top, and bolted it into place so that Samantha could set down her tray on it.

"Thank you, Jim!" she said. He was already hurrying back into the summer-house to fetch a third chair.

"Sorry about the delay," said Samantha. "The telephone rang just as I was about to bring the coffee out, so I took the message. It was Mrs. Conner. She says she's sorry, she can't manage tomorrow, but she'd like to come today instead."

"But what time today?" asked Susan.

"About twelve o' clock. I hope I did right, Sue, when I said I thought it would be all right for her to come at twelve o' clock. I said I'd have to ask you first, and then I told her that if you said it *wasn't* all right we'd let her know straight away."

"Otherwise she is definitely coming at midday today?"

"Yes, that's right, she's coming at midday unless we ring her now to say 'Don't come'. Thanks a lot, Jim. I'll have my chair just there beside Sue."

"Well, that's fine, Sam, as it's only five past eleven now. Yes, that's all right - you needn't worry about it at all!"

"That's good!" said Samantha, settling herself in her deckchair and giving Jim an encouraging smile. The three chairs were now drawn up round the table, with Susan's chair in the middle. "I thought it would be all right," she continued.

"It is!" said Susan cheerfully. "Now then, let's have our coffee - and then we'll have to find Jean Grookes to let her know - but there'll be plenty of time for that before twelve o' clock." She was already pouring out coffee into the cups.

Jim was feeling rather worried as Susan passed him his coffee, and he only managed a momentary smile as he thanked her for it. The fact was that the news that Samantha had brought was, for him, decidedly disturbing news. He had not yet met Rachel Conner, but he had heard from Samantha that she was a very attractive woman.

That was all very well – in a way it was exciting to know that very soon he would surely be meeting her – but he knew only too well that attractive women were his most serious weakness: he was far too easily attracted to beautiful women, usually with more or less disastrous consequences.

Rachel Conner was going to be the new Guide of Rhodes Castle. Susan had already interviewed her briefly, and had been happy enough to offer her the job to take the place of Jean Grookes, who was retiring because of ill health. For several weeks while she had been too ill to work Jim had been standing in for Mrs. Grookes, back once again in his old job as Guide of Rhodes Castle. Then they had heard that Mrs. Grookes was giving her notice. Being the Guide once again, even if only on a temporary basis (while he also continued his duties as Estate Manager) had afforded Jim a good deal of happy nostalgia, but when Susan had asked him whether he wanted to continue permanently as the Guide, as before, he had declined.

"Darling," she had said, "it's entirely up to you to do *whatever* you like to do here!"

"But, Sue, darling," he had answered, "it isn't really me in charge here – it's you! I'm only the Estate Manager."

"But that's why *you* should make the appointments, darling – if you want to." Then Jim had told her that, in any case, he thought that it would be best for him to stay just as he was, the Estate Manager; and so a possible quarrel had been averted.

"My word, it's really gorgeous out here!" said Samantha, when she had taken a first sip from her cup of coffee.

"It's perfect!" agreed Susan. "Darling, shall we tell Sam about what we were discussing just before she came here?"

"Oh, yes, let's tell her!" said Jim, opening his eyes with a start. He had been trying unsuccessfully to re-establish the happy mood of his daydream.

"No need to, if you'd rather not," said Samantha, but she managed to say it in a way which clearly indicated that she was very interested to know what they had been discussing.

"Oh, but we've got no secrets from you, Sam, dear," said Susan, "have we, darling?" (Jim nodded his agreement.) "We were just saying how much it reminded us, being out here, of that morning when we sat here, Jim and I, on the day when we had to say good-bye, when I went off after lunch to stay for a few days with Norma Beck at Broadstone."

"And you, Jim, set off in the fog the next morning to return home to Cockermouth. Yes, I was reminded of that morning too."

"Sam, dear, was there anything of any importance in the post this morning?" asked Susan, suddenly remembering something else.

"Oh, yes, so there was!" said Samantha. "There's a letter from Cockermouth." She pulled a letter from a pocket of her apron, and handed it to Susan.

"Oh, good, it must be Dad's answer at last to say when they're coming," said Jim.

"You'd better open it, darling," said Susan, handing the letter on to Jim.

He glanced at the envelope before opening it, and saw that it was addressed to "Mr. and Mrs. Sandy" in his father's handwriting. He opened it at once, and took out the following letter:-

140 Lorton Road,
Cockermouth.

Wednesday, 28th April 65

My dear Susan and Jim,

Jackie and I would be delighted to come down to stay for a few days at Rhodes Castle. We can come, as you suggested, on Friday week, May 7th, but will ring you up a day or two before that to confirm arrangements definitely, and let you know just when, and at what station we should be arriving. I think it will have to be a stay of just three days with you as I have to be back at work at the mine at least by the following Wednesday, so that'll mean travelling back on Tuesday. But we're really looking forward to coming down at last and seeing Rhodes Castle and its wonderful grounds for ourselves! Things are going really well at the mine now – or, I should say "mines", as we're interested in three mines now. The results of our first assays on Jackie's New Level at the Cobalt Mine look very promising for zinc, and might almost be commercially viable, although we don't know about that yet: further tests will be necessary. Then we were up at Carrock Mine the other day – meeting Professor Wadden by arrangement, and doing a bit of prospecting – and that evening we came back with something rather special in the mineral line! I must bring it along to show you when we come south, if I remember to.

Well, Jim, that's all I've time for now, so I'll have to close.

All's well here, as I hope it is with you.
With our love and best wishes, A.S.

"Dad says they can come Friday week," said Jim as soon as he had read the first sentence of the letter.

"Oh, good!" said Susan. "I'm so glad they can come!"

Jim was hastily reading through the rest of the letter, his eyes skimming over the details to take in only the main drift of it. Then he handed it over to Susan.

"Do you think I could read it aloud, darling?" she asked.

"Yes, do," said Jim.

"If you want me to know what's in it," said Samantha.

"What's Jackie's New Level?" asked Susan when she had finished reading the letter aloud.

"It's a new level that we've started in the old Cobalt Mine up in the fells, above Dad's Leadthwaite Mine; he calls it 'Jackie's Level' because she thought there'd be enough zinc up there to be worth mining."

"And there is?"

"Yes, there must be; that's what he means by the first results of the assays from that level being very promising. But I wonder what he can mean by bringing back 'something rather special' from Carrock Mine?"

"Well, darling, it must be something that he thinks you would find especially interesting. What do they mostly get from that mine anyway?"

"Well," said Jim, "I think it's been closed for a few years now; they don't get anything from there now, but they used to mine wolfram there."

"And your Dad's thinking of re-opening it to mine it again?"

"Yes, he is thinking of possibly re-opening part of it to mine wolfram again - if the results of preliminary prospecting look good enough."

"Perhaps that's what he means by coming back with 'something rather special in the mineral line'. What is wolfram, anyway?"

"It's an ore of tungsten," said Jim; "iron and manganese tungstate, I think. Anyway they used to mine a lot of it there. I expect that's what the old men started the mine for in the first place."

"The old men?"

"Oh, that's what they always call the miners of long ago; the books always refer to them as the 'old men'."

"Well, it all sounds most fascinating to me!" said Susan. "You must take me to see this Carrock Mine, darling, the next time we come up to stay with your Dad at Cockermouth."

"I shall; I most definitely shall!" said Jim eagerly. "I'm sure you'll find it fascinating even if we don't find anything interesting in the mineral line, as Dad evidently has."

Susan took a mouthful of coffee, and glanced round to her right, where she saw that Samantha was lying back in her deck chair, gazing lazily up at the cherry blossom, just as she and Jim had been doing.

"Sorry, Sam," she said, "I'm afraid we've been boring you with all this talk of mineralogy."

"That's quite all right!" said Samantha calmly.

"I don't know anything about it, you know - except for what Jim's told me."

"And I don't know anything about it at all!" said Samantha. "But - to change the subject - when are the Padgates coming, Sue? Is it tomorrow?"

"Yes, tomorrow evening they're due to arrive."

"By car or by train?" asked Jim.

"Oh, by car, so we won't need to meet them at the station," said Susan. "But you see, darling, this means that we will be able to have a dinner party for your Dad and Jackie with Aunt Nora and Uncle Geoffrey as they're staying on for over a week, Aunt Nora said."

"Oh, good! Dad and Jackie should be very pleased about that, I should think. But which day would be best for a dinner party, Sue?"

"What about Sunday - a week on Sunday?"

"Excellent!"

"Very well, we'll do a dinner party for the guests on Sunday week. But shall we ask anyone else? The Becks, perhaps?"

"Why not?" said Jim. "Yes, let's ask them."

""Well, darling, we will, but it is rather short notice; I don't know whether they'll be able to come."

"I haven't seen the Becks for ages," said Jim. "In fact, I don't think I've seen either of them since that time when we all stayed with your Great Aunt Alice at Knebworth, before you brought me here for the first time."

"Ah, yes, when you came down here to be our Guide. Well, darling, we'll try them. I'll write to Norma today."

Presently Samantha looked at her wrist-watch.

"Don't forget the time, Sue," she said. "It's nearly a quarter to twelve."

"Good heavens!" exclaimed Susan, opening her eyes with a jerk.

Like Jim, at her side, she had been gently indulging herself in very pleasant daydreams while reclining lazily in her deckchair. "So it is!" she added, glancing at her own watch and hauling herself into an upright position on the chair. "Come on, darling, we must go in now to meet Rachel. She may well arrive a bit earlier than twelve o' clock, you know, and it wouldn't do for us to be still out here being thoroughly lazy in our deckchairs."

"Of course not!" agreed Jim, who had already jumped to his feet, and was folding up his chair.

"Where do you want to meet her?" asked Samantha.

"Oh, well, I think we might as well meet in the Green Drawing Room," said Susan, "unless, that is, we meet outside first. And look here, Sam, you'd better come with us. We might as well offer her a drink of something first while we talk, and then we must go and try to find Jean Grookes."

"All right, I'll come if you like. But I thought that Mrs. Grookes was still off work?"

"No, she's just back today, and the idea is that she'll work with Rachel all next week so that she'll get properly used to the job before Jean finally leaves us at the end of next week. Oh, thank you, darling!" Jim had just taken her deckchair back into the summer-house, and had now come back to collect the other two chairs.

Samantha already had the tray in her hands with all the coffee things gathered onto it.

"Shall I bring the table?" said Susan. "Right, oh, Sam, we'll catch you up in a minute."

Samantha was already setting off to walk back to the Castle, the tray in her hands. A minute later Jim and Susan, hand in hand, were following her after Susan had closed and locked the door of the summer-house.

CHAPTER TWO

As they were walking round to the front of the Castle Jim was experiencing a strange mixture of thoughts and emotions. What he had heard from Samantha about Rachel Conner being a very attractive woman was certainly disturbing; yet at the same time he was aware of an eager anticipation of the meeting which was about to happen, an anticipation which definitely amounted to a feeling of rising excitement. Heavens! he thought. I certainly hope that Sam was only bluffing when she told me that I'd find Rachel a very attractive woman! I just *don't want* any more excitement of that sort in my life now that I'm married to my darling, Sue!

They were coming round to the front of the Castle, rather than following their accustomed and shorter route through the archway into the bailey and the back door as Susan was quite expecting Rachel Conner to arrive somewhat earlier than the arranged time of twelve o' clock. "It would be handier, really, if we could meet Rachel by the front door when she arrives," she said, "than having Jack show her into the Hall first, and then having to fetch her through to the Drawing Room to meet us." (Jack was the butler.) Jim had at once agreed with this proposal, but he did not have much time after that to suffer on account of the contradictory emotions he was experiencing. As they rounded the south-western corner of the Castle, to come out onto the broad sweep of gravel at the front of the Castle, a small green car came into view, moving slowly up the drive from the direction of the Inner Lodge.

"Good!" said Susan. "Here she is! I thought she'd probably come a bit early, as she seems very keen to meet the rest of us."

Jim was still holding her hand, but he was afraid by now that Susan might well be able to detect his rising excitement through an increase in pressure from his hand. I mustn't let Sue know what thoughts are going through my head right now! he told himself, wishing that he could let go his grasp of her hand; but at the same time he was being careful, he thought, not to vary the pressure of his hand in any way. Nevertheless, as the car passed the ponds on either side of the drive, he was doing his best to catch a glimpse of the driver to get a first impression of what she looked like. In this, however, he was unsuccessful as the car was still too far away.

They saw the car stop by the steps leading up to the front door, and at the same moment they saw the door opened from inside, and there was Jack, the butler, welcoming Mrs. Conner as she stepped out of her car. Susan now let go Jim's hand as she slightly quickened her steps.

Jim was feeling very glad that she did not seem to have noticed anything unusual through the touch of their hands.

Half a minute later they had all met by the front door.

"Good morning, Lady Dalmane," said Rachel Conner, extending her hand to Susan.

"Good morning, Mrs. Conner!" said Susan cheerfully, shaking her hand. "This is my husband, Jim."

It sounded so wonderful to Jim to be introduced by Susan as "my husband" that he hardly noticed Rachel Conner smiling at him as they shook hands and exchanged a "How-do-you-do?" A moment later, indeed, as Rachel Conner was introduced to Samantha, he was feeling that his introduction to the new Guide had been decidedly an anticlimax. It's all right, he thought, she isn't beautiful after all - thank heavens!

His first impression was of a small, rather ordinary-looking, middle-aged woman - almost a rather drab-looking woman - with shoulder-length blonde hair and greenish-brown eyes. In these two features she bore a superficial resemblance to Samantha; but Jim, looking at the two women together as they shook hands, saw that in fact Rachel looked altogether different to Samantha. Was it just that Samantha was taller than Rachel, looked obviously younger than her, and had larger and perhaps paler eyes? Or was there, perhaps, some more fundamental difference between the appearance of these two? But there was no time to wonder now as Susan, having dismissed the butler, was inviting the new Guide to come into Rhodes Castle.

"I know you'll be wanting to be shown exactly what your Guide job will involve," said Susan as they entered the Hall, "but I don't think we'll be able to meet Jean Grookes until one o' clock - that's right, isn't it, darling?"

"Yes," confirmed Jim, "she should be down at the Visitor Centre by one o' clock to start conducting the second tour of the day."

"Right; so, in the meanwhile, I thought that we might as well sit down in the Green Drawing Room again, and perhaps have a drink, while Jim can tell you something about how the work is organized." Susan had given Mrs. Conner her initial interview in the Green Drawing Room while Jim had been busy standing in for Mrs. Grookes.

"Thank you very much, Lady Dalmane," said Rachel Conner politely.

"You'd better come with us now, Sam, to see about the drinks," said Susan. Samantha had been standing to one side unobtrusively while her mistress had been talking, but now, as Susan lead the way down the passage, she took up the rear, walking behind Jim. "Oh!" she continued as she opened the door of the Green Drawing Room.

"I should have asked you first, Mrs. Conner, how long can you stay here with us today?

Perhaps you'll need to hurry back home soon?"

"Oh, no, that's quite all right, Lady Dalmane; I won't need to go home at least until three o' clock - or I could stay probably until about four o' clock, if you like?"

"But what about lunch? Do please have a seat, Mrs. Conner." Susan indicated an armchair for her guest.

"Thank you very much, but I shan't really need any lunch today as I had a snack at twenty past eleven, just before I left home to come here."

"Well, then, have a drink, won't you - tea or coffee? If you'll excuse us, though, we won't have a drink with you as we've just finished our cups of coffee. Or would you rather have sherry?"

"I'd love sherry, thank you!"

"Dry or sweet?"

"I'd like dry sherry, please."

"And a glass of cream sherry for you, darling?"

Jim preferred the strong, sweet taste of cream sherry to the dryness of Fino sherry. "Yes, please!" he said.

Samantha slipped out of the room to fetch the drinks.

*

Five minutes later Susan, Jim, and Rachel Conner were sitting in the Green Drawing Room with their drinks while Jim was telling Rachel more about what her work as Guide would entail. Samantha had left them to return to her other duties.

"You'll find that it can be a very busy job at times," said Jim, "and as you can't be everywhere at once to keep an eye on people we have decided that, starting from this summer, there are going to be two assistant guides to work under you; so they should be able to keep an eye on people while you are doing the conducted tours. When did we say that those two new assistant guides were to start from, Sue? June, wasn't it?"

"Yes, it was in June," said Susan. "But we'll let you know more about that later, Mrs. Conner."

"Oh, yes, that'll be quite all right," said Mrs. Conner.

While they were talking Jim was trying all the time, mainly by a purely subconscious effort, to avoid eye contact with Rachel Conner.

This, of course, was not easy for him as for most of the time he was speaking directly to her, telling her in some detail about the work of the Guide at Rhodes Castle. However, he was more or less aware, all the time that he was speaking, of an inner voice urging great caution on him in the matter of glancing at Rachel in the presence of his wife, Susan.

"So how long does a tour last?" asked Rachel Conner presently. "Presumably there is a fixed timetable which the Guide is supposed to keep to, and a fixed itinerary for the tours?"

"Oh, yes, indeed there's a timetable which the Guide is supposed to keep to, more or less. The complete tour should last for two hours with a quarter of an hour's break in the middle; so, you see, the ten o' clock tour goes around the Castle grounds until eleven o' clock, finishing up at the Visitor Centre for people to have refreshments and go to the toilet; and then we go round the inside of the Castle - the rooms that are open to the public - from about eleven-fifteen until midday. And that's it; the minibus takes the people back from the Castle to the Visitor Centre, and the tour is over."

"And the one o' clock and half past three tours follow the same pattern, I suppose?"

"Exactly so; and as for the itinerary, that is more or less fixed too, always starting by visiting the church, and going on from there as Mrs. Grookes will show you. But sometimes, for one reason or another, you may find that the tour is getting behind schedule; and then the thing to do - if you feel that it's necessary - is to leave out part of the tour."

"At the Guide's discretion?"

"Just so: it's always ultimately a matter of your own discretion as to where you take your party, and how long you stay in each place; but remembering that the important thing, really, is that you should always aim to get the tour finished at the right time. But don't worry about it, Mrs. Conner; it's not really as difficult as it sounds by any means. I'm sure you'll soon get used to the routine of it."

"Yes, indeed, I'm sure you will," said Susan. "So the idea is that Jean Grookes will do the whole tour with you as the apprentice, as it were, this afternoon, finishing at three o' clock. And then, if you like, you can come and do a few more tours in that way until you feel confident enough to take the people round on your own."

"Thank you very much, Lady Dalmane," said Mrs. Conner politely.

About half an hour later Jim, Susan, and Rachel Conner, having finished their drinks and discussion in the Green Drawing Room, came to the white gate at the bottom of the inner drive. The gate, as was almost always the case, stood open, but there was a notice beside the gate with the legend: "PRIVATE. Visitors By Appointment and Guided Tours Only beyond this point". It was five minutes to one. Beyond the drive gate and the notice they could see people milling around, waiting for the One o' clock tour to begin. Jim's eyes were already searching for Mrs. Grookes in the crowd, but a moment later he spotted her standing close to the Castle minibus; this minibus was used to carry the tour parties between the Visitor Centre and Rhodes Church (a distance of about half a mile) in order to save time.

"Ladies and gentlemen, would you take your seats in the bus now, please, if you want to come on the next guided tour. We shall be leaving in about four minutes from now." They heard the Guide shouting her order to the assembled crowd.

"I'd better hurry on, and get in with them!" said Mrs. Conner. She and Jim and Susan had already quickened their steps, but they had now almost reached the place where the minibus was standing at the entrance to the large car park at the Visitor Centre.

"Yes, but I just want to introduce you quickly to Jean Grookes first, before you all set off," said Jim, who was already feeling very relieved by the thought that he was about to lose the close company of Rachel Conner, for a time, at least.

A queue now formed by the door of the bus as people began to board it while Mrs. Grookes, the Guide, stood by the door, checking numbers as each passenger stepped up into the vehicle.

"Shall we join the queue?" asked Mrs. Conner, looking round for Jim.

"Well, I should think that... eh, what's that?" Jim suddenly spun round with a start, hearing a loud cheerful voice call out from somewhere just behind him.

"Hi! Hello, there, Mr. Sandy!"

"Oh, good heavens!" gasped Jim as he instantly recognized the tall man with an enormous, Western-style, cowboy hat on his head.

"Well, so we meet again, Mr. Sandy! It's been a while since we last met!" said the man, beaming with pleasure as he extended his right hand.

"It certainly has!" agreed Jim, feeling rather dazed as he shook the man's hand with a somewhat limp grasp. He had last met this enthusiastic American tourist, Jack Wonstannley, and his wife, in much the same place on a day in early June 1961, nearly four years ago; but he had never expected to see them again. Jim had already seen that the man's rather shy little wife was there; and another man who had been talking with her also seemed to be part of their group. However, remembering the time (he glanced at his watch) he was feeling decidedly flustered. He knew that the American man would be longing to talk with him about Beryl Buxton, the former Castle servant, and that he would jump at the chance of seeing over the inside of the Tower (which had been closed to visitors on his last visit to Rhodes Castle) because of its special association with the ghost of Mrs. Buxton (she had died there, apparently by suicide on a June day of 1951). However, what mattered right now was to get Mrs. Conner, who was standing unobtrusively just behind him, into the bus. They had been slowly moving forwards towards the bus even while they had been talking.

"Well, now, Mr. Sandy, I was just going to say... oh, sorry, sir, you're busy right now."

Jim Sandy waved a hand to silence that tiresome American man. He was already talking to Mrs. Grookes.

"Hello, Mrs. Grookes! I've brought along Mrs. Conner, the new Guide, to meet you and to come with you on this tour so that she can find out what the job is really like – if that's all right?"

"That's fine!" said Mrs. Grookes, glancing at her watch. She saw that it was now about a minute to one o' clock, which meant that the tour would probably start a little late, but that would not really matter. "Pleased to meet you, Mrs. Conner!" Rachel Conner had stepped forward, and the two women shook hands. "Now, if you would like to step into the bus, and take that empty front seat on the right-hand side, just behind the driver, I'll join you there in a minute."

Jim, taking an anxious glance behind him, saw that the American visitor, with his wife and his friend, was keeping as near to him as he could; obviously he was longing to speak again at the earliest possible opportunity. Behind them he noticed that there were only three or four other people in the queue for the bus. He also that Susan was standing to one side of the queue, looking on calmly, as if she were completely unconcerned about anything that might be about to happen. He decided on the spur of the moment that he had better board the bus briefly himself.

"Now, sir," he said, turning at the top of the steps to address the American tourist, who was boarding the bus immediately behind his wife, "please take a seat wherever you will." He waved a hand vaguely towards the rear end of the minibus, where there were still a number of empty seats. "But I'm no longer the Guide here, so I'm not coming with you." Jim was squeezing himself out of the way while the three American tourists pushed their way past him, looking for the nearest vacant seats on the left-hand side of the bus.

"Mrs. Grookes is your Guide today," said Jim, "but if you want to say anything to me, please be quick about it, sir - I must get out now."

"Oh, right, thank you!" said the American man, who had just sat down beside his wife. "But in that case could I please have a quick word with you, Mr. Sandy, at the end of this tour? That'll be right here, I take it?"

"Yes, the bus will stop here at the end of the tour," said Mrs.

Grookes, climbing into the minibus behind the last of the passengers.

"Yes, of course you can," said Jim quickly. "I'll see you later - at about three o' clock, I mean, at the end of the tour. That'll be all right for you?"

"Oh, sure, it will be! Thank you very much, Mr. Sandy!"

"And I'll see you too at three o' clock, Mrs. Conner?" said Jim, turning for a moment to the new Guide, where she was sitting beside Mrs. Grookes in the seat behind the driver's seat. "Good-bye for now, and good luck!"

"Good-bye!" said Rachel Conner, turning for a moment to give Jim a pleasant smile.

"Sorry, Mrs. Grookes, I'm delaying your start," said Jim, glancing again at his watch, and seeing that it was now almost a minute past one. "I'm off now!" The driver had already started his engine, and was waiting for Mrs. Grookes to give him the word to set off.

Jim hurriedly descended the steps and left the bus without another backward glance. As he saw Susan still standing there, where he had left her, it was almost as if he were not really seeing her, for the picture that was burning brightly in his mind's eye was an image of Rachel Conner sitting in that seat behind the driver's seat, and smiling at him. It was a picture which seemed to be floating provocatively in the space between himself and Susan, and he knew that at the same time it was both enthralling him and infuriating him. His opinion of Rachel had changed significantly since his first sight of her. She *was* attractive, but attractive in a rather subtle way. Almost he was feeling slightly dizzy as he approached his wife, and he even wondered whether he must be looking rather odd to her.

"Sorry, Sue, but I had to have a quick word with that man before they set off," he said rather breathlessly.

"That's all right, darling!" said Susan. "But you'd met him here sometime before?"

"Yes, indeed I have. Do you remember that American man I told you about before - the man who was desperately keen to see Beryl Buxton's grave in the Servant's Graveyard? Well, it was him."

"Oh, yes, I remember you telling me about him."

"Well, I never thought that I would ever see him again, but, all of a sudden, there he was; and he was desperate to try to talk to me, just when I didn't want to talk to him, when I had Mrs. Conner to introduce to Mrs. Grookes."

"Well, never mind, darling, I expect he pretty soon realized that you were too busy to talk just then. Look, there they go now."

The bus was just pulling out of the car park to set off down the drive on the first leg of the tour. Looking round for a moment, Jim and Susan saw the American man flourish his hat in their direction. They waved back to him. Jim tried, but failed, to catch another glimpse of Rachel Conner's face.

"Darling, we'd better get back now to look for our lunch," said Susan. "It's high time for lunch, you know!"

"Why, yes, so it is!" agreed Jim, suddenly thankful for the idea of having his lunch with Susan, as it would be just the sort of distraction he was needing at the moment. Not that I'm feeling at all hungry just now, he thought, but I've *got* to get that woman, Rachel, out of my mind; and lunch with Sue would distract me nicely.

They had turned, and were beginning to stroll back towards the Castle.

"I should think that you'll be able to get a word with that man when they come back at the end of the tour," said Susan.

"Well, yes, that's what I said to him just now. I'm going to meet him, and his wife and his friend, when they come back at the end of the tour. No doubt he'll want to talk about Beryl Buxton again."

"No doubt he will. But this time he's going to be shown round the inside and outside of the Tower, as well as the Servant's Graveyard, so that should please him very much!"

"Oh, he'll be absolutely thrilled, I should think, when he knows that the tour now includes that part of the front of the Castle. He was *so* disappointed that other time when I had to tell him that I wasn't allowed to show him into the Tower Library."

"And he might even see the ghost! But I suppose that he'll feel that at least he's in with a good chance of seeing the ghost!"

"Oh, yes, I'm sure he'll feel that," agreed Jim, "and that should satisfy him well enough! But I don't think he has any *real* hope of seeing a ghost while he's among all that crowd of the other tourists."

They were both looking up the drive as they were speaking at the handsome Great Tower and the southern facade of the Castle, all brightly lit up in the strong sunshine of the early afternoon. He's got no chance of seeing that ghost today; it's far too bright! thought Jim, as he tried to remember what it had really been like on that foggy morning as he had been leaving the Castle, when he had indeed met that strange, shadowy figure of a woman. That *must* have been Beryl Buxton, he told himself.

As they walked back to the Castle they continued to chat happily enough, mostly about the American tourist and his obsession with Beryl Buxton and her ghost, but Jim felt that his answers to the points his wife was putting to him were becoming more and more vague. The truth was that, try as he might, he could not make himself properly concentrate on any other subject while that fascinating but distressing image of Rachel Conner remained firmly fixed in his mind's eye.

CHAPTER THREE

At lunch in the Castle Jim was, for most of the time, silent while he was eating. That day he and Susan were having their lunch with Samantha in the Servants' Common Room (this was their usual arrangement when there were no guests staying at the Castle).

Jim was giving himself a sharp talking to. Although he was aware that the image of Rachel Conner was now (thankfully!) fading from his mind, he knew that some severe inner discipline was going to be needed in this matter of "dealing with her" Yes, discipline is necessary, Jim, and it's necessary right now! This must not, and *will not* happen again - this silly feeling of excitement when I think about her. She is *not* attractive - yes, I know that she is rather attractive *in a way* - but that should *not* make me feel excited. I am NOT falling in love with her - I can't fall in love with her - that's unthinkable! And why is it unthinkable? Because of Sue, my own Sue, my darling, beloved Sue - my *only* love.

At this point Jim's inner monologue ended as another memory suddenly came back to him. He had just glanced up from his plate at Susan, who was sitting opposite to him at the head of the oblong table, and chatting happily with Samantha, on her left. Then, suddenly and unexpectedly, those very poignant memories of his last couple of hours in Susan's company on the day before he had left Rhodes Castle were in his mind again. The effect on him was electric as he saw in his mind's eye the tears streaming down

Susan's face as she hurried from the room – the very room where they were now sitting – to catch a train at Yetminster station that would take her away to Bournemouth. The memory was so heavily charged with emotion that even now, as he let it sweep over him, his eyes were beginning to grow misty as his tears gathered once again. However, the extreme poignancy of his memory was not only bringing tears to his eyes; it was also bringing to his mind an immense feeling of relief, and even of joy. His reactions to his own memories of the circumstances and emotions of that parting from Susan were proof to him that he was still very deeply in love with her. There was absolutely nothing for him to worry about in respect of any feeling that might come to him when he thought about Rachel Conner.

"Darling... Jim, darling, are you alright ?" There was decidedly a note of anxiety in Susan's voice. Jim looked up on the instant, and saw that both the women were looking at him anxiously, but, even as he looked up, he smiled broadly.

"Oh yes – yes, I'm quite all right, honestly I am!" Jim pulled himself together, and tried to sound as if he meant what he was saying.

"Oh, good! But are you sure there's nothing the matter, darling? You've been very quiet, you know, for the last five minutes or so."

"I'm feeling absolutely fine!" said Jim. "But I expect that I have been pretty quiet. I've been... thinking."

"I expect it's come as rather a shock for you, meeting that American visitor again?" suggested Samantha helpfully, and Jim looked at her gratefully. "Sue's just been telling me about that."

"But Jim, darling," said Susan, "I'm sorry that we've been ignoring you while we've been talking about things. And I shouldn't worry either about that American man. No doubt he'll just say what he wants to say when you see him again at three o' clock, and then you'll know what to answer, if he needs an answer;

and anyway I'm going to come down with you in the car to have a word with Rachel Conner."

"And I'll tell you what, Jim," said Samantha. "You've been so lost in your thoughts that I don't mind betting that you've no idea what you've just been eating!"

"Why, you're quite right, Sam!" Jim suddenly broke into a laugh as he saw the amusing side of the situation. "I really don't know what I've just eaten!"

"Well then, darling, let me tell you what it is: it's a very nice shepherd's pie that Cook's made for us!" said Susan. "So why not have some more?"

"Yes, I'd love some more, thank you; and this time I'll remember to enjoy it!"

They were all smiling now as Jim passed his empty plate to Susan, who had the shepherd's pie on a mat in front of her. I'll tell Sue later what I was really thinking about, thought Jim. She'll understand.

As Jim took his second helping of shepherd's pie, and began to eat it (this time with a real appreciation of what he was eating) he was feeling incredibly light-hearted and happy. The memory of the tearful farewell to Susan had been an effectively cathartic thought: it had cleared all thoughts and images of Rachel Conner clean out of his mind, and, more importantly, it had convinced him that the love between himself and Susan was as strong as ever; there was no possibility that falling in love with anyone else was going to have the least effect on it.

"Jim, darling, I'm going to write to Norma Beck to ask her to come for a week on Sunday," said Susan a little later, when they had finished their lunch, "so you should find me in the Study at a quarter to three."

"And then you're going down to the Visitor Centre in the car?"

"Yes, that's it; and then, when I've had a quick word with Rachel, and you've had a word with that American man, we'd better go down to Yetminster to the Post Office."

"Right, oh!" said Jim, I'll come along to the Study at a quarter to three - if I remember the time!"

"Where are you going to be?"

Oh, I think I'll probably stay in the Green Drawing Room this afternoon, as I haven't really any work to do in the Estate Office today."

*

It was nearly ten minutes to three when Jim and Susan came into the Hall of the Castle on their way out to the front door. Susan's red car was parked just outside the door. Jim had spent a comfortable and (he thought) a rather lazy afternoon reclining on the sofa in the Drawing Room (with his shoes taken off) while he was looking through the pages of "The Times", and reading the parts of it that interested him.

Meanwhile, Susan had been at the desk in the room which had been her late husband's Study, and which was now her Study, while she was writing her invitation to Norma Beck, and doing some other written work. Now she had put the sealed envelope in her handbag, to be ready for posting, and had slung the bag over her shoulder.

"Come along, darling," she said, "we'll get down to the Visitor Centre now to wait for them coming.

*

It was just after three o' clock when Jim and Susan, sitting in Susan's car, saw the Rhodes Castle minibus draw into the car park to stop close to the spot where they were parked. They stepped out of the car, and a moment later saw the door of the minibus opened by Jean Grookes, so that the tourists could disembark.

Jim, realizing that he might well be about to see Rachel Conner again, was feeling very calm and composed. He had resolved that, if possible, he would not talk to her, or even look at her, but that, if he did see her, it would have no significant effect on his feelings. They saw the wife of the American tourist emerge from the bus, followed by the friend, and then by the man himself. Good, thought Jim, it looks as if Mrs. Conner is going to let all the others get out of the bus first, and then get out with Mrs. Grookes; so I probably won't need to say anything more to her today.

The American man flourished his large cowboy hat in an expansive gesture as he stepped down from the bus, and came straight over to Jim and Susan.

"Hello there again!" he held out his right hand to Susan. "Good afternoon, ma'am. May I introduce myself? I'm Jack Wonstannley, and this is my wife, Ella, and this is our friend, Doctor Philip Oakley."

"I'm pleased to meet you!" said Susan, allowing the man to shake her hand heartily. "I'm Lady Susan Sandy, but most people still call me Lady Dalmane, my late husband's name."

"Oh, ma'am, I was really sorry to hear that Lord Dalmane had died. They told us about that in the village where we're staying."

"Did they? Well, this is Jim Sandy, my new husband, whom you've already met." Susan was smiling broadly as she turned to Jim, at her side, to introduce him as "my new husband". Gosh, that still sounds wonderful! thought Jim.

"So we meet again, Jim!" said Jack Wonstannley, shaking his hand heartily. "And may I offer you my hearty congratulations, sir, on your marriage to Lady Dalmane? And so you, ma'am, are the Countess of Saint Helens?"

"I am the Countess of Saint Helens. Did you guess that?"

"Well, ma'am, I guess I kind of half guessed it!" Jack Wonstannley chuckled, but Susan had now turned to his wife.

"So where exactly are you staying?" she asked when she had shaken Ella Wonstannley's hand, and she had made a neat little curtsey.

"At 'Ye Olde Black Sheepe' in Yetminster, ma'am."

"Oh, at the pub in the village. That must be a nice place to stay, I should say." Susan glanced round towards the minibus for a moment, and saw that all the tourists had now disembarked; but Mrs. Grookes and Mrs. Conner were still standing in the bus in conversation.

Susan turned quickly to Dr. Oakley, beginning to be impatient to get the introductions completed as soon as possible.

"How do you do, Doctor Oakley?"

"How do you do, ma'am?" The doctor's bald head was not covered by any kind of hat, but he made a very slight forward inclination of his head as he shook Susan's hand. She felt that he must be a shy but very clever man, a view which was reinforced for her a moment later when Jack Wonstannley spoke again.

"Doctor Oakley is our expert in psychical research – and a really brilliant scientist."

"Oh, really?" Susan wondered for a moment what the man meant by "our".

"Oh, sure he is!" said Jack. "But I guess, ma'am that he's too modest to admit it."

Susan glanced round for a moment towards Dr. Oakley, but saw that he had turned his head aside, as if in complete indifference to any remarks which might be made concerning his scientific expertise.

"Now, if you'll excuse me for a minute or two," she said, "I must go into the bus to have a word with our new Guide."

"Of course! But, if you please, ma'am, I would like to ask you a favour – after you've spoken with your new Guide."

"Well, if you don't mind waiting here for a minute or two, I could have a word with you after I've had a word with Mrs. Conner; and in the meanwhile I'll leave you with Jim."

"Thank you, ma'am; thank you very much."

Susan gave him a quick smile, and hurried up the steps into the minibus. Jim, meanwhile, having shaken hands with Ella Wonstannley and Dr. Oakley, politely asked whether they had enjoyed their tour of the Castle.

"Oh, yeah, sure it was great!" said Jack Wonstannley happily. "And especially we enjoyed looking around inside the Tower Library."

"That was where you particularly wanted to go last time, wasn't it?"

"Indeed it was, sir; and I can tell you that I'm *really* pleased to have had this opportunity to be in there."

"But no sign of the ghost today?" Jim, knowing what the American visitor was thinking about, could not resist a smile as he mentioned the ghost.

"Oh, no - no sign of Beryl Buxton today!" Mr. Wonstannley chuckled. "Well, sir, I guess she'd think it was a bit too crowded in there this afternoon to put in an appearance for us!"

"Yes, I should think so," agreed Jim. He was wondering whether it would be wise to tell the man that he had, in fact, seen the ghost himself

"Well, as a matter of fact, sir, that is what I should really like to talk to the Countess about," said Jack Wonstannley. "I'd like to ask for permission to go in there tonight - just Doctor Oakley and myself - to do a bit of serious ghost hunting."

"Oh, I see! Yes, you'd certainly have to ask Susan's permission to do that; but she should be coming out of the bus any time now."

"That's fine, sir; I'll wait here for as long as it takes. I don't mind waiting here - in fact, come to think of it, I *ought* to wait here as we've arranged to meet our daughter, Mary, here. She'll be coming here on her bike, she said, and she reckoned to be here soon after three o' clock."

Jim glanced round quickly to see whether there was any sign of a girl on a bicycle, but at that moment he saw Susan emerge from the bus. He could see no one riding a bicycle.

"Ah, here comes Sue now!"

"I'm sorry to keep you waiting, Mr. Wonstannley," said Susan at once.

"Oh, don't mention it, ma'am!" said Jack Wonstannley. "As I just said to your husband, we ought to be waiting here to meet our daughter."

"Oh, yes? Well then, Mr. Wonstannley, perhaps you would rather have a chat with me later in the Castle? I was, in any case, about to go down with Jim to the Post Office in Yetminster."

"Then don't let me keep you now, ma'am, if we could talk later.

It was quickly arranged that the Wonstannleys and Dr. Oakley would call at the Castle later, probably between four o' clock and half past four, when Susan and Jim would be back from Yetminster. Susan pointed out for them that there were other attractions at the Visitor Centre which would help them to pass the time; in particular, she recommended that they should try the film show which was designed to supplement the Guided Tours, or to replace them for those visitors who did not want to walk. Susan and Jim were about to say good-bye again (for the time being) when they were all startled by the ringing of a bicycle bell and a sudden screeching of brakes as a girl appeared on a bicycle, and pulled up close to the place where they were all standing. The girl seemed, at first, to be slightly out of breath; evidently she had been riding hard.

"Hi, Dad!" The girl put a foot to the ground to steady herself, but did not get off her bicycle.

Jim glanced round again, and saw a plain-looking young girl, who was surely still in her teens. She was wearing a white top and pale coloured shorts, while on her head was a wide-brimmed hat of the same style as her father's.

"Hello there, Mary!" said her father cheerfully.

"Mary, darling, come and be introduced to the Countess," said her mother.

"Oh, sure!" said Mary. She propped up her bicycle against the wall of the ticket office.

"This is Lady Susan Sandy, the Countess of Saint Helens," said Ella Wonstannley. "Lady Sandy, this is our daughter, Mary."

"How do you do, ma'am?" Mary took off her hat with her left hand, while she shook Susan's hand with her right.

"You look to me like a keen cyclist," said Susan, noticing a large blue rucksack strapped onto the luggage grid of the cycle.

"Oh, yeah, sure I like cycling!" replied Mary. "I'm gonna do a cycling tour of Britain, you see. ma'am - leastways I hope to!"

"Are you really? Well, good luck to you, Mary; I hope you'll enjoy it. But perhaps we'll see you later this afternoon with your parents, who are going to call at the Castle for a short talk with me and my husband? You'll be very welcome to join us if you'd like to."

"Oh, thank you, ma'am, very much!"

Susan looked at her watch.

"Gosh, Jim, we'd better be going now! I'm sorry we can't stay to talk now, but we'll see you all later. Good-bye!"

Susan and Jim stepped into Susan's car, closed the doors, waved their hands, and drove away. As she headed the car down Stable Road towards the exit to the road to Yetminster via the West Lodge, Susan said, "That girl seems to take after her father!"

"In what way?" asked Jim.

"Well, she must be a very energetic person to be planning a cycling tour of Britain before she goes back to America."

"Yes, she must be! But it'll take her a long time, of course, to get right up to John O' Groats! I say, Sue, we might even see her again when we're up in Scotland in June?"

"Yes, I suppose we might."

There was a moment's silence in the car in which Jim reflected that he would not be in the least concerned if he never saw Mary Wonstannley again. He knew that she was not the sort of girl who would ever seem attractive to him. Then, thinking that it was wise to change the subject, he mentioned something else.

"That American man was telling me that what he really wants is to be allowed to come into the Castle tonight to hunt for Beryl Buxton's ghost. He told me that, Sue, just before he came out of the bus, so I said he'd have to ask your permission."

"Oh, good heavens!" said Susan. "What a character he is, with his obsession about that ghost!" She laughed at the thought of it. "Well, darling, I suppose we'd better let him come in tonight to try his luck as he seems to be quite set on the idea of hunting for that ghost. Did you tell him that you've actually seen that ghost?"

"I haven't told him that yet - but I think that I will tell him."

"I would, if I were you. And presumably he'll want to take that other chap, Doctor Oakley, in there with him. It'll be the Tower Library where they'll want to be, I suppose?"

"Yes, I think so," said Jim. "He said that Doctor Oakley was an expert in psychical research."

"And that, no doubt, means that he is considered to be an expert in the study of paranormal phenomena - ghosts, and all that sort of thing."

"Yes, that's what he must be."

"Well, darling, thank you for warning me in advance about this. We've got a little time now to think it over - whether or not to allow them into the Tower Library tonight - but, on the whole, I don't see why we shouldn't say Yes to them, do you? Jack Wonstannley certainly seems to me to be a very honest and trustworthy sort of man; and we can surely hope that his silent friend, the doctor, is of the same sort."

"Oh, I think that Jack Wonstannley is perfectly all right from the honesty point of view," said Jim. "I don't think that things would be stolen if we allow them to work in there tonight, although I can't imagine at all what sort of things they might actually want to *do* to hunt for a ghost."

"Nor me either, darling," said Susan.

"And there's another thing to consider: do you they'll want to stay in there all night?"

"Oh, surely not," said Susan. "At any rate, I don't think that we ought to give our permission for that. But I expect they'll want to set up some equipment in there - cameras, and that sort of thing - and then, maybe, they'll want to stay there for a while to see whether anything happens."

"And then, when nothing's happened, they could leave at about midnight, and come back in the morning to see whether they've captured anything unusual on film. I bet they don't, though!"

"Well, I wouldn't be so sure. After all, *you* had that strange experience on the morning when you were leaving us. But I know what you mean: a ghost is not likely to appear to order, as it were, especially when people are deliberately searching for it."

*

Jack Wonstannley was having a very satisfactory afternoon. As soon as the Guide had ushered the touring party into the Tower Library, the last room on the tour, he had spoken to his friend, Dr. Oakley, at his side in a loud whisper.

"This is the place, Phil - Beryl Buxton's haunted room - the place to set up our equipment!"

"'Sh! Be quiet a minute!" hissed Dr. Oakley. "I want to hear what the Guide's saying!"

They had missed a few words from Mrs. Grookes's speech, but they now listened to the remainder of it.

... "there is not much in this room, other than the books, which is of great interest in itself; but the most interesting feature of this room is its association with the newest ghost in the Castle. Beryl Buxton, whose grave we saw in the Servant's Graveyard, is assumed to have died here; her body was found just outside that window over there, and the cause of death was later established as the result of a fall from a considerable height, presumably from the top of the Tower..."

Mrs. Grookes went on to say a little more about Beryl Buxton and her ghost while the people gathered round her to listen.

Jack Wonstannley and Dr. Oakley were listening just as keenly as the rest of the party but, while they were listening, their eyes were roving eagerly around the room, noting features which were likely to be of use or interest when it came to making their own private investigations later on.

Presently Mrs. Grookes came to the end of her speech.

"Now, has anyone - apart from Mr. Wonstannley - got any questions?" she asked.

There was general laughter at this remark, and Jack laughed with the others. He had already asked the Guide many more questions than anyone else.

"Well, Mrs. Grookes, I guess I'm sorry, ma'am, that I've asked more than my fair share of questions," said Jack Wonstannley.

"Oh, don't worry about that; I was only joking," said Jean Grookes. "Of course you can ask me anything you like at any time."

But, for once, Jack Wonstannley could not think of anything else that he wanted to ask about in connection with Beryl Buxton.

"Thank you, ma'am," he said meekly, "but I don't think that I need to ask you anything else just now."

Mrs. Grookes allowed her party of tourists a few more minutes to look around the Library before she gathered them together to return to the minibus. Dr. Oakley was already looking around the room closely, mostly down at floor level.

"Good, there's a power point down here that I guess would do okay to plug in the photon beam." He pointed behind the reading desk, where there were, in fact, two power points, into one of which was plugged the lamp on the desk.

"Yeah, that'll be good!" said Jack Wonstannley. "And look here,

Phil: we could set up the automatic camera right here beside this desk."

"And that way it could take pictures either through the window, or of the interior of this room."

Ella Wonstannley, who had been looking through the titles of some of the books in the room (but had not seen anything which interested her) came up to the two men.

"How are you getting on?" she asked. "I guess you're mighty pleased, Jack, to have got into this Tower Library at last!"

"You bet; I sure am mighty pleased to have got in here at last!" said Jack. "Now Phil and me's just checking out where we're going to set up our equipment tonight."

"If you get permission."

"Oh, yeah, of course. But the Countess says she's gonna have a chat with us later in the Castle, so I'll ask her then."

*

In the Green Drawing Room of Rhodes Castle Susan and Jim were taking tea with their four American guests from the touring party. Susan had got back soon enough to have a cup of tea with Jim alone, before the guests arrived. Jim had remarked that it must be an unheard of privilege for people from one of the tour parties to be asked into one of the private rooms of the Castle to have tea with the Countess.

"Well, darling, I dare say it's perfectly true that I'm granting these people an unheard of privilege," said Susan, "but remember, Mr. Wonstannley *does* apparently already have a connection with the Castle. Didn't he tell you on that last occasion when he was here that his father used to work here as a valet to John's father, Andrew?"

"Oh, yes, I remember; he did say that," said Jim.

"Well then, I think it's fair enough that he should have an opportunity to have a talk with me, as that's apparently what he wants."

Jim had wholeheartedly agreed with Susan on that point; and a little later there had been a knock on the door, and the butler had shown in the four American visitors. Susan welcomed them, and invited them to sit down wherever they cared to (there was a sofa in the room which could seat three people comfortably, and two armchairs in addition to the one in which Jim was sitting).

Jack, the butler, was waiting quietly by the door. Susan asked her guests whether they would like some tea, and, having received affirmative replies from all of them, asked the butler to bring them tea and biscuits. She then immediately began to engage her guests in small talk, asking them first how well they had enjoyed their afternoon at the Castle and the Visitor Centre.

"Oh, it's been really *most* enjoyable, ma'am, thank you very much!" said Jack Wonstannley. "And we went to the film show, as you suggested, and that was just great!" He looked round at his wife, who was sitting beside him on the sofa. Dr. Oakley and Mary were sitting in the other armchairs.

"Yeah, we thought that the film show was just great!" agreed Ella Wonstannley. "It's a real good way, I reckon, ma'am, for people to get to know about the history of this place."

"And how about you, Mary?" asked Susan. "You didn't feel bored, I hope?"

"Oh, no, ma'am, not at all! I think it's a great film – I wouldn't mind seeing it again!"

"Well, maybe you'll find an opportunity to do that sometime," said Susan, smiling. "I'm so glad you've all enjoyed it." She sensed that the shy and silent Dr. Oakley had also been enjoying his afternoon at Rhodes Castle, but did not want to ask his opinion at the moment; so, wisely, she did not press him, and did not look round in his direction. "But I think, Mr. Wonstannley," she continued, "that the real highlight of the visit for you has been to see inside the Tower Library?"

"Ah, yes, ma'am; it most certainly has been the real highlight, as you say."

"So perhaps you would be glad to have an opportunity to be in that room to have another look around without the other visitors and the Guide being present?"

"Oh, well, but that would be just *wonderful* ; that would really be most kind of you, ma'am, to allow us to be in there again."

"Not at all; that should be no trouble," said Susan. "Was that what you wanted to talk to me about? Or was there something else?"

"Well, that was it, ma'am, really; at least..." Jack Wonstannley paused as the door opened and the butler came in, carrying a tray with tea and biscuits on it. He set the tray down on Susan's desk, and retired from the room unobtrusively. Jim stood up to pass around the cups and saucers and plates as Susan began to pour out cups of tea.

"Yes, do go on, Mr. Wonstannley," she said. "I can be listening to you while I'm pouring out the tea."

"Well, ma'am, what I really wanted to ask your permission for was this: we would like to set up some special equipment in the Tower Library, and maybe leave it there for a few days, You see, we have some special equipment which may help us to detect the presence of a ghost - if there is one in there."

"Oh yes? And what is this equipment, exactly?"

"Right: there's our camera to start with. That's actually an automatic camera that can take pictures of things at night by infra-red light while there's no one in the room. Don't ask me how it works, ma'am; I really have no idea, but Doctor Oakley could tell you more about that than I can. Then there's an instrument called a 'photon beam', and another one which can detect slight changes in a magnetic field. I guess they're all what you could call sophisticated pieces of equipment, but I think Phil could explain how they work, if you want to know, as I certainly can't!"

Susan now looked at Dr. Oakley, noticing that he was now looking keen to speak.

"May I tell you something about this apparatus, ma'am?" he asked.

"Oh, yes, please do," said Susan, hoping that he was not about to launch into a very long and technical dissertation which would be unintelligible to her, and boring for all of them, herself included.

Dr. Oakley began to explain what their equipment was and, briefly, how it was supposed to work. Susan did not understand all that he was saying as he occasionally used scientific jargon with which she was not familiar, but she did nevertheless follow the general drift of his explanations. She also realized that he was trying to explain things concisely, rather than in an unnecessarily long-winded manner.

Susan gathered that the camera could be used either manually, in the usual way, or automatically on what Dr. Oakley called the "auto-pilot", and that the function of the other equipment was to detect any slight changes or variations in the electromagnetic field, such as might conceivably be caused by a supernatural presence.

"In other words by a ghost?" she said.

"Yeah, that's it, ma'am," said Dr. Oakley, "although, mind you, variations in the field could very likely be caused by other factors for which one could give a perfectly reasonable scientific explanation."

"Yes, I suppose so," said Susan. "Well, I hope you get some interesting results when you get your equipment set up. I suppose it isn't very bulky, by the way?"

"Oh, no, ma'am, it's not at all bulky; we're gonna bring it all in just one suitcase, you see," said Dr. Oakley.

When Susan took leave of her guests about a quarter of an hour later it had been arranged that Mr. Wonstannley and Dr. Oakley would be returning to the Castle at about nine o' clock to set up the ghost-hunting apparatus. Then they would stay in the Tower Library with the apparatus for a while, but they would be leaving at least by half past eleven. Then, if necessary, they would come in again the next night, and the night after that, and so on, under the same conditions for up to a fortnight. At the end of the fortnight (or perhaps sooner, if they had "caught" anything interesting on film) they were returning to America, so the equipment would then be packed up and taken away.

Jim had reminded Susan that there would be guests staying in the Castle for much of this period, but Susan had said that that would not matter at all, and she had added that she thought that Jim's father, as a scientist, would probably be most interested in the ghost-hunting apparatus.

"Oh, he certainly will be," Jim had said, "and Jackie will be interested too."

"Oh yes, she's a scientist as well, isn't she? And Uncle Geoffrey will be interested in it too, I expect. You won't mind our guests going into the Tower Library just to have a look round in the day time, will you, Mr. Wonstannley? I'm sure they would all be most careful not to touch or meddle with anything that you've put in there.

Jack Wonstannley told Susan that he thought it would be "just fine" if her guests wanted to look at their apparatus, and Dr. Oakley then agreed with him on that point.

"But just before we go, ma'am," he said, "I'd like to tell you that what we're hoping to do, with Phil Oakley's help - and, we hope, some interesting photographs - is to write a book about the ghosts of Rhodes Castle."

"Oh, really?" said Susan. "But you'd be wanting to base it, presumably, at least partly on what's already in print on that subject?"

"Oh, yes, ma'am - with your permission, of course."

"We'll see about that later," said Susan. "If you want to base your book partly on copyright material I don't think I'd have any objection. Perhaps you would like to borrow one or two of our books while you're staying over here? I believe the best one for you would probably be 'The Haunted History of Rhodes Castle', by Andrew Dalmane, my late husband's father."

"That would be most kind of you, ma'am," said Jack. "I guess that would really be most helpful to us."

"Very well, then, you might as well take it with you now as it's in the Tower Library. Jim, darling, I think you'll know just where that book is?"

"Yes, I think so," said Jim; "at least, if no one has moved it since I did the inventory of all the things in there. I should be able to find it all right." He remembered that he had, in fact, glanced inside the large red-backed volume by Lord Andrew Dalmane on that morning when he had been compiling the inventory of the books and other paraphernalia in the Tower Library.

Susan lead the way, and the whole party now moved through to the Tower Library. Once through the doorway Jim went straight over to the bookshelves on the right-hand side of the room, where, looking down towards the bottom shelf, he at once saw the gold lettering on the back of the large red volume he wanted.

"Good, here it is," he said. He handed the book over to Susan, who was standing just behind him. The American visitors, especially Jack Wonstannley and Dr. Oakley, were again looking keenly around at everything they could see.

Susan looked quickly at the closed pages of the book to see whether any dust had accumulated there, but, seeing no dust to blow away, she handed the book on to Jack Wonstannley, who thanked her again profusely, and promised to take great care of it, and to return it to her before he left England at the end of his holiday. Susan then told him that probably she would not see him again that evening, but that she would definitely make an arrangement with her butler whereby the Tower Library would be open for him that evening.

"Do let us know as soon as you get some interesting results," said Susan as she shook Mr. Wonstannley's hand.

"Oh, sure I will!" said Jack Wonstannley, giving his hostess a hearty handshake. "Good-bye for now, ma'am."

"Good-bye, Mr. Wonstannley; we'll see you again soon!"

Susan and Jim came to the front door, and said good-bye to the others, and waved to them as they drove off in their hired car.

"They seem very hopeful of getting some positive results, don't they?" said Susan as they returned to the Green Drawing Room.

"It's what I told them about the time when I saw Beryl Buxton that's convinced them that something is likely to happen," said Jim. "Mind you, I can't really believe that anything supernatural *will* happen for them."

"Oh, well - you never know what may happen!" said Susan.

CHAPTER FOUR

"Good heavens! Well, I never!" exclaimed Lord Padgate. "Fancy putting up all that equipment to try to catch a ghost on film! I should think it's more likely to frighten off any ghosts that may be around - make them decide not to show themselves. What do you think, Nora?"

"Oh, I expect you're right, Geoffrey," said Nora Padgate, agreeing with her husband. "Not that I really know anything about ghosts."

"But you have a ghost of your own at Dallam Hall, haven't you?" asked Susan.

"Oh, yes, we have our resident 'Blue Lady', and Geoffrey and I have both seen her at times," said Lady Padgate. "But what I meant was that I don't know one could do anything, as it were, to 'trap' a ghost - which, it seems, is what these American visitors of your's are trying to do."

"It does seem like that, doesn't it?" said Lord Padgate. "No, I should think that it's most unlikely that this camera and the other equipment here will catch anything in the supernatural line."

Lord and Lady Padgate of Dallam, Susan's Uncle Geoffrey and Aunt Nora, had arrived by car at Rhodes Castle about ten minutes earlier.

Susan had met them in the Hall, and had shown them upstairs to their rooms herself after she had asked them whether they had

had a good journey. When they had come downstairs again she had told them briefly about Jack Wonstannley and Dr. Oakley, and their plan to try to trap the ghost of Beryl Buxton in the Tower Library.

"Oh, do let's go and see this equipment they've set up in there before we have our drinks," Geoffrey Padgate had said. Susan had already invited them to come and sit down in the White Drawing Room to have their drinks before dinner.

"Well, there you are, you've seen the equipment they've set up in here so shall we move next door now to sit in the Drawing Room?" said Susan. She and Jim stood aside while Nora Padgate, followed by her husband, left the room. Jim, coming out last from the Tower Library, closed the door behind him.

"Ah, but I do love this room!" exclaimed Nora Padgate as she entered the White Drawing Room. "There is such a feeling of light and elegance in here... I think it's utterly charming!"

"I knew you particularly liked this room," said Susan, who did not herself at all care for the severe formality of her best sitting-room, "so that's why I chose it for our drinks this evening. Now do, please, find yourself a seat anywhere you like, Aunt Nora; and you, Uncle Geoffrey. What would you like to drink? Sherry for you, Aunt Nora? Or gin? Or whisky?"

"Oh, sherry for me, please, my dear," said Nora Padgate. She made straight for the armchair in a corner of the room nearest to the long open shelves of the china display cabinet, as Susan had thought that she would.

Geoffrey Padgate asked for his usual gin and tonic, and went over to the sofa, but did not sit down.

"And sherry for you, darling?" asked Susan, smiling at Jim.

"Yes, please, Sue," he said. He did not really like the very dry Fino Spanish sherry which Susan drank, but he told himself that he was trying to acquire a taste for it.

Jack, the butler, who had already been sitting in the room with his drinks tray, was ready to stand up the moment Susan and her guests came in. The silver tray, on which stood a number of decanters and glasses, was resting on a small, elegant, three-legged table in the north-eastern corner of the room. The White Drawing Room stood right on the south-eastern corner of the ground floor of the Castle, so that it had windows looking out both to the south and the east.

The butler poured sherry into a glass for Nora Padgate, and Susan handed it on to her.

"You say that you like the feeling of light in here, Aunt Nora," she said, "and it is always pleasantly light in here in the daytime, but it's a pity it faces the wrong way for the evening sunshine."

"But it gets the morning sun very nicely, as we remember from our last visit," said Geoffrey Padgate. "Thank you, Susan." He took his glass of gin and tonic from Susan as she handed it to him.

"Do, please, sit down," said Susan. "Don't wait for me."

Jim and Geoffrey Padgate were standing near the sofa, waiting for Susan to sit down first, but now they both sat down. They had both been looking out through the south-facing windows at the low-angled rays of the evening sun shining on the ponds and on the parts of the gardens beyond the ponds. It was a quarter to eight, and it had remained sunny and warm all day. As soon as they were all sitting down with their drinks Geoffrey Padgate raised his glass.

"Now, Susan, I propose a toast to you and Jim: happy days, and many of them!"

They all repeated the toast and drank.

"Indeed, many of them!" said Nora Padgate. "It was wonderful news that you and Jim were getting married, but I was so sorry that we couldn't come to your wedding."

"Yes, it was a shame that we couldn't come, but we were abroad at the time, as you know," said Geoffrey Padgate. He took another sip from his glass and then added: "Do you know, Susan, this evening reminds me of another evening when we were sitting in here having drinks, Nora and I, with you and John. You don't mind me mentioning John's name, do you?"

"Oh, not at all," said Susan quickly. "No, I don't mind any more being reminded of John, I promise you."

"That's good. But what I was going to say is this: here we were on that other evening, quite a few years ago, and you told us you were planning to allow visitors to come into some of the rooms of this house, including this room; and then I think I said that you ought to get one of your servants to make an inventory of all the things you had in all your public rooms."

"Yes, I remember that evening," said Nora Padgate. "I was admiring all the lovely things on those china shelves, wasn't I?"

"Yes, I remember," said Susan.

"Then you told me, Susan," said Geoffrey Padgate, "that you were going to get your Guide to do this inventory job; and I think that you told us then that he was a very young man, quite new to the job, but that you had great confidence in his abilities."

"Maybe I did," said Susan. She saw that Jim was looking up at her in some surprise, and realized that he knew nothing about the episode they were discussing, as he had not been present in the room with the Padgates at that time.

"We're talking about you, young man, as I expect you've gathered," said Geoffrey Padgate to Jim, who was sitting beside him on the sofa. Susan was sitting on the other end of the sofa. "I hope you don't mind?"

"Not at all," said Jim politely.

"Well, Jim, isn't it amazing and wonderful how your circumstances seem to have changed over a few years? When Nora and I were here last time you were just a fairly junior servant of the Castle; but now, having married the Countess of Saint Helens, you are really the Heir to Rhodes Castle."

"Oh, good heavens - but I wouldn't really say so!"

"But, darling, you really *are* the Heir to Rhodes Castle!" said Susan. "Uncle Geoffrey is quite right. You're my husband, so, when I die, all this will become your's!"

"But I shall never be the Earl," said Jim. The smile had now left his face as he suddenly looked serious.

"That doesn't matter," said Geoffrey Padgate. "I'm just saying that the general principle applies: that when a couple are married, and one party dies before the other, all the assets of the deceased partner pass to the surviving one; so you, Jim, would be the heir to the Castle."

"Well, I've never thought of my position in that way before," said Jim.

"But who *is* the Earl of Saint Helens anyway nowadays?" asked Nora Padgate. The others looked at her gratefully for changing the subject. "I suppose the title must have passed to John's brother... What was his name?"

"Dick Dalmane," said Susan. "Actually, I don't think he is, officially, the next Earl of Saint Helens *yet*, but he is bound to be the next holder of that title presently as he was John's closest living male relative. But what do you think, Uncle Geoffrey?"

"You mean, how do I think the rules for the succession of the title should apply in this case?"

"Precisely."

"Well, to be honest, Susan, my dear, I'm afraid I really have no idea of how this case should be decided officially."

"But apparently Dick Dalmane is already using the title, Earl of Saint Helens," said Jim. "We had a letter from him recently, didn't we, Sue, which made it clear that he's already claimed that title for himself."

"Yes, that's quite true," said Susan. "Actually, we've had an invitation from them to meet them sometime soon at their London house.

Dick had written: 'The Countess of Saint Helens' – meaning his wife, Jane – 'and I would be delighted if you and Jim could come to visit us soon' – or some words to that effect. So, you see, if his wife is now styling herself 'the Countess' then he is now calling himself 'the Earl of Saint Helens'."

"What cheek! What impertinence!" exclaimed Nora Padgate indignantly; and the others nodded their heads in agreement.

"Indeed, that sounds to me like the height of impertinence," said Geoffrey Padgate. "Have you considered yet what, if anything, you're going to do about this?"

"Well," said Susan, "we have decided in the end, after a good deal of deliberation, that we'll accept their invitation and pay them a very short visit – definitely no more than one night! You see, Jim and I were planning to go up to London for a week in any case towards the end of this month."

"Oh yes," said Geoffrey Padgate, "but what I really meant was whether you'd decided that any action ought to be taken, as it were, to thwart the ambitions of your late husband's brother? But perhaps not yet?"

"Well, I should think not yet; at least not until we've had a chance to talk with Dick and Jane face to face."

"And then, perhaps, you might have to have a word with your solicitor?"

"Yes, I may have to do that, but I hope it won't come to that."

"We're hoping that we're going to persuade them to be sensible," said Jim.

"Well, good luck to you, my dears," said Nora Padgate. "But I think that it's really quite brave of you to think of staying with those people if they're really as rude as it sounds as if they are."

"Well, they're not exactly rude people," conceded Susan. "'Rude', perhaps, is not the right word for them; but it was surely damnable cheek to write to me insinuating that they already *are*, in fact, the Earl and Countess of Saint Helens! Oh, well, we mustn't be too upset about it: I dare say they mean well by inviting us to their house... What's that, darling?" Susan saw that Jim was nodding his head as if in complete agreement with what she was saying.

"Oh, I certainly think they mean well," he said, "and I'm glad we've decided to pay them a visit. Perhaps... well, perhaps they can't help having grand pretentions, as it were?"

"Grand pretentions!" Susan suddenly laughed, and the others were now all smiling. "Well, darling, that's a generous thought, I'm sure... Now, would anyone care for a little more to drink? I don't think that dinner will be quite ready yet, but Sam said she would come in and tell us when it's time to move through to the dining-room. A fill-up for your glass, Aunt Nora?"

"No, thank you, my dear; I've had enough."

"Uncle Geoffrey?"

"Thank you, Susan, my dear. Just half a glass for me, please."

The butler came and took Lord Padgate's glass, and refilled it for him. Jim, who still had a little sherry left in his glass, refused any more when it was offered to him, but Susan had her own glass refilled.

"I'm sorry that I can't be more helpful as to how the rules apply for the succession of a title," said Geoffrey Padgate when he again had his glass in his hand. "I mean, in the non straight-forward cases, like your's. You see, that's something I've never had to bother my head about, having simply inherited my title of Baron Padgate of Dallam from my father."

"Yes, like John simply inherited his title from his father," said Susan. "And I dare say that John never really considered how his title of Earl of Saint Helens would be passed on, as we never had any children. Or perhaps he may have considered it privately, but I don't remember him ever talking about it with me."

"H'm!" said Geoffrey Padgate. "Isn't it funny? Here we are, three members of the English aristocracy, and you, Jim, the husband of a Countess: here we are in this room, and yet between us we can't answer a perfectly simple question about the succession of a title!'"

"How disgraceful!" remarked Susan, smiling broadly. "What do you think, Aunt Nora?"

"Well, Susan, my dear, I'm afraid that I shall have to go to the bottom of the class with the rest of you as I really don't know the answer to this problem. Mind you, as I said before, I can't help thinking that in this case the title of Earl of Saint Helens *must* pass presently to Dick Dalmane."

"But when?" asked Geoffrey. "And how?"

"Doesn't it have to be conferred by someone?" suggested Jim.

"Ah, yes, I think it does have to be conferred by someone," said Geoffrey. "And I suppose that that person would probably be the Prime Minister; or else, possibly, the Lord Chamberlain... or the Lord Chancellor."

"Not by the Queen?" asked Jim.

"Yes, that might possibly be the case. You see, the system is that the Sovereign confers honours on people, but only on the advice of her Prime Minister; so it's really the P.M. who has the final say in decisions of this sort. Isn't that right, Susan?"

"Oh, yes, I think so," said Susan.

"Well, that's how it is: twice a year, generally, an Honours List is published of the people selected to be honoured, and these people are then invited to come along to Buckingham Palace to receive their Honours personally from the Queen. And I think, Jim, that it's quite possible that such an Honour might be extended to *you* presently."

"What! To *me*?" Jim was shocked and, indeed, incredulous to hear it suggested that he might be invited to Buckingham Palace to receive an Honour from the Queen.

"I'm sorry if you find that a rather shocking idea, but, you see, you have married a Peeress of the Realm, which means that it might be considered appropriate for you to have some title - perhaps 'Sir James Sandy, Baronet'?"

"But... I haven't done anything to earn it!" Jim saw that the others were all smiling as if they found this idea of a title for him rather amusing, but now he looked hopefully at Susan.

"Never mind, darling," said Susan quietly. "I'm almost certain that, if they do decide that you ought to have a title, as Uncle Geoffrey suggests, you wouldn't have to go to the Palace to receive it personally from the Queen. You'd just be granted a title, and that would be that. But perhaps it won't happen anyway."

"Oh, don't worry about it, Jim," said Geoffrey Padgate. That sort of honour is conferred, I think, by letters-patent, and not personally by the Sovereign at an investiture."

"Oh, I see," said Jim. He would have liked to ask Lord Padgate exactly what letters-patent were (although he had an idea that they were a kind of legal document), but decided that he would ask that question some other time.

There was a short pause in the conversation while Geoffrey Padgate drained his glass.

"Were you, by any chance, Susan, thinking of speaking in the Lords when you're up in London later this month?" he asked presently.

"Yes, indeed," said Susan. "I was thinking of speaking in the House when we debate the Railway Bill later this month. We don't know yet when that'll be but, when we do know, we can pick our dates, and go up to London for a week."

"Staying at your house in Roehampton?"

"That's right, we'll be staying for most of the time at John's London house in Roehampton; then we'll move on to stay for just one night with Dick and Jane at East Sheen; and then finally we'll probably have a night or two at Jim's mother's house in Ealing."

"Mum wants us to come and stay for at least one night while we're up in London," said Jim, "and we're hoping to meet my brother, Ben, who's at Westminster School as a boarder; but if it's a weekend he could be at home."

"Won't he be almost finished at Westminster now?" asked Susan.

"Oh, yes. Mum says he's doing his last term at Westminster now, and going on to Oxford in the autumn. He's a lot brighter than I am, academically!"

"Oh, darling, I wouldn't say that!"

While they had been speaking the door had opened and Samantha had come in. She spoke at once to Jack, the butler.

"Dinner is served!" announced the butler in a loud voice.

"Oh, good!" said Susan. "You two will be ready for it, I'm sure, after your long journey. Now, if we're all ready, shall we make our way through to the dining-room?"

"Is that your small dining-room?" asked Nora Padgate. "I seem to remember that you have two dining-rooms?"

"Oh, yes, we'll be using the dining-room today, not the Party Room."

"The Party Room?"

"Well, it's called the Banqueting Hall really, the huge room next to the dining-room, but I usually call it the Party Room."

"Shall I lead the way now to the dining-room?" suggested Jim. The butler had by now gathered up all the empty drinks glasses onto his tray. He opened the door into the Hall, and then stood aside to allow the gentry to leave the Drawing Room before him.

"That's a good idea," said Susan, "as our guests may, perhaps, have forgotten the way."

"I think I *have* forgotten the way," confessed Nora Padgate. "At least, I'm sure I've forgotten how many doors you have to go past down that long passage."

"Right, if you'd like to follow me, I'll lead the way," said Jim.

"It's actually the fourth door on the right down the passage." They had come out of the White Drawing Room, and were standing again in the Great Hall of the Castle. Nora Padgate, who had been the last of the four of them to leave the Drawing Room looked back hopefully over her shoulder as she left the room.

"I think, perhaps we'll go back there for our coffee after dinner, if you like," said Susan, reading her thoughts correctly, and remembering how fond she was of the White Drawing Room, "but we'd better follow Jim down the passage now, and not get left behind."

"Of course," said Nora Padgate.

"I do like the way you've had notices attached to all the doors," said Geoffrey Padgate as he passed the first door on his right and read the notice: "VISITORS' TOILETS". "They're discreet, but obviously useful."

"Yes, they certainly are useful for our visitors," agreed Jim.

"You see, we've had a notice put on the door of every room that's open to the public to say what that room is, and 'PRIVATE' notices on the doors of all the other rooms to keep people out of our private rooms."

"You do have all these things very well organized here," said Geoffrey Padgate. I think that maybe Nora and I could learn a lesson or two from you while we're staying here."

"Maybe we could," said Nora Padgate. "How many rooms do you have open to the public, Susan?"

"Well, let me think," said Susan. "Actually, I'm not very well up on facts of that sort, but I do know that we have a total of thirty rooms altogether on the ground floor, and I think that just five of them are included in the visitors' tours. That's right, isn't it, darling?"

"Yes," said Jim. "There's the Great Hall, the Banqueting Hall, the Ballroom, the White Drawing Room, and the Tower Library. And upstairs there's the Earl's Library, the Chapel, and the Flag Room."

"I suppose that's where you keep the flags for the flagstaff on the Tower?" said Geoffrey Padgate.

"Yes, that's it, and it's on the second floor of the Tower, and there's a trapdoor in the ceiling to give access to the top of the Tower. Have you been up there?"

"Oh, yes, we had a look out from the top of the Tower the last time we were staying here."

"And you get a wonderful view from up there, I remember," said Nora Padgate.

"Indeed you do," said Geoffrey Padgate, "but I don't actually remember the Flag Room, although I suppose we must have passed through it to get up to the top of the Tower."

"You must have gone through the Flag Room," confirmed Jim, "but here's the Dining Room. Shall we go in now?"

"Do come in, please," said Susan. "They'll be waiting now to serve the dinner."

The two men stood politely to one side to allow Nora Padgate to walk into the Dining Room first, followed by Susan. Jim had just seen the door through to the Servants' Common Room close, and knew that the butler had gone by that way (rather than by the passage) to reach the kitchen with his tray of decanters and glasses.

The Dining Room of Rhodes Castle was an elegant, although not very large room; it was almost square in shape, but was slightly longer in the direction of the passage than it was the other way. In the centre of the room stood a round table, a table large enough for eight places to be laid on it, if necessary, but today it was laid for four people. It seemed to be at least as bright that evening in the Dining Room as it had been in the White Drawing Room, although the sun was not shining in directly at the windows, which faced north-west, and looked out onto the large paved area of the Castle Bailey; but it was bright enough for the two silver candlesticks which stood on the table to gleam conspicuously, almost as if they were directly reflecting the sunlight. (In fact the evening sun could never shine directly onto the rooms facing onto the Bailey along the south-eastern wing of the Castle because they were always shaded by the two floors of the south-western wing.)

"Now, Aunt Nora," said Susan, would you like to sit here; and, Uncle Geoffrey, could you sit on the opposite side, please, over here?"

Susan had drawn out from the table the chair nearest to the door from the passage for her aunt while she had been speaking. Nora Padgate sat down in her chair, while her husband went round the table to take the place opposite to her's.

"You were saying how much you'd enjoyed the view from the top of the Tower," continued Susan, "so I thought that perhaps we might go up there tomorrow morning after breakfast - if there's time. I'll have to go to church tomorrow morning, as it's Sunday tomorrow, and I dare say that you might like to come with us?"

"Oh, but we'd love to come to church with you tomorrow, wouldn't we, darling?" said Nora Padgate enthusiastically. "Rhodes Church is such a lovely little church!"

"Yes, indeed it is," said Geoffrey Padgate. "Will that be Mattins, Susan?"

"No, it will be Communion, actually, as it's the first Sunday in the month - it'll be a sung Communion service with four hymns."

"And will you be reading, Susan?" Geoffrey Padgate remembered that John Dalmane had read the lessons when they had attended a service of sung Mattins on their last visit to the Castle.

"Yes, I'll be reading the Epistle," said Susan. "Ah, good, here comes the soup!"

"Thank you!" said Nora Padgate as the housemaid set a steaming bowl of soup in front of her.

"It's pea and ham soup - home-made, of course," said Susan.

"Delicious!" said Geoffrey Padgate, sniffing the pleasant aroma hungrily as Samantha set his bowl of soup on the table. "I do congratulate your cook, Susan, for her wonderful work in the kitchen.

But perhaps Mrs. Garten is not still your cook?"

"She is, actually. I'm very lucky, mind you, to have inherited Julia Garten, as it were."

"She's German, isn't she?"

"Well, no, she's English really, as she was born in England; but then the family moved over to Germany when she was very small, and she went to a German school with her brothers and sisters – a big family they were – and she was brought up as if she was a little German girl.

And presently she met and married a German man, a doctor, and they lived at Koblenz until about ten years ago, when Klaus, her husband, changed his job and came over to England; and then Julia took a job here with us as cook. But soon after that Klaus became seriously ill, and died; so I don't think think Julia will ever want to move back to Germany as she has no relations living over there."

"Has she any children?" asked Nora Padgate.

Oh, yes, they had three little boys before Klaus died. You see, Julia isn't very old – she's only in her forties, I think – so hopefully she'll want to stay with us for a good long while yet."

"And she lives near here?"

"Yes, they live in the village of Leigh, which is just a few miles away."

"Well, she's certainly an excellent cook," said Geoffrey Padgate.

"I remember that we had some marvellous German dishes at dinner when we were last staying here."

"Did you?" said Susan. "I can't actually remember that, but, as a matter of fact, tonight's main course is going to be one of Julia's special very German creations: sausages in a tomato and garlic sauce."

"That sounds very good!"

"It is; but I hope that you won't mind that we're not having a roast tonight?"

"Oh, not a bit!" said Nora Padgate. "Susan, my dear, you shouldn't have worried so much about us; whatever your cook has prepared for us will, of course, be absolutely excellent."

While they had been talking and eating their soup Sandra, the kitchen maid, had come in with the main course things on a tray. These things were then transferred to a hot electric plate warmer which stood on a small table between the windows. Then, as Sandra was leaving the room, the butler came in with two bottles of red wine to accompany the main course. Meanwhile the housemaid remained standing silently by the table with the plate warmer, waiting to collect the empty soup bowls when that course was finished.

Jim was not saying much as he ate his soup; in fact he was lost in his own thoughts, but he did notice the various unobtrusive comings and goings of the servants who were waiting on them. The other three diners, in animated conversation, noticed nothing of this. He had been startled by the news that he was now the lawful Heir to Rhodes Castle, and he was thinking over the implications of his new situation. In particular, he wondered what might happen when Dick Dalmane became the next Earl of Saint Helens, for evidently he certainly *would* become the next Earl; and this, Jim thought, would probably happen quite soon - perhaps within the next year or two. Would he then want to come to live in Rhodes Castle? That was a disturbing thought; and Jim, considering it, heard little of the conversation of the others around the dinner table.

Presently, when the soup course was finished, the housemaid stepped forward to collect the empty bowls. Then the main course was brought to the table, and the large dish, in which were the sausages in their German sauce, was set in front of Susan, and the cover removed. A delicious, piquant smell filled the room as Susan began to serve the dish onto the pile of plates in front of her. At the same time the butler came over to the table to fill the wine glasses.

They had just started to enjoy the main course when the telephone rang. It stood on the small table where the butler had set down his tray with the wine bottles. He answered it immediately.

"Rhodes Castle." A pause, and then, "Yes, I'll get her for you. Hold the line, please. It's Mr. Sandy who wants to speak to you, my Lady."

Susan had already pushed back her chair and stood up to answer the telephone. She picked up the telephone receiver. The butler, meanwhile, quickly transferred her dinner plate to the plate warmer in case it should be a long call.

"Hello! Susan Sandy speaking... No, that's quite all right... Oh, but that would be delightful!... Oh, yes, Mr. Sandy, I'm quite, *quite* sure about that... Yes, I'll be delighted to see the Twins as well as yourself and Jackie; and I'm sure Jim will be jolly pleased too!" (Susan for a moment glanced round at Jim, and saw him smile back at her and nod his head.)... "What's that?... No, of course I don't mind at all. Of course you can come on the Saturday night... Yes, I'll pick you up at Sherborne station on Saturday night at whatever time you say... No, it'll be no trouble at all... Right... Very well, I'll expect another call from you on Thursday or Friday evening to confirm the time... Oh, yes, about this time would be perfectly all right... Good-bye, Mr. Sandy."

Susan replaced the receiver and returned to her place at the table, while Jack, the butler, with quiet but prompt efficiency once again set her dinner plate before her.

"Well, Jim, that was your Dad, as you must have guessed, and he says that the Twins will definitely be coming with him when they come down here for the party, but they'll be arriving on Saturday night, he says, rather than Sunday night, because of the trains."

"Oh, good!" said Jim with genuine pleasure. "I'm so glad that Carol and Victoria will be coming too."

"Well, your father says they were very determined to come, if they're asked to, and that they've made all the necessary arrangements to take a few days off work. Jim's twin sisters, Carol and Victoria, are coming to our party here a week tomorrow along with their father and stepmother," explained Susan to her guests.

"Oh, splendid!" said Nora Padgate. "So we'll look forward to meeting your sisters, Jim, and your father and your stepmother."

"But not your mother, Jim?" said Geoffrey Padgate. "She lives in London, I believe?"

"Yes, she lives in London," said Jim, "but she didn't really want to come, although we did ask her. She lives with her partner, you see - at least, I think she's married him now."

"Yes, I can quite understand that she would probably rather not come to a party here."

"How old are your sisters now, Jim?" asked Susan.

"They're... let me think... they must be twenty-two, but they're going to be twenty-three very soon; their birthday is later this month."

"Oh, how nice to be just twenty-two! I *am* looking forward to meeting Carol and Victoria, you know!"

"But you've met them before, Sue," Jim reminded her. "Surely they were at home, and you met them that time you came up to stay with us, and we went to the Grasmere Sports..." Jim's voice trailed off into silence, and a frown appeared on his face.

"Yes, I know I met them then." Jim suddenly saw that Susan was smiling at him in a way which clearly meant: "We don't want to think or talk about that time any more"; and instantly the frown left his face, and he found that he was smiling back at her. The occasion of Susan's last visit to his home in Cockermouth, when he had taken her to see the Grasmere Sports, held very painful memories for Jim as it had also been the occasion of a serious split between them, when Susan had even gone as far as to tell him that she had broken off her engagement to him. That had happened when Susan had discovered that he had spent a night in bed with Jackie Rothwell, the woman who was now his stepmother. However, it was abundantly clear that Susan now regarded all that episode as something which was definitely in the past, and, moreover, something which should remain buried in the past. Jim, therefore, was now more than happy to let that painful memory slip away from his mind just as if it had never troubled him at all.

"Did you say they'll be coming to Sherborne station, Sue?" he asked her.

"Yes, it'll have to be Sherborne station because they'll have to come via London, your father said. Apparently it wouldn't be possible to come the other way, via Bristol, as there isn't an early enough connection from Cockermouth to catch the through train to Bournemouth."

"Ah, yes, that would be the Pines Express, no doubt," said Geoffrey Padgate. "It *does* leave Manchester pretty early in the morning, I think, so I suppose that passengers from the Lake District wouldn't be able to join the train at Crewe. But the other way round, going north, if I remember right, the connections for the Pines Express should work out all right."

Jim and Susan both knew that Geoffrey Padgate, who was a Director of British Railways, had an almost encyclopaedic knowledge of the passenger train timetable.

"I've travelled back to Cockermouth from here, starting by taking the Pines Express from Stalham," said Jim.

"Well, your father and his party are still planning to travel back that way when they leave us on the Tuesday morning," said Susan; "but, anyway, I'm so glad they're all coming."

"So how many people are you expecting altogether for this party?" asked Nora Padgate.

"Oh, well, let me see," said Susan. "There's Nigel and Norma Beck..."

"Oh, good!" said Jim. "So the Becks can come!"

"Yes, I've heard from Norma that Nigel's going to be on holiday next week and the week after, so they can both come. Then there are four people coming from Cockermouth; that makes six. Then there are you two, Aunt Nora and Uncle Geoffrey, and that makes eight. And of course there'll be Jim and me. And perhaps there'll be my sister, Denise, and her husband Rupert, but we haven't heard yet whether they can come, or not. So there could be twelve of us altogether."

Nora Padgate said that it certainly seemed that there would be a good number of guests to make for a jolly party. Then she repeated an invitation which she had first made over the telephone a few days earlier when she had rung up Susan to confirm that she and Geoffrey were definitely coming to Rhodes Castle.

"But we do hope that you and Jim will be able to come to stay with us for a few days, or longer if you like, at Dallam Hall."

"Oh, do come to Dallam Hall, please!" pleaded Geoffrey Padgate.

"We'd love to come to Dallam Hall, and we *will* come, won't we, darling?" said Susan.

"Yes, we'll certainly come," said Jim.

"But I don't think we can say yet exactly when we could come," said Susan. "Perhaps in late July, or August...?"

"That would be fine with us, I think?" said Geoffrey Padgate, looking across the table to his wife for confirmation of this opinion.

"Oh, yes, that would certainly be fine with us," said Nora Padgate.

Jim and Susan thanked the Padgates very much for their invitation, but then Geoffrey Padgate, while apologizing for the general dreariness of his home town and its environs, suggested a further idea which immediately appealed to Jim.

"I know that Warrington is not usually considered much of a town to visit – in fact, some people would call it, I suppose, 'a bit of a dump' – but there are, in fact, some interesting old railway relics tucked away among the little lanes right in the middle of the old town, and we could go to see them."

"Oh really?" said Jim. "That sounds interesting!"

"You mean that area around Three Pigeons Alley – was that its name?" said Susan.

"Yes, I mean that area," said Geoffrey Padgate. "And you've seen it once before, Susan, so you know what it's like – and, so far as I know, nothing much has changed around there as, luckily, the council is not allowed to knock down the old locomotive shed."

"Yes, it's certainly a good thing if those old railway buildings are not going to be swept away. John and I both thought that that area was, in a way, most charming and very interesting."

Then, for Jim's benefit, Geoffrey Padgate explained that what they were talking about was the shell of the old building which had once been the train shed and station at the southern terminus of the first railway line built from Warrington.

"There used to be some rusty old tracks still on the ground there in my young days, I remember," he said, "but I'm afraid they've long ago been swept away."

"What a shame!" said Jim. "I really like looking at things like that."

Presently the main course was finished, and the servants carried away the dirty dishes and brought in a choice of two dessert dishes, and the meal and the talk went on. Following the news that all of his family from Cockermouth would shortly be coming down to the Castle, Jim was now in a much less introspective mood, and was joining in the general conversation much more easily and happily; and in fact this happier mood remained with him for the rest of the evening until bed time. However, as they climbed into bed together

Susan revealed that she had been aware of his discomfort when the topic of the heirdom to the Castle had been raised.

"Darling," she said, "you've been thinking about what Uncle Geoffrey said about you becoming the Heir to Rhodes Castle some day, haven't you? And you're unhappy about it?"

"Yes, I have been thinking about that," admitted Jim, "and it has rather worried me."

"Well, darling, I think that you should put all that worry out of your mind, if you can. It just isn't worth thinking about, or worrying about, you know."

"Yes, Sue, darling, I do know that. I'm not thinking about it any more."

CHAPTER FIVE

The train from London to Exeter pulled into the down platform of Sherborne station. Jim and Susan were standing near the middle of the platform, waiting for it. The train stopped.

"We'll probably have to move up or down the platform a bit to meet them," said Susan.

"Yes," said Jim, but for the moment neither he nor Susan moved from the spot where they were standing and watching passengers emerging from the train. A few seconds passed. Many passengers had already disembarked from the train, but so far there was no sign of Jim's family. He was seized with a sudden feeling of panic as the thought came to him that they had probably missed the train, having arrived at Waterloo too late to catch it. Desperately his eyes moved rapidly over the doors of the train, first towards the front end and then towards the rear; and then he suddenly spotted his sister, Carol, as she emerged from the train, carrying a small suitcase. His sensation of relief was instantaneous.

"There they are!" he cried as Victoria stepped down onto the platform immediately behind her sister. He waved an arm happily, and saw Carol wave back to him.

"Good!" said Susan.

Jackie and Arthur Sandy had followed the Twins in stepping down onto the platform. Mr. Sandy was carrying a suitcase, and Jackie a handbag and another small bag, but Victoria seemed to be carrying nothing. Jim and Susan were now hurrying along the platform to greet their guests from Cockermouth.

"I say," said Jim, glancing at his watch, "the train must have got in a little early!" They had been told that the train was due to arrive at Sherborne at one minute past eight, but it was now, according to Jim's watch, about half a minute before eight o' clock.

"Well, that's good, isn't it? Hello!" Susan waved a hand in greeting to her guests. The next moment there was a general embracing and shaking of hands. Jim hugged each of his sisters, and then offered to take Carol's suitcase for her.

"All right!" she said, handing it over.

"Gosh, I'm so glad that you could come!"

"Well, we're jolly glad that we've been able to come," said Carol, "aren't we, Vicci?"

"Yes, we certainly are!" said Victoria. "And we want to see *everything* now that we are here, don't we, Carol?"

"Yes, that's it, Jim, we want you to show us everything that we ought to see," confirmed Carol; and both girls laughed as Jim said, "We'll do our best!"

"Hello, Twins!" said Susan happily as she also embraced each of them in turn. "Yes, of course we'll do our best to show you everything that you ought to see on this visit."

Jim had already greeted his father and his stepmother, Jackie, so now the whole party began to walk back down the platform towards the exit.

"Have you had a good journey?" he asked his father. Mr. Sandy and Jackie, with Jim, were bringing up the rear while Susan and the Twins were walking on ahead.

"Yes, we've had an excellent journey, thank you - by this train, at least," said Mr. Sandy, "and, in fact, I think we've arrived here a minute or two early."

"We have arrived here early," said Jackie, looking at her watch.

"Yes, this train seems to have moved really fast once it got away from London, with only a few stops," said Mr. Sandy. "But the 'Royal Scot' was rather different; it got us into Euston about a quarter of an hour late. However, luckily that didn't matter as we still had plenty of time to get to Waterloo via the Northern Line to catch this train, the six-five."

"So, all in all, we've had a really good journey," said Jackie.

"And isn't it a beautiful evening now?"

"It's lovely now," said Jim, "and it's been like this for most of the day."

"Here we are," said Susan, as she came to her car which was parked just outside the station on the station forecourt. "My word, you people have done well to bring so little luggage with you. We can easily fit your suitcases in the boot - and that bag, Jackie, if you want to put it in there with the cases." They stowed the suitcases and Jackie's bag in the boot.

Susan invited the others to get into her car. She asked Jackie to sit in the front seat beside her, and apologized to the others, saying that it might be rather a squeeze for four people in the back seat.

However, when they had all climbed in, and shut the doors, they found that really it was not an uncomfortably tight fit for four people after all. Mr. Sandy had got in behind Jackie, and the Twins were sitting on the right-hand side of the car, behind the driver, while Jim had squeezed in between his father, to his left, and Carol, to his right.

"You'll have to sit in the front seat next time, Mr. Sandy," said Susan. "Are you sure you're not too uncomfortable where you are?"

"Oh, I'm perfectly comfortable sitting here, thank you, Lady Dalmane," said Mr. Sandy politely.

"By the way, is it all right for us to call you, 'Lady Dalmane', or should we be saying 'Lady Sandy'?" asked Jackie.

"I should call me just 'Susan', if I were you," said Susan. "Some people still call me 'Lady Dalmane', and others call me 'Lady Sandy' now, and that's really who I am – but I think you might find that rather confusing!"

"So do I!" agreed Mr. Sandy, smiling. "I think we'd better stick to 'Lady Dalmane'."

While they were talking Susan was driving her car out of the station car park. They came out onto the street, where Susan turned right, and then right again a few moments later at another junction.

"That's the tower of Sherborne Abbey, you're looking at," said Susan, seeing Carol and Victoria twisting their heads around to see the top of the Abbey tower, which was glowing a mellow reddish colour in the low-angled golden rays of the evening sunshine. "By the way, do any of you know Dorset at all?"

"No, we've never been to anywhere in Dorset before today," said Mr. Sandy, "so it's all a splendid new adventure for us."

"Well, I'm sure you'll find a lot that's well worth seeing," said Susan, "both in Sherborne and out in the country... Ah, here we are at the main road."

Susan had to give way and attend to the traffic for about half a minute as they came to the junction where they were going to join the main road southwards from the town.

"This is the main road to Dorchester, the A352," explained Jim, "but we don't have to go far along it before we turn off for the Castle."

"About how far?" asked Carol.

"About a couple of miles to the place where we turn off the main road."

"But how far is it from here to the Castle?" asked Victoria.

"Oh, that would be about six miles, I suppose, from where we are now," said Jim.

"But how far until we can see the Castle in the distance?"

"Oh, gosh!" Jim thought quickly for a moment. His mind had gone back in a flash to the very first day he had himself seen Rhodes Castle, which had also been in the evening after a long and very memorable train journey down from the North with Susan. "Well, the road runs through Rhodes Park for a mile or two before we get to the South Lodge, which is where the main drive begins; and there's a place on the road - the public road - where you can see the Great Tower in the distance. That would be... about four miles from here. Would you think it was about four miles, Sue?"

"Yes, I'd say it's about four miles," said Susan. "I know the place you mean, darling."

"How are things going on at home, Dad - and at the mine?" asked Jim a moment later, thinking it well to change the subject.

"Things are going very well at home, thank you," said Mr. Sandy, "and at the mine; at least, we should say 'the mines', shouldn't we, Jackie?"

"That's right," said Jackie. "We have an interest nowadays in two other sites as well as our own Leadthwaite Mine as potential venues for extending our activities."

"Gosh, that sounds exciting!" said Jim. "And - I say - you said you'd found something particularly interesting in the mineral line?"

"Ah, yes," said Jackie, "we did find something at Carrock the other day when we were there with the professor. At least, you found the stuff in the beck there, Arthur."

"But what is it?" asked Jim.

"Ah, well - I'll tell you later, Jim," said his father. "At least, I won't tell you as I expect you might know what it is when I show it to you - but that had better wait until we get to the Castle."

"That's right, Mr. Sandy!" laughed Susan, half turning her head for a moment to smile at him. "Keep us in suspense!"

There seemed to be nothing to say in answer to that so Jim was silent for a moment, as many thoughts and speculations passed rapidly through his mind. He had glanced round quickly at his sisters, and had seen by the smiles on their faces that they had evidently seen this thing which had been found in the beck at Carrock Mine. He reasoned that it must be a rare mineral:

something worth making a fuss about. Well, what rare minerals were supposed to be found around Carrock Mine? He thought of the very rare tellurides of bismuth that supposedly had been detected there. If his father and Jackie had found, and taken away, a piece, or pieces, of rock containing one of those minerals (such as joseite) in amounts big enough to identify with the naked eye, then, surely, that *would* be quite some discovery! But that, surely, would be very unlikely. The thought that they might have found gold passed through his mind, but then he thought that it was, if anything, even less likely that they could have discovered gold; after all, so far as Jim knew, no gold had ever *definitely* been found at Carrock, in spite of many rumours and popular stories about it being there.

They came to the place where Susan turned off the main road to the right onto the smaller road which ran through the Rhodes Park to Leigh, but Jim, lost in his thoughts, hardly noticed it.

"Here we are in the Park," said Susan. "It's on both sides of the road from here onwards."

"You mean, this is Rhodes Park?" said Jackie.

"Yes, this is our parkland surrounding the Castle - Rhodes Park."

"So we'll soon be coming to the first place where you can see the Castle?" asked Victoria.

"Yes, quite soon," said Susan.

"It's about another two miles, or slightly less," said Jim, coming out of his mineral daydreams. "It's just before we get to South Lodge, where we turn off into the drive through the main gates."

"Oh, good!" said Carol. "We'll very soon be seeing it, Vicci."

"I'll point out the place when we come to it," said Jim.

His mood had changed again. With mineralogy forgotten, he had easily picked up the feeling of light-hearted gaiety and excitement of his sisters. In fact, he was strongly reminded of how he had himself felt on the first day on which he had seen Rhodes

Castle. On that evening, he remembered, he had been just as eager to catch his first of the Castle in the distance as Carol and Victoria now were. It was altogether a good feeling, and it was not in the least spoilt, either, by the presence of Jackie, sitting in the front passenger seat.

Remembering his past unwise adventure with Jackie, and its almost disastrous consequences, he had been a little apprehensive about how he would feel about meeting her this time, but he had been pleasantly surprised to find that now he did not seem to be attracted to her at all.

I certainly don't want to feel attracted to Jackie again now that Rachel has come into my life! Jim told himself. He had not seen Rachel Connor again since the day when he and Susan had briefed her on the details of the Guide job. However, he had often found himself thinking about her and fantasising about her in many an idle moment. Then he would tell himself sharply that it was quite pointless to fall in love with another man's wife, and that it would bring him nothing but misery to do so. He would remind himself of how deeply he was still in love with his darling wife, Susan, and would argue to himself that there was no room in his heart for anyone else.

As the car came to the last straight stretch of the road before the turning-off at South Lodge, Jim was in an easy, carefree mood: all amorous and worrying thoughts were far from his mind.

"There you are," he said, pointing out of the window. "There's the tower of the Castle."

The eyes of all the passengers in the car turned to the right to look that way.

"There it is!" said Victoria.

"I see it!" said Carol.

"Is that the tower called the Great Tower?" asked Mr. Sandy.

"Yes," said Jim, "that's the Great Tower."

"And here's South Lodge and the beginning of our drive," said Susan as she turned to the right off the public road.

"My word, what magnificent drive gates you've got here!" said Mr. Sandy as the car swept through the open gates.

"And what a superb avenue of trees lining your drive!" said Jackie. "I like the way it leads one's eye up to the Great Tower in the distance."

"It is pretty good, isn't it?" agreed Susan.

"Is that the tower that's supposed to be haunted?" asked Mr. Sandy.

"Yes, that's the one."

"Haunted?" said Carol. The Twins looked at each other doubtfully.

"Oh, don't worry about that!" said Jim, smiling. "The ghost very rarely appears."

"But you've seen it yourself, haven't you, Jim?" said Victoria.

"Yes, it's true: I have seen the ghost. But that was out-of-doors, and not in the Tower Library, which is supposed to be the most haunted room in the Castle."

"You saw it out-of-doors? But where?" asked Victoria.

"I met the ghost one very misty morning in the inner part of the drive - beyond that white gate you can see in the distance."

"But who is this ghost?" asked Carol. "Do tell us, Jim. We don't know anything about it."

"Well," said Jim, "her name was Beryl Buxton, and she used to work here as a servant; but that's quite a long story, so I'll tell you about it later. There are other things to look at now."

"Of course," said Carol.

"That road we've just passed on the left leads to Rhodes Church.

And that small house you can see on the left-hand side of the drive further on is called the Inner Lodge; and the Visitor Centre is just off this road to the right at the crossroads there."

The visitors were looking around them, admiring everything that they could see as the car moved up the drive. They came to the Inner Lodge crossroads (where Stable Road, to the left, lead down past the stables to West Lodge) and, slowing down, passed through the open white gates into the inner part of the main drive. Jim now became silent for a moment as his eyes began to scan very carefully the prospect of the Castle lawns. He had remembered Rachel Connor. Oh, don't be ridiculous! he told himself sharply. She won't be here now. She must have gone home long ago! But, powerless to stop himself, his eyes went on with their diligent search.

The others, meanwhile, were continuing to talk enthusiastically.

"I say, Arthur, look at that huge tree!" said Jackie, looking at the heavy branches of the great cedar tree.

"It's a cedar, I suppose?" said Mr. Sandy. "And the ponds do look lovely, don't they, and the fountains?" He glanced round for a moment towards his son, but saw by the blank look on Jim's face that he appeared to be lost in his own thoughts.

"Well, here we are at the Castle," said Susan. "Yes, that's a cedar tree, and it's very old certainly, but I can't remember how many hundreds of years old it's supposed to be." Looking around, she noticed her aunt and uncle sitting on a bench on the lawn, enjoying the evening sunshine. "There's Aunt Nora and Uncle Geoffrey," she said, waving to them. "They're Lord and Lady Padgate, and they're staying here with us," she added for the benefit of her latest visitors. "I'll introduce you to them in a minute, when we get out of the car."

Lord and Lady Padgate, who had drinks glasses in their hands, stood up to be ready to be introduced to the other members of Jim's family.

*

Some ten minutes later they were all sitting down in the White Drawing Room. Susan had received a discreet message from Samantha to the effect that dinner was ready, more or less, but that it would be possible to "keep things hot for a quarter of an hour, or so" while people sat down to talk and relax and enjoy a short drink before dinner.

After Jim's family had been introduced to Lord and Lady Padgate they all went into the Great Hall of the Castle. Jack, the butler, and Samantha had emerged from the front door to carry in the guests' heavier luggage.

"Jack and Samantha are going to carry your suitcases up to your rooms now," Susan had said when they were assembled in the Great Hall, "but I expect you would like to wash your hands first after your journey..." She broke off, seeing her guests staring around in wonder at the stags' heads and banners high up in the Penumbral Gloom of the dark Hall. "Well, what do you think, Jackie?"

"Oh, I think it's very nice," said Jackie cautiously, looking round at her husband as if trying to divine what he thought about it.

"And very impressive," said Mr. Sandy.

"And have you detected anything supernatural in there with this equipment?" asked Jackie.

"Not yet," said Susan," but perhaps we will presently. At least, when I say 'we' I suppose I should really say 'they'. There are two men – two of our visitors actually, who are evidently very interested in ghosts – who came here to ask my permission to set up that equipment in the Tower Library a few days ago... Do you remember when that was exactly, Jim, darling?"

"Oh, well..." (Jim thought for a moment). "Yes, it was the evening before the day the Padgates arrived, so it was just over a week ago."

"So it was," said Susan. "And, you see, they've been calling in every night and every morning since then to check their camera and their other instruments to see whether they've 'caught' anything; but so far they haven't."

"But for how long are they going to have their equipment in there?" asked Jackie. "Presumably you've set a time limit on this experiment?"

"Oh, yes indeed," said Susan. "At least, they've set their own time limit on it, really. You see, they've come over from America to stay here for, I think, three weeks?" (She looked round at Jim, who nodded to her.) "Yes, and at the end of their three weeks they're going to dismantle their equipment to take it away with them."

"I'd like to see this equipment – if I may?" said Jackie.

"And I'd be interested to see it as well," said Mr. Sandy.

"Well then, we'll call in next door to have a quick look at what they've got in there before we go into the Dining-Room for dinner," said Susan.

"We've seen it," said Nora Padgate, "and we both thought it was rather an amazing thing to do: to catch a ghost on film! At least, I think you thought, Geoffrey, that it would be more likely to frighten off any ghosts that might be about the place!"

"Well, I believe I did say that," said Geoffrey Padgate.

During a moment's silence Mr. Sandy, having taken a sip from his glass of sweet sherry, whispered to Jackie at his side.

"Shall I bring out that box now?"

"You'd better ask Susan first," Jackie whispered back to him.

"Lady Dalmane," said Mr. Sandy, "would it be all right for me to bring out our little mineral box now to show people what we've found?

Or perhaps there wouldn't be time now before dinner?"

"Oh, do let us see it now!" said Susan, smiling at him. "I'm sure we're all longing to see what's in it; and, of course, dinner can wait a few more minutes, if necessary."

"All right – here it is then."

Mr. Sandy dipped his left hand into the inside pocket of the jacket he was wearing, and slowly drew out a small wooden box. Meanwhile with his right hand he was holding his wife's hand. Arthur and Jackie smiled lovingly at each other, enjoying the atmosphere of mounting suspense they were creating. Mr. Sandy stood up to offer the box to Susan first.

"No," she said, "let Jim see this first; it'll mean much more to him than to me." She put out her hand for the box to pass it on to Jim.

Jim, in his turn, stood up to take the box, and everyone else also rose to their feet, eager to catch a glimpse of whatever rare mineral specimen might be contained in that little wooden box.

"I'll put it on this little table so that we can all see what's in it," he said.

The box was of polished wood with a hinged lid which was fastened with a brass catch; it was slightly bigger than the average jewel-box (about 3 inches x 1.25 inches). Jim unfastened the catch and lifted the lid, already straining his eyes for a first glimpse of what he should find inside the box even before the lid was fully raised. Around him and behind him several other pairs of eyes were also straining for a first glimpse. However, the lid, once opened, revealed a temporary anticlimax.

Inside the box, resting on a purple cushion, there was a small piece of carefully screwed up tissue paper. Evidently the real contents of the box were wrapped up in that piece of tissue paper. With fingers that trembled slightly, in spite of his best efforts to open and smooth out the paper carefully and calmly, Jim opened the paper; and as he did so he drew in his breath sharply as he immediately caught sight of something which, at a first glance, might have been taken for some yellowish dust. However, he also noticed at once in two slightly larger pieces of the mineral a bright metallic lustre – not a sparkle – which excited him considerably.

"Gosh...! My word...! It's gold, isn't it?"

"It is indeed gold!" said his father.

"Oh, isn't that lovely!" exclaimed Nora Padgate admiringly.

"My goodness, it certainly is lovely!" said Susan. "You *have* been lucky, Mr. Sandy, if you've really found gold!"

"Is that real gold that you've got there?" asked Geoffrey Padgate. "Are you sure it isn't just fool's gold?"

"Oh, yes, we are *quite* sure that this is not fool's gold," said Jackie. "What we've got here is a small quantity of gold dust which Arthur, my husband, found in the river close to Carrock Mine."

"What? By panning?" asked Geoffrey Padgate.

"Yes, by panning for it," said Jackie.

Jim was staring in bemused amazement at the tiny pieces of gold lying on their piece of paper in the box. The others, except for his father and Jackie, were also staring at the gold dust over his shoulder.

"I can't really believe that this is gold!" he murmured thoughtfully.

"Have a closer look at it, Jim," advised his father. "Here, try looking at it through this lens." Mr. Sandy took from a pocket a powerfully magnifying jeweller's lens and handed it to Jim.

"May I pick up one of the larger bits to get a proper look at it?" he asked.

"Of course you may! It won't do it any harm to be handled."

Carefully Jim picked up the largest of the little pieces of gold.

He placed it on the palm of his left hand and, inserting the lens into his right eye, proceeded to examine it closely.

"It's *very* beautiful!" he said presently. Looking up, he saw the faces of the Twins, smiling at him over his shoulder. "I expect you knew about this before?" he said.

"Yes, we've been shown it before," said Carol, "but we'd sworn to keep it absolutely a secret, you see. Anyway, we wouldn't have wanted to spoil this moment for you by telling you what Dad had found before he was ready to show it to you."

"Just so," said Victoria. "But, you know, we can hardly believe either that Dad really has found gold! It's amazing! It's wonderful!"

It *is* amazing!" said Jim, who was again studying closely the tiny lump of gold in his hand by means of the lens. Then he remembered that Susan was waiting to have a look at it. "Here you are, Sue," he said, taking the lens out of his eye, and handing it and the gold over to Susan.

"My word, it does look beautiful!" she murmured as, with the lens in her eye, she carefully studied the nugget of gold in her turn. She thought for a moment and then asked a question.

"Does it look as if its edges have been rounded off because it's been underwater for a long time?"

"That's just how it is, Lady Dalmane," said Mr. Sandy. "It must have come out of the rock originally, and most probably it has come out of a quartz vein. But this is what we call 'alluvial gold' or 'placer gold'. You see, when small scales or grains of gold have been rolled along underwater on a river bed for a long time, and sometimes for a considerable distance, that tend to lose their distinctive crystalline shape, and they end up as agglomerations of gold with soft rounded edges."

"I see," said Susan.

"And then we can properly call them nuggets of gold," said Jackie. "This, in fact, is a very small nugget that you're holding in the palm of your hand now, Lady Dalmane."

"Well, it's absolutely lovely!" said Susan.

"Do you suppose there's more of this gold where this came from?" asked Geoffrey Padgate. He was standing behind Susan as if he was trying his hardest to catch a glimpse of the tiny nugget. "What do you think about it, Mr. Sandy?"

"I think there's sure to be more gold where this came from," said Mr. Sandy. "Wouldn't you say so, Jackie, darling?"

"Oh, yes, I'd say it's almost certain that there'll be more gold in the rocks where this came from - probably a lot more," said Jackie. "But whether there's any more gold to be found in the river - well, that's another matter. You see, these grains of gold may have been washed down by the river a long way from their source which, very likely, will be a quartz vein in the Skiddaw Granite. And frankly we have absolutely *no* idea - at least not yet - of where this gold-bearing vein might be in relation to the place where we did our panning in the river."

"But you're going to find it, Dad, of course?" said Victoria.

"And when you have found it you'll start mining gold by the ton, and then we'll all make our fortunes!" said Carol.

Mr. Sandy laughed.

"Oh dear, I wish it was as easy as that - but I'm afraid it isn't!"

"Oh, well, Dad, I know that there will inevitably be some practical difficulties to be overcome first; but if you do find a vein in the rock with plenty of gold in it, then surely you will be starting a gold mine there presently?"

"Oh, yes, I agree with you, Carol; of course I do," said her father. "If all goes well, nothing could be nicer or better than to have a viable mine working there presently. But first things first; and the first point is that, as things stand at the moment, we have no right to do *anything* on the land there - and perhaps no right even to be there - let alone having any mining rights. So, you see, the first step would have to be to negotiate with the landowner there for permission to make some exploratory borings to find out what lies beneath the surface."

A few minutes later, when Nora and Geoffrey Padgate had both gasped with pleasure at the close-up sight of the gold, and it had been safely returned to its box, Susan lead the way, and the party went out into the Hall, still talking excitedly of gold. Susan pointed to the door of the Tower Library as they passed it, and suggested that her latest guests might like to go in there to have a quick look at the scientific equipment which had been set up for ghost detecting. Mr. Sandy and Jackie both said that they would be very interested to see it, so now the whole party moved into the Tower Library.

"Gosh!" exclaimed Jackie.

"Good heavens!" said Mr. Sandy.

"Well, there it is," said Susan. "That's the camera, you see, but Jim and I don't really know what these other gadgets are, or how they're supposed to work."

"No, we don't," said Jim, "but I *think* that this thing which looks rather like a sort of lamp must be what they call the 'photon beam'."

"Ah, I see!" said Jackie. "That must be what that mirror over there is meant for. That thing that looks like a lamp must send out a beam of radiation of some sort which is reflected back to it by that mirror." She was looking at a small circular mirror mounted on a tripod which was standing against the wall of the room opposite to the lamp.

Jim realized with some admiration that Jackie's keen scientific mind seemed to have already worked out how the equipment was supposed to work, even before it had been explained to her.

"Well, I'll tell you what," said Susan: "it won't be long before Jack Wonstannley and Doctor Oakley come in, as they do each evening, to examine their equipment and switch things on, ready for the night; and, if you'd like to meet them, I could ask our butler to let us know in the Dining Room that they've arrived. No doubt they could explain what they're up to better than we can."

"That sounds like a splendid idea!" said Mr. Sandy. "Thank you very much, Lady Dalmane."

"We'd better go and have our dinner now," said Susan. "They usually come in at about nine o' clock, or a little after that, to look at their equipment, so it might mean going through there to talk to them before we've finished our meal – if you don't mind doing that."

"We won't mind at all, thank you, Lady Dalmane," said Mr. Sandy.

They were just beginning the dessert course when Jack, the butler, came into the Dining Room to tell Susan that Mr. Wonstannley and Dr. Oakley had just arrived. Susan was serving helpings of sherry trifle from a huge bowl in front of her on the table, but now she passed a helping to Victoria and stood up.

"We'd better go through and talk to our American ghost hunters now as they may not want to stay very long, and then we can come back to our dinner," she said to Mr. Sandy, who was sitting to her right (Jackie was sitting to her left).

"Oh, they're American, are they?" said Mr. Sandy.

"They are indeed. Now, if you'll excuse us, Twins, and you, Uncle Geoffrey and Aunt Nora, we'll leave the room – I take it you don't particularly want to come and talk to these people now?"

"I think we'd rather stay here, Susan, thank you," said Nora Padgate with a glance across the table at her husband, who nodded to her.

"And you two?" Susan was now looking at Carol.

"We'll stay here too, thank you," said Carol, and Victoria nodded her head in agreement. Jim, however, had risen to his feet.

"Jim, darling, don't you think that you ought to stay here to look after these people?" said Susan. "But I don't think we'll be out of here for very long."

"All right," said Jim, sitting down again. His place at the table was opposite to Susan's place on the round dining table. Carol was sitting to his right, and Victoria to his left.

Susan, Mr. Sandy, and Jackie now left the room to go to talk to the ghost hunters.

"Hello there, Lady Dalmane!" exclaimed Jack Wonstannley cheerfully, turning round as Susan and the Sandys entered the

Tower Library. Dr. Philip Oakley also turned his head for a moment, but said nothing; he appeared to be busy doing something with his camera.

"Hello, Mr. Wonstannley," said Susan. "Hello, Doctor Oakley. I've brought in a couple of friends of mine, scientists, who would be most interested in knowing a little bit more about this equipment of your's, and how it works."

"Oh, yeah, sure; we'll show them."

"This is Arthur Sandy, the father of my husband, Jim, and this is Jackie Sandy, his wife, and Jim's stepmother. And this is Jack Wonstannley and Doctor Philip Oakley, from California."

When they had all shaken hands Susan asked Jack Wonstannley whether they had yet had any success.

"Yeah, I guess we've had *some* success – in a way!" said Jack Wonstannley. "At least, our camera has at last taken a few pictures last night."

"But were they not the sort of pictures you're hoping for?"

"Ah, I guess you're right there, ma'am!" chuckled Jack. "Indeed, they're not at *all* what we were hoping for!"

"They're here if you want to see them," said Dr. Oakley. "I've just printed them." He handed a packet of photographs to Susan, who handed it on to Mr. Sandy.

"Oh, my goodness!" Mr. Sandy laughed suddenly as he looked at a photograph of a moth in flight against a shadowy background of one of the bookshelves of the Tower Library. "Look at this, Jackie," he said; but Jackie was already looking over his shoulder, and Susan was also trying to see what the camera had captured. There were six photographs altogether, and Mr. Sandy, glancing rapidly through the rest of them, saw that they were all studies of the same moth. He handed them on to Jackie.

When they had all seen the photographs Susan handed them back to Jack Wonstannley.

"Obviously, you must be very disappointed by these?" she said.

"Oh, sure, yeah, I guess it's disappointing," said Jack Wonstannley, "but, in a way, I reckon it's a good thing to get these photos - it shows that our equipment *does* work okay automatically in the dark - in the infra-red."

"So you think that if it had been a ghost moving about, rather than a moth, you might have captured it on film?" said Mr. Sandy.

"Why not?" said Mr. Wonstannley.

"Yes, indeed... but what do you think, darling?"

"Well," said Jackie, "I would say, scientifically speaking, that it's doubtful whether anything as insubstantial as a ghost *could* be recorded on film. But I don't know, really."

"Ah, that's it; we don't really know either," said Mr. Wonstannley. "But may I ask you, Mrs. Sandy, what your line in science is?"

"I'm a geologist. My husband and I are both mining engineers and geologists."

"Oh, so you're into mining?" said Dr. Oakley. "That sounds interesting. Do you work a mine, then?"

"Yes, we do," said Jackie. "We're currently working a mine in Cumberland, where we come from, for barite - barium sulphate." Jackie paused, and glanced meaningly at her husband, and caught his eye.

"Oh, sure! That's interesting," said Dr. Oakley.

"Yeah, I guess that must be a most interesting profession, and a satisfactory one," said Mr. Wonstannley; "leastways, if you're lucky enough to strike it rich, as you might say."

Mr. Sandy and Jackie looked at each other meaningly, and each of them knew that the other one also knew that nothing whatever was to be said about gold. For the present time the fewer people that knew about the discovery at Carrock, the better.

"That's just so," said Mr. Sandy, "and we have been pretty lucky recently at our Leadthwaite Mine, haven't we, Jackie?" (Jackie nodded her head.) "And we're thinking of extending our operations into zinc mining, as the results of some preliminary prospecting look very promising."

Susan looked at her watch. "If you don't mind me saying so, Mr. Wonstannley," she said, "we ought to be going back to the Dining Room soon to re-join my other guests, and to finish our meal."

"Oh, I'm so sorry, ma'am, if we're keeping you from your meal by talking here," said Jack Wonstannley politely. "We didn't know you were having your meal now."

"Never mind!" said Susan. "Of course you didn't know, but you said you were going to show Mr. Sandy and Jackie how this equipment of your's works, you remember?"

"That's right, ma'am; we'll do that right now."

"Shall I explain how things work?" suggested Dr. Oakley. "I reckon I could explain things quite briefly if you're in a hurry to get back to your meal."

They thanked him very much, and Dr. Oakley went straight into an explanation of how his equipment worked. Some five minutes later, when they returned to the Dining Room, Mr. Sandy and Jackie were feeling perfectly satisfied that they now knew how the equipment and the camera they had seen was supposed to be able to detect the presence of any ghosts that might appear in the Tower Library. Jackie, however, was sceptical about their chances of success.

"Frankly, I don't believe that that equipment they've got is capable of detecting ghosts (if there *are* any ghosts!)," she said.

"Well, you may be right, but I prefer to keep an open mind on it," said Mr. Sandy.

"Here we are again," said Susan. "I'm sorry we've been away so long while you've been finishing your meal, but I expect we'll soon catch up with you now!" She had seen as soon as she had come into the Dining Room that the others had finished eating their dessert, and were now chatting happily among themselves.

"It's quite all right," said Carol.

"We don't mind," said Victoria.

"Have you had a satisfactory talk with the ghost hunters?" asked Geoffrey Padgate.

"Oh, yes, *very* satisfactory, thank you," said Mr. Sandy. "We've both been quite fascinated by Doctor Oakley's explanation of how his equipment is supposed to work."

"Only I don't believe that that equipment is ever going to work for them," said Jackie. "At least, not in the detecting and catching of ghosts, but it works alright for photographing moths, and things like that, as we've seen for ourselves!"

"Oh, really? So they've only managed to capture moths on film so far?" said Geoffrey Padgate. "Well, I did say that that equipment was more likely to scare off any ghosts that might be there than to catch them!"

"And maybe that's what has been happening," said Nora Padgate.

"Oh, yes, maybe it is," agreed Jackie, "but, as I said to my husband just now, I don't believe that they're using the right equipment to catch a ghost - if *any* sort of equipment would be right for that - although I certainly think that what they've thought up is very clever - their equipment *is* very ingenious. I give them all credit for that!"

CHAPTER SIX

The evening sunshine, reflected from the large gilded mirror over the fireplace, was gleaming softly off the sweeping golden arms of the chandelier which hung in the centre of the ceiling of the White Drawing Room. The chandelier was, in fact, one of the great treasures of the Dalmane family of Rhodes Castle; its arms were made of silver plated in twenty-four carat gold. It was one of the fixtures of that room which, along with the china display shelves of the north wall and the mirror over the mantelpiece (above the fireplace in the middle of the east wall) always particularly delighted Nora Padgate. This evening she was standing by the fireplace with her husband, chatting with Susan's sister, Denise Allerby; while in another corner of the room Susan was talking with Denise's husband, Rupert. Jackie and Arthur Sandy were sitting on the large sofa (which stood along the south wall of the room) but Jim and the Twins were not in the room at all. Jim had gone in the car to pick up Nigel and Norma Beck, when they arrived by train from Bournemouth at Stalham station, but Carol and Victoria were, for the moment, walking outside in the garden, enjoying a beautiful May evening in the sunshine. They had, however, promised to come back into the Drawing Room to mix politely with the other guests as soon as Jim should arrive back in the car with the Becks.

"I *do* like the colour of your dress!" said Nora Padgate, looking admiringly at the very tall, elegant figure of Denise Allerby, who was wearing a bright pink party dress which she liked to put on for parties.

"Thank you!" said Denise. "My husband calls it my 'shocking pink', but he does like it! And I think that Jim rather likes it too. I remember that I wore it when we had a party at my mother's house for Sue and Jim when they were engaged to be married. Where is Jim, by the way?"

"Sue said that he'd gone in the car to fetch two more friends of their's who are coming to the party, so he's picking them up at Stalham station."

"Oh, I see," said Denise.

"So we're going to be quite a jolly party here tonight," said Geoffrey Padgate. "Twelve of us altogether, in fact; and I believe Sue said that everyone will be staying here tonight."

"So quite a lot of the many spare rooms here are going to be occupied tonight," said Nora Padgate. "I *do* think it's very jolly having so many of us here all at the same time!"

"Oh, yes, I quite agree with you, Aunt Nora," said Denise. "I'm very glad that Rupert and I decided that we could come, but, of course, it's a pity that Mum and Dad couldn't come... Ah...! Here come those other guests."

Nigel and Norma Beck had just come into the room, closely followed by Jim. Then, a moment later, Carol and Victoria appeared. Like everyone else in the Drawing Room they were formally dressed for the party; both girls were looking very attractive in black party dresses.

Susan greeted Norma Beck with a kiss on the cheek and Nigel Beck with a warm handshake. She had not seen Norma for a few years, and was pleasantly surprised to see how well she looked; indeed, she thought that Norma looked, if anything, even a little younger than the woman she had remembered. Certainly she looked a little plumper than the dreadfully thin, ill-looking person she had remembered. But she *was* ill on that day when we met them at Cockermouth station, she reminded herself.

The Becks were introduced to all the other guests, and drinks glasses were handed to them, and the small talk in the room continued.

Like Nora Padgate, Norma Beck was immediately struck by the formal beauty and elegance of the White Drawing Room. She had seen the room once before on a short visit to the Castle, but this was the first time her husband had been there. She told Susan that she thought that it was a particularly beautiful room.

"I particularly love that big gilded mirror over the fireplace," she enthused. "So wonderfully elegant - particularly now with that very tall woman - your sister - reflected in it!"

"Oh yes," said Susan, "but I wasn't too sure myself, to tell you the truth, that I care for the colour of Denise's dress: it's rather startlingly bright!" To herself Susan was saying, "It's downright vulgar, that shocking pink!"

"Perhaps," said Norma Beck. "But no matter: I do admire this room very much! What do you think, Nigel, dear?"

"Oh, I agree with you very much, Norma, my dear, about this being a lovely room," said Nigel Beck. "There's a great feeling of light in here, isn't there... light and elegance?"

"Indeed there is," said Geoffrey Padgate, coming up to them. "My wife and I both admire the elegance of Rhodes Castle, and this room in particular; in fact, the drawing-room of our own place, Dallam Hall, seems almost dark and dreary, compared with this!"

"And where exactly is your place, Lord Padgate?" asked Norma beck.

"Warrington. Dallam Hall is just outside Warrington - which, I admit, is not exactly the most attractive place in England!"

"Ah, but I expect it has character and history," said Norma Back tactfully.

"Oh, it does indeed!"

"We don't really know Warrington, although we have passed through it by train," said Nigel Beck. "In fact... yes, we *have* seen Dallam Hall. Do you remember, Norma?"

"Oh, yes, of course I remember: we came past Dallam Hall that day we travelled south in the train with Susan and Jim; and after we'd passed through Warrington station Susan pointed it out for us. If I remember right we saw a handsome building of red sandstone."

"That's the one," said Geoffrey Padgate. "I don't know whether I'd really call it 'handsome', mind you; perhaps 'imposing' would be a better word to describe it. But Nora and I really think of it as a rather ugly house, to tell you the truth."

"Wasn't it built by one of your ancestors who had a connection with the railways?" asked Norma Beck. "I seem to remember Susan telling us something like that."

"Yes, that's correct," said Geoffrey Padgate. "An ancestor of mine was one of the first directors of the Warrington and Newton Railway, and it was he who had the present Dallam Hall built where it is now - within sight of the railway lines. But Dallam Hall was the seat and home of the Padgates of Dallam for centuries before that."

"But not the same house?" said Nigel Beck.

"No, it was a different house on a different site; and then the old Dallam Hall was pulled down when they built the new one on the present site."

*

They were just finishing the dessert course when an incident occured which changed the whole feeling of the evening for everyone present in the Banqueting Hall.

It had been a well organized and most successful dinner party. The conversation had flowed easily around and across the long table, and everyone had been in a relaxed and cheerful mood. They had been talking about the hauntings of their various stately homes. Nora and Geoffrey Padgate had been telling the others about the Blue Lady of Dallam Hall, but Geoffrey Padgate had said that a postcard which they sold to their visitors, a card showing a picture of a lady wearing a long blue dress was, in his opinion, certainly a fake.

"That was never a ghost, you know, that figure in blue floating along our Gallery," he said.

"Floating?" said Denise.

"Well, I've no doubt that the lady was, in fact, merely walking along the passage when the photo was taken."

"But they've made it look as if she was floating – not touching the ground – like a ghost?"

"That's exactly what they've done; but, mind you, it has been done quite cleverly."

"We have a ghost at Soken Hall, my parents' home," said Denise.

"Apparently he was a former Marquis of Walton who was a keen horseman, and so, not surprisingly, he's usually seen riding round the rooms and passages on his black horse – or so they say – but I've never seen him myself. But you've seen Tom at Soken Hall, haven't you, Sue?"

"Oh, no, I've never seen him," said Susan. "I've only heard tell of him from Father, who has seen him..." Her words faded into silence.

For a few seconds nobody spoke. There was not a sound to be heard in the Banqueting Hall. Then all their heads turned together towards the door into the Dining Room.

John Dalmane, Susan's former husband, the late Earl of Saint Helens, was coming into the Banqueting Hall from the Dining

Room, next door. No one saw the door move; the Earl simply appeared as if he had come straight through the closed door. He moved swiftly and completely silently down the long hall as if he meant to come to talk with Susan, who was sitting at the head of the table, at the other end of the Banqueting Hall.

No one moved or spoke. It was as if the temperature in the Banqueting Hall had suddenly dropped to some point well below freezing, although no one actually felt cold. As Jim said afterwards, describing his feelings to Susan, he would not have been entirely surprised to have seen icicles hanging from the ceiling during those long seconds when the ghost was moving through the Hall.

Jim was longing to get up, to hurry to his wife's side, and to put an arm around her shoulders, but he found that he could not do it. It was as if his legs simply would not work while the ghostly figure was visibly present in the room.

Only the heads of the dinner guests turned as they watched Lord Dalmane until he came to the door opposite to the one through which he had entered the Banqueting Hall. Then, without the slightest pause or break in his stately movement they saw him pass through the closed door which lead into the Great Hall. This done, the apparition vanished instantly.

For a few seconds longer still no one in the Banqueting Hall moved or made a sound. Then Jim suddenly found himself springing to his feet. In a moment he was at Susan's side to comfort her. He had noticed, as they had all noticed, that the ghostly figure had kept moving at a stately pace through the Hall all the time except for one moment when it had briefly stopped right behind Susan's chair. Susan, however, had already buried her face in her hands, as if the episode was too much for her to bear, but Jim did not pause to consider that she might not have been aware that the apparition had stopped right behind her chair.

As he jumped to his feet Jim's thoughts and feelings were in such a state of commotion that he hardly noticed that several other people in the room were also at that moment violently giving vent to their pent-up emotions. He hardly heard Norma Beck's shriek, or saw her collapse forward dramatically onto the table; and he scarcely noticed Nigel Back rushing round the table to come to his wife's aid (luckily there was no question of Mr. Beck and Jim colliding as they were both moving round the table in the same direction).

"Sue, darling!" said Jim gently, putting an arm protectively around his wife's shoulder.

Susan looked up at once as Jim touched her. For a moment she gave him a half-smile, but she did not speak. Jim thought that her face looked strangely white and lifeless. But probably we all look rather white just now, because of shock, he thought. He kissed her gently on the cheek, and thought that her face did not seem as warm as usual.

"Darling... are you all right?" he continued.

Susan looked into his eyes for a moment, and seemed to draw comfort from her husband's kiss.

"I'm all right, Jim, darling," she said in a quiet voice. Then she looked round the room, and seemed to pull herself together. "But look, there's Norma with her head on the table!" she continued in a crisper voice. "Is she all right?"

"I'll go and see..." began Jim; but at that moment they suddenly saw Norma Beck jerk her head upright. Clearly she had not fainted, as Jim had feared for a moment.

"Oh, Nigel!" she gasped. "It was *awful*!" Quick! Let's get out of here!"

"But, darling, do you *really* want to go now?" asked Nigel Beck in what Jim thought sounded like a rather shaky voice.

"Yes, yes! Let's go right now!"

"Oh, well... but..."

Luckily for Mr. Back they were all suddenly distracted at that moment by a knock on the door through from the Great Hall. The butler, white faced, rose to his feet, but before he could come to the door it opened, and in came a rather breathless Jack Wonstannley.

"I sure beg your pardon, Lady Dalmane, for coming in uninvited..." he began, but then broke off, evidently aware of the look of shock on all the faces in the Banqueting Hall. "Oh...! I see that you've just seen the ghosts too in here?"

Jim, with an arm still around Susan's shoulder, looked quickly into her eyes to see whether she meant to answer Jack herself, or whether he should speak for her; but it was at once obvious to him that his wife, in spite of her shock, was fully in command of the situation.

"It's all right, Mr. Wonstannley," she said. "Yes, we've just seen my late husband pass through this way..."

"Oh, ma'am, but I *am* sorry for you!" said Jack Wonstannley. "That must have been a *dreadful* shock for you, ma'am."

"I dare say it was!"

"But you've just seen him too in the Tower Library?" asked Jim.

"Oh yes, sir, we have just seen him. Or at least, to be precise, sir, we've just seen *two* ghostly figures in there."

"Two? You mean, one of them was Beryl Buxton?"

"That sure was Beryl Buxton, the female figure; and the other one - well, I guess I kind of knew somehow, my Lady, that that must have been John Dalmane, your late husband - although I never actually met him before."

"When he was alive, you mean?"

"Precisely so, ma'am."

"Anyway, Mr. Wonstannley, you might as well have a seat and join us in here for a few minutes now that you've come in. Oh, thank you, Jack, we'll have that chair just here, beside my chair." The butler, with conscientious forethought, was bringing forward a spare chair. At a sign from Susan he set the chair a little back from the table, to the right of her own chair. Then, while Mr. Wonstannley sat down, she remembered Mrs. Beck. She quickly looked round the table again towards Mrs. Beck, but saw that she was sitting down again and appeared to have regained her composure.

"Are you feeling better now, Norma?" she asked.

"Oh, yes, thank you!" said Mrs. Beck with surprising calmness.

"But are you leaving us now?"

Norma Beck looked quickly round to her husband to see what he thought.

"Just as you like, Norma, dear," whispered Nigel Beck.

"No, we'll stay here, thank you," said Norma Beck.

"Very well, so we'll stay," said Nigel Beck, and Susan and Jim could hear the relief evident in his voice. "But I think that we've all just had a pretty nasty shock," he added, looking around the room at the faces of his fellow guests.

"Yes, it has been a very nasty shock for all of us," agreed Susan, "and I'm *so* sorry that this has happened to spoil our evening."

"But it wasn't your fault at all, Sue," said Denise, and Susan noticed that she was now standing beside her; "but I suppose you could almost say that it might have been my fault as I think I was just talking about ghosts at Soken Hall - that might have been enough to make a ghost appear here!"

"Oh no, of course not - really, Denise, what an idea!" said Susan almost crossly. "Anyway, I think that we've said quite enough about ghosts for this evening, except that I'd just like to ask Mr. Wonstannley exactly what he and Doctor Oakley have seen in the Tower Library; and then I suggest that we'd all better move back to the Drawing Room. Is that all right?" She looked round the room quickly, and saw general nods of approval. "Now, do tell me, Mr. Wonstannley, what happened just now in the Tower Library?"

Jack Wonstannley told Susan that he and Dr. Oakley had suddenly, without any sound or warning, seen the figure of John

Dalmane coming through the door from the Hall without opening it. Then the second ghostly figure had simply appeared in the middle of the room; it had appeared spontaneously, he said, as if from nothing, and it was the figure of a woman, clad all in black "Well, no, I guess she was wearing a long black dress down to the ground, ma'am, but her head was bare, and her hair was hanging down around her shoulders; and I knew at once that she was Beryl Buxton."

"You must have been very pleased, though, to see Beryl Buxton at last?" said Susan.

"Well, ma'am, to be truthful: yes, I guess I was mighty pleased to see her - in a way. But I can tell you that it came as a sickening shock to see those two figures just appear like that, out of nothing."

"Yes, of course. But do go on, Mr. Wonstannley. What happened next?"

"Well, ma'am, what happened next was that those two figures moved silently together through the library until they came to the window; and then they simply went through the window and disappeared. And that was all there was to be seen. But we kept very quiet, ma'am, while those two ghosts were crossing the room - we never said a word to each other - but I looked round at Phil, and he pointed to the camera, and nodded to me, ma'am, so I knew that meant that the camera was active, that it was taking pictures. So I reckon that maybe we might have some pretty interesting pictures when we get them developed and printed!"

"Indeed, yes, and I hope that you will indeed get some interesting pictures of those ghosts," said Susan. "But you never know: I suppose it's just as likely that the film, when developed, will simply show nothing but the room and the ordinary things in it."

"Oh, yes, ma'am, and that's just what's so fascinating, ain't it? Well, I guess we should know the answer to that by this time tomorrow, or a bit sooner, maybe. We'll let you know, ma'am, just as soon as we have the answer, what it is."

"Well, thank you very much, Mr. Wonstannley; I'll be very interested to know whether you've managed to capture them on film, or not. But have you any idea yourself of what you expect the result to be?"

"Yeah, well, I guess we *will* get those two figures captured on the film - after all, there really was no doubt that they were there in the room with us for a little while - and you people in here all saw Lord Dalmane, I guess?"

"Yes, I think we all saw him," said Susan.

"But, on the other hand, Phil reckons that when the film is developed and printed there'll be no sign on it of those two ghostly figures; so we'll just have to wait and see who's right, ma'am, presently."

"But you've got some other instruments in there. Perhaps one of them may have picked up and recorded something unusual happening even if the figures don't come out on film?"

"That's just what I was gonna say, ma'am: if the photos haven't worked then maybe our other instruments may have picked up something. I guess we'll soon find out one way or another. Anyway, ma'am, I mustn't keep you from your dinner any longer. Phil and I's gonna be off now, but we'll see you again tomorrow, ma'am, with a full report, I hope, on what we've found out."

"Very well, Mr. Wonstannley, but I think people are ready to leave this room anyway." Susan looked round the room for a moment, and saw that everyone was standing up and talking; the appearance of the ghost of her former husband had certainly had the effect of breaking up the party. "Shall we go back to the Drawing Room now for our coffee, darling?"

"Oh, yes, I think we'd better do that," said Jim, who was still standing quietly at his wife's side.

"Good-bye, Mr. Wonstannley, until we see you again tomorrow," said Susan, rising to her feet to shake Jack Wonstannley warmly by the hand. "And thank you so much for coming in to talk to me. To tell you the truth, it was *very* comforting having you to talk to after that shattering experience!"

"Oh, don't mention it, ma'am; it's always a pleasure to talk with you!" said Jack Wonstannley, beaming happily. "Good-bye - until tomorrow!" He gave a cheery wave with his right hand, and left the Banqueting Hall by the way he had come in from the Great Hall.

Back in the White Drawing Room Susan and Jim and their guests were drinking glasses of port wine to steady their nerves, and discussing amongst themselves what the unexpected and shocking apparition in the Banqueting Hall might mean.

"There's one thing about it," Susan had said as she and Jim had left the Banqueting Hall: Jack Wonstannley didn't really seem shocked at all. But I suppose he must be very pleased, really, to have actually met Beryl Buxton at last."

"Yes, I suppose he must be," Jim had said, "although I don't think that *anyone* could fail to be at least a little shocked on meeting a ghost. My goodness, Sue, I'm sure I'll always remember what a shock I got on that morning when I saw that shadowy figure in the mist."

In the Drawing Room Jim went over to join the rest of his family who, he saw, were clustered together in a group around the fireplace. He had already seen that his sisters were both looking very pale, but that Jackie and his father were looking less shocked than anyone else - with the exception of Jack Wonstannley - and perhaps the Padgates. But the Padgates know all about ghosts in haunted stately homes, he reminded himself, so, of course, they can't have been much upset by what's just happened here.

"Hello, Jim!" said Jackie. "Come and join us. We're just discussing the question of whether those ghosts are likely to have been captured on film, or not, but I think those American ghost hunters are going to be disappointed when they've got their film developed and printed."

"But I'm not so sure about that," said Mr. Sandy. "I'm keeping an open mind about that, but I reckon that they won't be disappointed anyway – whether or not the ghosts have been photographed – since you could say, either way, that that would prove something, scientifically speaking."

"Oh, yes, I know what you mean, Dad," said Jim.

"But are you all right, Jim? You're looking very shocked, if you don't mind me saying so."

"Well, I dare say I am, Dad; but, yes, I'm sure I am all right, really."

"But what about Susan?" asked Jackie. "It must have been a particularly shocking experience for her!"

"Yes, I know," said Jim. He looked anxiously round the room, but felt comforted when he saw that his wife was talking with her sister, Denise, and Denise's husband, Rupert. "Sue's all right," he said, "although it has, of course, been a *particularly* unpleasant experience for her. He was thinking, as he said this, of that moment when the ghost had paused just behind her. Did she know about that? "Anyway, I'll be having a private talk with Sue just as soon as I can," he added.

"I'm sure that would be a good idea," said Jackie.

"But what about you two?" asked Jim, now addressing his sisters. "I'm so sorry that this has happened, you know."

"Oh, I'm all right now," said Victoria. "It was a bit of a shock, seeing that ghost – but that's all. But what do you think, Carol?"

"Yes, I'm all right too," said Carol. "But you really needn't apologies, Jim, for what's happened. It certainly wasn't your fault."

"No, of course it wasn't," said Victoria. "And you told us it was haunted, Jim, and now we know for certain that it is!"

Jim knew that the Twins were feeling all right again, but he sensed that most of the other guests were really as ill at ease as he was himself, in spite of a superficial air of calmness.

*

Susan and Jim were lying in bed and talking over the events of the evening as neither of them was yet feeling ready for sleep.

"But what does it all mean?" said Susan. "Presumably John must have appeared for some reason - not just to frighten us or upset us - but for what reason ?"

"Sue, darling, do you know, that's the very question I was just turning over in my mind? *Why* did he appear?"

"And why did he stop for a moment just behind my chair?"

Jim was very relieved to hear Susan say this as he had felt an extreme reluctance to mention to her this matter of the ghost pausing behind her chair. She might not have known that had happened, he had told himself, so, if she doesn't know about it, perhaps it would be best that she should remain ignorant. However, now that she had mentioned this matter first he was glad that they could talk about it.

"Well," he said slowly, "I wonder if perhaps he was wanting to say something to you - to give you some message - but he couldn't?"

"H'm, yes... I rather think that that's what it really was," said Susan. "But I don't think that ghosts can talk like ordinary living people. At least, I don't think that I can remember any case in which a ghost is said to have actually spoken."

"No, I can't either. But..." At this point a sudden idea came to Jim like a flash of inspiration. "perhaps he wanted to say something to you by putting some thought directly into your mind."

"Oh, you mean by a sort of telepathy? Well, darling, do you know, I really think that perhaps that *was* what was happening when John was standing just behind me."

"But surely, Sue, that sort of thing can't *really* happen?" Jim suddenly wished that he had never mentioned the idea that the ghost might have transferred some message telepathically into her mind. Surely any such message from 'the other side' would be something sinister, or even threatening?

"Oh, but I'm not so sure," said Susan. "I think that John *must* have been trying to tell me something so, if we could just be quiet for a moment, perhaps it will come to me, whatever it is he wants to say to me."

For about a minute neither of them spoke as, reluctantly, Jim agreed to Susan's request for silence; but he was filled with a strange sense of foreboding. He was longing to say something, anything; not just to break the silence, but to break (as it seemed) some evil spell - for it was as if, temporarily, Susan's mind had been taken over by some external force. However, this idea was only very vaguely formed in Jim's mind : all that he was really aware of during those seconds of complete silence was a great feeling of uneasiness.

"I know what it was now," said Susan suddenly, speaking quite calmly as before. Jim, for a moment, felt less tense at the sound of her voice. "It's really quite clear to me now what John was wanting to tell me... only I'm not too sure, darling, whether I ought to tell you."

"Oh, Sue, darling - perhaps you'd better not tell me!" Again Jim was filled with alarm and dread, and yet he realized that he was also longing to hear what Susan was about to tell him.

"When I was thinking about it again just now," said Susan, ignoring her own idea that she ought not to disclose her supernatural "message" to Jim, "it was as clear to me as if I could actually hear John's voice, talking to me. He just said: 'I'll see you again, darling, very soon'. That was all. I'm pretty sure that that was all that he wanted to pass on to me."

"Oh, no... no!" moaned Jim wretchedly.

"Jim, darling! You mustn't be upset, my darling!" Susan's voice changed abruptly as, aware of her husband's distress, her voice became much more sympathetic.

"Sue, darling, I'll *try* not to be upset," said Jim. "But, you see, surely what that message meant - if it meant anything - was that...

you're going to die soon, and then John will see you again - but I won't see you any more!"

Susan did not answer him immediately. There were a few long seconds of tense silence, and then, very gently, she spoke again.

"I'm sorry! Jim, darling, I'm so *very* sorry for you... and I'm sorry I told you that. I definitely shouldn't have upset you by telling you that."

"But, Sue, darling, you were quite *right* to tell me that! We've got no secrets from each other, have we? And it's the truth - it surely *must* be! I know it too, Sue, darling!"

"Well, if you know it too... But, darling, *do* let's forget all about it now - if we can!"

"Yes, I'll try to," said Jim seriously.

"That's right, my darling. Come to me, Jim, my darling!"

They clasped each other tightly, and kissed and cuddled each other for a little while, but Jim soon found that Susan was slackening her clasp on him; and her voice, gently reassuring him that all was well, faded into silence. Susan had fallen asleep.

*

For hour after hour Jim tossed about restlessly on his side of the bed while Susan remained asleep, and while the same depressing, worrying thoughts repeated themselves endlessly in his mind. Eventually, however, he sank into an uneasy state of sleep, but even then he could not escape from the dreadful thought that Susan was soon to die. Now that thought became even more unpleasant as the subject of some very worrying dreams. Presently he woke suddenly in considerable distress, but his mind was so tired and confused that it was a little while before he realized that the bedside light was switched on, and that Susan was clasping his hand, and looking anxiously into his face.

"Jim, darling, it's all right now – it is *really* all right now!" she said quietly. Jim was very relieved to hear her voice, comforting him quietly, but he was dimly aware that she had been speaking to him before. "Darling, you've been having some dreadful nightmares, I think?" she continued.

"Oh, yes...! Oh, Sue, darling, it's been absolutely dreadful...!"

"Never mind, darling, it's all over now, and you're awake again!"

"Am I?" said Jim doubtfully. "It doesn't feel at all as if it's all over!"

Then Susan assured him that she knew exactly what was on his mind and troubling him so badly; she told him that he had been thinking about a possible message from her former husband to the effect that she might die soon. Jim, perhaps because he felt exhausted by the terror of his dreams, was content mostly to listen to the gentle, soothing sound of her voice in silence, although occasionally he put in a word or two himself. However, Jim was more tired than he realized at that time, and he did not understand that his brain did not want to think about what Susan was trying to tell him. He was simply happy to let himself feel comforted by the sound of Susan's voice.

Susan soon realized that what she was saying was having the desired effect on her husband, and, after a while, when she received no answer to the question, "Are you feeling better now, darling?" she understood that he had fallen asleep. Hopefully this time he would have a more peaceful sleep. As for herself, Susan doubted whether she would sleep any more as she now felt rather wakeful, but she knew that, in any case, it would not be very long until she ought to think of getting up.

But I hope Jim gets some decent sleep now, my poor darling. The funny thing is, though, that I don't feel at all upset now by what happened last night – I feel remarkably calm – but I'm sure I shouldn't! It's odd, really... as if John must have put some calming influence on me!

CHAPTER SEVEN

When Jim came out of his bedroom he met the Twins at the top of the stairs. He was feeling very tired and worried, and could only think of the dismal prospect of Susan dying soon, so the cheerful voices of the Twins, breaking in on his morbid thoughts, came as something of a shock to him.

"Good morning, Jim!" they greeted him, one after the other.

"Good morning," said Jim. "I hope you've had a good night?"

"Splendid, thank you!" said Carol.

"Yes, a lovely night, thank you - very comfortable!" said Victoria.

"But, Jim, you don't look as if *you've* had a very good night," said Carol seriously, now looking carefully into his face.

"Well, er... as a matter of fact, I must admit that I have had a rather restless night," admitted Jim. "Actually, I think I had some rather troublesome nightmares while I was asleep."

"Oh, Jim, how dreadful!" exclaimed Victoria.

"Oh dear, I am sorry for you," said Carol. "It must have been that ghost?"

"Yes, it must have been. But have you two *really* slept all right? You haven't had any nightmares or worrying dreams?"

"Oh, no, I certainly haven't," said Carol. "I've had a very peaceful night, actually."

"And so have I," said Victoria. "In fact, I think I had some really rather lovely dreams... but I can't remember anything of what they were about now."

It was clear to Jim that the Twins had not been at all seriously upset by the appearance of the ghost at supper the previous evening.

"Well, look here, shall we go down to breakfast now?" he suggested. "Sue must be down there already... Ah, here comes Dad, and Jackie."

Mr. Sandy and Jackie were coming along the passage from their room. They exchanged "Good mornings!" and, in answer to Jim's question, said that they had had a very comfortable night, thank you. It seems that I'm the only one who's had a bad night! thought Jim. But I hope that Sue's all right; she certainly seemed very calm when she was comforting me in the night. And then I must have dropped off to sleep, and Sue must have slipped out of bed very quietly when it was time to get up, and she must have dressed and left the room while I was still asleep. But, mercifully, there weren't any more nightmares!

They went downstairs and in the Dining Room met Susan and the Becks. Nigel and Norma Beck had almost finished their breakfast, and were thinking of packing up their things in time to leave for their train, but Susan, to keep them company, had only so far eaten the cereal course of her breakfast.

"Good morning!" said Susan cheerfully as the Sandys came into the room. "That's right, come in and sit down anywhere you like." She waved a hand to show that there were plenty of places laid at the table. "I hope you've all had a comfortable night?"

"We've had a lovely night, thank you," said Mr. Sandy. "Very comfortable indeed."

"And we've had a splendidly comfortably night too," said Carol.

"That's good," said Susan. "But I am *so* sorry about last night; it was so upsetting, what happened, wasn't it?"

"Oh, don't worry about that, Lady Dalmane," said Jackie. "Actually, we found it most interesting, didn't we, Arthur?"

"Indeed!" said Mr. Sandy. It was *fascinating* to meet a real ghost here, Lady Dalmane!"

"You see, we're scientists, Arthur and I," said Jackie, "and so we tend to find those sort of things fascinating."

"Well, I'm so glad you can take it that way," said Susan. "That's right, do sit down, and my maid will bring you whatever you want for your breakfasts."

They thanked her, sat down at the table, and said "Good morning" to the Becks, who were smiling at them.

Jim, unsmiling, sat down after the others had sat down. He had not said a word until he mumbled a "Good morning" to the Becks when they greeted him. Carol for a moment looked across the table at her brother, and saw that he was lost in thought, still worried, no doubt, by the nightmares he had suffered.

"Well, we'd better be moving now, Norma dear," said Nigel Beck.

"I'm sorry that we'll have to say 'Good-bye!' so very soon after saying 'Good morning', but we've got to think of catching our train back to Bournemouth, you see"

"Yes, of course; we quite understand," said Jackie.

"What time did you say the train left?" asked Susan.

"It's the nine-one from Stalham," said Nigel Beck.

"Well, Jack, our butler, will take you to the station whenever you're ready," said Susan, "but I hope you'll excuse me if I don't come with you."

"But of course you must stay here to look after your other guests, Lady Dalmane," said Norma Beck. "We don't mind at all."

"And I think we should be ready to leave in about ten minutes from now," said Nigel Beck. He looked at his watch, saw that it was five minutes past eight, and glanced at his wife, who nodded her head in agreement. "Please excuse us."

Nigel and Norma Beck left the room and, as they left, Susan turned round to tell them that the butler would be upstairs in a few minutes to carry their luggage down for them. Meanwhile, Samantha was waiting on the four Sandys, taking their orders for cereals, coffee, tea, and toast; while Jack, the butler, was at the side table, dispensing food as required, and Samantha carried it over to the breakfast table on a tray.

*

At the breakfast table plans for the day were being finalized. The Becks, driven by Jack as chauffeur, had left the Castle to catch their train, but none of the other guests had yet come downstairs for their breakfasts. Mr. Sandy and Jackie and the Twins had all decided that it was an excellent morning to go for a walk after breakfast so that Jim and Susan could show them around the grounds; and then, perhaps, they would want to walk on a little further afield. Susan, however, was a little bothered by the idea of going out for a walk before her other guests had even appeared from their bedrooms. But I expect they'll be getting up soon, before we set off, she thought. And maybe they'll want to come too?

"Shall we walk the path that goes through the Whitfield Copse?" suggested Jim. He now felt keen to join in the conversation of the others to try to distract himself from his obsessive and most unwelcome thoughts.

"That's just what I was going to suggest," said Susan. "It's a very nice walk; and we could go on, if we want to, over the Whit Field and down to the brook."

"And then, if we want to make it into a round, we could go on past Leigh Brook Copse, and come back by the West Lodge and Stable Road."

"I'm sure that anything you suggest will be fine, Lady Dalmane," said Jackie.

"About how far would this be?" asked Mr. Sandy.

"Oh... a bit over a mile, I suppose," said Susan. "What do you think, Jim darling?"

"I should say it's about a mile and a half, probably," said Jim after a moment's thought.

"Then I'm sure it'll be fine!" said Mr. Sandy. "What do you think, Twins?"

The Twins both said that they thought that the walk would be fine and not a bit too far, but then Susan reminded them that she wanted to be back at the Castle at least by twelve o' clock so that she would be able to say good-bye to her sister, Denise, and her husband before they left. "But we should easily be back long before midday if we set off for the walk quite soon - ah, good, here comes Aunt Nora, and Uncle Geoffrey."

The Padgates came into the Dining Room. Susan asked them whether they would like to come on their morning walk after they had finished their breakfast, but they said that they thought that they would rather stay at the Castle, sitting in the garden in the sunshine (if the weather stayed fine). Then the same question was put to Denise and Rupert, who had just appeared in the Dining Room, but they also decided that they would not come on the walk. Well, it's a good thing that those late-comers don't want to come with us as that would have meant a considerable delay while they eat their breakfasts, thought Susan.

"Shall we say that we'll meet in the Hall in about a quarter of an hour, those of us who are going out walking?" she suggested. "Is that all right for everyone?"

Everyone said that it would be all right. Susan, excusing herself to her later breakfast guests, then left the room, and the other walkers followed her.

Jim, as he left the Dining Room, was again glum and silent. He felt that he would like to have a little time on his own to think before joining the other walkers, so he slipped quietly out of the

Dining Room into the servants' common room (next door) on his way to the back door into the Bailey. Then, as he opened the back door, he saw someone coming towards him across the Bailey - and instantly his day was completely changed for him.

It was Rachel Connor. Jim's feeling of tiredness and his obsessive worries about Susan vanished as if they had never bothered him. He did not have to think about what he would have to do next; already he was walking briskly towards the door which lead into the Estate Office, having noted that Rachel was also heading for that door.

Rachel Connor recognized him, and waved a cheery hand in his direction. "Hello, Jim!" she called out.

"Hello, Mrs. Connor!" he shouted back joyfully. In another few seconds he was at her side. "How are you getting on with your work here?" he asked her.

"Oh, very well, thank you."

Jim was in time to open the door of the Estate Office for her, and to stand aside for her to enter the room before him.

"Thank you very much, Jim!" said Rachel, and smiled at him pleasantly. Jim felt a thrill of excitement pass right through him.

"Are you coming in here too?"

"Well, no," said Jim, wishing that he could think of something else to say to her to keep the conversation flowing. "I, er... I don't think I've seen you since the afternoon when you did the tour with Mrs. Grookes?"

"Yes, that's right, Jim; and now Mrs. Grookes has gone so I've got to manage the guided tours on my own."

"But you're finding that all right?"

"Oh, yes indeed, thank you. So far, so good! I'm just coming in to report for work now."

"Well, I mustn't keep you," said Jim. "Good-bye, Mrs. Connor, and all the best to you!"

"Thank you, Jim. Good-bye!"

"He waved a hand cheerily, and saw Rachel smile at him once more before she closed the Estate Office door behind her. They had been standing to talk in the open doorway.

Jim almost felt like dancing, or shouting for joy; so great was the effect that Rachel Connor had had on his emotions. However, he did not dance or shout, but merely contented himself with walking slowly back across the Bailey towards the door through which he had come out of the Castle, and exulting inwardly as he walked.

When he met the others again he found that they were almost ready to set off on their walk. He should have been aware that he would look somewhat different to the others because of his encounter with Rachel Connor, and, in fact, he was vaguely aware of this. But it doesn't matter a bit if they think I'm a bit different now, he told himself happily. It won't even matter if Sue guesses that I've seen Rachel and been talking with her – my goodness, it *has* been wonderful! – and I do feel quite different now! And anyway, it's most unlikely that Sue will realize that I've just met Rachel – so long as I don't mention her name. I must be careful not to do that.

"Hello, Jim!" called Victoria, seeing him coming up to join them.

"Ah, there you are," said Carol. "Are you ready to come with us now?"

"Oh, yes, I'm quite ready now," said Jim.

"You look as if you're feeling much better now?"

"Yes, I am," said Jim shortly.

"Hello, darling!" said Susan. "Well, that is good that you're feeling better. So we might as well set off now, if we're all ready?"

As he walked Jim was longing to mention the name, Rachel Connor, but he managed not to. Realizing that it would be best to avoid conversation with his wife for the next hour or two – until the intensity of his crush on the new Guide had died down a little (as he believed it would) – he tried to stay with his family for the whole of the walk. However, when they returned to the Castle at about twenty minutes past eleven he found that the flames of his new infatuation were still burning as brightly as ever. He had been telling himself while walking that he was not in the least worried by this new situation in which he found himself. It definitely *doesn't* mean that I don't love Sue any more, he told himself firmly. It just means that I have a new love in my life which will run along parallel, as it were, with my love for Sue. But, of course, I'll have to be very careful not to let Sue know how I'm really feeling, as I don't want to upset her.

They had not been back at the Castle for more than five minutes when Samantha appeared to ask Susan to come to the telephone. They had all gone into the Green Drawing Room to sit down and rest after their walk, and Jim was happy enough to stay there, chatting with his father and Jackie and the Twins. Susan could have taken the call without leaving the room (as there were telephones in nearly all the main rooms in the Castle), but now she followed Samantha into the Great Hall to take the call there.

Susan had guessed that it would be Jack Wonstannley ringing up to report on some developements arising from last night's ghostly encounter, and so it was.

"Ah, hello there, Lady Dalmane!" he said cheerfully. "And how are you this morning, my Lady?"

"I'm fine, thank you!" said Susan.

"Oh, that's great! Well, ma'am, I just thought I'd ring you briefly to let you know that we've just discovered something rather interesting, as you might say, about what happened last night."

"Oh yes, tell me!" said Susan. "Did the ghosts get caught on film, then?"

"Ah, ma'am, but that's just what's so interesting. No, they didn't. You see, ma'am, Phil's just finished developing the films – we haven't had time to do prints from the negatives yet – and he's just told me that there's absolutely no sign of any ghosts on any of our negatives. But what's *really* interesting, ma'am, is that we've recorded some slight variations, or fluctuations – that's what Phil called it – in the electro-magnetic field – and those fluctuations exactly co-incided with the appearance of those two ghosts in the Tower Library!"

"Gosh!" said Susan. "My word! So you really have captured something from what happened last night?"

"I'd say we certainly have, ma'am; sure, we've got those old ghosts captured – in a way – although not on film."

"So you think the pictures, when they've been printed, will be just photos of the Tower Library looking as it always does, without the slightest sign of any ghosts in it?"

"Exactly so, ma'am. And Phil has shown me the negatives, and I've had a good look at them myself, ma'am – so I reckon I know what I'm talking about!"

"Well, well, that is most interesting news, Mr. Wonstannley; I really am so glad that you've got a positive result recorded on one of your gadgets. Thank you so much for letting me know about it."

"Oh, it's a pleasure, ma'am!"

"Well, Mr. Wonstannley, I'll pass on this interesting news to the others; they'll be glad to hear about it," said Susan. "So good-bye for now, and we'll see you this evening." She hung up the receiver, and returned to the Green Drawing Room when Jack Wonstannley had said good-bye to her.

Well before the end of the day Jim realized that he was feeling more like his usual self. The euphoria had passed – helped by animated conversation during the walk and afterwards – but his feeling of light-hearted happiness persisted. What was more, it was perfectly obvious to him that Susan had not guessed anything of the real reason for his change of mood since breakfast. He was reassured, but was still aware of the need for caution and to have his wits about him; even to mention Rachel's name carelessly in conversation could have serious consequences for him. No, I mustn't talk to anyone about her! he kept telling himself firmly. But he longed to mention that name aloud, as it rang in his head all the time.

CHAPTER EIGHT

"Doesn't it seem oddly quiet now that there are just the two of us left here?" said Susan. All the other guests had gone, and Susan and Jim were sitting on their own in the Dining Room, having their dinner.

"I know," said Jim. "I was just thinking the same thing. But it's been lovely having all those guests to stay here!"

"I'm especially glad that your family could come, all four of them," said Susan.

"Yes, it's been lovely having them here, and they've certainly had a super time... Ah, here comes Sam."

Samantha came into the Dining Room from the direction of the Kitchen, bringing the main course of dinner on a tray. Susan and Jim had finished eating their soup, but were in no particular hurry to press on with their meal. Samantha placed a dish of lasagne and hot plates on mats in front of Susan and then set the vegetables on the table.

"I've got my brother-in-law's address in Croydon, if you want to know it," she said.

"Oh, yes, we'd like to know it!" said Susan eagerly. "Do you mean that you've actually got it with you now, written down?"

"Yes, I've got it here," said Samantha, removing a folded piece of paper from the pocket of her apron.

"Look here, do sit down, Sam, if you're not too busy now to stay here with us for a few minutes while we talk. There are plenty of empty chairs here!" Susan pulled out the empty chair to her right for her maid to sit down on. Jim was, as usual, sitting opposite to Susan across the round dining table.

"Thank you, Sue," said Samantha, sitting down at the table and handing the piece of paper to Susan. "Yes, I could stay here for a little while, if you like... but you'd better not let the food get cold."

It'll stay hot for a minute or two. I must just look at this first, and then I'll serve the lasagne. Susan unfolded the piece of paper, read the address on it, and thought for a moment or two. Jim was looking up at her expectantly.

"Do you know where it is, Sue?" he asked.

"I don't think I do," said Susan. "It's 481 Cedar Road, Croydon."

"It's Addiscombe, really," said Samantha, "as apparently it's on the Addiscombe side of Croydon town centre."

"Oh, really?" said Susan. But I'm afraid I'm none the wiser yet.

We must get out our street atlas of London after supper, and have a look. Now then, I'd better get back to serving dinner. What about you, Sam, as I'm keeping you here?"

"No, thank you, Sue," said Samantha quickly. "I won't have any now, thank you. You see, I've just finished eating my supper."

"Yes, of course. But I hope you don't mind us eating our's while we talk?"

"Oh, that's quite all right! Do you know the Croydon area at all, Sue?"

"Well, a little bit, but not really. I remember passing through Croydon once when on the way from London to Brighton, but I think we used the by-pass when we came back; it's called the Purley Way, I believe. Is that all right for you, darling? Another spoonful?" Susan was offering Jim a large helping of beef lasagne, which she knew was something he was particularly fond of.

"No, thanks, that'll be enough - to start with anyway!" said Jim happily. "Thank you, Sue. Have you ever been to this place in Croydon, Sam?"

"No, I've never been there," said Samantha. "In fact, I've never been to Croydon at all. But I don't think that even Roger has been there to stay with his brother since we got married."

"So you don't know whether it would be fairly easy to find this house, coming by car, I suppose?" said Susan.

"I don't know, really," said Samantha. I only know that Rog said it was very near East Croydon station - I can remember that - so I suppose that if you could find that station you'd be nearly there."

"I expect so," said Susan. "Anyway, we could surely find our way easily enough from East Sheen to East Croydon station using our good street map of London."

The idea of including a short visit to Croydon in their trip to London had come about when Susan had heard from Samantha that her husband, Roger Burton, would be staying in London at the same time as she and Jim were on their trip to London. Roger reckoned that, as he expected that the case he was working on would last for at least a week (with a client who lived in Central London) his best plan would be to stay with his brother while the case was on at the Central Criminal Court. His brother lived with his wife in a detached house with a large garden in East Croydon (or Addiscombe); in fact, at number 481 Cedar Road. It had been arranged that Roger Burton would stay there at night while his client's case was being heard in court, as it would have been far too far to think of commuting each day between Rhodes Castle and London. Samantha had told Susan about this arrangement a few days earlier, and then she had come up with what promised to be one of her inspired good ideas. She had suggested that Jim and Susan might like to have an informal chat with her husband after they had stayed a night with Dick and Jane Dalmane.

"Because you see, Sue, there might be... well, legal implications arising, as it were, after you've heard what those other Dalmanes want to say to you. And if there's anything in what they might say on which you might want Roger's professional advice, he'd be only too happy to give it to you, I'm sure."

"Well, Sam, do you know, I think that's a very sensible idea," Susan had said. "I think, in fact, that it would probably be a *very* good idea to call on Roger after we've done the Dalmane visit."

"It would only be informal advice that Roger would give you," Samantha had said, "and, of course, he wouldn't charge you anything for it."

"Yes, but it might be very helpful to have some advice from your husband straight away, after talking with Dick and Jane. And then, later on, when we've come home to Rhodes Castle, we could make another appointment - a proper appointment - to talk with Roger in his office, and, if necessary, start a legal action against them. But that's assuming, of course, that they're absolutely set on the idea of becoming the Earl and Countess of Saint Helens - and, perhaps, even of taking over Rhodes Castle and turning us out - although I can't really imagine that they would want to go that far. But let's hope that they'll be sensible, and abandon any silly ideas they may have of assuming my late husband's title illegally."

Samantha had then told Roger, her husband, about her good idea, and had passed on the substance of her conversation with Susan and Jim.

Roger had contacted his brother again, and the upshot of it was that there was now a standing invitation for Jim and Susan to come on any evening of their trip to London to the house in Cedar Lane, Croydon, so that they could have an informal chat with Roger Burton. "And then you would know what your legal options would be - in case you need them," Samantha had said.

At the end of their dinner Susan and Jim returned to the Green Drawing Room to sit there while they drank their coffee, looked at the map of London, and discussed their travel plans. Before she sat down Susan went straight to a bookshelf and took out from its place a street atlas of London, which was in the form of a book.

"You'd better sit beside me on the sofa, darling," she said, "so that we can study this together."

Samantha came into the room with two cups of coffee on a tray. Jim sat down beside Susan on the sofa as she opened the book at the pages marked: "Key to Sectional Maps".

Susan turned to the pages where there were maps of Croydon and Addiscombe. She and Jim bent over the maps.

"There's East Croydon station anyway," said Susan a moment later.

Jim, noting where her finger was pointing, was already searching diligently amongst the small print of the names of the lesser streets and roads in that part of Croydon.

"There it is!" he said a few moments later. "There's Cedar Road, Sue."

"Good! Yes, that's it; but it *is* close to East Croydon station, isn't it? At least, one end of it is. Do you know, darling, we could probably walk there from the station if we decide that we'd rather go there by train than by car - as the roads of South London might be rather congested in the evening rush hour?"

"Oh...! Well, I suppose they might be," said Jim doubtfully.

"You sound disappointed, darling?" said Susan. "Were you looking forward to a drive across South London in the car?"

"Yes, I was, really. But... Sue, darling, if we were to decide to go by train where would we have to start from? Presumably we'd have to take the car for a few miles anyway from East Sheen to find the right station to get us to Croydon?"

"Well, yes, I think that is a point which I hadn't considered. But I don't really know which station we'd have to head for to get a train to Croydon, without having to change somewhere on the way.

I suppose Balham, probably - or Streatham, perhaps. But then if we were going by car the whole way I should think that our best route would probably lie in that direction anyway."

"So there wouldn't be much point in taking a train?" said Jim.

"That's right, darling; I don't think that there would be much point in taking a train if we had to cover perhaps almost half of the distance by car first in order to arrive at the right station for East Croydon."

"Then let's have a look now at some more of these maps to find the best route for driving to Croydon from East Sheen."

For the next three quarters of an hour, having decided that they did not want to watch television that evening, Jim and Susan continued to pore over the maps of London while they drank their coffee and discussed their travel plans. As he began to calculate the shortest practical route from East Sheen to Croydon, using only main through routes (so that, hopefully, they would not get lost) Jim knew that he was becoming keener and keener to be off to London with Susan in two days time. He had by now forgotten about Rachel Connor, while thoughts of London filled his mind and fired his imagination. His brother, Benjamin, who was now in his last term at Westminster School, had said that London was "a great place to be in". I'm sure it is! he thought.

I must go and see Ben at Westminster, if I can.

When he went to bed that night Jim was still happily thinking about his forthcoming trip up to London. But later that night, as the daylight of the early dawn was beginning to come through the curtains, a dream came to him which changed his feelings completely.

He dreamed that he was once again sitting in a classroom of his old school in Cockermouth. It was not the first time he had dreamed of being back at school, so that, in itself, did not make the dream unusual. However, there were two things about this dream which did make it unusual and remarkable. The first was that the school in his dream was not, in fact, in Cockermouth at all; but he did not discover this fact until some time after he had woken up, and was trying to recall all the images from the dream. The school in his dream was in London. He assumed (afterwards, when he had woken up) that it had been somewhere in South London in a part of the capital that he had never yet visited, with the details supplied entirely by his imagination. The second remarkable feature of the dream was the presence in it of Rachel Connor.

At first Jim was not aware of the presence of Rachel Connor in that classroom. It seemed to be a summer afternoon; the sun was shining in through the windows, and the atmosphere in the classroom was warm, drowsy, and quiet – in fact, for a school classroom, it was very quiet indeed. Looking around the room, Jim saw that the other pupils in the room seemed to be adults rather than children. At the front of the classroom the schoolmaster, in a black gown, was fast asleep, his head resting on his table.

It seemed that there was an essay to be written. Jim had seen that most of the other pupils were busily writing, whereas, on his own sheet of paper on the desk oin front of him, he had so far written only his name. He looked down at it glumly for a moment. What on earth was he supposed to be writing? I've no idea what I'm supposed to be writing, he thought presently, so I'll give up trying to write anything. It won't matter; it must be almost the end of the class anyway.

And then, somehow, he found that he was looking with particular interest at the woman who was sitting at the front of the class, directly in front of the teacher's desk. Why, I'm pretty sure that must be Rachel Connor! he thought, now staring with great attention at the back of a blonde head of hair.

The woman turned her head and, recognizing Jim, gave him a warm smile. Oh, joy! he said to himself, it *is* Rachel! But how soon will I be able to talk to her? And just then the silence in the classroom was abruptly broken by the loud ringing of a bell somewhere outside the room.

The teacher awoke with a jerk and sat up crisply, as if he had been in full charge of the class all the time.

"Time's up!" he said sharply. "Stop writing now, and hand in your essays. Leave them on my desk as you go out. You can go home now." He stood up, and left the room at once through a door in the wall just behind his desk.

There was now a great bustle of activity in the room as the students hurriedly gathered up their belongings and made for the open door, leaving their essays in a pile on the teacher's desk as they left the room. Jim, however, with an eye on Rachel, who had not yet moved from her desk, stayed where he was. Hopefully in a minute or two they would be alone in that classroom, and then he would be able to talk with her - and perhaps even kiss her, or make love to her. But that was not to be. Just before the last of the other students had left the room Jim saw Rachel suddenly look at her watch, and stand up quickly. He hurriedly rose to his feet himself. Rachel was coming over to have a word with him.

"I've got to get home to Deptford now," she said, "so I'm sorry, Jim, that I can't stay to talk with you."

"Oh, I see!" Jim thought quickly. "Would you like a lift home with me, Rachel?" He was almost sure as he made this offer that it would be rejected, but to his considerable surprise she accepted it gratefully.

"Oh, that would be very nice; thank you very much, Jim! I was going to walk home, but, as you're offering me a lift, I'll take your very kind offer!"

"That's all right," said Jim. "But is it far, Rachel, to your home in Deptford?"

"Oh, no, it's only about two miles from where we are now in Lewisham." Rachel Connor deposited her completed essay on the teacher's desk with the other essays, but Jim was perfectly happy to leave his almost blank sheet of paper where it was, on his desk.

They left the classroom together, and walked down a long corridor towards an open doorway where the sun was shining in brilliantly.

Passing through that doorway, they found themselves in a huge car park which was still fairly full of parked cars. Now Jim was, for a moment filled with panic.Where was his car? He supposed that he must have parked it somewhere in that vast car park, but he realized now that he had no memory of whereabouts that might be. Dismayed, he turned to Rachel at his side.

"I'm sorry, Rachel, but I can't remember where I parked my car, but I think it must be *somewhere* in this car park. I'll start searching for it at once."

"That's all right," said Rachel. "There's a bench just here so I'm going to sit down while you go looking for your car – so long as it doesn't take you too long to find it. I've got to get home soon, you know."

Jim set off at once to walk up and down the rows of parked cars, looking for his own car, telling himself as he searched that he must not be too disappointed if, in the end, he could not find it since it had already become a uniquely enjoyable afternoon simply by talking with Rachel. However, as he searched the car park, row by row, he began to realize that in the end he was not going to find his car, so, when he came to the corner of the car park furthest away from the back door of the school, and had not found the car, he was not surprised to find that it had been an unsuccessful search. He would have to hurry back now to the bench where he had left Rachel to apologize to her, and to explain that he could not, after all, offer her a lift. Bother it! he said to himself. Now which way ought I to go from here? He was feeling confused as he looked around the car park, but a moment later his confusion turned into alarm and shock as he realized that he could no longer see the familiar old brick buildings of the school. But surely the place could not have just vanished into thin air – or could it? I must try to find Rachel again anyway, he told himself. Surely she can't have vanished too!

Disappointed and alarmed as he was, still nothing could overcome his feeling of elation resulting from his conversation with Rachel. Where is she? he wondered. But at that moment the whole car park suddenly vanished – and Jim woke up. However, so powerful and vivid had some of his dream images been that it took Jim a little while to realize that he was now awake, lying in his own bed, and that beside him lay Susan. But Susan was also awake, having been disturbed by Jim's dream.

"Are you all right, darling?" she asked him.

Jim blinked his eyes once or twice before answering to try to get it into his mind that he was now awake; that dull ordinary reality was once again the familiar background to his existence. "Yes, I'm all right," he said slowly and rather doubtfully. He sat up in bed and looked about him. There seemed to be quite strong daylight coming through a gap in the curtains, so he supposed that it must be early morning, but he hoped that it was still nowhere near the time for getting up. Oh, if only he could be asleep again to get back into that gorgeous dream!

He looked round at Susan, and saw that she was lying down comfortably in her side of the bed, but he noticed that her eyes were open; she was watching him. However, although he saw her, he was still seeing vividly in his mind's eye an image of the desks in that classroom and of Rachel Connor smiling at him.

"Have you been dreaming, darling?" asked Susan. You seemed to be saying something in your sleep a little while ago. Was it an upsetting dream?"

"Oh, no! It was... a gorgeous dream, and I wish I could get back into it again... but I don't really want to talk about it just now, Sue, darling."

As he settled down to try to get back to sleep Jim realized that he ought to be worried by what he had just heard Susan say when she had said, "you seemed to be saying something in your sleep". Had he then spoken Rachel's name aloud when he had been searching for her in that car park? He could not remember shouting out her name, but he supposed that that might have happened.

However, he was feeling dozy and comfortable, and the lovely images of Rachel, as he had seen her in the dream, were burning so brightly in his mind that he felt that he could not care less whether Susan had heard him speak her name aloud, or not. Ah, what a gorgeous woman she is! he told himself happily. Now, let me see: what, exactly, did she look like? What was she wearing? But no sooner had he thought about it when, straight away, he was seeing that school classroom again, and Rachel in particular. As his focus of attention zoomed in on her he saw at once that the top half of her was clad in a tight-fitting black jersey which emphasised the outlines of a magnificent pair of breasts; but what she was wearing below her jersey he could not see. Anyway, that did not matter. What *did* matter was that he could still see very well in his mind's eye what he wanted to see, and it pleased him very much that these dream images had not yet faded away to the point where they would become forgotten. He knew, of course, that dream images – even vivid or beautiful ones – are usually forgotten very quickly on waking up; so the fact that he could still "see" much of what he had been dreaming about well after the dream had ended told him that it had been an unusual as well as a memorable dream.

He remained awake for quite a long time, but the dream images of Rachel gradually faded away from his conscious mind; however, he was not aware that the images were fading away. Presently he was asleep again. He either had no further dreams, or, if he did dream again, he remembered nothing of it when he woke up the second time. He woke up, in fact, with the wonderful images of

Rachel still so firmly fixed in his mind's eye that he was inclined to believe that he had indeed slipped back into that marvellous dream.

*

For the whole of the rest of that day images of Rachel continued to haunt him: delighting him and exciting him, but also (in a way) maddening him. From time to time, and mostly when he was on his own with nothing else in particular to think about, he would seriously concentrate on those delightful images and try to analyze them. In that way, he thought, perhaps he would happen on the secret of that woman's powerful attraction for him.

He realized, in fact, that there must be something a little irrational in being so strongly attracted to someone who was obviously a great deal older than himself. My goodness, he thought, she must be well into her fifties – perhaps even getting on for sixty years old! Then *why* does she hold such a powerful attraction for me? As he remembered looking closely into her face for a moment when he had been talking with her at the Estate Office door he saw that her face was certainly not like an attractive young female face; the lines of advancing age had been clearly visible on her face. But there was certainly *something* about that face that was, at least for him, utterly and devastatingly charming.

Jim now made a discovery that was to vex him considerably whenever he thought about Rachel, and, in particular, whenever he tried to see her clearly in his mind's eye. It was simply that the delightful images were inclined to become very blurred and indistinct, or even to vanish altogether, the more he tried to force his mind to think of them. He knew, of course, that it was just because he was trying too hard to see her that he could not see her in his mind's eye, and that his best plan, therefore, would be to stop concentrating so hard on recalling the image he longed to see. He knew this, but he was unwilling at that time to put that plan into action. Jim was sitting on the sofa in the Green Drawing Room, and in his hands was "the Times" newspaper; its pages were open, but he was not reading, or even attempting to read the paper. At that moment he was alone in the Drawing Room; Susan had been there with him, but she had left the room a few minutes earlier. Jim supposed that she had only left the room temporarily, probably to visit the toilet, and that she would very soon be back with him. I've only got a minute or two to concentrate on now on seeing Rachel, he told himself, but I can't see her - and that's really maddening!

A minute later the door opened and Susan came back into the room. Jim moved up a bit on the sofa to make more room for her to sit down beside him, and immediately recommenced reading the newspaper.

"Thank you, darling," said Susan, "but I'm not going to be sitting down any more in here just now. I'm going to take my sewing through to the Sewing Room as it'll be easier for me to work in there. And I expect you'll be going back to the Office quite soon, darling?"

Jim looked at his watch as if he had only just thought of the time because of Susan's reminder. In point of fact he had known, when he had sat down after lunch with the newspaper, that he would have to return to the Estate Office by two o' clock. This had meant that he would only have about twenty minutes for sitting on the sofa with Susan. However, becoming lost in his efforts to recall his dream, he had recently quite forgotten the time.

"Gosh, it's ten to two already!" he said. "Yes, I'll soon have to be returning to the Office - but I think I could have just another five minutes with this paper."

"All right, I'll see you later, darling." Susan was already standing in the doorway, taking with her the garment on which she was going to work in the Sewing Room. She closed the door after her.

Oh, how wonderful! Rachel, I love you! thought Jim as Susan left the room. He had been seeing very clear images of Rachel

Connor's face even while he had been talking with Susan. Which just goes to prove, he thought, that the best way to see her now is by trying *not* to see her - in fact, by thinking of something else. That way seems to work well enough!

Jim looked at his watch again, saw that it was almost two o' clock, and rose to his feet, taking his newspaper with him. He already knew that he was not ;ikely to find very much to do in the Estate Office in the way of necessary work, but he liked to be at his desk for the right hours, even though he had set those hours himself, for himself.

In a sort of happy dream Jim came into the Estate Office through the door from the Bailey. He could not but fail to remember that this was the last place where he had seen Rachel in the flesh, and now he saw her again in his daydream and, as that image flashed vividly in his mind for a second, he smiled broadly, but he did not try to hold onto the image. It'll come again! he told himself as he put down "The Times" on his desk and went over to the other door (from the outside of the Castle) to unlock it. The notice on the outside of this door read:

RHODES CASTLE ESTATE OFFICE

OPENING HOURS
MONDAYS TO FRIDAYS

10 a.m. to 12noon
2 p.m. to 5 p.m.

Jim sat down in the wooden chair drawn up to the large desk which stood in the middle of the room. For a moment he glanced at the correspondence which was lying on the desk, waiting to be dealt with, but then he picked up the newspaper again. Later! he said to himself decisively. I'll deal with the typing in a little while, when I've finished reading what I want to read.

But then, as he saw Rachel again in his mind's eye, he thought, Gosh, if only I could have her in here as my secretary!

The possibility of appointing a secretary to help Jim in the Estate Office had, in fact, been discussed and rejected. Jim had told Susan, when she had suggested it, that, for the time being at least, the amount of work to be done would not justify the appointment of a secretary. He had said that he could quite well do all the typing himself, and that he would much rather be occupied and busy in the office than idle; and all this was perfectly true. Both of them, however, had understood the real reason for having no secretary to help in the running of the Estate Office, knowing that such an appointment would almost certainly be of someone female, and probably young and (in Jim's eyes) dangerously attractive. And Sue and I both know perfectly well that that simply would not do for me! he had told himself.

When five o' clock came, and Jim had met no one in the Office, he locked the doors and left via the Bailey, bringing with him a reminder for Mr. French at South Lodge that his rent was now overdue. After he had had his tea with Susan he meant to get on his bike and ride round to South Lodge to put the reminder through the letter-box. An afternoon of work in the Office had had the effect of damping down to some degree the strength of his infatuation for Rachel Connor, and Jim realized that this had been a good thing. The excitement caused by thinking about Rachel had not left him, but it had been pushed to the back of his mind while he had been compiling letters and typing them. Now, suddenly, a completely different kind of thought came to him as he walked across the Bailey. Gosh, we're off to London tomorrow morning, Sue and I! That'll be good – *very* good – and I'm certainly looking forward to it very much!

CHAPTER NINE

Jim and Susan were well on their way to London. They had stopped for a lunch picnic by the bridge over the River Mole on the road from Cobham to Leatherhead, the very bridge where several years before they had rested while on a long evening walk. On that occasion the walking party had started from Esher station in the south-western suburbs of London, bound for a camping site on Ranmore Common on the North Downs.

That had been a very memorable occasion for both Jim and Susan, and it had been Jim's idea that today they should stop for their picnic by this particular bridge so that they could "wallow in old memories", as he had put it. Susan had agreed to this idea readily, even though it had entailed a detour from their planned route. "It doesn't matter a bit which way we go as we've got all day to get to London!" she had said.

"Well, not quite all day – I told Claire that we'd probably arrive by tea-time, or a bit sooner. But that still leaves us with lots of time to spare so we will go by that longer way, via Leatherhead. I think that's a lovely idea!"

John and Claire Walker were the long-term tenants who lived in Susan's London house; in effect, they were the caretakers. In order to make the long journey by car from Rhodes Castle less tiring Susan and Jim were having a number of stops along the way to rest and refresh themselves, and so that they could take turns with the driving. Jim had been driving for the first leg of the journey as it had been easy enough, after leaving Sherborne, to find the right road; all he had had to do was to keep going eastwards along the A30 in the direction of Greater London. They had stopped at a cafe at Hook, just off the main road, for morning coffee, and then Susan had taken over the driving for a while, presently leaving the A30 at Bagshot.

Jim put his cup to his lips and tipped his head backwards to drain the last drops of tea from the cup.

"Do you want any more, darling?" asked Susan, after a glance into the flask to see whether there still was any tea left in it.

"No, thanks, Sue, I won't have any more now," said Jim dreamily. For the past few minutes he had not been saying anything while he had been staring into the deep, dark pool of the river just below the bridge, where the water hardly seemed to be moving at all.

"Were you remembering just how it was the last time we sat here?" asked Susan.

"Indeed I was," said Jim. Actually, I was having a lovely daydream about it. Oh, Sue, darling, we had such a *wonderful* time on that walk, didn't we?"

"I know; I was just thinking about it too."

"And later on we had to step across the electrified rails of that railway line. Gosh, that was really terrifying!"

"But we managed it! And after that you carried me, Jim, darling, when I was too tired to walk any further."

"Oh!" said Jim. "That lovely road in the moonlight! Oh, heavens, it was *so* wonderful that night!"

For a few moments they both remained silent, lost in their thoughts. Jim was feeling strangely peaceful, and he guessed that Susan was feeling as he was, happy and peaceful, as indeed she was.

Certainly the day and the place had a lot to do with this feeling of peacefulness. It was becoming very warm for a day in mid May;

the sun was shining, and there were small puffy white clouds in the sky, but very little wind. It was, in fact, almost perfectly calm where Jim and Susan were sitting on the grass by the bank of the river. And it was very quiet. Having left the main road about half a mile back, and taken the small country road which lead over the river bridge, they had also left nearly all of the motor traffic behind them. As Susan had pointed out, it had been around lunch time (about ten minutes to one) when they had arrived at the bridge, and not many people were out and about in their cars - at least, not on that road. From time to time there came the sound of a passing car, but in between these times there were good periods of silence, with only the occasional songs of blackbirds and thrushes and other birds to be heard. The feeling of rural peacefulness was further enhanced by the fact that the hawthorn trees and bushes thereabouts were in full bloom, and the air was full of the heavy and rather soporific scent of the may blossom.

Jim put an arm around Susan's waist and, gently pulling her towards him, planted a kiss on her lips. A moment later they were locked together in a loving embrace, but their embrace only lasted for about a minute. Susan had offered no resistance to it, but now she pulled away from him slightly.

"Darling," she reminded him in a quiet voice, "we must remember the time."

"Oh, bother the time!" said Jim. "Sue, darling, it's just *so* lovely to be here... just the two of us!" And thank heavens that I'm *not* thinking about Rachel today! he said to himself.

"Yes, I know it is," said Susan quietly. "I've felt it too, darling - the specialness of this place and the memory of the wonderful things that happened to us on that walk. But I think that we ought to move on now, all the same. You're keen to be seeing London, aren't you?"

"Oh, yes, of course I am!" Jim suddenly sat up straight and then jumped to his feet, remembering that he was indeed keen to be seeing the outskirts of Greater London, so as to know that they had nearly reached their destination for that day. "I feel quite ready to go on now.

Shall I drive now for a bit, Sue?"

"Yes, of course, if you'd like to!"

They had discussed the route they meant to take beforehand, and had decided that, having taken the diversion via the Leatherhead road (for the bridge over the River Mole), the best way would be to head on as if for Leatherhead town centre, and then turn off onto the Kingston road. "That way takes us into London via Chessington," Susan had explained; and Jim had seen this for himself when he had looked at the map after Susan had finished studying it.

*

Half an hour later they were driving along a tree-lined road in a built-up area. To either side of the main road, as far as they could see, were houses and the lesser roads of suburbia.

"So this is Chessington?" said Jim.

"Yes, this is Chessington."

"We're in the outskirts of London now?"

"For all practical purposes we are," said Susan, "as I don't think we'll pass through any more bits of open country between here and Roehampton."

"Gosh!" said Jim. "London! But it doesn't seem at all long, does it, since we were sitting on that lovely river bank?"

"No, it doesn't. But we haven't come all that far from our picnic place. I suppose we've only come about eight or nine miles from there.

Look here, darling, if you'd like me to drive before we get onto the Kingston By-Pass we'd better change over soon."

"Yes, please, Sue! I would like you to drive now," said Jim.

"I'll stop as soon as I see a place where I can pull in easily."

A moment later they passed the opening of a rather wider road to the right, and then Jim spotted a good place to stop the car on the left, where there were no other parked cars.

"That's good!" said Susan. "That was Moor Lane we've just passed, so we're into Hook now." Like Jim, she had been looking out carefully, but she had also been remembering landmarks on a once familiar road.

"Oh, yes," said Jim when he had parked the car. "You were telling me before about how you used to come this way when you had a friend who lived in Chessington. Have we passed her house yet?"

"I don't really know, but I think we must have passed the place where I used to turn off for Helen's house as we've passed Moor Lane - that bigger road we've just passed - and I think it was somewhere to the south of there. But I dare say she'll be married now, and living somewhere else, as she was about the same age as me."

Susan and Jim changed places and then drove on again, soon coming to a new road interchange with an underpass where they gained access to the Kingston-By-Pass (the A3).

"Gosh, I'm glad I'm not driving now!" said Jim as their car passed beneath the busy by-pass road. "It looks complicated here."

"It is!" said Susan shortly. She was concentrating hard on her driving, and swerved slightly to find the correct traffic lane. "Good!" she said a moment later. "We've done that right, and come out onto the by-pass - in the right direction!" She saw a sign which had the distance to Central London marked on it, and so knew that they were travelling in the right direction.

Jim's feeling of light-hearted happiness had remained with him while he had been driving the car but, now that he no longer had to concentrate his mind on driving, he was, if anything, in an even happier frame of mind. The fact that he knew that this strangely happy, peaceful mood would not last could not affect him in the least. Sooner or later something would remind him of his new love for Rachel, but, for the moment, his old love for Susan reigned supreme in his mind. He was happy, too, to think that he would (hopefully) soon be seeing his brother, Benjamin, at Westminster School. Nothing very definite had been arranged about a meeting there, but Jim had written to his brother to give him the dates on which he could come to see him, and Ben had written back to say that he would be very pleased to meet him and Susan, but that he could not give any definite day or time for a meeting since his duties as Captain of the School (Head Boy) kept him very busy for most of the time.

Well, thought Jim, perhaps we could go up to Westminster this evening as there's going to be plenty of time left today for us to do whatever we want to? It's only about a quarter past two now, and we must be nearly at the house in Martin Lane, so we should be arriving there in the next few minutes...

"Jim, darling, I was thinking that perhaps it would be a nice idea if we went down to Westminster this evening to see whether we could meet your brother?" said Susan a little later.

Jim was a little startled to hear her speak his thought aloud as if she had known what he had just been thinking, but, in his present carefree state of mind, he could not let that worry him.

"Yes, why not; but do you know, Sue, I was just thinking the same thing?"

"Were you really?" said Susan. "Well, we should arrive at our house in Martin Lane in three or four minutes from now, I should think, as we're off the by-pass now."

"I thought we were. This is Roehampton Vale, isn't it?"

"Yes, it is; and do you see that set of traffic lights down there, some way ahead of us?"

Jim nodded, seeing lights about a quarter of a mile ahead of them at a road junction.

"That must be the place where Roehampton Lane turns off to the left, where we leave this road," continued Susan. "Yes, it is; it's on that sign. We're almost there now."

"Oh good!" said Jim. "I say, Sue, what a *lovely* part of London this is! It looks almost like the country around here, doesn't it, with all these big trees round about?"

"Yes, I know. Roehampton *is* a lovely area – and especially so at this time of the year with the trees all coming out into leaf."

"They're just about in full leaf here."

"Yes, I would say they are. And that nice green area on our right is Putney Heath. It's really very pleasant around here – a nice area for walking."

"Let's walk here this evening, Sue, when we've come back from Westminster?"

"Bless you, darling, we will!" said Susan happily. "Why not? It looks as if the weather will stay nice at least for the rest of today."

"And let's hope for tomorrow as well, and the rest of the week!"

They had come to a temporary stop in a traffic queue, which pleased Jim well enough as there was a great deal to see, looking around him. Then the lights changed to green, and they moved off again. Susan turned to the left into Roehampton Lane.

Two minutes later she parked the car outside a large detached house with a small garden area in front, on the street, and a larger, walled garden behind the house. The houses were only on the left-hand side of the street (with Roehampton Lane behind them); on the other side was Putney Heath. Trees hung over the pavement on that side of the road, and behind them was the open grassland of the Heath.

"Gosh, what a lovely place!" said Jim as he opened the front passenger door of the car. "And I see we've got the Heath right opposite the house, We won't even have to use the car when we want to walk on the Heath."

"That's right; we won't need it," said Susan. "Look, darling, there's a gate in the fence just over there, almost opposite to our house."

Jim thought how very odd it sounded to hear Susan talk of the place as "our house". He would have to try to get used to the idea that this handsome house, which had been Lord Dalmane's London house, now belonged to Susan, which meant that it was really his as well as her's.

As Susan opened the boot of her car to start removing their luggage the front door of the house opened, and a smartly dressed rather elderly man appeared. He came down the garden path and opened the garden gate. Susan looked up and recognized him, as the butler greeted her.

"Good afternoon, Lady Dalmane!"

"Good afternoon, Ron. This is Jim, my husband."

"Good afternoon, Mr. Sandy, sir," said the butler politely. "Let me take the luggage for you, ma'am. There's no need for you to touch it."

"Hello!" John Walker had appeared at the front door. "Do come right in, you two. Claire will be with us in about five to ten minutes, I should think. She's just slipped out to buy something at the shop round the corner."

When Susan had introduced Jim, as her husband, to John Walker, her tenant at Number One, Martin Lane, John Walker invited them to come into the sitting-room to have a cup of tea.

"But you've arrived much sooner than we'd expected," he said. "You must have started quite early this morning?"

"Well, yes, we did start quite early," said Susan.

"Then you must be rather tired by now, I should think?" said John Walker. "Come in and sit down, and we'll have some tea. Or perhaps you'd like to wash your hands first after your journey? The bathroom's upstairs, but I think you know the way, Susan."

"Yes, I do," said Susan, "We'll call in there first, I think, and then join you in the sitting-room."

As Jim followed Susan up the stairs he had the curious feeling that he somehow recognized this John Walker. But I *can't* have ever seen him before, he said to himself. But his face does seem somehow familiar...

*

They had not been sitting in the sitting-room for much more than five minutes when Claire Walker arrived in the room. The tea had just been brought in by the butler, and then they had heard a woman's voice downstairs, saying something to the butler. As Claire Walker entered the room Jim, to be polite, rose to his feet, but even as he stood up and looked at her, he saw, at the first glance, that her face also seemed familiar to him. Certainly her's was not, in his judgement, an attractive face; he knew at once that he was never going to fall in love with this woman. That was certainly a relief to him, but that was not the point; what really startled him now was the strange feeling that he had seen her once before somewhere else. Could it be possible that he had indeed met this couple before? But, of course, there was no time now for Jim to wonder about this any more. Already he was shaking her hand and saying, "How do you do, Mrs. Walker?" as Susan introduced him.

"Pleased to meet you, Jim," said Claire Walker; but Jim thought for a moment that he had caught a rather odd, quizzical look on her face. Almost as if she recognizes me! he thought.

"Do sit down, please, and we'll have some tea," she continued.

"But I do apologize for not being here when you arrived."

"That's all right, Claire," said Susan. "We don't mind; and I don't think you were expecting us quite as early as this."

"Well, we weren't, really," said Claire Walker. She put her hand to the teapot, but then paused. "Do you both like plain china tea?" she asked. "I know you do, Susan." She looked round at Jim.

"Yes, please, that'll be lovely!" said Jim.

"I know it's rather early to be having afternoon tea, but I thought you'd be wanting something now," said Claire as she began to pour out the tea.

They thanked her, and told her again that it would be lovely to have a cup of tea. Jim had already seen that there were slices of cake on a plate, and had decided that he would be able to eat a slice when it was offered to him, although he did not feel hungry after their recent lunch picnic.

As he slowly ate a slice of cake, and waited until his cup of tea should have cooled enough to allow him to take a sip of it, Jim was leaving most of the conversation to Susan. He kept taking discreet glances at the faces of his host and hostess; and as he did so he was becoming more and more convinced that he had met them somewhere before.

Soon, however, he began to feel that he ought to accept the fact that this particular enigma was likely to remain an enigma for him. But he did not mind. He was pleased by the fact that they were sitting comfortably in an attractive, elegant drawing-room: a room which had the added bonus of a good view. The room was on the first floor, overlooking the street, which meant that they were looking out over the pleasant scenery of Putney Heath.

Presently the conversation returned to the subject of Jim and Susan's journey of that morning. John Walker asked which way had they come?

"We didn't come the shortest way," said Susan. "The shortest way, I think, would have been to stay on the A3 when we came onto it at Cobham, but we turned off instead onto the Leatherhead road because we wanted to come round by that way."

"Yes; but presumably you did most of the journey from Sherborne along the A30?" It seemed that John Walker had a good memory for details from road maps of Southern England.

"Oh, yes, indeed we did; we kept on the A30 as far as Bagshot - didn't we, darling?" Susan looked hopefully at Jim.

"Yes, we did," he said. "We left the A30 at Bagshot. Afterr that we were heading for Leatherhead on a lesser main road because we were heading for a nice picnic place that we knew about."

"Near Leatherhead?"

"Yes, it was quite near Leatherhead, and just off the main road, beside the River Mole."

"Oh, really? That sounds interesting!"

"It's a lovely place that we'd been to once before, so we decided that we wanted to see it again," said Jim. He suddenly noticed that both John and Claire Walker were looking at him very keenly.

"I think we know where you mean!" said Claire, smiling at him.

"There's a little road that leads off the main road to a bridge over the River Mole. If I remember correctly, it comes just after you've gone through the village of Stoke D' Abernon."

"My goodness!" exclaimed Jim. "So you've been there too?"

"Yes, I think so, but it was several years ago. Do you remember that long walk we did, darling, starting from Esher station?" Claire was now looking at her husband.

"Oh, yes, indeed I do!" he said. "It was a long evening ramble, actually, and we were in a party of walkers lead by Captain Clark, and bound for somewhere up on the North Downs, where we were going to camp for the night."

"Good heavens!" gasped Jim. I see..."

His enigma had suddenly been solved for him. Claire and John Walker had been with him and Susan on that long walk from Esher station. They had been in the party of walkers who had rested with them on that bridge over the River Mole; that was where he had seen them once before.

About half an hour later Jim and Susan were on their way again, heading for Central London. "It'll be just as well," Susan had said, "to get to Westminster well before the evening rush hour gets under way, and I should think that we ought easily to be there between three o' clock and a quarter past three. She was driving, and as they came to Putney Bridge she slowed the car down so that they were able to catch a glimpse of the river on the Putney (upstream) side of the bridge.

"There's the place where the Boat Race starts from," said Jim eagerly, recognizing for a moment The Embankment, the hard from which boats are launched, and a row of boathouses.

"Yes, that's it." Susan was concentrating on watching the traffic, and could not take her eyes off the road ahead to glance down at the river.

"I believe this is where Ben comes when he does his rowing," said Jim. "That happens on Tuesday, Thursday, and Saturday afternoons, he said."

"So you're hoping that you can go with him tomorrow afternoon?"

"It would be very nice if I could! But which way are we going now, Sue?"

"I thought we'd best go through Chelsea via the King's Road, as I think I know that way best. Then we'll head for Victoria station and Victoria Street – if we can!"

They experienced some slight difficulties in finding the way to Victoria station after they had passed Sloane Square, but presently they found themselves at the western end of Victoria Street.

Oh, good!" said Susan. "There's the front of Victoria station, and this is Victoria Street. We should be at the Abbey in a few minutes."

They were at the Abbey within a few minutes of leaving Victoria.

Both of them were glad that the traffic had not been too heavy, and that they had not got seriously lost, but now Jim was keenly on the look-out for the landmarks his brother had told him to look out for. As soon as he saw the twin towers of the west end of Westminster Abbey across Broad Sanctuary he was already on the look-out for the archway which would lead them into Dean's Yard.

"There it is!" he said, pointing to the right; but Susan had also spotted it and was heading the car in that direction. They passed through the arch, and immediately saw a world quite different from the busy London streets outside Dean's Yard.

"Oh, this is nice!" said Susan as she stopped the car for a moment to look around. In front of them was a quiet green square with the various buildings of the Abbey, the Abbey Choir School, Westminster School, and Church House around it.

"You've never been here before, Sue?" asked Jim.

"Never! I've never been through that archway before, although I think I must have noticed it when I've been to the Abbey before."

Susan had no difficulty in finding a place where she could park her car, but Jim was already busy looking around, trying to see his brother. It was three o'clock, and there were not many people about in Dean's Yard at that time, so that Jim thought it would be easy to spot his brother if he should happen to see him; he was assuming that he would have no difficulty in recognizing Ben although it had been many years since they had last met.

As they stepped out of the car they heard the Westminster chimes for the hour sounding from the nearby clock tower of the Palace of Westminster, followed by three dull strokes from Big Ben.

It's three o' clock," said Jim, "so I suppose it's still a bit too early to meet Ben."

"What time did he say that school ended today?" asked Susan.

"A quarter past three on Mondays, so we might as well have a bit of a look round the place first. Look, Sue, that must be the archway that leads into Little Dean's Yard." He pointed to a narrow, ancient-looking archway through the buildings on the eastern side of the square, a way large enough only for pedestrians.

"We'll go in there," said Susan, but they had hardly had time to pass through the dark archway when they saw a number of boys emerge from a doorway somewhere to the right, followed by a tall man wearing a black gown over a red cassock. I wonder if he's the Headmaster? thought Jim as they exchanged a quick "Good afternoon!" with the man before he disappeared through the archway behind them.

"Hello there, Jim!" One of the boys hailed them, a tall, fair-haired youth, wearing a black gown over his smart grey suit.

Benjamin Sandy had recognized his brother before he had had time to spot him.

"Oh, hello, Ben! I wasn't really expecting to see you just now!"

"Weren't you?" said Ben, smiling at them.

The two brothers shook hands, and Jim introduced his wife.

"This is my wife, Susan. Sue, this is my brother, Ben."

"How do you do, Lady Sandy?" said Ben politely, smiling at Susan.

"I'm pleased to meet you!" said Susan, smiling back at him as they shook hands. But a moment later Ben was glancing at his wrist watch.

"I'm afraid I'll have to go in a minute," he said. "I've just come out of a meeting of the Monitorial Council, but I'll have to go up School now for Latin Prayers." (At Westminster School "up" means "to" or "into") "I'd love to show both of you around the place a bit, but I can't do that now."

"All right," said Susan, "we mustn't make you late for your Latin Prayers, but shall we meet you again afterwards, if you're free then?"

"I could be for a little while, Lady Sandy," said Ben. He looked again at his watch. "Latin Prayers are said at a quarter past three, and that lasts for about ten minutes, and it's nearly ten past three now. Shall we say that I'll meet you in just over a quarter of an hour, at about twenty-five past three? There are some wooden benches over there, to the left, by Ashburnham House if you want to sit down."

They thanked him, and waited where they were as he hurried off to talk with two other senior-looking boys, also wearing gowns (which showed that they were Queen's Scholars), who were waiting to have a word with him. Then Jim and Susan saw the three of them walk hurriedly off towards the School Gateway, which they could see on the opposite side of Little Dean's Yard.

"What a nice lad your brother is, Jim!" said Susan rather dreamily.

Jim looked at her. For a moment he thought he saw a rather odd expression on his wife's face as she watched Ben Sandy and his two friends until they disappeared from their sight up the steps which lead into the large assembly hall known as "School". What did it mean, that rather intense expression on her face? Was she beginning to fall in love with Ben? He decided to say nothing to answer her point about Ben.

"Shall we have a look around?" he said after a moment's pause.

"We might as well," said Susan, "and then we can sit down on one of those benches your brother told us about."

"All right."

They took a leisurely walk around the Abbey Cloisters for a while, much admiring all that they saw, and then sat down on one of the wooden benches outside Ashburnham House to wait for Ben Sandy to meet them again. At twenty-five minutes past three, exactly as he had arranged it, Ben came down the School steps and came straight over to speak to them again. He invited Jim and Susan to come to join him for lunch the next day in College Hall, the place where the Queen's Scholars ate their meals. He assured them that there was always room for one or two guests at the High Table. To Jim's surprise, Susan at once accepted the invitation, saying that it would be "very nice" to take lunch with the Queen's Scholars in the ancient and historical setting of College Hall.

"But you're going to be in the House of Lords tomorrow, aren't you?" Jim ventured to remind her.

"Darling, it's all right," said Susan. "Debates in the Lords never start at least until the middle of the afternoon, so, you see, there'll be plenty of time for us both to lunch here with Ben. Don't you want to?"

Jim thought that he now detected a hint of sarcasm in his wife's voice.

"Oh yes, of course I'd *love* to have lunch in College Hall tomorrow with you and Ben," he said quickly.

"Just as you like," said Ben politely.

"Well, it's a splendid idea!" said Jim. But is it really such a splendid idea? he wondered. He had just noticed Susan and Ben exchanging smiles that were almost furtive.

"Thank you very much, Ben!" said Susan. "Yes, we'll accept your very kind invitation. But where, and when, would you suggest that we meet you?"

"Well, Lady Sandy, lunch is always at one o' clock sharp, and morning school ends at ten to one, so I would suggest that we all meet at around five to one by the archway into Dean's Yard where I first saw you - over there." Ben pointed to the narrow dark archway which was the entrance to Little Dean's Yard from Dean's Yard.

It was agreed that they would meet for lunch the next day by the archway. Then, as Ben said that he could spare them about half an hour before he would have to return to his official duties, he offered to show them around the old buildings and gardens of the School and the Abbey Cloisters.

"Did you see the Little Cloister?" he asked.

"No, I don't think we saw that," said Susan.

"Well, I think you ought to see that, and I'll show you round College Garden as well. They're both extremely old gardens, you know."

As they walked around, admiring the ancient buildings and gardens of the School and the Abbey, Susan and Ben were soon chatting happily together, but Jim, mostly lost in his own thoughts, was saying very little. Damn it, Sue fancies him! he told himself irritably as they walked again through the Dark Cloister on their way to the Little Cloister. But, no, I mustn't be jealous – no, I've really no right at all to feel jealous of Sue, seeing that I've fallen in love with Rachel! But (thank heavens!) I'm really *not* in love with Rachel today...

"I say, what a lovely garden!" he said aloud, suddenly startled out of his cogitations by the apparition of a little walled-in green space in the middle of which a fountain was playing.

"Gosh!" said Susan happily. "Who would have thought that there was a little garden here, hidden away amongst these cloisters?"

"You could say, it's one of the better kept secrets of this place," said Ben. "Probably not many of the tourists who flock here to see the Abbey discover this quiet little corner – in spite of the fact that it is signed from the Dark Cloister with an arrow on the wall, as you may have noticed."

Well before they came to the end of their guided tour Jim had all but forgotten that he had been tempted to have jealous thoughts when he had thought that he had spotted signs of infatuation on Susan's face. He was, in any case, beginning to doubt that idea.

"You've guided us round this place very well, Ben," said Susan as they once again came back into Little Dean's Yard, by the wooden benches. Ben had taken them into Ashburnham House (which belongs to Westminster School) to see the elegant rooms of the School Library and the magnificent Georgian staircase, which they had both admired very much. "Thank you very much!"

"Thank you, Ben," echoed Jim.

"That's all right," said Ben, "but" (he looked at his watch) "I ought to leave you in a minute or two, if you don't mind."

"Of course," said Susan. "You've got duties to attend to as Captain of the School. That means you're Head Boy really, doesn't it?"

"It does mean that, Lady Sandy. Yes, I'm Captain, but only for the rest of this term as I'm leaving the School at the end of this term."

"So Jim has told me," said Susan.

"And you used to be the Guide at Rhodes Castle, Jim, weren't you?"

"Yes, I was the Guide," said Jim, "but now I'm the Estate Manager."

"Oh, well, you'd better tell me about it tomorrow," said Ben. "I must go now. Good-bye, both of you, until we meet again tomorrow!"

They said good-bye to Ben, and walked back through the archway. A minute later they were on their way again in Susan's car as she set off to drive back to Roehampton.

CHAPTER TEN

"It's absolutely gorgeous out here!" said Jim happily.

"Yes, it really is lovely," agreed Susan, "and so wonderfully quiet! You'd hardly know you were in London, sitting here in this garden," "Yes, it's lovely," said Claire Walker. "But surely, Susan, you must have eaten your meals in the garden here before, when you've been staying here with John - your former husband - haven't you?"

"Well, actually, Claire, I don't think I ever remember eating out here before in this delightful garden, although Jim and I sometimes take our breakfast out to the Private Lawn when we're at home at Rhodes Castle; but this, I think, is even better than it is at home. You and John really must come to stay with us at the Castle sometime."

"Oh, thank you, Susan; I'm sure John and I would be really delighted to come to Rhodes Castle sometime," said Claire. "Now then, help yourselves, won't you? Would you like some sugar with your cereal, Jim?" She pushed a glass sugar bowl across the table in Jim's direction.

"Thank you," said Jim.

"I suppose John has already gone off to work?" said Susan. "We haven't seen him this morning."

"No, I don't suppose you would have seen him this morning," said Claire. "Not that he sets off for work all *that* early; but remember that we really are having our breakfast quite late!" She glanced at her watch. "Yes, it's about five to nine now. But, of course, we didn't want to be early as we want this week to be a sort of holiday for you and Jim."

"Yes, and we're certainly enjoying being quite laid-back and lazy while we're staying here!" said Susan.

"We certainly are!" said Jim.

"Your husband works in the City, doesn't he?" asked Susan.

"Yes, he works for one of the big international finance companies," said Claire. "His office is in Cannon Street, not far from the Bank of England – but what exactly he does when he's in there I really don't know, and I've never cared to ask. Anyway, he likes to arrive there before nine o'clock, if he can, so he usually sets off from here well before eight to go down to East Putney station, and in that way he can get straight through to the City without a change by the District Line. But what, exactly, are your plans for today? I think you said you'd been asked out to lunch somewhere, but I didn't quite take it in when you told me last night."

"Yes, we've been asked to lunch at Westminster School with Jim's brother, Ben."

"Oh, yes?"

"And after that I'm off to the Lords to attend a debate, and Jim's going down to Putney to spend the afternoon rowing with his brother. That's right, isn't it, darling?"

"Well, almost right," said Jim. "Actually, I think I'll only be watching them rowing, but not rowing myself." He looked up from his almost empty cereal bowl, saw that Claire was smiling at him, and found that automatically he was smiling back at her.

For a moment as she smiled Jim felt a familiar thrill of attraction pass through his body, but the moment passed, and Claire's face once more seemed ugly to him. Gosh, he thought, is there something rather fascinating about this woman after all? Or is it only her bust, as usual, that attracts me? She certainly *does* have a pretty nice pair of breasts under that tight-fitting top she's wearing this morning! And then, quite unexpectedly, there was suddenly a wonderful image of Rachel in his mind. For a second he felt tempted to try to hold onto that new image, to revel in its loveliness while it was there; but almost at once another thought came to him, and it was as if this new thought was springing from another part of his brain to rescue him from an unwanted infatuation. Stop! this new thought said to him (it was almost as if the word were shouted in his mind). I must *not* think about Rachel now!

"Ready for some toast, Jim?" asked Claire.

"Jim came out of his daydreams with a start, suddenly realizing that he had finished eating his bowl of cereal.

"Yes, please," he said as Claire passed the toast rack to him. "Thank you," he said, taking a piece of toast.

It was one o' clock and, having met Ben, as arranged, by the archway of Little Dean's Yard, they had been taken by him to the steps which lead up into College Hall from the Deanery Coutyard. As they had passed through the courtyard Ben had pointed out the Dean's house on the eastern side of the courtyard, and the windows of the ancient chamber known as the Jerusalem Chamber on the north side, immediately beneath the massive structure of the Abbey.

They had spent much of the morning until just after midday shopping in Harrod's, and had taken Claire with them; she had begged a lift with them, having explained that she was also going out to lunch with a friend who lived in Thurloe Square. Jim had left Susan and Claire to spend a happy time in the Ladies' Fashion Department while he had spent a very boring hour wandering aimlessly around the store. He had not really wanted to buy anything, but had found it necessary to make a few small purchases to fill up the time, which had been passing maddeningly slowly. Eventually, at about ten past twelve (as they had arranged) he had seen Susan coming towards him where he was already waiting for her by the main entrance from Brompton Road. Claire had disappeared. Susan told him that she had walked round to her friend's house in the nearby Thurloe Square, intending afterwards to come home by the District Line from South Kensington station. Then, having regained the car, which Susan had managed to park in Egerton Crescent (just off Brompton Road), they had driven to Westminster to meet Ben.

"Well, what do you think of this?" asked Ben as he lead his guests into College Hall.

Jim and Susan took a quick look around the high-ceilinged ancient room, which at that time was full of boys sitting at a number of long tables, waiting for lunch to be served.

"My word!" said Susan. "What a gorgeous place to have one's lunch! But this looks like a very ancient and historic room, Ben?" Her eyes, like Jim's, had already focused on the far end of the room, where the High Table stood on a dais two steps up from the rest of the room.

"I like those shields on the wall!" said Jim admiringly. Like Susan, he was looking at the well-decorated wall behind the High Table.

There were three large coats-of-arms painted on the wall up there with some smaller heraldic devices beneath them.

"It is a very ancient room," said Ben. "I'll tell you about it - and about those shields - later. We mustn't keep the Master waiting.

Could you follow me, please?"

As he followed Ben and Susan towards the dais Jim suddenly found that he was wondering where they would be asked to sit; or, at least, to stand first (he remembered that they would have to remain standing while Grace was said). He was hoping that Susan would not be asked to sit next to Ben.

It turned out, however, exactly as he had feared. The Master of the Queen's Scholars, who was standing quietly at his place at the centre of the High Table, shook Susan warmly by the hand as she arrived, said "How do you do, my Lady?" in a respectful voice, and then offered her, as the guest of honour for that day, the place at his right-hand side. Then he shook Jim's hand and offered him the place at his left.

When the Grace before Dinner was said they sat down (it seemed to Jim interminably long - more like a short church service than a grace).

Jim was feeling rather isolated and nervous as he sat down between the Master, to his right, and an unknown Queen's Scholar, to his left; but he knew that he felt annoyed, seeing that the figure sitting at Susan's right hand was none other than his brother, the Captain of the School and Captain of the Queen's Scholars.

Food was brought up to the High Table on trays from the kitchen (which was just beyond the opposite end of the room where they saw a serving hatch where the more junior Scholars, and those who were not Queen's Scholars were queueing to receive their helpings). Dishes of food and piles of plates were unloaded onto the table in front of the robed and cassocked figure of the Master of the Queen's Scholars, but Jim already knew that, whatever the meal might be, he was not feeling hungry. He mumbled a "Thank you" when a plate of mince, potatoes and cabbage was presently set before him. He had the uncomfortable feeling of being trapped in a place where he did not belong, and mentally cursed his brother for inviting him and Susan to this very formal lunch.

Meanwhile, the boy sitting next to him on his left was doing his best to make polite conversation. He introduced himself by name, and explained that he was, as Jim had guessed, the Deputy Captain. "And I believe that you, sir, are Mr. Sandy, and that your wife is Lady Sandy, the Countess of Saint Helens?"

"Yes, that's right," said Jim.

"And you are the older brother of our Captain, Ben Sandy?"

"Yes, he's my brother."

After that they ate in silence for a few minutes while Jim knew that the boy was trying to think of something else to say which might start a conversation. He knew, of course, that it was largely his own fault that they were not managing to start a polite conversation, but in his present sullen mood he felt no inclination to try to be sociable.

He kept glancing whenever he could to his right to see how Susan was getting on, and was infuriated to see that, each time he glanced her way, she was chatting easily and happily either with the Master of the Queen's Scholars or with Ben. I'd like to wipe that silly grin off his face! he thought angrily as his feeling of jealousy flared inside him like bubbles in water when it is coming to the boil.

Presently the plates and dishes of the first course of lunch were taken away, and bowls of jam sponge cake in custard were brought in for the second course. In spite of his sour mood caused by his fit of jealousy Jim realized that it had not by any means been a bad lunch, considering that it was a school meal (for a moment he tried to remember what the meals had been like at his old school in Cockermouth). He was now in any case beginning to feel a little more cheerful again, realizing that the meal was almost over. However, as he put his spoon down in his empty bowl, he happened to overhear what the Master was saying at that moment.

"Have you met Doctor Radhauer, our Headmaster, Lady Sandy?"

"Well, we haven't really met him yet," said Susan, who had also finished her lunch. But we did see him, just for a moment, yesterday afternoon - didn't we, darling?" Jim had managed to catch Susan's eye, and was suddenly smiling back at her.

"Yes, it was just as we were arriving when we saw him," confirmed Jim, addressing his words to Susan, rather than to the short, dark-haired figure sitting between them in his scarlet cassock and black gown.

"We just exchanged a quick 'Good afternoon' with him," said Susan, "but I expect he was busy, and didn't have the time to talk with us then."

"Doctor Radhauer is a very busy man, my Lady," said the Master; "but perhaps, if you would like to have a talk with him, we might be able to arrange something."

"If you like, sir, I could go round to the Headmaster's house now to ask him; he's almost certain to be there now?" suggested Ben helpfully.

"Why, that's a good idea, Ben!" said the Master. "Yes, you go and do that now, remembering to tell him that Jim is your brother, and that his wife is the Countess of Saint Helens. You did say, my Lady, that you would be staying in London for the rest of this week?"

"Yes, we are," said Susan, "and I think we're quite free tomorrow afternoon, aren't we, Jim? You're not going rowing with Ben tomorrow are you, darling?"

"No, only today, I think," said Jim.

"We don't do rowing on Wednesdays, Lady Sandy," said the Master politely. "Sport at Westminster is done on Tuesday, Thursday, and Saturday afternoons."

"Yes, I see," said Susan. "I remember now that Jim did tell me that before."

The Master looked up and down the High Table to see that everyone had finished eating his meal. He glanced at his watch. It was nearly half past one.

"If you would like to stand with me now, Lady Sandy, we will close lunch with the Grace," he said gravely.

As he stood up with everyone else Jim felt a sudden wave of apprehension. Were they in for another very long Grace? But he need not have worried; a few seconds later it was over.

"Off you go now, Ben," said the Master, "but perhaps you could report back to me presently on how you get on with the Headmaster?"

"Yes, sir, I will do that," said Ben. Then, turning quickly to Susan, he said, "If I could see you again, my Lady, as soon as I've spoken to the Headmaster I could let you know whether he can see you, or not. So shall we say that I'll see you again by the Archway, hopefully, in about five to ten minutes?"

"That'll be fine!" said Susan. "We'll wait there."

Ben Sandy hurried out of College Hall on his way to the Headmaster's house, which was in Dean's Yard.

The Master of the Queen's Scholars politely suggested that Susan and Jim might like to accompany him out of the Hall. None of the boys in College Hall had moved from their chairs. They were not allowed to leave the Hall during lunch time (without special permission) until the Master had left the room.

When they had returned to the old archway leading into Little Dean's Yard the Master took his leave of Susan and Jim, having shaken them both warmly by the hand, saying how pleased he had been to meet them. Jim was smiling as he shook the Master's hand, but a moment before he had been scowling again. He had seen the smile on Susan's face when Ben had said, "If I could see you again, my Lady". He was, in fact, rather hoping that Susan would notice the frown on his face, and would ask him about it so that he would then be able to give his grievance an airing.

Susan, however, seemed to be quite unaware that anything might be wrong. She had evidently not picked up any danger signals from Jim's face.

"We could come here again tomorrow afternoon, I suppose, even though it's not a rowing day tomorrow?" she said

"Oh, yes, of course we could," said Jim. "You mean, if we're invited to meet the Headmaster tomorrow?" Pull youself together!

he told himself sharply. Forget this silly jealousy! It's all absolute nonsense!

"Yes, it might be rather fun to meet the Headmaster," said Susan.

"I suppose it might be. But perhaps, Sue, you might want to go back to the Lords again?"

"I shouldn't think so," said Susan. "I expect I'll be able to say what I want to say this afternoon. You wouldn't like to come with me, darling, would you? You could sit in the Gallery, you know, to listen to us debating?"

"Well," said Jim slowly and thoughtfully. "I *would* like to come with you, Sue, into the Lords to hear some of your debate. Yes, I'd like to do that very much... but I don't think I could do that today because I've told Ben that I'm coming down to Putney with him this afternoon, and I'm really looking forward to that as well."

"Well, darling, if I were you I'd stick to your plan and go rowing with Ben this afternoon. In any case, I might as well stay in the House until about six o'clock, or so; and then it would be time to go home. I suppose you would have come back from rowing by then?"

"Oh yes, surely by six o' clock, I should think. But Sue, how am I going to find you again when I come back? I've never been into the Houses of Parliament before, so I'm sure I'd never find you in there!"

"Oh, I don't know," said Susan. "It's not actually as confusing as one might think, finding one's way inside the Palace of Westminster.

But... I'll tell you what." She saw the doubtful look on Jim's face.) "I'll come back here. That'll be easier for you. Shall we say that, whatever happens, I won't stay in the House any later than six o' clock?"

"Oh, good! Yes, that's a good idea, Sue," said Jim with relief.

"Right! Shall we say, then, that whoever gets back here first will be sitting on one of those wooden benches - where we sat yesterday afternoon? Ah, here comes Ben, and it looks as if he's got something to tell us." Ben Sandy had just come out of the front door of a house a little further along the same side of Dean's Yard as the spot where they were now standing. They saw that he was hurrying towards them, clearly with some message or invitation to pass on.

"The Headmaster has asked you to come to tea with him tomorrow afternoon, if you can," said Ben as soon as he had come within talking distance.

"Oh good, that'll be very nice!" said Susan cheerfully. She looked round quickly at Jim, but thought that he was looking rather doubtful.

"That's all right," he said.

"At what time?" asked Susan.

"Four o' clock in the sitting-room of his house, which is just along here," said Ben. "So what I would suggest, Lady Sandy, is that I meet you here tomorrow afternoon at about five to four; he's asked me to come as well."

"Oh, good! So we'll see you tomorrow afternoon, Ben!" Susan was smiling happily, but Jim, seeing the exchange of smiles between his brother and his wife, was frowning again.

"I must rush off now, Lady Sandy, if you'll excuse me, as I don't want to be late arriving down at Putney. I'll see you here in about five minutes or so when I've changed, Jim. Is that all right?"

"All right," said Jim sulkily, without looking up at his brother.

Ben did not appear to notice that anything might be wrong. They watched him as he ran across Little Dean's Yard and disappeared into the open doorway of College, on the further side of the Yard. They waited for a few seconds in silence where they were while Jim continued to stare down morosely at his feet.

"Darling, what's the matter?" said Susan gently in a quiet voice.

Jim pulled himself together.

"Oh, well, it's, er... I didn't like the way that Ben was smiling at you, Sue."

"Oh, don't be ridiculous, Jim!" said Susan, almost crossly.

"Really, it's absurd to say that!"

"I'm sorry to upset you, Sue." Now Jim was beginning to sound, and feel, distressed. "I'm sorry... but..."

"But what?"

Jim felt suddenly agitated as he realized that he did not know what to say in answer. There followed a few tense seconds of silence before Susan spoke again.

"Look at me, Jim, darling!" Jim looked up into his wife's face, and saw that she was looking grave and unsmiling. Until that moment in their conversation he had been avoiding direct eye contact with her.

"It comes to my mind," continued Susan, "that perhaps I have as much reason to feel jealous because of you as you may have to feel jealous because of me." She paused a moment as she saw a look of shock suddenly come into Jim's eyes. He had suddenly understood what she was leading up to, and felt absolutely horrified that she had somehow divined his most secret thoughts and desires. "Yes, I know that there is a certain person, a member of our staff back at home, to whom you feel a very strong attraction... but you didn't know that I knew that, did you?"

Jim's face had gone quite white with shock as he listened to Susan's revelation. She, however, had seen the signs of contrition there on his face, rather than of resentment or anger. She had been speaking very calmly and quietly, but now she offered Jim her hand. Jim drew her gently into the darkest recess of the ancient archway before he answered her.

"Sue, darling, I am most dreadfully sorry about that. Yes, I'm very, *very* sorry, my darling Sue." Tears were now beginning to roll down his cheeks and, for the moment, overwhelmed by the emotion of the moment, he could say no more.

Susan looked quickly around her and saw that, thankfully, they were alone, although she remembered that Ben might re-appear at any moment.

"Do you still love me, Jim?" she asked quietly.

"I do, Sue!" answered Jim passionately. "Oh, Sue, my darling, I really, *really* do love you - I promise you I do! I... what is it, darling?" He was suddenly worried as he felt Susan pull away from his embrace; he had been hoping to kiss her, and that she would then tell him that he was forgiven.

"Here comes Ben," said Susan.

Damn! thought Jim. If only he could have had another minute or two alone with Susan he could surely have put things properly right between them.

"Are you ready to come with me now, Jim?" asked Ben cheerfully.

"Yes, I'm ready," said Jim dully.

"Do you want to come with us, Lady Sandy?" asked Ben.

"Well, thank you so much for asking me, Ben," said Susan, "but, no thank you; I think we'd best stick to our original plans, which means that I'm going to walk round to the Lords now to take part, I hope, in this afternoon's debate, but Jim's going to go with you now to Putney.

That's right, isn't it, darling?"

"Yes," said Jim, wishing that he could change the plans and say decisively that he was going with Susan to the House of Lords; but he felt that he could not now do that.

"Then we might as well all walk together through Dean's Yard anyway," said Ben, who now looked quite different; gone were his dark grey suit and black gown, and in their place he was wearing pale trousers and a pink tie, and a pink blazer with his white shirt.

When they had passed through the larger archway that lead out to Broad Sanctuary they went their separate ways.

"Good-bye, Jim," said Susan "See you later by that bench in Little Dean's Yard.

"Good-bye, Sue, darling!" called Jim. There was no time for more. Susan was already hurrying away from them in the direction of Parliament Square.

"We'd better cross here by the lights," said Ben. "Quick, let's get over now while we can!"

Jim found himself being hurried across the eastern end of Victoria Street, where the traffic lights controlling the junction with Great Smith Street were holding up the traffic for them. As they turned the corner to walk up Tothill Street towards St. James's Park station he had a quick final glance in the direction of Parliament Square, but he could no longer see Susan. I wish I could have gone with her, he thought sadly. Why did I think I wanted to watch Ben rowing at Putney?

"Have you brought any money with you?" asked Ben suddenly, breaking into his gloomy thoughts.

"Oh, yes, I've got plenty of money with me," he said, slipping a hand into the inner pocket of his jacket as he spoke to make sure that his wallet was there. "I suppose I might need some money to buy something at tea-time?"

"Well, you needn't bother about that, Jim," said his brother kindly. "I've enough to pay for both of us for tea, but you will need a fair bit of money, I should think, for your train fare from St. James's Park to Putney Bridge, and back again."

"Oh, of course, we're going by the Underground. Sorry, I'd forgotten about that."

"I don't know what a return ticket will cost you, Jim. You see, I don't need to buy a ticket to travel as we're all issued with season tickets at the start of each term. I'd be quite happy to pay for your ticket but, quite frankly, I'm afraid I haven't brought enough money with me."

"Oh, don't worry about that, Ben; I can easily pay for my own fare." Jim was quite annoyed that his brother should want to talk with him about anything as trivial as money when there were very serious matters pressing on his mind. But after all, he said to himself, Ben doesn't know what's on my mind... unless I tell him. Yes, perhaps I should...

They came to the other end of Tothill Street. They had been walking at quite a brisk pace, and now Jim saw before him on the left-hand side of the street the tall building which was the headquarters of London Transport at Number 55, Broadway, and also the entrance to St. James's Park Underground station.

"We must be close to St. James's Park now, I suppose?" he said.

"Yes, we are," said Ben. "If you turn up the next street to the right, Queen Anne's Gate, you come out onto Birdcage Walk, where there's a way into the park. But, of course, we can't do that now." He lead the way into the Underground station, where Jim bought his return ticket to Putney Bridge.

As they went down to the platform for westbound trains Jim suddenly realized that his mood was changing again. He suddenly felt cheerful again, remembering that he had for some time been greatly looking forward to this expedition to Putney. I might as well enjoy myself, he told himself. After all, I can always talk to Ben later about Sue, if I want to.

On the platform they saw that there were a number of other Westminster boys, who had been walking ahead of them, waiting for a train. Just then a train appeared from the tunnel and drew into their platform, but it was a Circle Line train, so they did not board it.

"The next one from this platform is for Ealing Broadway," said Ben, reading from the illuminated train departures notice board above their platform, "so we might as well take it."

"But wouldn't it be better to wait for a Wimbledon train?" said Jim. He remembered that Putney Bridge was a station on the Wimbledon branch of the District Line.

"Not necessarily," said Ben. "We could change at Earl's Court and take a Wimbledon train from there, and with luck we'd get to Putney Bridge much sooner than we would if we just wait here for the next Wimbledon train. You see, they run through from Edgeware Road as well as by this way."

"Oh, I see," said Jim, remembering that Ben was an experienced traveller on the Underground (and particularly on the District Line).

He decided at once to trust his judgement on the matter of which train they ought to take.

When they arrived at Earl's Court they stepped out of the Ealing train onto Platform Three of the District Line station. Jim had just expressed his surprise on seeing that the line beyond the junction to the west of Gloucester Road station was above the ground.

"Yes, and most of the line beyond Earl's Court down to Putney Bridge is above ground as well, as you'll see," said Ben.

"But where exactly are we now?"

"We're at Earl's Court."

"Oh, yes, I know that, of course; but what I meant was, in what part or region of London is Earl's Court?"

"Ah, well..." Ben thought for a moment. I suppose we must be in West Kensington, more or less. But look, there's a Wimbledon train coming into Platform Four now from Edgeware Road. We'd better be ready to board it when it stops."

They boarded the Wimbledon train when the doors opened, along with the other Westminster boys who had travelled with them from St. James's Park

"Good!" said Jim as soon as he had entered the train. "There's more room in this train than there was in the other one."

"We'll probably find it more crowded on the return journey," said Ben.

The journey by the Underground continued. So Ben was quite right to decide on changing at Earl's Court as we had hardly any time to wait there, thought Jim.

Soon the train came to Putney Bridge station. Jim followed his brother and the other Westminster boys onto the platform and then down the steps to go out into the street outside the station. He had been looking out through the windows, surprised to see that the railway line there ran along an embankment, high above the level of the surrounding streets and houses

"Ben lead the way along the street called Ranelagh Gardens, which leads from the station to Putney Bridge Approach. As they came onto the bridge Ben suddenly asked Jim a question.

"How's Dad getting on nowadays, Jim? I gather that he's been staying with you lately at Rhodes Castle?"

"Yes, he and Jackie and the Twins came down to stay with us for two nights," said Jim. "Work at the mine is going on very well, he said."

"But is it really true that he's found gold?"

"Oh, so he told you that, did he? Yes, it is true. But when did he tell you that?"

"He rang up two nights ago to tell me that they'd been down to see you, and that he'd brought a little sample with him of what they'd found."

"Well, it's true," said Jim. Dad had a little box with him, and he passed it around to show us what was in it; and there was a little dust in that box and a tiny nugget of gold."

"Gosh! So maybe Dad will really be making a fortune soon out of this gold?"

"Well, I don't know whether he really will. But look here, Ben, you'd better keep quiet about it at least until Dad has had time to do some more prospecting to try to find out whether this discovery is likely to be worth going on with - or not."

"Oh, yes, of course I'll keep quiet about it," said Ben, "but I bet he's been pretty excited by this discovery!"

They had walked across the bridge, and now Ben lead the way to the right, onto Lower Richmond Road, and from there down onto the Embankment. Jim, as he walked with his brother, could not help feeling a little annoyed that he had chosen this time to talk about their father and the discovery of gold. He would have liked to be allowed to stop on the bridge for a moment to ask Ben about what could be seen from there, looking towards the boathouses on the Putney side of the river. But, of course, it's all so familiar to him that he doesn't really notice anything, he thought.

They walked past a row of boathouses and came to the Westminster School Boathouse, where Ben pointed out the School Flag which was flying on a small flagpole on the balcony. He lead the way into the boathouse, where Jim saw some long, narrow boats stacked upside-down on trestles and neatly stacked oars. He would have liked to have been allowed to linger there for a moment to look around, but Ben was already hurriedly climbing the staircase which lead up to the first floor.

"Sorry, Jim, but I'll have to hurry on now as our boat is already down on the hard, and it looks as if most of the rest of the crew are already there. Now look, this door leads into the Tea Room, and you can get out onto the balcony by going through there." Ben opened a door for a moment, and then closed it again, giving Jim a momentary vision of a room where there were a number of tables with chairs, like a cafe. "And this door leads into the Changing-Room. I should come in here now, if I were you, but I'll have to leave you in a minute when I've changed."

Jim found himself swept into the Changing-Room, a long room above the open space on the ground floor where the boats were stored.

"All right," he said rather doubtfully.

Ben was already flinging off his clothes at high speed. Then, without slackening his pace for a second he drew on a pair of white shorts and a white vest from his clothes bag. Then he hung his blazer, shirt, tie, and long white trousers on a peg which, as Jim noticed, had his name printed beside it. Ben sat down for a moment on the row of clothes lockers underneath the row of pegs to tie the laces of the light gym shoes he used for rowing. Then he quickly stuffed his bag into the empty locker beneath his peg.

"Must rush down now!" he said briefly, but not breathlessly.

"Coming with me?"

"I might as well," said Jim, thankful to be leaving the Changing-Room, where he had been feeling very uncomfortable with nothing to look at except some of the other boys who had travelled with them from Westminster; they were also changing, but rather more slowly than Ben had changed.

They descended the stairs rapidly. When he had taken his oar from the place where it was kept Ben hurried down the hard to the spot where the boatman and most of the crew of the First Eight were waiting with their boat.

"Sorry I'm late!" he called out as he ran down the hard.

"It's all right, Ben, you're not the last today! Sherwood hasn't arrived yet," answered one of his friends.

"But here he is – Mike's coming now!" said another member of the First Eight crew.

Ben turned for a moment and saw that Mike Sherwood, who rowed next to him at Number Seven, was running down the hard, carrying his oar; and he also saw that Jim was standing on the hard, waiting to see the Eight paddle off when the boat was launched.

The school boatman was holding the boat carefully as the members of its crew took their seats in it, starting with the boy who rowed Bow. When Ben had taken his seat as Stroke (at Number Eight, near the stern), and the cox, a much smaller boy than any of the rowers, had climbed in behind him, the boatman pushed the boat out into the river.

The cox immediately gave the order to the crew to start to paddle the boat upstream.

Jim had been told by Ben roughly what he should expect to see that afternoon in the way of rowing. The idea was that the First Eight would be involved in one or two practice races against the Second Eight after they had done a bit of practice on their own to "warm up". At the moment they were paddling upstream against the tide quite slowly, so that Jim, walking along the hard past the boathouses, was easily able to keep up with them. He crossed the bridge over Beverly Brook at the end of the hard and the boathouses, and saw that the towpath continued along beside the river in the direction of Harrod's Depository and Hammersmith Bridge. To his left, behind a fence, lay the open space of Barn Elms Park. He realized that the view was, in fact, quite familiar to him although he had never walked there before; it was a view which he had seen several times before while watching the University Boat Race on television. It does look a little different, though, he thought, now that I'm actually walking on the towpath beside the river!

He walked slowly on, but saw that he was now getting ahead of the First Eight; they were now waiting, it seemed, for the boat of the Second Eight, which had just been launched. Jim decided that he would do as Ben had advised him, and not walk too far along the towpath in order to get the best possible view of the two crews when they were racing. I'll watch them from the End of the Fence, he told himself, remembering Ben's advice.

*

Jim met his brother again about three quarters of an hour later as he disembarked with the rest of his crew on the hard outside the School Boathouse.

"Hello!" said Ben as he stepped out of the boat. "My word, that *was* a close finish!"

"Did you win?" asked Jim.

"Yes, but only by a canvas! Didn't you see the end of the race?"

"No, I didn't get back here quite in time. You see, I was watching by the End of the Fence, as you suggested, and I saw the start of the race and waited there until the two boats had passed me."

"Were the others in front then?"

"Yes, they were; by about a length, I should think. Then I ran back towards the hard, but I wasn't quite in time to see the finish.

But where exactly was the finishing line?"

"By the U.B.R. Stone – the Boat Race Stone," said Ben. "It's just down there, you know, where you can see Kenilworth Court – that block of flats this side of Putney Bridge."

"It must have been a good race then?"

"It jolly well was! But look here, Jim, you'd better follow me in now." Ben was already walking back to the boathouse, carrying his oar.

"I'm going to have a shower now, and then I'll change, so I'll see you again in the Tea Room quite soon. Or come into the Changing Room again, if you like."

Jim followed his brother up the steep steps leading to the first floor of the boathouse. Ben opened the door of the Changing Room and went straight in, but Jim, after a quick look, did not enter there; he saw a brief vision of steam and naked and half-naked bodies (the showers were at the further end of the room), and decided at once to go straight into the Tea Room. He opened the Tea Room door and went in there, and saw at once that the place was arranged as a self-service cafe: there was a stack of trays on a trolley to the right of the door as one came in, and the idea, evidently, was to choose one's cakes, etc. from the front of the counter, and take a cup of tea, and pay for it there; and then to find a table and a seat. Jim looked around and hesitated. The place was not particularly crowded; there were empty chairs here and there, and he saw that there were two empty tables out on the balcony.

"Would you like some tea, sir?" asked one of the ladies behind the counter, realizing, from Jim's clothes, that he was a visitor, and not one of the boys.

"Oh, thank you, but I think I'll wait for my brother before I have tea," said Jim. He went out through the open door of the balcony, and sat down there in a chair where he could see into the Tea Room so that he would see his brother when he arrived there.

As he waited for him to arrive Jim soon began to feel that Ben was certainly taking his time over having a shower, and then dressing; however, he could not feel bored as he waited as there was still plenty of activity to watch on the river. Boys were sculling in little narrow boats, designed for a single rower, but Jim was more interested in watching the slow progress upstream, with pauses, of a Four. Ben had told him about the boys who rowed in what were amusingly called "Graveyard Fours"; they were those, he had been told, who were not good enough to row in any of the School's Eights. He thought that those in the "Graveyard Four" he was now watching were really doing not at all badly, although they were certainly moving much more slowly against the tide than the First Eight had done.

For most of the time Jim had been enjoying himself while he had been watching the First Eight in action on the river, but there had been a time, while he had been waiting for the two racing boats to come down the river past him, when his melancholy thoughts had threatened to return and poison his mood for the rest of the afternoon. He knew that he had by no means recovered properly from the shock he had received when Susan had revealed that she knew about his infatuation with Rachel. It had come as a new shock to him to discover that his jealous thoughts and the aftermath of that earlier shock were still troubling him; he had not yet fully exorcised them, but had merely pushed them to the back of his mind. Now, however, as he waited for Ben to come into the Tea Room, Jim was aware that his melancholy thoughts were once again threatening to take over his mind. But what should he do about it?

Should he confide in Ben, and pour out those most private and secret worries to him – or not? It was a difficult decision to make, but presently he decided that he would confide in his brother. And then he saw the Tea Room door open, and there was Ben.

Ben, now changed again into his blazer and white trousers had come into the Tea Room, and had taken a tray. Jim came in from the balcony to join him.

"Do you want to go out again onto the balcony?" asked Ben when they had loaded up their tray with the things they wanted.

"Yes, let's go out there," said Jim.

They took the tray out to the table on the balcony where Jim had been sitting before, and sat down there. Presently, as they ate their cakes and drank their tea, Ben noticed that Jim was oddly silent.

"You seem very thoughtful, Jim?"

"Oh, yes... I've got something on my mind." Evidently Ben had guessed as much, Jim realized.

"I thought, perhaps you had," said Ben.

Jim had been wondering how best to approach the matter that was on his mind, but now he decided at once to trust his brother and simply to say whatever words came into his mind.

"It's about Susan. I'm worried, Ben."

"Oh, no! You don't mean to say that she's ill?"

"No, no, she's not ill; it's nothing like that," said Jim. "But you see, Ben, the fact is... that I've fallen in love with another woman."

"Oh dear! I'm sorry to hear that, Jim. But who is this other woman, if you don't mind me asking?"

"She's working for us at the Castle."

"In what capacity?"

"She's the Guide, and we've only recently appointed her."

"Oh dear, that does sound like an awkward situation to be in! If you've only recently appointed her then, presumably, you could hardly be thinking of sacking her yet?"

"But would that have been your advice, Ben - to sack her?"

"Well, Jim, I really don't know the circumstances, do I? But, on the whole, it probably would be best for you if she were *not* on your staff at the Castle, so that you wouldn't be seeing her any more. But the question would then be: how can you achieve that without sacking her? What do you think, Jim?" Ben looked carefully into his brother's face, but deduced from the far-off expression which he saw there that Jim was deep in thought.

At that moment Jim had, in fact, just received another shock, although this time it was certainly a very pleasant shock. A wonderful vision had just swum into his mind. He was seeing Rachel Connor as if she was standing just in front of him, only a few feet away. She looked so real that it had almost seemed that he could have reached out a hand to touch her. But only for a fleeting moment. No sooner had he seen this enchanting vision than it disappeared again; even as a thrill ran right through his body like an electric shock it was no longer to be seen in his mind's eye, so that he was left feeling both thrilled and shocked at the same time. He understood that he must have immediately tried to grasp at the elusive vision, to hold onto it, and so had lost it.

There had been a brief silence. Ben realized, quite correctly, that Jim had not even heard the last point that he had put to him. Now, when he saw that Jim looked as if he was ready to attend again to their conversation, he put a different question to him.

"But is this woman married or single?"

"She's married," said Jim in a flat, dreary voice. "But, of course, that makes no difference because *I'm* married to Sue."

"Yes, I realize that," said Ben seriously. "Even if she had been a single woman, or divorced, or a widow, she could not possibly be your's..."

"For as long as I remain married to Sue," said Jim quietly.

Ben looked at him sharply for a moment.

"But you want that, of course?" he said. "You want to remain with Susan?"

"Oh, *absolutely*! Good heavens, Ben, I still really, really love my darling wife, Sue, and, of course, I want to stay with her for as long as I posiibly can. The very last thing that I want is that our marriage should break up because of this - because I'm in love with Rachel."

"I understand," said Ben seriously.

There was another short break in their discussion. Jim looked away from his brother for a moment and saw that the "Graveyard Four" which he had been watching before had now turned round, and was heading back towards the hard. But he could take no interest now in what was happening on the river.

"Well, Jim," said Ben presently, "you're in a difficult position certainly, but I'm glad that you've told me about it. I'd like to help you, but I don't really know yet what I could do to help you - except to pray. So I'll do that, Jim; I'll pray for you." Ben smiled as he saw Jim staring at him in amazement. "You're surprised to hear me say that?" he continued.

"I am indeed!" said Jim. "I had no idea that you were religious, Ben."

"But I wouldn't say that I am, particularly," said Ben, still smiling at his brother's evident surprise. "To be honest, though, I've only trealized quite recently that I have a calling to serve the Lord in the ministry of the Church; and so what I'm going to do, you see, is to study theology."

"I thought you were going to study the Classics – Latin and Greek?"

"Oh, yes, I shall be continuing to study the Classical languages while I'm at Oxford, so that, hopefully, I'll get my M.A. degree presently; but after that I'm hoping to study theology."

"So that you can be ordained?"

"Yes, that's the idea."

"Good heavens! You do surprise me, Ben!"

"Well, yes, I suppose I have sprung something of a surprise on you by telling you this. But it seems to me that the fact is, Jim – if you don't mind me saying so – that we hardly know each other nowadays; or at least I suppose we could have said that that was true up to yesterday."

"Oh, yes, I quite agree," said Jim. "We've been apart for far too long, living entirely separate lives. Look here, Ben, it's high time that you came to stay with us at Rhodes Castle. Perhaps you'd like to come and stay with us for a week or two, sometime after the end of this term?"

"Oh, thank you, Jim, that would be lovely; I'll have quite a bit of free time, I should think, after this last term at Westminster ends round about the twentieth of July, and I'm not due to go up to Oxford until... Oh, here comes Mike!" The door from the Tea Room opened, and Mike Sherwood stepped out onto the balcony.

"Do you mind if I sit with you, Ben?" he asked.

"No, that's fine; there's plenty of room here!" said Ben cheerfully.

Jim looked up for a moment at the large, powerful-looking youth with rather curly fair hair who stood before them, and frowned for a moment, while inwardly he was cursing this intruder for interrupting his private conversation with his brother.

Mike took another chair that was standing nearby, and pulled it up to the table to the left of Jim's place.

"Mike, this is my brother, Jim, who has come down to watch us rowing today. He lives at Rhodes Castle with his wife, the Countess of Saint Helens. Jim, this is my friend, Mike Sherwood who rows with me in the Eight."

"How do you do?" said Mike Sherwood, offering Jim his hand.

"Pleased to meet you!" said Jim, now smiling as he took Mike's hand and shook it. He was now feel;ing secretly rather pleased at being introduced as the husband of the Countess of Saint Helens, but he thought that Mike, understandibly, looked and sounded a little nervous. I must put him at his ease, he thought. "So you row at Number Seven in the First Eight?" he continued.

"Yes, I do," said Mike. "But you, Jim... your wife is a countess?"

"Yes, she is, but I'm not an earl. You see, what happened was this: when I first met Susan, my wife (as she now is), she was married to the Earl of Saint Helens; but then the Earl died, and some time after that *I* married the Countess. So that's how it is that we live at Rhodes Castle, the seat of the Dalmane family, the hereditory Earls of Saint Helens."

"But where is Rhodes Castle?"

"It's in Dorset, about seven miles from Sherborne."

"Oh, I see. Thank you for telling me," said Mike rather clumsily.

"And are you a Queen's Scholar too?" asked Jim.

"No, but I'm an Honorary Scholar."

"What's that, exactly?"

"Honorary Scholars at Westminster are day boys; we don't board in College, as all the Queen's Scholars do."

"Mike lives very close to where we are now," explained Ben. "In fact, he lives in Kenilworth Court, just down the river from here, so he's jolly lucky being a day boy *and* a rowing man."

"Well, yes, I am lucky to live in a flat overlooking the river here at Putney," admitted Mike Sherwood. "Kenilworth Court is a good place to live for anyone interested in boats or rowing."

"Yes, it must be," said Jim.

As he continued to chat with Mike and Ben, Jim soon forgot to be annoyed that his private talk with his brother had been cut short. When they had finished their tea the three of them left the boathouse and began walking along the Embankment together in the direction of the tall block of flats known as Kenilworth Court. They passed the short street called The Platt, and came to the entrance to Kenilworth Court. Mike Sherwood, when he had said good-bye to Jim and Ben, disappeared into the flats.

"Well, Jim, you were saying that I ought to come and stay with you and Susan at Rhodes Castle, and I was saying that I'd love to..." As they came again to Putney Bridge Ben picked up their former conversation as easily as if it had never been interrupted at all.

Jim told his brother that he would have to consult Susan first, of course, and they would have to check their diaries, but he thought that sometime during August would probably be a good time for Ben to come to stay with them. As they continued to chat on their way back to Putney Bridge station, and afterwards on the District Line on their way back to St. James's Park station, Jim came to realize that the feelings of jealousy which had assailed him so fiercely at lunch time had been nothing less than absurd, just as Susan had told him that they were. He remembered that she had said, "Really, it's absurd to say that", when he had told her that he had not liked the way that Ben was smiling at her.

And Sue was absolutely right about that! he told himself. Now, however, having had a good heart-to-heart talk with his brother, Jim was feeling entirely differently about that whole episode. In short, he now knew that Sue had been in the right, and he had been in the wrong.

When they arrived back at Westminster School, after an uneventful journey on a through train to Upminster from Putney Bridge station, Jim was once again feeling thoroughly happy and hopeful. As they came into Dean's Yard he remembered that Susan would have spent her afternoon in the Lords, where she would, very probably, have taken an active part in the debate. Now he was suddenly in a hurry to get back into Little Dean's Yard, wanting to see her again, and hoping that she would be there to meet him. He remembered that she had told him that she would not stay in the House of Lords any later than six o' clock, and that they were to meet again by the benches in Little Dean's Yard. It was only a quarter to six. Would she be back yet, or would he have to wait for her? Without really knowing what he was doing he suddenly broke into a run, temporarily leaving Ben behind. As he came through the archway his eyes were already carefully scanning the Yard in front of him. Oh, good, there she was, sitting on the first bench! He saw Susan raise a hand, and waved back joyfully to her.

"Hello, Sue!" he called out cheerfully.

"Hello, Jim, darling! Hello, Ben!" came Susan's answer.

Jim stopped for a moment to glance over his shoulder. Yes, there was Ben, just behind him.

"Have you had a nice time at Putney?" asked Susan.

"It's been lovely! How's your afternoon been, Sue, darling? Did you get a chance to say what you wanted to say?"

"Indeed I did!" said Susan. "Do you have to go now, Ben?"

Ben was looking at his watch, and seemed to be in a hurry to leave them.

"Yes, I think I really ought to leave you now, Lady Sandy," he said, "but I'll see you tomorrow afternoon, as we arranged it, at five to four by the Archway."

"All right, we'll see you then. Good-bye, until tomorrow."

"Good-bye, Ben," said Jim. "and thanks ever so much for your help!" He added this in a subdued voice, aware that Susan would not know to what help he was referring. However, he was quickly aware that there was no need for such caution. Susan was evidently not interested in the contents of any private discussions between himself and his brother.

Ben hurried off towards the entrance to College.

"So you've had a good afternoon in the Lords, darling?" said Jim.

"Excellent!" said Susan. "Look here, shall we sit down while I tell you about it?" She sat down again on the bench, and Jim sat down beside her. "Yes, there was a big majority in favour of my Amendment, so we passed it all right – in fact, only a handful of peers voted against it."

"Oh, that's splendid, Sue! But I do wish I could have been there to hear you persuading them to vote with you, Sue, darling!"

"Oh, well!" said Susan, and laughed. "Perhaps you'd better come with me to the Lords tomorrow afternoon, after we've finished having tea with the Headmaster?"

"I'd simply *love* to come with you!" said Jim happily.

CHAPTER ELEVEN

As they drew near to the end of their journey at East Sheen both Jim and Susan were feeling apprehensive. Then Jim, who was doing the navigating with notes and an open street map, while Susan was driving, saw a sign which read: "Borough of Barnes: EAST SHEEN" on the top of a direction sign, and, for a moment, felt a flash of something that was almost like panic pass through him. But only for a moment.

"Here's the 'East Sheen' sign, Sue, where we have to turn right at the traffic lights," he said.

"I've seen it," said Susan.

There was no delay for them at the junction as the lights were green for them. Jim, however, was privately disappointed that the lights were not at red. He knew thsat he was dreading the imminent meeting with Dick and Jane Dalmane, but he also knew that his fear must be quite illogical. They were coming to the Dalmanes' house as invited guests and, no doubt, they would be politely (if not warmly) received when they arrived there.

As Susan turned the car to the right off the Upper Richmond Road, coming into Sheen Lane, Jim was already reading out the next part of their written directions. "The first turn to the right, Archer's Road, about fifty yards after the traffic lights, and exactly opposite the turning to the left to Barnes Central Library and the Council offices."

"Here it is!" said Susan. "That was very easy to find. Now, what was their house number?"

"Number Four, and it's on the right-hand side of the road."

They saw that the first house on the right in Archer's Road was number 2, so they pulled up outside the next house where they was the number 4 on the stone gates. They were in a quiet, tree-lined, suburban road. There was no one to be seen anywhere, and no traffic moving in the road, and altogether it seemed to Jim to be most unnaturally and ominously quiet.

Susan had switched off the engine of her car, but neither of them had moved from their seats. Jim saw that Susan was looking at the house as if she were trying to see whether anyone was peeping out through a window, expecting to see them.

"It doesn't look as if there's anyone here, does it?" she said, almost as if she were talking to herself rather than to Jim. "But it must be the right house, and they must be in. We'd better ring the doorbell."

"Yes," said Jim, but he paused to glance at his watch. "It's about half past six now," he said.

"So that must be all right as we said we'd try to get here between six and seven o' clock."

They went through a garden gate between large, ornate stone gate posts, and up a garden path towards the front door. They saw that the house, an elegant Georgian three-storeyed building, had a handsome stone portico like all the other houses along that quiet street.

Susan was on the point of ringing the doorbell, but the door was suddenly opened from the inside by a smartly dressed butler. The butler, who had never seen them before, seemed to guess who they were.

"Lady Sandy?" he said in an enquiring voice.

"Yes, indeed!" said Susan, "and this is my husband, Jim."

"Come in, my Lady," said the butler, making a stiff little bow towards her, but (so far as Jim could tell) ignoring him completely.

"You'll have some luggage to bring in, my Lady?" he continued as they stepped through the front door of the house.

"We haven't brought much, but it's in the boot of the car if you'd like to bring it in."

"He must have been peeping through the window in the door to have seen us coming!" whispered Jim to Susan as the butler went back to the car to collect their suitcases. There was a small square window of plain glass in the front door above a heavy metal door-knocker. The electric bell-push for the doorbell was to the left of the door.

"Oh, do come in, Susan, my dear!" said a woman's voice in a strangely affected, drawling accent. "Come in, Jim." Looking up, Jim and Susan, who had hardly had time to look around them, saw a short, fat woman with blonde hair who had appeared in the hall. "So Rodney let you in as soon as you arrived? You haven't been waiting out there, have you?"

"Oh, no, that's all right," said Susan. "Your butler opened the door for us as soon as we arrived."

"Well, that's all right, but I'd meant to do it myself," said Jane Dalmane.

"Thank you!" said Susan, now addressing the butler as the latter put down their two suitcases in the hall.

"You'll be wanting to lock your car now, my Lady?" suggested Rodney, the butler politely. "Perhaps I may do it for you?"

"Thank you very much, but I'd rather do it myself," said Susan. "I'll be back in a moment." She turned to go back to her car.

"Now do come in and meet my husband," invited Jane Dalmane to Jim. "They've arrived, Dick!" she suddenly shouted over her shoulder.

"Just coming!" another voice shouted back.

Jim shook Jane Dalmane's hand and mumbled a polite, "How do you do, Lady Dalmane?" to her. Then, glancing over his shoulder for a moment he saw with relief that Susan was back in the house. At almost the same moment a door on the left of the hall opened, and a man, whom Jim recognized as Sir Richard (Dick) Dalmane, emerged from the sitting-room.

Jim had seen the late Earl's brother, Dick Dalmane, and his wife, Jane, only once before, long ago (it seemed) in the days when he had been working as the Guide of Rhodes Castle, but he had never been introduced to them before. On that other occasion, he remembered, he had only been able to peep at Dick and Jane Dalmane through the high hedge which separated the Visitor Centre from the main lawn. Now, as he remembered that occasion when he had not been supposed to meet or see the visitors, he could not resist a sly grin as he shook Dick Dalmane's hand.

"Have you had a good journey?" asked Dick Dalmane, apparently thinking that they had travelled that day from Rhodes Castle.

"Oh, yes," said Susan. "The traffic on the roads between here and Westminster wasn't bad at all, with the rush hour being more or less over when we set off."

"Oh, of course; you've come on from Westminster this evening, haven't you? I was forgetting that you've already spent several days in London since you left the Castle."

"That's right," said Susan.

"Do let's sit down in the sitting-room while we talk," said Jane Dalmane. "That's it in here, if you'd like to follow me." She showed them the way into the sitting-room, where the butler quietly pulled out armchairs for the visitors. Then Jane nodded to the butler, who went off to bring in the drinks tray.

"So you've come on from Westminster School this afternoon?" she said as soon as they were all sitting down.

"Yes, indeed," said Susan. "In fact, we had tea with the Headmaster this afternoon, and then we came on to you."

"That sounds a bit intimidating!" chuckled Dick. "Tea with the Headmaster! But perhaps it wasn't frightening? Perhaps you already knew the Headmaster?"

"Oh, no!" said Susan. "We'd never met the Headmaster before, but we didn't find it a bit intimidating, having tea with him this afternoon

– did we, darling?"

"No, we didn't," confirmed Jim. "We just found that he seemed a very nice, polite man, and so ir seemed perfectly easy making conversation with him. But my brother was there too, and that helped to make things go smoothly."

"Your brother?" said Jane.

"My brother, Benjamin, is the Captain of the School - the Head Boy in other words - and so he arranged this meeting for us."

"He's quite pally with the Headmaster, I suppose?" said Dick

"Well, yes, I dare say he is," said Jim.

"Ah, good, here comes Rod with the drinks tray," said Jane. "Now, my dears, do let's have a drink while we talk, and then we'll have our dinner."

The butler put down his drinks tray on a small table close to Jane Dalmane's armchair. They were offered a fairly wide choice of drinks, including plain tonic water if they preferred something non-alcoholic, but both Susan and Jim chose the dry sherry.

As he slowly sipped his drink (wishing privately that it had been a sweet or medium rather than a dry sherry) Jim did not join in the general conversation very much, which left him plenty of time to think about things. Dick Dalmane, he thought, quite reminded him of John Dalmane, although he was rather shorter and perhaps not so handsome as the late Earl. But he had at once noticed a change in Jane Dalmane's appearance which, he thought, was a change for the better. Her hair, he remembered, had been a most unnatural shade of silvery-white on that last occasion when he had seen her, but now it seemed to be a much more natural shade of blonde. She rather reminds me of someone now with that honey-blonde hair, he thought. With a shock he suddenly realized who that person was. Why, it's Rachel! Her hair is exactly the same shade of blonde as Rachel's hair! And with that thought he was instantly transported away from that sitting-room in East Sheen, and was seeing again the gorgeous head and face of Rachel Connor. Damn! he said to himself. I didn't want to think about Rachel at all while we're away in London. And I was thinking about her yesterday afternoon as well down at the boathouse in Putney. Oh dear, oh dear - why does this woman, Jane, have to remind me of Rachel when I only want to forget her?

Jim's train of thought was suddenly broken when the conversation between Susan and the Dalmanes took an unexpected turn. Susan had been telling her hosts about their plans for the rest of their stay in London before they returned home.

"We're planning to return home on Sunday after we've spent two nights staying with Jim's mother in Ealing," said Susan. "Then, of course, we'll be back at home again in Rhodes Castle at least until the summer when we're hoping to go up to the Hebrides again."

"Oh, Susan, but how *lovely*!" said Jane enthusiastically. "It must be so lovely up there - and you and Jim have been there before, I believe?"

"Yes, indeed we have; and it certainly is lovely up there, as you say."

"Well, I hope you'll enjoy that holiday when it comes," said Dick. "And then you'll be returning to the Castle, no doubt?"

"But of course!"

"Well, Susan - I might as well tell you this now - we're going to move into Rhodes Castle early next year," said Dick in a flat, matter-of-fact voice.

"What?" said Susan sharply. "I beg your pardon?"

"I said, we will be moving in to Rhodes Castle, Jane and I, early next year: on February the first, to be precise. You'll be getting a letter from my solicitor shortly to confirm the details, but I thought that it would be a more friendly approach, shall we say, to tell you in advance our plans for moving into the Castle."

"Friendly!" expostulated Susan. "Well, of all the...!" She cut herself off short, suddenly unsure of what to say next as she caught Jim's eye, watching her anxiously. "Dick, you must be out of your mind to be thinking of moving into Rhodes Castle," she continued, now speaking with very deliberate calmness. "I think you must have taken leave of your senses!"

"Oh, no! My husband has certainly *not* taken leave of his senses!" said Jane quickly, springing to the defence of her husband. "You see, Susan, the fact is that Dick is now *officially* the new Earl of Saint Helens. He's had a letter to confirm that - haven't you, Dick?"

"Yes, I have recently received a letter to confirm that," said Dick Dalmane. "I'm sorry, Susan; perhaps I should have told you that first?"

"But what is this letter you're talking about?" asked Susan. "And from whom?"

"It's a letter from the Lord Chancellor to me, advising me that I shall officially take the title of the Earl of Saint Helens at a short ceremony to be held in the House of Lords in about a month's time - I forget the exact date. Of course, to be strictly accurate, I'm not the Earl of Saint Helens *yet* - but I soon will be - and Jane will be the new Countess, of course!"

"Oh, well, Dick, let me *congratulate* you on your elevation to the Peerage!" said Susan sarcastically, laying a cold emphasis on the word "congratulate".

"Thank you!" said Dick, appearing not to notice the coldness of her tone.

"Oh, but it *is* wonderful news for us, you know," said Jane. "Dick to be the Earl of Saint Helens, and I to be the Countess of Saint Helens. It's as it should be."

"Is it?" said Susan sharply. "And what am I to be then? What title do you think would be right for me? Will I have to be known as the Dowager Countess of Saint Helens, do you think? We can't have *two* Countesses at the same time, you know!"

"Ah, well," said Dick, "I think you must be right about that, Susan, although I must confess that I don't really know the answer to your question."

"Don't you?" said Susan, now softening her tone somewhat. "Well, listen, Dick. Don't get me wrong about this: I don't mind in the least if I'm to be demoted, as it were, from Countess to Dowager Countess. No, honestly, I really don't mind what my title is to become when you and Jane become the Earl and the Countess. And I *am* pleased that this has happened for you at last."

"Well, Susan, it's really kind of you to say that, but I'm sorry that we've upset you by pointing out that we shall be exercising our rights, and moving into the Castle next year."

"But that, Dick, is just absurd, as I said before. I shall have to have a word with my solicitor if you really mean to think of evicting us. In fact, I'm expecting to be able to have a talk with him tomorrow evening. I must do that."

"Then you'd better do that, Susan. We don't mind, do we, Jane, darling?"

"Not a bit!" said Jane. "You see, we are already in touch with our solicitor about these matters. But, as Dick said, we really are sorry to have upset you by this news."

"Ah, well, it's only the absolute absurdity of this idea of us having to move out so that you can move in that has upset me," said Susan. "But... what do you think about it, Jim, darling?"

"I entirely agree with everything you've been saying," said Jim slowly, choosing his words carefully, and suddenly smiling as he caught Susan's eye. He had known perfectly well that he must leave all the talking to his wife while they were discussing their possible eviction from the Castle, unless or until she asked him to voice his opinion.

Sue's the boss! he said to himself.

"Well, there you are, Dick; we're of one opinion on this matter, you see!" said Susan, answering Jim's smile with a warm smile of her own. Up to that point in the conversation, since Dick Dalmane had first mentioned their intention to move in to Rhodes Castle, she had been looking very serious.

It seemed that Dick Dalmane was trying to think of something to say to answer Susan's assertion positively, without losing face, but almost at once she cut him off by continuing.

"But enough! I really don't want to hear any more on this subject now, if you don't mind!"

"Very well," said Dick quietly, "we won't talk about it any more."

"Will you have a little more to drink, my dears, before we go through to dinner?" asked Jane as casually as if no contraversial subjects had ever been thought of that evening, let alone discussed.

"I'll have another half glass of sherry, thank you," said Susan politely, with just a hint of a smile in Jim's direction.

He understood that she was signalling to him that she was showing that she was bearing no grudge against Dick and Jane for daring to mention to them the matter of their possible eviction. Sue's forgiving them, he said to himself. He also accepted a fill-up of his glass.

*

For the rest of that evening, and especially a little later when they were all sitting at the dinner table in the Dalmanes' dining-room, they were all being rather careful in what they said. Jim understood that their host and hostess, in particular, were being careful that no remarks they introduced into the conversation might cause further offence to their guests. He guessed, however, that they did not at all regret having mentioned their intention to move into the castle presently, and he often found himself wondering whether it might turn out that they were really in the right after all: that they would indeed have to leave Rhodes Castle. It was such an unsettling thought that he found, when it came to dinner time, that he did not feel as hungry as usual.

He also wondered, from time to time, whether their hosts had forgotten their manners by not asking them whether they would like to visit the bathroom. But he need not have worried. When they were ready to move from the sitting-room Jane Dalmane suggested that perhaps they would like to "wash their hands" before dinner. Then, while she lead Susan upstairs to the bathroom, the butler discreetly showed Jim the way he should go.

When they had all sat down at the dinner table, and the servants had brought in the first course, it seemed at first that conversation was a little difficult. There were one or two decidedly uncomfortable periods of silence while they were all trying to think of something to say, something that would not serve as a reminder of the conversation in the sitting-room before dinner. It was not long, however, before a chance remark by Jane Dalmane again suggested to Jim what unpleasant people his host and hostess really were.

"Darling, did you get that book you wanted from the library today?"

"No," said Dick. "They wouldn't let me have it."

"You mean, they hadn't got it?"

"Oh, yes, they had it all right, but the man behind the counter said that I was not going to be allowed to borrow any more books until I brought back the Dalmane Family History, and paid the fine on it."

Jim wondered how long overdue the book was for return to the library, and how big was the fine they were asking for.

"But what did you say then?" asked Jane. "You told the man who you are, I hope?"

"I did indeed," said Dick, "but it made no difference. He said, 'I'm sorry, sir, it doesn't matter who you are. I'm not allowed to let you take out any more books until "The History of the Dalmane Family" is returned to the library, and the fine paid on it.' And so then I said I'd have to write a sharp letter of complaint to the Barnes Chief Librarian. And so I shall!"

"Yes, indeed!" said Jane. It's absolutely *disgraceful* behaviour of the library staff! Don't you think so, Susan? I hope that your local library never treats you in that way, if you use it?"

"Well, as a matter of fact, we never do use our local library," said Susan, glancing into Jim's face as she answered. He had understood by the look on Susan's face that she entirely disagreed with Jane Dalmane's assertion that the Barnes library staff were behaving disgracefully towards her husband.

"By the way," said Susan, "I think I know the book you mean. Is it the one by my Uncle Tom – 'The History of the Dalmane Family' by Thomas Bellingham-Smith, my mother's brother?"

"That's the one," said Dick.

"But have you not considered the possibility of purchasing a copy of the book to keep for your own library?"

"Ah, well... yes, I have, of course, considered that possibility," admitted Dick grudgingly.

"But we don't want to buy the book!" said Jane sharply. "Why should we when we can get it from our local library just over the road in Sheen Lane? And I don't see why anyone else should really need to read it as it's a book about *our* family."

Neither Susan nor Jim could think of anything to say in answer to that. What beastly, mean people they are! thought Jim; and he knew that Susan was thinking along much the same lines.

For the rest of the meal the conversation returned to being mostly polite small talk on relatively unimportant matters. It was clear to both Jim and Susan that their host and hostess were being careful to steer the conversation away from the awkward subjects of moving house and using the public libraries.

*

"Well, I really can hardly believe it!" said Susan. "To think that Dick had the bare-faced cheek to tell us quite calmly that they're intending to move into the Castle early next year!"

"Yes," agreed Jim. "Such cheek really *is* almost unbelievable!"

"It certainly is!" said Susan.

Jim and Susan had just said Good-night to their hosts, and had shut the door of their spare bedroom. It was a light and pleasant room at the front of the house on the first floor, overlooking the quiet street outside. Susan, having first pulled the curtains and switched on the bedside light, had pulled off her shoes and flopped down onto the comfortable-looking double bed. Jim, following her example, had done the same, and now they were both lying on the bed, still fully clothed.

"But what a jolly good thing it is that we can go and talk to our solicitor tomorrow night!" said Jim.

"I know, darling. I was just thinking the same thing myself. What a good thing we made that arrangement!"

"But in the morning, Sue, darling, what do you think we ought to do? We can't go to Croydon to talk to Roger until the evening, but I suppose we ought to leave this place as soon as we can?"

"Absolutely! As soon as we possibly can! It would almost be nice, wouldn't it, to get away without having to see Jane and Dick again for breakfast – but, of course, we can't do that. But I vote that we leave here right after breakfast!"

"And I second that!" said Jim. "But what about after that? Have you got any plans in mind, Sue?"

"Well, what we ought to do first, I think, is to go straight back to Claire in Martin Lane."

"But she knows that we're coming back there for tomorrow night, doesn't she?"

"Oh, yes, she knows that, but we might as well call in there at around ten o' clock, or so - if we find her in then, as I hope we will - to confirm our arrangements and to leave our main luggage there for the rest of the day while we go out touring."

"I say, Sue, do you think we ought to tell Claire about what they've said to us about moving in to the Castle next year?"

"Why not?" said Susan. "Yes, I think we might as well tell her that. I'm sure she'll be most sympathetic when she hears about the rudeness of these people."

There was a short pause of a minute or two in their conversation while Jim tested the comfortableness of the bed by lying down properly with his head resting on the pillows. They had both been lying in a semi-reclining position, their heads propped up on the headboard of the bed with a pillow.

"I say, Sue," he said presently, "this bed is *really* comfortable!"

"Oh, splendid!" said Susan. "So at least we should have a comfortable night here; and that's one good thing about coming here!"

"And it's a good thing, isn't it, that we've got our own bathroom?"

"Oh, yes, it certainly is; I wouldn't like to run the risk of meeting Jane or Dick again this evening!"

A door from the spare bedroom opened straight into a small guests' bathroom. They had looked at it earlier in the evening, and had pronounced themselves well satisfied with what they had seen.

"But Sue, darling, do you think it's going to be all right?" asked Jim presently.

"You mean, all right when we've had a talk with Roger tomorrow evening, and told him about their intention to evict us from the Castle?"

"Yes, I mean that. It *is* pretty worrying to have a threat like that hanging over us."

"Yes, I know it is," said Susan, "but I really am sure, my darling, that we needn't worry about it. I'm sure that Roger will be able to deal with them in one way or another – that is, if they really mean what they say – as I'm afraid they do!"

"But there's another thing, Sue," said Jim. "About that business of the library books: doesn't that just show how mean and beastly they really are?"

"Absolutely! Yes, that's the sort of people they are – but I must say that I applaud the library staff for the stance against them they've evidently taken! Really, I think that Dick's arrogance in saying, 'Don't you know who I am?' and then assuming that he can keep a book out for as long as he likes without paying the fine on it, is insufferable."

"I agree with you, Sue; Dick's attitude is insufferable."

"And so is Jane's. She backs him up, you know, in the stand he's taking against the Barnes Public Libraries – and against us!"

"Do you know, Sue, I expect that, if he is forced to give that book back to the library presently, he'll be wanting to borrow our copy of it; and, of course, he'll be expecting to be able to borrow it when they move in to the Castle next year?"

"To borrow it?" said Susan. "To simply take it, more likely, I should think... Oh well, darling, shall we try to forget about them now for a while as they're rather odious people?"

"A good idea, Sue! Let's forget about them!"

Chapter Twelve

"Oh, hello! I wasn't really expecting to see you until later in the day," said Claire Walker as she opened the front door, looked out, and saw Jim and Susan standing outside.

"Well, I am sorry, Claire, if we're being very awkward by dropping in when you weren't expecting us," said Susan. "But we could go on now, if you like - if it's not convenient for us to come here now - and return later on?"

"Oh, not at all, my dears, not at all," said Claire kindly. "Do come right in now!"

"Are you sure it's not inconvenient? Perhaps you were thinking of going out about now? We did think of ringing you up this morning, you know, to let you know we were thinking of dropping in, but somehow we didn't."

"My dears, it really is quite all right. Do come in, and we'll have a cup of coffee, and you can tell me how you've been getting on. I really don't need to go out for a while yet." Claire Walker opened her front door wider, and stepped aside for her visitors to enter the hall.

Jim and Susan thanked her, came into the hall, and shook hands with her.

"You were staying at East Sheen last night, weren't you, with your late husband's brother and his wife?" said Claire.

"Yes, we were," said Susan.

"So I suppose it didn't take you very long to get here?"

"That's right, it hasn't taken us very long," said Jim. "The morning rush hour seems to be over, more or less, and" - he looked at his watch - "Gosh, it's not quite five to ten yet! It must have taken us less than ten minutes to get here. Don't you think so, Sue?"

"Yes, I think it was just about twenty to ten when we left Jane and Dick's house," said Susan. "And I suppose it's only about three miles?"

"Yes, I would say that the crossroads at East Sheen must be about three miles from where we are here in Roehampton," said Claire.

"Anyway, my dears, shall we go through to the kitchen - if you don't mind sitting in there while we have coffee?" She lead the way down a passage which lead out of the hall. It was surprisingly dark in that rather narrow passage; although it was late May Jim noticed that there were electric lights on there.

"Here we are, my dears," continued Claire as she lead her guests into a large room on the left at the end of the passage. "This is my kitchen, Jim - I don't think you've been in here before?"

"No, I haven't," said Jim, looking around him.

"Are you on your own here at the moment, Claire?" asked Susan, guessing that they had been shown into the kitchen as there were no servants about the place.

"Well, not quite on my own, actually," said Claire. "Cook is probably upstairs at the moment, but she's off duty, and there's no one else in the house now. So, my dears, if you'd like to find yourselves some chairs we'll sit down at the table to have coffee. That's it, Jim, if you would like to take that one over there by the grandfather clock, and put it down at this end of the table - that's right, Susan, that one can go over there."

Susan had picked up a chair which had been standing in front of one of the windows, while Jim was fetching another chair which had been standing beside a grandfather clock which stood to the right-hand side of the door (for anyone entering the room).

"But I'm glad to see you again!" continued Claire. "Do sit down, Jim. Don't wait for me. I'll sit down when I've got the coffee ready."

"It looks rather dull and dreary outside now?" said Susan, who was looking out of the window. There were two elegant sash windows on the southern side of the room (the front of the house), overlooking the narrow strip of front garden and the street.

"Just what I was going to say," said Claire. "You've been lucky with the weather so far for your stay in London. Now tell me, Susan: how did you get on last night with the Dalmanes? Was your visit there really as bad as you'd feared it might be?"

"Well, as a matter of fact, Claire," said Susan with a quick glance at Jim, "I'd say it was even worse than we'd thought it might be!"

"Worse?"

But Susan had heard the tone of disbelief in Claire's voice and so knew that it was time to tell her what had actually happened in The Dalmanes' house. She told of the threat of eviction that was now hanging over them and said that she would have to consult her solicitor who, luckily, was in London at the moment.

"He's staying at his brother's house in Croydon," said Jim, and we'd made an arrangement before we left home on Monday that we could drop in there any evening, if we wanted to talk to him. So we're going there this evening."

"Well, I'll wish you luck, my dears; and, of course, you can let me know how you got on when you come back here later in the evening," said Claire. "Anyway, coffee's ready now, so let's have it."

Jim was not saying very much as he ate and drank, but he was using his eyes. He allowed his gaze to wander around the room, approving well of all that he saw there, but he found, to his annoyance, that it wanted to settle on the pleasantly well-rounded figure of Claire Walker, who was sitting to his right. He was quite certain that he did not feel seriously attracted to her, but the well-rounded outlines of her bust, emphasised by the tight-fitting, short-sleeved black top she was wearing, could not have failed to draw and hold his attention. He was secretly glad, too, that they would be coming back there after their visit to Croydon to spend one more night with Claire and John Walker before moving on to his mother's house for their last two nights in London.

"I like the way you've arranged this room," said Susan presently.

"But do you usually use this end of the room as your dining-room when you haven't got people staying here?" About two thirds of the large room was carpeted and tastefully furnished like a dining-room, while the other part of the room, where there was the Aga cooker and kitchen sink, was uncarpeted and clearly served as the working kitchen area.

"That's right," said Claire. "We don't normally use the dining-room when there are just the two of us at home as it's more convenient to use this room as a dining-room."

"When they had finished their coffee and biscuits, and were on the point of leaving, Claire asked them where they were planning to go that day. She was standing at the open front door to see her guests off.

"We're going into the City to have a sight-seeing morning," said Susan. Jim wants to see St. Paul's Cathedral, and the Monument, and the Tower of London."

"And Tower Bridge too, if there's time," said Jim. "Then we're both going down to Putney to watch my brother do his rowing. He's in the Westminster School First Eight, you see."

"And then we're off to Croydon to talk with Roger, our solicitor," said Susan.

"And then we're coming back here," said Jim, hoping that he did not sound as if he were unnaturally keen on the idea of returning to the house in Martin Lane.

"Good luck with your legal talk!" said Claire. "And let us know later how you got on there."

*

"Now then, Susan," said Roger Burton when he had closed the sitting-room door and sat down in an armchair, "I gather that you've spent a night with Sir Richard and Jane Dalmane, and that, as a result of that visit, you have some problem that you'd like to talk over with me?"

"That's right," said Susan. "We do indeed have a problem, and we'd like you to advise us on what to do about it."

"I'll do my best," said Roger Burton.

Jim and Susan had found Jeremy Burton's house, number 481 Cedar Road in East Croydon, with surprisingly little difficulty. They had been welcomed into the house by Jeremy Burton (Roger Burton's brother), and had then been introduced to Jeremy's wife, Lydia. Jim saw a diminutive woman with dark hair and dark eyes who smiled at him as they shook hands. Then from another room appeared the person they had come to see, Roger Burton, the solicitor. There had been more shaking of hands.

"Now, if you don't mind, Susan," said Lydia Burton," Jeremy and I will withdraw into the kitchen as you'll want a little time to have a private talk with Roger.

Roger Burton had then lead the way into a large airy room at the back of the house. a room which had a french window looking out over a lawn behind the house. He invited Susan and Jim to sit down in armchairs before he sat down himself. Now that it was early evening the day had faired up considerably, having been dull and cloudy for much of the day with some rain in the middle of the day, but now the sun was shining again, and the clouds had almost completely disappeared from the sky.

"Well, in a nutshell, Roger, it's like this," said Susan. "Dick and Jane Dalmane have told us that they're intending to move in to Rhodes Castle in February of next year."

"Good heavens!" said Roger Burton. "Do you mean to say that they simply announced that as if they were assuming that the Castle now belongs to them?"

"That's exactly what they did," said Susan, "and Jim and I think that it's the height of impertinence!"

"Yes, we do!" agreed Jim.

"It may well be that," said Roger seriously. "But tell me, Susan, was that all that was said on that subject? Surely they gave you some grounds - or excuse, shall we say - for assuming that the Castle has somehow become their's, so that they can just move in whenever they want to?"

"I was just coming to that," said Susan. "Dick told us that he is now officially the Earl of Saint Helens, or that he very soon will be; so, you see, he's reckoning that by holding that title he now has the right to take Rhodes Castle as his Seat, to come in and live there - and to turn us out!"

"And, no doubt, to turn *us* out too?" said Roger.

"Oh, yes, of course; I was forgetting that you and Sam live with us in the Castle. So what do you think, Roger?"

"Well, Susan, I wouldn't worry about it at all. No, really I don't think that any of us need have any fear that they could be evicting us because, frankly, they would *not* be within their rights to think of doing that."

"Oh, good!" said Susan. "I hoped that you would say that!"

"Well, if you'll give me a little time, I'll check up on the relevant points of the law as soon as I get home; but I'm already pretty well sure that they haven't got a case at all for moving into the Castle."

"So what do you think that we ought to do next, Roger?"

Roger Burton thought for a moment.

"Well, really the best thing to do for a start would simply be to try to persuade them to be sensible," he said.

"Do you think it would be a good thing if you were to write to them?" asked Susan.

"That's exactly what I was going to suggest. Yes, I'll write to them, Susan, with your permission, telling them that you've informed me, as your solicitor, of their intentions in this matter, and I shall advise them strongly to do the sensible thing, and abandon this ridiculous idea of moving into Rhodes Castle. Have they, by the way, actually said that they're intending to serve an eviction order on you presently?"

"Well, no, I don't believe they have," said Susan after a moment's thought. "What I think that Dick actually said, if I remember it correctly, was that we should soon be getting a letter from his solicitor to confirm the details of what they're intending to do. I think he just said that, but I think that I was so shocked to hear about getting a letter from his solicitor that I didn't ask him whether that would actually take the form of an eviction order, or not."

"Ah, I see," said Roger Burton. "Yes, I'm sure that you must have been very shocked indeed to hear about getting a letter from his solicitor; but, all the same, Susan, I'm inclined to think that it's a good thing, in a way. You see, what I mean is that it would be a good thing if I were to write to their solicitors, as well as to them personally. But the snag in that plan is, obviously, that we don't know yet who their solicitors are. Presumably you don't know that?"

"No, we don't know that yet," said Susan. "But of course we will know as soon as we receive the letter from them."

"Yes, that's right; and then, perhaps, if you would be so kind as to pass the information on to me, or show me the letter when you receive it, I would be in a position to write a formal letter, with your permission, to their solicitors. But - if I could just mention one thing, Susan – it's a good thing that we are not Sir Richard's solicitors!"

"My goodness!" Susan suddenly laughed. "I hadn't thought of that, but, yes, it would be very awkward for you if you had to represent both sides, as it were, in this arguement."

"It would indeed – it would be all but impossible, I should think! But very fortunately for you we are not representing Sir Richard and Lady Jane Dalmane, so we can put that idea out of our minds. So, as I was saying, if I have your permission I'll write to their solicitors as soon as I can."

"Oh, yes, please do that; you have my full permission to write to their solicitors. And your's, darling...? Jim, darling?" Susan turned to her husband, but saw by the far-away look on his face that Jim was entirely lost in his own thoughts, and had probably heard nothing of what she had just been saying.

"What's that, Sue?" he said, startled from his reverie as he suddenly turned his head towards her. His armchair was facing the large window overlooking the garden and, looking at the view and becoming lost in his own thoughts, he had completely lost the thread of Susan's conversation with Roger Burton. Now, suddenly, he was all attention again. "I'm so sorry, Sue, but I'm afraid I haven't heard what you've been saying."

"Darling, I don't think you've been paying attention!" said Susan reprovingly, but she said it with a smile, and Jim saw that Roger Burton was also smiling at him.

"I'm sorry!" said Jim. "But yes, that's true; I haven't been paying attention."

"It *is* a nice view from here, looking out over the garden, isn't it?" said Roger Burton.

"It is," agreed Jim. "As a matter of fact, I've been watching some squirrels out there... Look, there's one of them over there now! Just at the bottom of the trunk of that pine tree." He pointed to the spot at which he was staring.

"Oh, yes, I see it!" said Susan excitedly. "Oh, isn't that lovely!"

"Yes, they are fascinating to watch, aren't they?" said Roger. "I was watching two or three grey squirrels out there yesterday evening.

It's funny, though, that we don't seem to see so many of them back at home –"

"Oh, there's another!" Susan interrupted him. "Sorry, Roger! You were saying?"

"I was just going to say that Sam says that she's seen quite a few in the Whitfield Copse."

"Jeremy says that you see lots of them around here," said Roger, "but he says there are too many of them, really, and that he regards them as pests; but Lydia likes to see them coming into the garden, so they leave them alone, but don't actually encourage them to come by feeding them."

"Of course you had the red squirrels round about you, darling, when you were living in Cockermouth, and they're really much nicer than these grey ones," said Susan.

"Oh, yes," said Jim. "But I've only seen the red squirrels once or twice in the Lake District. But, look, one of those greys has appeared again – over there – and it's eating something."

They all saw a grey squirrel which was sitting on its hind legs, its bushy tail over its back, while it held something in its paws and nibbled at it.

"But that reminds me, Roger, that perhaps it's time you were eating a meal?" said Susan. "When do you have your supper here?"

"Well, we have it about now, actually."

"Then we must go! I thought that would probably be the case; and we've stayed here long enough anyway, and we don't want to delay your supper. But you've been very helpful, Roger; I'm so glad that we've had this opportunity to talk with you today."

"It was Sam's idea that you might like to come here," said Roger.

"Well, it was a brilliant idea, so do thank her, won't you, from both of us. Come on, Jim, darling, we'd better find Lydia and Jeremy now to tell them that we must be going." Susan rose to her feet while she was speaking, but Roger, who was sitting nearer to the door, jumped to his feet to open it for her.

Jeremy Burton had heard them, and had come out of the kitchen into the hall.

"Are you off now?" he asked.

"Yes, we really must be off now," said Susan, "but thank you so much for letting us come here to talk with Roger."

"Just coming!" shouted Lydia's voice from the kitchen, and a moment later she too appeared on the scene.

"Have you been watching the squirrels?" asked Jeremy. "We have the same view over the lawn from the kitchen windows as you have in the sitting-room.

"Yes, we've been watching them," said Jim.

"They seem to like our pine trees," said Lydia. "But there are a lot of grey squirrels about in this part of South London, you know: you see them all over the place in gardens, in the parks, and on the Addington Hills."

"I suppose the open countryside is not all that far away from here?" said Jim.

"That's right, it's not all that far to get out into the country - I suppose it would be about four or five miles if one went out through West Wickham, which is the way we usually go."

"I see," said Jim politely, although he could not really understand what Lydia Burton had told him without looking at a map.

Jeremy opened his front door for the visitors. Outside they had seen that the sun was now shining in an almost cloudless sky, but Jim and Susan had already seen the dramatic improvement in the weather as it had happened while they had been driving from Putney to Croydon.

"What a beautiful evening it's turned into!" said Susan. "But we've got to be off now as we don't want to keep you from your supper; and anyway Claire will have our's ready for us when we get back to Roehampton."

Susan thanked Roger again for his helpful advice, and their hosts for making them welcome in their home, and then they left them. As they drove away down Cedar Road and George Street in the direction of Croydon town centre Jim had taken the driving seat. Their plan was to return to Roehampton by exactly the same route on which they had come, via Streatham, Wandsworth, and the Upper Richmond Road. Jim had decided that it should be perfectly easy to find the right route (with help from Susan, if necessary). It was twenty minutes past six as they pulled up temporarily at the traffic lights at the intersection of Croydon High Street and North End, but the traffic was not heavy, the evening rush hour being well and truly over.

Jim was happy enough to concentrate on driving the car safely and carefully, but he could not help feeling glad that they were now returning to the house in Martin Lane. He was glad, too, that no thoughts or images of Rachel Connor had disturbed his mind that day.

However, his daydreams in the sitting-room of the Burton's house (when he had not been actively involved in watching the squirrels) had been mostly concerned with thinking over the day's sight-seeing experiences in the City of London.

*

When they arrived once again outside the house in Martin Lane, Roehampton, they saw that John Walker was there, mowing the two narrow strips of lawn outside the front of the house. They saw him wave an arm as Jim parked Susan's car and switched off the engine.

"Hello!" he called out. "Do come in! I've gathered from Claire that you may need to move in here soon?"

"But I'm pretty sure, now that we've had a talk with our solicitor, that we won't need to," said Susan. "Ah, here comes Claire."

The front door of the house stood open as the evening had now turned quite warm, and Claire had come out to greet them.

"Hello again, my dears!" she said. "I hope you've had a good day, since I last saw you?"

"Excellent!" said Susan, smiling happily.

"Well, do come in now, please," said Claire, "and you can tell us about your day when we've sat down. Perhaps, as it's turned into such a beautiful evening, you'd like to sit in the garden for a drink - in the main garden at the back, I mean, where we have breakfast?"

"That would be lovely!" said Susan.

A little later, when they were sitting at the garden table with their before-dinner drinks, Susan invited John and Claire to come to stay with them at Rhodes Castle.

"It's been so nice staying here," she said. "Jim and I have really enjoyed it, so now we'd like you to come and stay with us sometime - wouldn't we, darling?"

"Oh, yes, indeed!" said Jim, trying not to sound as pleased as he suddenly felt.

"Well, thank you, Susan, that's a very kind offer! But you know that you've really only been staying in your own house while you've been here with us?"

"Oh, yes, I realize that," said Susan, "but I must say that it doesn't really feel like staying in our own house while we're here."

"No, it doesn't," said Jim. "It feels like we've been staying in *your* house, but we've enjoyed being here very much!"

"It's been wonderful!" said Susan. "But do come to the Castle to stay sometime soon, if you can. I can't say exactly when would be best until I've looked in my diary, but I think we'd probably be free to have you sometime in the autumn."

"That's very kind of you!" said Claire. "Yes, I'm sure we'd love to come to see Rhodes Castle to stay there with you sometime."

CHAPTER THIRTEEN

Jim and Susan were having their breakfast on the private lawn at Rhodes Castle. They had arrived back at the Castle in the afternoon of the previous day, having finished their very succesful trip to London with two nights staying at Jim's mother's house in Ealing. Now, on a beautifully warm morning of early summer, inspired by the example of the breakfasts they had eaten in the garden of the house in Roehampton, they were again enjoying an outdoor breakfast. They had seen Samantha only briefly the previous day, and even more briefly when she had brought out with the butler one of two trays laden with breakfast things, but they had been able to tell her that her idea had been a great success: that they had had a very useful talk with her husband, Roger. Both Jim and Susan, however, (and especially Susan) were hoping for an opportunity soon to have a proper, long chat with Samantha to tell her more of what they had seen and done in London.

"Sam's coming back," said Jim presently, having swallowed a mouthful of toast and marmalade. "She must be bringing out the post."

"Yes, I expect so," said Susan. Samantha was coming uphill towards them across the short grass of the private lawn. They saw that she had an envelope in her hand. "Have you got some post for us, Sam?"

"Yes, I have," said Samantha. "I thought that you'd want to see this letter now, Sue. It's from America."

"America? It must be a letter from Jack Wonstannley!"

Samantha handed over the letter. Susan quickly ran her eye over the handwriting and the American stamps and the postmark on the envelope.

"Has this just come this morning?" she asked.

"Well, no, it came yesterday morning, I think," said Samantha. "Of course there's been a lot of other post come for you while you've been away, but I thought that you'd be particularly interested in this one."

"You're right, Sam - quite right! I'm sure we'll be particularly interested to see what Jack has to say." Susan had been opening the envelope while Samantha had been speaking, and now she pulled out the letter which had been folded inside it. "It is from Jack Wonstannley," she said as she took a first quick glance at the writing.

"I'd better be off now," said Samantha, who was evidently ill at ease standing there while her mistress read a personal letter which did not concern her.

"It's all right, Sam, if you want to stay here," said Susan. "I was just going to read it aloud to Jim, but we don't mind at all if you want to stay here?"

"But I really ought to be going now," said Samantha.

"Oh, well, if you're busy now, Sam, we mustn't keep you, but we would like to have time to have a proper chat as soon as we can. Perhaps we could manage to meet at coffee time later this morning?"

It was arranged that Samantha would join Jim and Susan for morning coffee at around eleven o' clock in the Green Drawing Room. Then, as Samantha hurried away to return to her work in the Castle, Susan picked up the letter from Jack Wonstannley and began to read it aloud. This is what Susan read:-

145 Presidio Avenue,
San Francisco,
CALIFORNIA,
U.S.A.

My Dear Lady Sandy,

This is to let you know that Ella and I and Phil very much enjoyed our trip to England, and we are extremely grateful to you, ma'am, for allowing us to come into Rhodes Castle to carry out some psychical research in the Tower Library. Now, I'd like to let you know, ma'am, that Phil has just told me that he reckons that work we did in there has turned out really well.

Sure enough, though, those photos when they were printed showed no signs of any of those old ghosts! Well, ma'am, I guess that you could call that some kind of a disappointment, in a way, but - as I think I told you when I spoke with you on the phone - we have some really good evidence that something odd did indeed happen in there, and that was just at the exact time when we saw those ghosts. I've enclosed a copy of a print-out we made, showing what Phil calls fluctuations in the electro-magnetic field.

Now let me try to explain it. I gather that the x-axis (that's the horizontal line at the bottom of the graph) shows the time, and the y-axis shows variations in the field intensity (whatever that may mean - don't ask me!). So, you see, the other line on the graph is supposed to show how the field varies with time; and Phil says that that spike that you see on the line exactly coincides with the time that we saw those two ghosts. But Phil says that we haven't actually proved anything by getting this result, but, ma'am, I'm sure you'll agree that it does make it look very likely that that there spike is directly associated with the appearance of the ghosts. So, in short, I think we're onto something right enough!

Well, ma'am, we got back home to San Francisco safe and well late on Monday (our time), and after I'd had my sleep I wrote you straight away and posted it by air mail, so I hope this will get to you pretty soon. By the way, ma'am, Phil says that he'll be moving to L.A. sometime in the fall as he's gonna take a better paid position in the university there, but I sure will be keeping him in touch, and he'll be doing the same sort of research there, only I guess with better facilities. So what that means is we're soon gonna be able to start writing our book on the Ghosts of Rhodes Castle – and we'll be keeping in touch with you, ma'am, about that.

Well, I guess that's all I have time for now, so I'll close with very many thanks, ma'am, for all your help and hospitality.

Your's very sincerely,
Jack Wonstannley.

"Well, there you are, darling," said Susan, who had now picked up the piece of paper with the graph printed on it, and was looking at it.

"They seem to think that their work has been a huge success!"

"I would think it has," said Jim. "May I see that graph, Sue, darling?"

Susan handed over the graph. Jim stared at it thoughtfully for a few seconds.

"I see they've written 'Time by stop-watch' at the end of the time axis," he said.

"Yes, so that they could correlate what happened with the exact time that it happened. I'm sure they've been most meticulously careful over their work in the Tower Library."

"But what do you think, Sue? Do you think that they've really proved anything by getting this reading printed out on this graph?"

"H'm!" Susan looked thoughtful, and for a moment gave Jim no answer. She picked up the letter and glanced through parts of it again. "'Phil says that we haven't actually proved anything by getting this result...' Well, maybe not... but I think that they really *have* proved that something unusual happened when we saw those ghosts."

"And that means that Jack Wonstannley must be really very pleased by the way it's turned out," said Jim. "Just remember, Sue, how he was always saying that he was longing to meet the ghost of Beryl Buxton. And now he has!"

"Yes, I'm very glad for him," said Susan. "I'm sure that this book that they're planning to write deserves to be a great success. I'll tell you what, darling; do you think that perhaps we should write back to him to wish him and Phil Oakley good luck with the research and the writing?"

"Oh, yes, let's do that!" said Jim.

*

The rest of their breakfast on the private lawn passed very peacefully and happily for Jim and Susan. As if by some unspoken agreement they spoke no more about Jack Wonstannley or Philip Oakley, or the ghosts they had seen in the Banqueting Hall and the Tower Library.

The private lawn was a peaceful place that morning, but it was also a spiritually uplifting and a refreshing place.

Later in the morning, when he and Susan were sitting together on the sofa in the Green Drawing Room, waiting for Samantha to bring in the coffee, the mood of light-hearted jollity was still with both of them.

They had decided to treat the day (it was a Monday) as a holiday as they had only returned from their travels in the late afternoon of the previous day. "We need time to adjust ourselves to the routine of ordinary life," Jim had said, and Susan had agreed with him; so he was not going to return to his usual work in the Estate Office until the morning of the next day.

Samantha came into the room, bringing the morning coffee and biscuits on a tray.

"Oh, thank you, Sam!" said Susan. "Now do come and sit here in this armchair. You're going to stay here with us for a little while, aren't you, while we talk and drink our coffee?"

"Yes, I can stay for a while, if you like," said Samantha. She looked quickly at her watch. "It's not quite eleven o' clock now, so I think I could stay until about a quarter past - or perhaps a little longer, if you don't mind, Sue?"

"Oh, that'll be fine!" said Susan. "But, Sam, before we tell you more about what we've been up to, you haven't really told us yet about how things have been going on here. Have you got Roger back at home yet?"

"No, not yet," said Samantha. "He rang up last night to say that he'll have to stay in London at least until Wednesday as the case is going on longer than he thought it would, but he hopes to be back at home by the end of the week. And I hope he'll be back too!"

"I'm sure you do! But apart from that, Sam, I suppose everything else here has been going on as normal?"

"Oh, yes, I would say that everything's been going on all right while you've been away - except that Rachel Connor isn't here, as apparently she's ill."

"Oh, really? But what's the matter with her?"

"I don't think it's anything very serious," said Samantha."

Apparently Mr. Connor rang up yesterday morning to say that Rachel wouldn't be coming in to work because she's got flu, or at least some illness of that sort; but I can't really tell you much more than that because I didn't speak to Mr. Connor. Jack took the call."

"All right," said Samantha. "But, by the way, Sue - I hope you won't mind me mentioning this - you called a Planning Committee meeting for tomorrow morning, you know, before you and Jim went away."

"My goodness!" said Susan. "So I did, and I'd quite forgotten all about it!"

"I thought perhaps you might have forgotten that."

"I had forgotten it. Thanks ever so much for reminding me about it. I think I said it would be at nine o'clock in the morning, didn't I?"

"Yes, you said it was to be at nine o' clock in the Tower Library."

Oh dear! thought Jim. That's another blow for me! Rachel would have been at the meeting, but now, of course, she won't be able to come because she's ill.

The idea of having a Rhodes Castle Planning Committee had, in fact, originally come from Jim. Both he and Susan had known for some time that there was a serious need to raise more money by any reasonable means to offset an increasingly large deficit in the Castle accounts.

As Estate Manager, Jim had direct access to the various accounts and bank balances. One day, earlier in the spring of that year, he had told Susan that he thought it would be a good idea for them to institute a planning committee so that they could raise money for the Castle by having various social events, open to the public. Susan had been very pleased with his idea, and so they had set up the Rhodes Castle Planning Committee under Susan as its chairman.

At the first meeting quite a number of potentially good ideas had been put forward, but only one of them, so far, seemed likely to be a candidate for "further action". This idea was that they should have a fund-raising concert as soon as they could. Jim had agreed to take on the role of Honorary Secretary to the Committee, and in this role he had been very busy, making telephone calls and writing letters, in order to secure (if possible) a date when the local choral society could come to give a performance for them, either in Rhodes Church or, possibly, in the Music Room of the Castle.

"You don't really want me to come to the meeting tomorrow, do you?" said Samantha.

"Oh, yes, I do!" said Susan decisively. "I certainly want you to be there with us, Sam, as you're usually very good at thinking up brilliant ideas!"

"Am I really?"

"But of course you are! Just think, Sam; if it wasn't for your brilliant idea Jim and I would probably never have met each other again, and we wouldn't be married now. And then your idea that we ought to have a talk with Roger at Croydon while we were in London has turned out to be wonderfully helpful for us; so certainly you must be there with us tomorrow!"

"I'll come then."

"But who else will be coming, Jim, darling?" asked Susan. "You made a list, I think, of the people we want to have on the Committee?"

"Yes, I made a list," said Jim, "but I don't think I can remember all the names that are on it until I look at it again. There aren't many names on the list yet, though - we may want to invite a few more people to join the Committee - but the Vicar is one of the names on the list, and we'll want him to come so that, hopefully, we can confirm the date for the concert."

"For a performance of Tracy Symon's Mass?"

"Yes, for that. But we've had a letter from the Vicar to say that he is intending to come tomorrow morning."

"So we have," said Susan. "Yes, I remember you telling me that before. And Jack will be there, of course, and the Head Gardener, and... I don't think we should be expecting anyone else to turn up, do you?"

"Well, no..." said Jim. The moment had come to mention Rachel Connor's name, and now he found that his heart was beating uncomfortably fast. "There's, er... well, Mrs. Connor won't be able to come tomorrow, of course, but we'd asked her to come as she's the Guide." He was deliberately avoiding his wife's glance as he said this.

"Oh, yes, I know that we've asked Rachel Connor to be on the Committee - but I expect she should be all right to come to next month's meeting." Susan's calm, even voice was giving nothing away of what she might really be thinking at that moment. Oh, damn it! Jim thought to himself irritably, I *should* be really pleased to know that I *won't* be seeing Rachel tomorrow... especially as I'll be with Sue at the meeting.

But Jim knew that he was not feeling at all pleased as he considered the consequences of Rachel Connor's forthcoming absence.

Suddenly he realized that his mood had become quite sullen, almost angry. Why had they had to mention Rachel Connor's name now? It did not occur to him at that time, however, that although he had been thinking about Rachel he had not actually seen her at all in his mind's eye. It was a little while later, when the conversation had turned to the subject of their trip up to London, when an exciting image of Rachel Connor suddenly appeared, as if from nowhere, in his mind. Immediately he felt exultant that he could see her again in his mind's eye, but he could not help also feeling a certain sadness as he reflected that he would not be seeing her tomorrow morning.

They were just finishing their coffee, and Samantha had just said that she ought to be getting back to her work, when there came a knock on the door.

"Come in!" said Susan.

Jack, the butler, came into the room.

"Begging your pardon, my Lady, for interrupting you," he said at once, "but I thought I ought to tell you that Mr. Connor has rung up to say that Mrs. Connor can't come in to work today because she's ill."

"And was it yesterday morning when Mr. Connor rang up to tell you that?" asked Susan.

Jim had been watching the expression on the butler's face carefully. He had not been scowling when Susan had asked him, "Was it yesterday morning when Mr. Connor rang up?" but he had definitely only smiled as Susan had, in the end, commended him for his initiative. He had also noticed that the only time that Jack had looked at Samantha had been when he had said, "I see that someone else has already told you about it..."; and even then he had only glanced in Samantha's direction for a fraction of a second. So he guessed that Sam had already told Sue about the telephone call from Mr. Connor, and he's annoyed because she's done that before he could do it, he thought. But I'm glad that Sue hasn't had to tick him off because of this!

CHAPTER FOURTEEN

Susan parked her car in the High Street in Sherborne in a place where parking was allowed. Jim and Susan were in the middle of the town and close to an archway between two shops which lead into a secluded courtyard. Having locked the car they walked through the archway. They had an appointment to talk with Roger Burton, the solicitor, in his office.

The letter from Richard and Jane Dalmane's solicitors had been delivered to the Castle on the morning of the previous day. As Jim and Susan had expected, it had turned out to be a formal legal letter demanding their eviction from the Castle by January 31st 1966. Susan had in fact guessed what was in the envelope as soon as Jack, the butler, had brought it to her. "This'll be the letter from Dick and Jane's solicitors," she had said, and so she and Jim had then braced themselves for a reading of the contents of the letter. Then she had taken out the letter from its envelope and had read out most of it aloud for Jim's benefit. They were in the Breakfast Room (as the morning had not been fine enough to make it worth while to eat out on the Private Lawn) and had nearly finished their breakfast when Jack had come in, but Jim, as he listened to what Susan was reading out for him, put down his last piece of toast on his plate as he listened in a state of increasing shock and horror.

"My goodness, that really does sound shocking!" he had said when Susan had finished reading it out aloud. It had turned out to be exactly the sort of letter they had expected – a formal notice of eviction – yet it had still managed to shock them both as Susan had read through it.

That evening Jim had gone up to the second floor and along the passages until he had come to the suite of rooms which constituted the Burtons' flat. They had already decided that it would not be fair to expect Roger Burton to deliberate on legal problems in the evening, when he was off duty, so Jim was merely going to tell him that the letter had come and, if possible to make an appointment to have a talk with him as soon as possible.

It was Roger Burton himself who came to the sitting-room door when Jim knocked on it.

"Oh, come in, Jim," he said. "Sam's just busy in the kitchen now, cooking our supper, but do come in and sit down if you'd like to talk."

"Thank you so much," said Jim, "but I'd rather not stay now if you don't mind. I've just come to tell you that we've had that letter from Dick and Jane Dalmane's solicitors, and so we'd like to talk to you about it."

"Ah, I see," said Roger. "And it's a notice of eviction?"

Jim nodded.

"Well, I could see you in the office tomorrow, if you like. You'd better bring the letter with you as I shall probably need to take a copy of it. Now, what time shall we say...? Let me think. Would half past twelve be about right for you?"

Jim said that half past twelve would be a most convenient time for them, and so it was settled.

"What's a Commissioner for Oaths?" asked Jim. "Do you know, Sue?" He had just read the notice on a brass plate beside the front door of the solicitors' office: "ROGER BURTON AND MICHAEL HOME.

SOLICITORS AND COMMISSIONERS FOR OATHS."

"Well, really, darling, I'm not too sure of that myself!" said Susan. "But I think it's got something to do with bequests - wills - and that sort of thing. But let's go in now anyway."

"We're a little bit early," said Jim. "It's only about twenty past twelve now."

"That won't matter. We can go and sit in the waiting room until Roger is ready to see us."

They went up three steps and in through the open doorway. For a moment, coming into the building out of the bright sunshine, it seemed rather dark inside, but then Jim saw a flight of stairs in front of them. Susan, who had been inside that office once before, was already leading the way up the stairs. Evidently the door through which they had come in gave access only to rooms on the first and second floors of the building. Then, as he hurried up the stairs after Susan, he saw a sign with an arrow pointing the way to the solicitors' offices on the first floor. At the top of the stairs they found a closed door with a notice, PLEASE ENTER, on it.

"That's it, darling, we go in here," said Susan, opening the door as she spoke, having waited a moment for Jim to catch her up. "This is the waiting room."

"Have you been here before, Sue?" asked Jim, as he followed his wife through the doorway.

"Yes, I've been in here once before," said Susan.

The first thing that Jim noticed when he came into the waiting room was that it was a large, airy, square room with windows on two opposit sides, but then, almost at the same moment, his gaze came to rest on a large desk in the middle of the room, and especially on a young woman seated at the desk, who appeared to be eating a lunch picnic. She put a partly eaten apple down on the desk as Susan approached her.

"Hello, have you an appointment here?" she mumbled, speaking with her mouth full of apple.

"Yes, indeed! I'm Lady Susan Sandy, and this is my husband, Jim," said Susan. "We have an appointment to see Mr. Burton at half past twelve."

"Just a minute!" said the girl. "'Scuse me!" She turned her head half aside and then, with a careful aim, she spat. Jim, watching her in fascination, saw an apple pip fly through the air, describing a parabolic curve as it descended into a strategically placed metal waste paper basket, where it landed with a satisfactory click. That was a good aim! thought Jim admiringly.

"He isn't ready just yet," continued the girl nonchalantly, having turned again to Susan. "He's got a client with him in the office now."

"I know we are a bit early," said Susan.

"Yes, you are a bit early. Would you like to take a seat, please, while you wait?" The girl waved an arm vaguely towards a number of empty chairs along one wall of the room, and then, picking up her apple again, at once resumed her lunch picnic as if she were annoyed at having any clients for either of the solicitors interrupt her while she was eating.

By one of the windows on the right-hand (west-facing) side of the room there was a small round table on which were lying some newspapers and magazines, and two empty armchairs were drawn up to this table.

Susan made straight for one of these armchairs and sat down in it without another glance at the girl at the reception desk. There was no one else in the room.

Before he sat down Jim took a quick glance out of the window, where he saw at once what he had expected to see: the courtyard through which they had walked to enter the building. Yes, there was that horse chestnut tree they had seen in the middle of the courtyard, and it was certainly a most handsome sight with its tall candles of white flowers fully open to the strong June sunshine.

"It's a pretty sight, that tree, isn't it?" said Susan, turning her head for a moment so that she could look out of the window.

Jim agreed with her. Then for a moment Susan turned her head to glance the other way, towards the desk where the girl was just finishing her apple.

"What disgusting manners that girl has!" she said in a low voice; but Jim realized that she hoped that the girl would hear her say it.

"I'm rather shocked to find that Roger can employ such a person to work in here!"

"Well... perhaps he doesn't know that his secretary eats her lunch at the desk in here." Jim did not quite know what he ought to say, but felt that Susan had expected him to answer her point.

"And spits out her apple pips into the waste paper basket in front of customers! It's quite disgusting! Perhaps I'd better mention it when we go in to talk with Roger."

Jim wanted to say, "I wouldn't do that if I were you, Sue", but he decided that it would be wisest to say nothing more on that subject, so he remained silent. And I mustn't look round at that girl! he told himself sharply. But had he really found something attractive in her? He had to admit to himself that he had, but why that should be was something of a mystery to him. Probably it had something to do with her behaviour, the very behaviour which Susan had already criticised as being rude and disgusting. Other than that she was certainly "nothing very special to look at" (as Jim put it for himself in his own mind). She was tall, reasonably slim, had an average figure and shoulder-length straight brown hair, but she certainly had a plain-looking face; in no way could he have thought that she looked beautiful. But he was sure that there was *something* about that girl, other than her unorthodox and perhaps rude manner of eating in public, which had attracted his attention. It was almost as if she were already familiar to him... Why, hadn't he seen her somewhere else before today? He puzzled over this little riddle for a few moments, but could find no satisfactory answer. Then his thoughts were suddenly distracted as Susan spoke to him again.

"Aren't you going to read something while we wait here, darling? We may have to wait a while, you know, before Roger will be able to see us."

Jim saw that Susan had picked up "The Times" from the pile of things on the table, and that she was already looking at the front page of the paper.

"Oh, yes, I suppose I might as well try to read something," he said.

"Did you want to look at 'The Times'?"

"Oh, no, that's all right, Sue; you carry on with it. I'll try one of these magazines."

He poked about among the pile of magazines on the table to find out what they were, but, as he had expected, he found nothing there that he thought would really interest him. I'm not really in a mood for reading, he thought. He drew out a copy of "Country Life" from the pile and began, not very hopefully, to turn over the pages. As he did so he heard a dull thud as something was tossed into the waste paper basket. Evidently the girl had finished eating her apple and had thrown away the core. He half turned his head, but remembered in time that it would be better not to turn round to glance at that girl. Had Susan already noticed that he had been attracted to her? It seemed, however, that Susan had not noticed anything of that sort which might have meant serious trouble for him later. She was calmly reading the newspaper as if nothing in the world was wrong. Jim tried again to interest himself in something from the pages of his "Country Life" magazine. But I don't think that I'm going to be able to keep my mind focused on this for very long! he thought.

Jim thought that the time must be passing very slowly as he and Susan sat in their armchairs in that waiting room. He frequently raised his eyes from the pages of his magazine to look out of the window, or glance around the room, but he was always careful to avoid looking again directly at that girl at the desk. He knew that she was now attending again to her office work as the sound of the typewriter keys, clattering away, came to his ears. But I *have* seen that girl somewhere before, he thought. I wonder where...?

It was about a quarter of an hour after their arrival when one of the doors at the other end of the room was opened and Roger Burton and another man, a client, appeared in the doorway. The client seemed very well pleased with the help and advice he had just received and, having thanked the solicitor profusely, shook his hand warmly.

Susan put down her newspaper on the table, and she and Jim looked up hopefully. Jim had already given up trying to read the magazine so there was nothing in his hands. The satisfied client, having said good-bye to Roger Burton, was leaving the room with a quick smile in the direction of the secretary as he passed her. The girl had stood up to have a quick word with Roger Burton before he called Susan and Jim into his office.

"I'll be with you in a minute, Susan," said Roger quickly. "What is it, Sandra?"

After about half a minute of private and urgent discussion with his secretary, Roger Burton again turned to Susan while the girl went back to her desk.

"I'm so sorry to have kept you waiting," he said. "Do come in now, please." He held the door open and stood aside while Sudsan, followed by Jim, came into his office. "Do have a seat, please, and we'll be able to talk," he continued).

They thanked him and sat down. There were two chairs already drawn up to the large desk where Roger Burton had his chair. Glancing around the room as he sat down Jim saw that the pictures around the walls had been carefully chosen to give the place an appropriately legal, although not oppressive, atmosphere. There was a watercolour of a courtroom scene (Jim supposed that it was a typical courtroom scene) and some pictures of judges, all dressed up in their wigs and gowns and robes.

"So I gather that you've now received the letter you were expecting from the Dalmanes' solicitors?" said Roger Burton.

"Yes, we have, and I've brought it with me," said Susan. She opened her handbag and brought out the letter in its envelope. "Here it is!" She handed it over to the solicitor.

"Thank you," said Roger. "And when did you get it?"

"It came yesterday morning."

"Ah, yesterday morning. Well, let's see what they say." Roger Burton took the letter out of its envelope and began to read it through carefully.

Jim saw that Susan was watching the solicitor's face carefully as he read the letter, as if she were watching to see whether any signs of emotion would appear on his face as he considered its contents; but for his part he could detect no signs of any change in his expression. He had so far said nothing, and was not expecting to say anything unless, of course, he was asked a question. His thoughts soon wandered away from the matter of the letter, and he found himself wondering again where he had seen that girl before. He remembered that he had heard Roger Burton call her "Sandra". So her name is Sandra, he thought. Now doesn't that ring a bell, so to speak? Then, suddenly, it came to him.

Sandra, the kitchen maid! Why until very recently she had been working at the Castle as a kitchen maid, but now she had a new job – and no doubt a better paid job too, working in a solicitor's office. Sam must have helped her to get this job here, working for Roger, he reckoned.

At this point Jim's train of thought was broken as Roger Burton, having finished reading the letter, spoke again.

"Well, Susan, this is just as we expected it would be, isn't it: a formal letter demanding your eviction from the Castle by the 31ˢᵗ of January, 1966?"

"Yes, indeed it is!" said Susan. "So what do we do now, Roger?"

"Well, I'm sorry to tell you that, as it stands, it seems to be a properly constituted legal document. I haven't discovered any flaws or loopholes in the wording which we might, as it were, be able to turn to our advantage. But don't worry about that, Susan, we'll manage this all right one way or another - we definitely will. And the thing to do now, as I said before, is for me to write to them."

"And you're going to return this letter when you write to their solicitors?"

Roger Burton thought for a moment.

"Yes," he said, "it would be a good idea to do that. At least... the best plan would be to have several copies of that letter. Then, you see, I could send a copy of it to Sir Richard and Lady Jane when I write to them, saying: 'This is the letter which your solicitors have written to my client, Lady Susan Sandy'. And then I shall need to retain one copy of it here in the office for future reference; and it would be just as well, I suppose, to enclose a third copy of it when I write to their solicitors to request them to withdraw and cancel their order."

"But won't that be a nuisance to you to have to make several copies?"

"Oh, no, not at all," said Roger Burton. "You see, we've just recently acquired one of those new photo-copying machines, a splendidly useful gadget - every solicitor's office should have one - so it'll be no trouble at all to run off as many copies of that letter as we want.

So I think, if you'll excuse me a moment, Susan, I'll just go through and ask Sandra to run off three copies of this letter right now so that you can take the original letter back with you." He got up, and went through to the waiting room, leaving his office door open behind him so that Jim and Susan could hear what was said.

"Sandra, could you let me have three copies of this letter, please? Could you do it right away, please, and bring them into my office when they're ready?"

"Yes, sir," said Sandra.

Jim could not resist the urge to turn his head for a quick glimpse back into the waiting room. He saw Sandra get up from her chair to take the letter over to the photo-copying machine. He now remembered having seen it standing in a corner of the room.

"Do you know, Susan, that you could almost say that we stole that girl from you at the Castle to bring her here to work as my secretary?" said Roger Burton cheerfully as he closed the office door behind him.

"Well, actually, Roger," said Susan, "I must say that I didn't know that - at least I'd quite forgotten, until now, that until very recently she'd been working at the Castle."

"That's right, she was a kitchen maid at the Castle, but I was needing a new secretary at the time, and so you might say that Sam 'found' her there for me."

"Oh, really? But presumably she'd already decided that she wanted to leave us?"

"Oh, yes, I imagine that she must have decided on trying a new job somewhere else."

"Someone ought to have told me that she'd handed in her notice," said Susan; and then, after a pause, having caught Jim's eye, "Oh, yes, I remember," she continued. "You did tell me, Jim, darling, that she was handing in her notice and leaving us. You told me... but I never really took it in. But look here, we're wasting your time, Roger, by talking about Sandra now. Shall we get back to business? So you're writing to their solicitors to ask them to withdraw this notice of eviction?"

"Indeed I am," said Roger. "In fact, I'm intending to do it this very afternoon as I haven't got any further appointments with any clients today."

"Well, that's splendid, Roger! But what will happen if they won't go along with your request? Or if they don't even bother to answer it?

"Ah, well, I think we must set a time limit for their co-operation. I think I should write: 'My client has instructed me to instigate a process of litigation in the County Court unless I receive a reply from you within four weeks of today's date, expressing your decision to rescind in its entirety the order which you have served on my client...' and so on. I think it should be something on those lines, but not necessarily with quite those words. I'll obviously have to think carefully about the best way to word it. But what do you think, Susan?"

"Oh, I should think that a letter like that would be simply fine - just what we need!" said Susan.

"And what about the time limit...? Come in!" There was a knock on the door as Roger Burton was speaking.

The door opened, and Sandra, the secretary, brought in the three copies of the legal letter which she had just produced.

"Here are the copies of the letter that you asked for, sir," she said; this time in a rather nervous voice, Jim thought. He saw her give an anxious glance into Susan's face, and then quickly look away again as if she were afraid that Susan would now make some complaint to her boss about her off-hand manner in the waiting room.

"Thank you, Sandra!" said Roger Burton as his secretary handed over the copied documents. "You may go now."

"Thank you, sir," mumbled Sandra as, without another backward glance, she left the room as quickly as she could and shut the door behind her. But Jim had noticed how Susan was staring at her disapprovingly as she hurriedly disappeared from view.

"Did you want to have a word with Sandra?" asked Roger Burton.

Evidently he also had noticed something in Susan's look.

"Well, yes, perhaps... but I could do that afterwards when we're ready to leave," said Susan.

"If you're happy to do that?"

"Indeed I am!" said Susan. "But, to get back to business, you were talking about giving them a time limit to answer, and I think you were suggesting that we set that time limit at four weeks?"

"Well," said Roger, "in my judgement, I think that in a case like this we shouldn't give them any longer than four weeks to comply before we start an action in the courts; but, to be fair to them, I think that we shouldn't give them less than four weeks either."

"That sounds all right to me," said Susan.

"So we'll say four weeks then. Mind you, I wouldn't want to place any bets on how this may turn out - whether they'll choose to comply with our request, or fight it. But, you know, if they go for the latter option, I have a strong feeling that, although we may start with an action in the County Court, things will go beyond that."

"You mean, it might have to go to the High Court?"

"It might indeed have to go on to the High Court; and if it did that would inevitably mean that the case would drag on for longer, and, of course, it would be more expensive for the litigants. But you see, Susan, if the case is heard first in the County Court, and they lose it - as we hope they would - they would very probably appeal, and then the case could be heard again in the High Court. But I suppose that another possibility is that *we* might lose the case in the County Court - although I think that very unlikely - and in that case we would want to appeal, no doubt."

"But could we appeal in those circumstances?" asked Susan.

"Of course we could. We could ask a High Court Judge to grant an injunction to forbid the Dalmanes from evicting you - and

Sam, and me – from Rhodes Castle; and that injunction could remain in force, if necessary, until a further appeal had been made to the Court of Appeal."

"And after that to the House of Lords?" suggested Jim suddenly.

He was not sure what had prompted him to break his silence and join in the conversation, and afterwards was rather surprised to find that he had spoken at that point. I'd only intended to listen, not to talk, he reminded himself.

"Are you interested in the law too?" said Roger, smiling at Jim.

"Well, you're quite right to say that the House of Lords is our highest and final court of appeal, and our case could, in theory go up to the Lords – but I should think that that would be a very unlikely outcome."

"Oh, I see," said Jim.

"Well, I suppose we ought to be thinking of going now to look for some lunch in town," said Susan, "and I dare say that you could do with your's too, Roger. But you've been ever so helpful, and we really can't thank you enough!"

"Oh, that's all right; don't mention it, Susan!" said Roger. "It's been a pleasure to advise you – and, anyway, this eviction threat potentially concerns us as well as you. And you're going away pretty soon on holiday, I believe?"

"Yes, indeed we are," said Susan. "We're setting off next week, in fact."

"On Thursday," said Jim.

"Yes, a week on Thursday, in the afternoon, we're taking a train up to London so that we can travel overnight on the sleeper to Scotland from Euston," said Susan.

"And we arrive at Inverness the next morning," said Jim, "and then we take a local train to Kyle of Lochalsh, and then the ferry to Stornoway."

"Oh, so you're not going to be sailing in the *Osprey* this time?" asked Roger.

"We're not going to be sailing this time because we've taken a self-catering cottage for a week," said Susan; "and as they let them from Saturday to Saturday it's important for us to arrive there on the right day and at about the right time."

"Yes, I can understand that, but I think I heard from Sam that you're going to stay with her Aunt Mave. I suppose you're planning to stay with her for one night when you arrive in Lewis, and then move on to your cottage?"

"That's exactly what we are planning to do as it will be quite late in the day, I think, when we arrive in Stornoway."

"And whereabouts in Lewis is the cottage you've taken?"

"Well, it isn't actually in Lewis at all, strictly speaking; it's in Harris, in fact – but, of course, it's all one island, as you probably know"

"It's at Tarbert in Harris," said Jim. "At least, it's not quite in Tarbert village but just outside the village: a cottage on the hillside with a south-facing view (according to the brochure) and a good view over East Loch Tarbert."

"It sounds absolutely delightful!" said Roger wistfully.

"Well, it certainly does!" said Susan. "And I bet you're wishing right now that you and Sam could come too!"

"Oh, my word, I certainly am! But, of course, it would be absolutely impossible and out of the question for us to come this time."

"I'm so sorry, really, that you and Sam won't be coming with us this time, but we'll send you a post card; and we'll be taking our cameras with us so that, when we've come back and had our films developed and printed, you should be able to get a good idea of what it's like around Tarbert... Well, Jim, darling, let's go and get ourselves some lunch now." Susan rose to her feet after a quick glance at her watch. "But perhaps you'd care to join us for lunch, Roger, so that we could continue our chat?"

"That's very kind of you, Susan," said Roger, "But I think that I won't come with you this time. You see, I have actually brought a picnic lunch with me so I'm going to eat it in here now."

"You seem to go in for picnic lunches in this office!" joked Susan. "When we came in, you know, your girl out there in the waiting room was eating her picnic lunch!"

"Was she? But I'm sorry if that's upset you, Susan. I could have a word with her if you like..."

"Oh, no, don't do that!" said Susan hurriedly. I'm not upset, or offended – but I think that, after all, I will have a quick word with her just now, as we go out.

"As you please," said Roger Burton. "Well, good-bye, Susan, and I hope that you two have a very happy holiday in Lewis and Harris. We'll look forward to getting your post card! And I'll keep you in touch, of course, of any developements in our business with the Dalmanes." He opened his office door for them, and shook them both warmly by the hand.

Susan and Jim thanked him and said good-bye, and then Susan went over at once to the reception desk. Sandra, seeing them coming out of the solicitor's office, at once pretended to be very busy with something that was on her desk, but at the last moment, as Susan spoke to her, she looked up from what she was writing.

"Do you know who I am?"

"Oh, yes, my Lady, I know that you're Lady Susan Sandy." Sandra's tone was now diffident and rather nervous, quite different from what it had been when Susan and Jim had first entered the waiting room.

"Did you remember who I was when we came in? You used to work for us at the Castle, you know, until quite recently."

"Well, I'm sorry, my Lady, but I didn't remember that – not at first anyway," said Sandra. "And I'm sorry if you thought I was rude to you when you came in."

"That's all right, Sandra," said Susan, now deliberately adopting a more kindly voice. "Don't worry about it! Are you enjoying your work here?"

"Oh, yes, very much, thank you, my Lady!"

"Good! We'll let you get on with your work now. Good-bye"

Susan and Jim left the room without waiting to hear Sandra's "Good-bye, my Lady". Jim had waited rather anxiously while Susan had been talking to Sandra, but he had been careful not to look at her.

They did not say anything until they had descended the stairs and left the building and were once again in the courtyard.

"I say, Sue," said Jim, "I thought you were going to scold Sandra for eating when we came in, and for spitting out her apple pips?"

"I was going to scold her," said Susan, "but then I thought that I wouldn't as she seems to have got the message anyway. Now where shall we go for lunch, darling? To The Buttery Restaurant?"

"Why not!" said Jim keenly. "They've always had a good menu when we've been there before."

"Then we might as well walk there, and leave the car where it is as we probably wouldn't find any better place to park it."

They had come back through the archway into the High Street, and were now passing the place where Susan had parked her car. Jim agreed with her, and so they walked on in the direction of the Abbey.

"I'd say we've done a good day's work in there," said Susan as they walked. "At least, Roger has."

"Yes," said Jim, "but – I've just thought of something – if he writes to their solicitors today, as he said he's going to, they should get his letter tomorrow morning, and then there may be an answer for us presently – but it could well come just after we've gone up to Scotland for our holiday."

"I thought of that too," said Susan. "But it won't really matter, will it? I was going to let Sam know the telephone number of our cottage in any case so she would be able to ring us up to let us know if an answer come while we're away. I'll have to tell her to open any mail that comes for me with a London postmark."

"Their solicitor's office is in High Holborn, isn't it?"

"Yes, it is, so I suppose it would have the postmark, 'LONDON WC2' on it – or perhaps 'WC1'."

"And then we would know, if Sam were to ring us up while we're at Tarbert, that we would have to deal with that straight away when we get back home."

"But hopefully there wouldn't really be anything to deal with anyway," said Susan, "unless they're going to take a really defiant attitude, and not back down on this threat."

"They will, though, I think?"

"Yes, I think they will. Anyway, here we are, darling, so let's put all these legal matters out of our heads, and think about lunch instead, and about our holiday plans!"

"I can't stop thinking about our holiday plans now since Roger mentioned them," said Jim as he followed Susan through the door of the restaurant while a waiter, who knew Susan, and had seen her coming to the door, politely held it open for them.

They found an empty table for two without any difficulty. Ten minutes later they were enjoying their lunch. Jim, who had agonized for some time over his choice, had finally decided on chicken curry, while Susan was eating lasagne. While they ate they continued to talk about holiday plans as if their problems had somehow become quite insignificant, as compared with their forthcoming holiday. When Jim told Susan that he had already started packing things for the holiday she was amused.

"But, darling, I expect you'll have to take some of the things out of your bag again in the next day or two?" she said.

"Yes, I expect I will have to," said Jim, "but there's something very nice about packing!"

"I know what you mean, darling!" said Susan.

CHAPTER FIFTEEN

"We're nearly there!" said Jim, standing up and looking out of the train window. "I can see the Thames now, and a bridge, and the Houses of Parliament on the other side of the river."

"That must be Lambeth Bridge," said Susan, standing up in her turn. Yes, we should be into Waterloo in about a minute, I should think, so it's time now for us to be getting our luggage down off the rack.

The train which had brought them up to London from Sherborne was now moving fairly slowly, so that it was easy enough for Jim and Susan to keep their balance as they reached up to the luggage rack to bring down their various pieces of baggage. They came into Waterloo station, the terminus of the line, where the train drew to a standstill at one of the long main-line platforms. Jim pulled open the sliding door of their first-class compartment. In the corridor outside people were already moving past their door, carrying their baggage.

"There's one thing about it, Sue," said Jim cheerfully. "We really don't have to hurry at all. We could let other people get out before us."

Susan looked at her watch.

"Good heavens, we certainly can!" she agreed. "We *are* early! It's only half past four now!"

"So we've got three hours from now until our train is due out of Euston. Whatever are we going to do, Sue?"

"I think we might as well have a meal when we get to Euston. I know it's awfully early to think of having dinner, but at least we could fill up quite a lot of time by eating slowly."

Jim and Susan had already decided that they would not travel by the Northern Line to Euston, but would take a taxi instead. It seemed to both of them that it would be the sensible thing to do as the Underground would be crowded in the evening rush hour and, in any case, they were bringing with them quite a number of pieces of baggage, so that a journey across Central London by taxi would undoubtedly be the easier option.

There were plenty of taxi cabs standing for hire in the taxi rank outside the main entrance to the station so that all too soon (as it seemed to Jim) they were on their way again. However, he was in a jolly mood, and was prepared to enjoy seeing again some of the sights of London, as he had just said to Susan.

"Look, there's the dome of St. Paul's," he said as they crossed Waterloo Bridge.

"Yes, you do get a good view of the City from here," said Susan.

Then they passed the imposing building of Somerset House on the Embankment, and went around Aldwych onto the broad thoroughfare of Kingsway. Here they encountered some slow-moving traffic, but there were no serious delays, and presently the road ahead cleared again. Soon after that they reached Euston station. While Susan was paying the fare Jim looked at his watch, and saw that it was just after ten minutes to five. It's a pity that journey through the middle of London couldn't have lasted rather longer, he thought.

They picked up their luggage and began to walk in the direction of the colonnade of the new station (Euston was being rebuilt at that time), but they had hardly taken more than three or four steps when Jim was startled by a sudden shout, and at the same moment he noticed that Susan was waving to somebody.

"Lady Sandy!"

"Darling, it's Nigel and Norma Beck!" said Susan with delight; but Jim had seen for himself who it was they were meeting.

"So it is!" he said. "Hello!"

The next moment the Becks and the Sandys, having pushed their way through a thinning crowd of people on the station forecourt, and put down some of their hand-held baggage, were greeting each other warmly and shaking hands.

"Well, this *is* a surprise to meet you here!" said Norma Beck.

"It certainly is!" agreed Jim.

"But, look here, are you in a hurry to catch a train?" asked Nigel Beck. "We mustn't hold you back if you are."

"Oh, no, absolutely not!" said Susan quickly. "In fact we've got far too much time - we've got hours to wait, literally, until our train is due out."

"Just over two and a half hours," said Jim, glancing at his watch.

"Well, do you know, *we've* got ages to wait here too!" said Nigel Beck.

"Well, I'll tell you what: why don't you come and join us for a meal in the station to fill up the time?" said Susan. "Jim and I had just decided, a little while ago when we got in to Waterloo, that that was what we'd better do."

"Yes, do come and eat with us," urged Jim.

"I'm sure we'd love to," said Nigel Beck. "Don't you think so, Norma, darling?"

"Oh, yes, I certainly do think so!" agreed Norma Beck. "I suppose we *can* eat a meal in the station?"

"Well, there used to be a sort of restaurant in the station where you could get meals," said Susan, "but, now that I come to think about it, perhaps it may have had to close because of all the rebuilding work that's been going on here."

"We'd better go in to see what we can find," said Nigel Beck, "but there are sure to be some eating facilities open."

The four of them, picking up their hand luggage, set off for the place where they had seen people going into the station through the arches of the colonnade.

"Are you setting off on a holiday somewhere?" asked Nigel as they walked onto the station concourse through the colonnade.

"We're off to Scotland tonight by the sleeper," said Susan.

"The 'Royal Highlander'?"

"Yes, by the 'Royal Highlander' to Inverness, and then we go on by train tomorrow morning to Kyle of Lochalsh. We've booked a holiday cottage on the Isle of Harris for a week."

"Oh, that'll be lovely!" said Norma, rather enviously, Jim thought.

"But are you starting a holiday too?" asked Susan.

"Well, not exactly a holiday, really," said Nigel, "although I am on a week's holiday at the moment. But we're going to stay with my Aunt Annie for a few days at her new house."

"Was that the one who lived somewhere near Knebworth?"

"Yes, Aunt Annie used to live at Datchworth, near Knebworth, but she's moved now to Brickett Wood, which is near St. Alban's. That's why we have to go from Euston now, instead of King's Cross. We take a train from Euston to Watford Junction and change there, and then catch another train on the St. Alban's Abbey line to Brickett Wood where, hopefully, Aunt Annie will meet us with her car - if we arrive at the right time."

"And that's why we mustn't start from here too soon," said Norma.

"What time was it, Nigel, that we're supposed to arrive at Brickett Wood?"

"Seven twenty-three. So we're to catch the six-sixteen from here first."

"Ah, so you've got over an hour to fill in first," said Susan.

"Our's is the seven-thirty - I think?" She looked at Jim, knowing that he would remember the time.

"Yes, our's goes at seven-thirty," said Jim. "Look, here's the restaurant!"

"Oh, good!" said Susan. "So let's go in now."

They had been ambling slowly along the broad concourse between the platform ends and a long row of shops, offices, and other rooms at the southern end of the station but, as he walked, Jim had been keeping a sharp look-out for a restaurant. He went up to the door and held it open for the others.

"It looks all right," said Nigel as he entered the restaurant after the two ladies had gone in before him.

"Have you been in here before?" asked Susan.

"Do you mean this restaurant or the new Euston station?"

"Well, either, really."

"I haven't been inside this station since they started the re-building, although, of course, I know about it - but I must say it looks, on the whole, *very* different from the ramshackle old place I can remember it was before.

"That's just what I was thinking," said Susan.

"Shall we sit down now?" said Norma suddenly. "I think Jim has found a table for us."

Nigel Beck and Susan both glanced round at Norma for a moment, and then noticed that Jim was indeed standing a little way off by a table laid for four, but, as they moved off in that direction Susan could not resist a brief smile. She was smiling because she had suddenly been reminded by what Norma had just said and, perhaps, by the way she had said it, of an occasion long ago (it seemed) when the same four of them had been at Knebworth, having travelled by train that day from Cockermouth. On that occasion Norma had certainly been ill, and her mood in consequence had been petulant and grumpy; and "Shall we sit down now?" had suddenly reminded Susan of the short terse remarks Norma had made on the walk from

Knebworth station to the house in Knebworth were they were staying that night.

They had seen that the place offered waitress service so they sat down at the table. The restaurant was not really crowded but, looking around, they could see no other empty tables laid for four people. Jim found himself sitting opposite Susan, with Norma Beck to his right, and Nigel Beck to his left, but he was rather disappointed that the place which the others had left for him was the one with his back to the door through which they had entered. This meant, of course, that he could not see out through the windows onto the station concourse; and this was indeed a disappointment to him. However, the thought uppermost in his mind as he sat down was that he knew there was a need to be careful about his behaviour; he must not appear to be looking out lustfully for attractive women. While the others had been in animated conversation when they had come in, Jim was already scanning the whole room carefully. He had been looking for an empty table for four, but he had also been casting rapid glances around the room to see what the waitresses looked like. He had quickly realized, however, that none of them looked in the least attractive to him. So it should be quite easy, he thought, to keep my resolve!

"Well done, darling, for finding us this table!" said Susan, smiling at him as she sat down. She pushed the menu card, which was in front of her place, towards Norma, on her left.

"I suppose we'd better not eat too much in here?" said Norma, looking up at her husband across the table.

"That's right, Norma, my dear," said Nigel. "My Aunt Annie is sure to give us a good meal when we get to her house - at about eight o' clock, probably - so it would be best to be hungry enough to eat it. We mustn't eat too much in here."

Norma took the menu, looked at it for a moment, and then made up her mind.

"I'm going to have just the soup," she said. It was obvious that she had not bothered to read right through the long menu which was arranged as an "a la carte" menu, with all the items priced separately.

Norma passed it across the table to her husband.

Nigel Beck took rather more trouble over reading through the menu than Norma had done, but in the end he also decided to choose the Soup of the Day. Susan and Jim decided that they were hungry enough to eat a two-course meal as they had eaten nothing since having an early lunch at the Castle at ten minutes past twelve before they had left to catch their train (the one thirty-four from Sherborne).

Susan asked Nigel Back whether they had ever been to Brickett Wood before.

"No, we've never been there before," said Nigel; "but, you see, Aunt Annie moved there recently from Datchworth so as to be nearer to the place where her older sister, my Aunt Letty, lives. Aunt Letty is now about ninety years old, you see, and I've heard from Aunt Annie that her health is now failing and that she's getting very frail. She lives now in an old peoples' home in Saint Alban's, and Aunt Annie visits her now and then."

"I see," said Susan. "And I suppose that this old peoples' home in Saint Alban's is only a few miles away from the place where your Aunt Annie now lives?"

"Yes, we think it must be. So far as I know, Brickett Wood is only about five miles from Saint Alban's - but Datchworth is much further away."

"But do tell us more about your holiday plans, Susan," said Norma suddenly. It seemed that she was bored by her husband's talk about his two aunts, and not really looking forward to staying with Aunt Annie at Brickett Wood. "When do you expect to arrive at your holiday cottage?"

"Oh, some time on Saturday, I think," said Susan.

"Not until Saturday?"

"Oh, yes!" said Jim. "It'll take us until the day after tomorrow to get to the Outer Hebrides."

"Good heavens! But couldn't you get there more quickly by flying?"

"I dare say we could," said Susan, "but we don't want to!"

"No, we don't want to," agreed Jim. "The crossing by ferry from Kyle of Lochalsh sounds much nicer."

"Oh, yes, I know what you mean," said Norma. "You'll see much more of Scotland that way, I should think, than if you were to take a plane from somewhere."

"I'm sure you've made a wise decision to go by train and then take the ferry," said Nigel. "I think we would have done just the same if it had been us going on this trip - don't you think so, Norma, darling?"

"Oh, good heavens, yes! I couldn't *stand* the idea of flying!"

"So the ferry goes from Kyle of Lochalsh, you say?" said Nigel. "But isn't that rather a long crossing?"

"Well, yes, I suppose it is," said Susan. It leaves Kyle of Lochalsh at midday, but I think it's meant to be five o' clock when it gets in to Stornoway."

"So you see," said Jim, "as it'll be quite late in the day tomorrow when we reach Stornoway, we're not going on to our cottage in our hired car until the next morning - Saturday morning."

"We're going to stay on the Friday night at a place where we've stayed before, the last time we went up to the Isle of Lewis," said Susan. "My maid has an aunt who lives at a cottage that's not all that far from Stornoway, so we've arranged to stay there on the Friday night. Then in the morning we'll set off for Tarbert in Harris to find our cottage."

"Is it in a town, or a village, or out in the country?" asked Norma.

"We think it must be out in the country from the information they've sent us," said Susan, "but apparently it's very near Tarbert."

"The brochure says that it's half a mile from Tarbert," said Jim, remembering the printed details, "and it says that it's 'very peaceful' and that it has 'good views over East Loch Tarbert'."

"It sounds delightful!" said Norma.

It seemed to Jim that time was passing quickly, almost too quickly, while they were happily talking and eating their food. From where they sat he could see an electric clock mounted on the wall at the back of the restaurant above a door which he could see was marked "TOILETS"; and there was also another door near it marked "PRIVATE", through which the waitresses came and went with their trays. He was glancing at the clock only occasionally, but he noticed that Mr. Beck was also keeping a wary eye on the time while he was eating his soup and talking.

They had all finished eating, and Susan had paid the bill for all of them, when Nigel Beck, having glanced at the clock, said that he reckoned that it was time for him and Norma to go out to look for their train to Watford Junction. They picked up, or put on, their various pieces of baggage (Jim and Susan were each carrying a rucksack on their backs) and came out again onto the station concourse. Lead by Nigel Beck, they now began to walk to their right towards the low-numbered platforms where, he said, they were sure to find the platform from which the six-sixteen was scheduled to depart. They had not gone very far, however, when they saw a large illuminated board with "MAIN LINE DEPARTURES" on it.

"We'd better stop and look at it," said Nigel.

"There's the 'Royal Highlander'," said Jim almost at once, pointing to the name on the illuminated signboard. "Departs seven-thirty p.m. from Platform Fifteen."

"There was no train at Number Fifteen when we passed it just a moment ago," said the observant Nigel, "But it's only about six o' clock now, so you would hardly expect it to be in yet... What's up, Norma?"

He noticed a broad smile on his wife's face, but was puzzled to know what could have suddenly amused her.

"I was just remembering how we waited for a train at Cockermouth station, the same four of us," said Norma, "and we had a long wait for the train that time - like this time!"

"You were ill that time," said Nigel, "and I was quite worried about you, having a long journey ahead of us, you know."

It was now Jim's turn to smile broadly, having been reminded of the day he had first met Susan.

"It was the best day ever!" he said quietly as he and Susan exchanged a quick smile. "The very best day of my life!"

"It was the day you and Susan first met each other, wasn't it?" said Norma.

"Indeed it was!"

They were walking on again, and now, for the moment, Jim did not want to say anything else. His mind was suddenly so full of memories of that never-to-be-forgotten day at Cockermouth station that he knew that all he really wanted now was to daydream happily: to try, as it were, to bring that most special meeting back to life so that he could feel once again the unspeakable pleasures of that unexpected rush of first love for his darling, Susan. And yet he knew at the same time that he could not do it. It was not just that walking on the concourse of Euston station with Nigel and Norma Beck (and many other people) there were far too many distractions around him for him to have the slightest chance of focusing his thoughts on so etherial a subject. And it was not only the distractions which would make that impossible. Jim knew in his heart that there had been something very special about the ambience of that occasion which he would never be able fully to recover.

"Here's our train," said Nigel. "I thought it would be at the platform now as it's due out in just about ten minutes from now."

"We'll come onto the platform with you to see you off," said Susan, and Jim was glad to hear her say it.

"Yes, we'll come with you onto the platform," said Jim, agreeing with Susan.

"Okay!" said Nigel. He was already leading the way onto Platform Four, and the others were following him.

"But do we just get into the train without showing our tickets to anyone?" asked Norma.

"Yes, I would say so," said her husband. "I'll just ask first, though, to make sure." he had just spotted two railway officials chatting together further down the platform.

"That's right, sir," said one of the men, when Mr. Beck had questioned him. "This is the six-sixteen to Watford Junction, and we'll be inspecting tickets in the train."

Jim suddenly felt an overwhelming desire to get into the train with the Becks, even if he should only stay there for a minute or two.

After all, it was quite safe to do so as the train was not due to start until sixteen minutes past six, and it was now only seven minutes past six (he checked the time).

"Can I take that for you?" he said to Norma, who was carrying what looked like a heavy bag.

"Oh, thank you!" she said as she stepped up into a carriage of the train, followed by her husband, and then by Jim with her bag.

"Well, I might as well get in too!" said Susan cheerfully as she also stepped up into the train behind Jim. They had entered a carriage near the front of the six-car suburban train, and were pleased to find that it was not yet very full.

"Good, here are some empty seats - let's sit here!" said Norma, making straight for a window seat, and sitting down.

Jim handed the bag he was carrying for Norma to Nigel Beck, who put it up onto the luggage rack. He saw the two railway officials still standing and chatting on the platform nearby.

"They must be our driver and guard, those two," he said.

"What! Surely you don't know them, Nigel?" said Norma.

"No, of course I don't; but that's a driver's cap that one of them's wearing."

"I think we'd better get out of this train now," said Jim.

"Yes, we'd better when we've said 'Good-bye' – we don't want to be carried off to Watford Junction!"

When they had said their good-byes Susan and Jim stepped down again onto the platform, but they remained there, standing by the window where the Becks were sitting.

"We might as well stay here until the train goes out?" said Jim hopefully.

"Oh, yes, we might as well," said Susan, "as there's only about another six minutes to go now until it's due to depart."

"Look!" said Jim a moment later. "Mr. Beck must have been right about that railwayman being the driver of this train – he's just getting into the cab now." The two railwaymen who had been chatting together were now going their separate ways: one towards the front end of the train, and the other towards the rear end.

"I would say so," said Susan, "and I believe that the other one is the guard. Doesn't it remind you, in a way, darling, of Mr. Ruddock and Mr. Blencow?" Susan was smiling happily, remembering once again the day when they had first met the Becks at Cockermouth station, when Mr.

Ruddock had been the driver of the 10.08 train, and Mr. Blencow, the guard – and she had met Jim for the very first time.

"Yes, I was thinking about them and remembering that day," said Jim. "I wonder if the Becks were reminded of those two as well?"

"I expect they were," said Susan. "After all, Nigel was, and still is, so far as we know, a driver himself."

Time now seemed to be passing slowly as they waited on the platform for the departure time of the local train to Watford Junction, but presently they were startled by the sound of a whistle blown sharply from somewhere behind them. Jim had just noticed that Nigel Beck, sitting inside the train, had been looking at his watch.

"They're off!" said Susan as she saw the train beginning to move.

She and Jim waved their hands, and saw Nigel and Norma waving back to them. Jim began to walk along the platform as he continued to wave a hand, but he very soon had to give up his attempt to keep pace with the Becks' window as the train was rapidly picking up speed. He glanced over his shoulder, and saw that Susan was again standing beside him.

"Well, they're on their way, darling, so we might as well go back now to see whether our train has come in?" she said.

Jim, however, did not answer her, and seemed, indeed, to be temporarily in a trance as his eyes followed the rapidly departing train. After a few more seconds the rear end of the train disappeared from their view under the bridge which carried Hampstead Road over the railway tracks.

"Right!" he said. "Let's go back now."

They walked slowly back towards Platform Fifteen and found, when they arrived there, that the "Royal Highlander" had com in, and was standing at the platform.

"Shall we get into the train now?" said Jim.

"I think we might as well," said Susan. But it's only twenty-two minutes past six now, so we've still got over an hour to wait for our departure!"

"Our reserved compartment is in Coach 'B'," said Jim, "so I expect it'll be up towards the front end of the train."

They began to walk along the platform, looking at the labels, each with a letter of the alphabet, on every carriage of the train.

"It's a good thing, you know, that in the end we didn't decide to take that later train from Sherborne," said Susan as they walked past Coach "F". "We'd have missed meeting the Becks if we'd taken the three thirty-four from Sherborne."

"Oh, yes, of course; I see what you mean, Sue. Do you know, I was just thinking that it feels... well, almost lonely here now that we've said good-bye to them?"

"I know just how you're feeling, darling," said Susan, "and I'm feeling exactly the same myself. It really has been very nice meeting the Becks here unexpectedly, and having this chance to have a good chat with them; and of course it's a pity that we've had to say good-bye to them. In fact, when I come to think of it, it's a pity that we couldn't have all travelled together to the Outer Hebrides. I'm sure Norma would really love the Isles of Lewis and Harris."

"Yes, she said, 'It sounds delightful', didn't she, when I told her what the brochure says about the cottage. And probably Nigel would have found it delightful too."

"Well, here we are, darling – here's Coach 'B'."

They stepped up into the first-class carriage, the second one behind the locomotive, and began to walk along the corridor, looking for their reserved compartment. By the time they had found it they had seen no one else in that carriage, although each door had its "RESERVED" sticker attached to it.

*

Presently the time reached half past seven. The train began to move, but Jim, revelling in happy memories and daydreams, failed to notice that their real journey had now begun. Susan looked up from the book she was reading and saw that his eyes were closed.

"Are you asleep, darling?" she asked quietly.

"Oh, no!" said Jim quickly, opening his eyes with a jerk.

"We've just started."

"Gosh, so we have!" said Jim. Looking out of the window, he was in time to see the platform ends of Euston station disappearing behind them. "It's lovely to think that we're on our way to Scotland now!"

"I'll say it is!"

"But, all the same, isn't it amazing to think that the next time we step out of this train we'll be in the heart of the Highlands – and yet here we are, right now, still looking out at Central London through these windows!"

"Yes, I know what you mean: we've got a long journey ahead of us now," said Susan. "But we won't be seeing these suburbs of north-west London for all that much longer, and then we'll feel that we're properly on our way."

That evening the weather was perfect. The sun was shining in a completely cloudless sky. The weather was so cheerful that even that even the constantly changing views of suburban London, seen through the train window, seemed delightful to stare at. Presently, however, the train left London behind them, but now Jim and Susan were no longer looking out at the ever changing view.

They had pulled down the blind across their window, and retired into their bunks to settle down early for the night. And about half an hour after that they were both asleep.

CHAPTER SIXTEEN

When Jim awoke he became aware quite slowly that he was in a train, and that the train had stopped moving. Where was he? Then, as he remembered that he and Susan were in a sleeping compartment of the "Royal Highlander" he raised himself from his bunk on one elbow and pulled back part of the blind from the window to look out into the darkness. He saw a platform of a station, lit by electric lights, a bench with no one sitting on it, and some station buildings, but not a sign of anyone about the place. He thought that the station, wherever it was, looked vaguely familiar to him. Could the place possibly be Carlisle? He looked at his watch, and saw that the time was one thirty-six, but, as he did not know when the "Royal Highlander" was scheduled to stop at Carlisle he was none the wiser. Was Susan awake? he wondered. He kept perfectly still for a moment while he listened carefully and, after a second or two, found that he could hear her steady breathing in the general quietness in the train and on the platform outside. He turned his head to look at Susan where she lay on the opposite bunk to his and saw that she was lying perfectly still, her head turned away from him towards the wall of the compartment. It was obvious that she was asleep.

Jim decided that he would have to look out through the windows on the corridor side of the compartment in order, hopefully, to find a clue to the identity of the station. Wherever the place was, it certainly seemed to be a large station with an overall roof to it. In his stockinged feet he moved very quietly across the floor, lifted a corner of a blind, and looked out across the corridor at the view on that side. So this *is* Carlisle! he said to himself happily as his gaze alighted on a station nameboard over there. After a moment's consideration he came to the conclusion that they must be standing at Platform Three, and that that other long platform which he could see beyond two empty centre roads must be Platform Four, the main southbound platform; and two bay platforms beyond that must be platforms Seven and Eight.

Then his attention was caught by a light in the window of a room behind Platform Eight. As he watched he saw the light suddenly switched off. A moment later a door beneath that window was opened and a man in railway uniform came out. He watched the man close the door and lock it, and then saw him begin to walk along the platform.

Why, thought Jim suddenly, that room is the station-master's office. It's the room where I had my interview for the porter's job at Cockermouth. Then I got into the train to Cockermouth from Platform Five and met Mr. Ruddock... but then at Penrith I met Jill Rose.

The sudden thought of his former girlfriend, Jill Rose - whose existence he had completely forgotten about - was somewhat distressing to him. It was as if he was feeling guilty for having allowed her to drop completely out of his life, in spite of the fact that he knew very well that this was the best thing that could have happened. At least, he said to himself, it was certainly the best thing for me that she should disappear completely from my life. Then the thought came to him that it would be good if he could return to Cockermouth. I think I'd like to get out of this train right now to go back to Cockermouth if there was a local train going that way now... but, of course, I can't; and anyway there wouldn't be any local train in the middle of the night.

Suddenly he noticed that their train, the "Royal Highlander", was beginning to move again, although it had been a very quiet start (he had heard no whistle blown). Good, he said to himself, we're on our way to Scotland, and we'll pretty soon be crossing the border. I must put all these melancholy thoughts out of my mind. He remained standing where he was for a little longer, looking out of the corridor window, thinking that perhaps he would be able to see the River Eden in the moonlight when they came to the bridge over the river (it was a few nights after the full moon, and the sky was clear, and the moon was well up in the sky). Presently, however, he realized that they must have crossed over the bridge without him noticing it as he saw that they seemed to be almost out of the suburbs of Carlisle. He looked round again at Susan and saw that she still seemed to be fast asleep. He crept quietly back into his bunk, lay down, and made himself comfortable; and now he hoped that he would soon fall asleep again. Soon, however, he realized that this was not likely to happen as he now had too much to think about. I wish I hadn't remembered Jill Rose, he said to himself sadly. I wonder what's become of her? I think I must have made her very sad when she realized that I simply wasn't interested in any sort of permanent relationship with her. But there was that nasty sister of her's, Julia... and her behaviour was absolutely disgraceful! She very nearly ruined everything for Sue and me – and she *would* have brought it all to an end if Sue hadn't been generous enough to forgive me.

For a long time, as the train moved northwards through the Southern Uplands of Scotland, Jim's mind continued to rake through many upsetting thoughts and memories connected with the Rose sisters, but eventually he fell asleep again.

*

It was about half an hour later, when daylight was beginning to fill the sky, when Susan woke up. She looked at her watch and saw that it was a quarter to four. She wondered whether Jim was awake, looked round at his bunk, and saw that he appeared to be asleep. Then, as he had done, she kept very still for a moment and listened carefully, but, because of the noise of the train, which was now moving quite fast, she could not hear the sound of his breathing. She pulled back a corner of the blind, as he had done, to look out of her window. My goodness, it's getting quite light now – it must be nearly the time of sunrise! But it looks really nice outside, so it looks as if we should be in for a pretty good day! As Jim had done, she pulled part of the blind away from the window so that she could look out. She saw fields near the railway line and, perhaps half a mile away, the line of a main road.

Further away she saw that the flattish country near the railway line rose up into hills. They were, perhaps, quite high, those hills, but she did not think that they could be the mountains of the Scottish Highlands although she thought that they must be somewhere in Scotland. Then she saw some houses by that main road, and then more houses, and then there were roads and streets and other buildings to be seen through the windows. They were evidently in the outskirts of a town, but Susan did not recognize the town of Stirling, never having been that way before.

The train passed near enough to some houses for her to notice that curtains or blinds were drawn across all windows; there was no one up and about at that early hour. They're all still asleep, she thought to herself happily, for certainly there was something very pleasant in being awake and watchful when everyone else was asleep.

Their travelling by train was over, and they had embarked on the Stornoway ferry at Kyle of Lochalsh. Now the ferry was sailing northwards along the east coast of the Isle of Lewis as it was approaching Stornoway harbour. Jim and Susan were standing on the port deck, watching the rugged coastline of dark rocks and many inlets go past them while they kept recognizing many coastal landmarks from their previous arrival at Stornoway, which had been on board Susan's yacht, the *Osprey*.

"That rocky headland we're just passing must be Raerinish Point," said Susan, looking up from the open map which Jim was holding, and pointing with a finger.

Jim was finding it difficult to hold his map steadily enough for them to read details from it as a fresh north-easterly breeze was making it flap about in his hands.

"Yes, I think it must be," he said. "I say, Sue, doesn't this remind you of that time when we first came to Stornoway, sailing along this coast in the *Osprey*?"

"And you were steering her that time, you remember?"

"I do indeed!" said Jim. "I was finding it quite scary, I think, knowing that I was in charge of the yacht; but it was wonderful all the same, coming here in our own yacht."

"It certainly was; but so is this! Just think, darling, somebody else is doing the steering just now, so that we don't have to bother our heads about anything but enjoying ourselves!"

Sue's quite right! thought Jim happily as they continued to watch that dark rocky coastline. Soon they could see the town of Stornoway ahead of them, spread out around the head of the deep inlet in the coast which formed Stornoway Harbour. They passed the small lighthouse on Arnish Point and, having already passed the promontary of Holm Point on the starboard side of the vessel, found themselves in the smooth sheltered water of the outer harbour. Very soon after that, as they approached the jetty, it was time for them to return to the lounge in order to take their places in the queue for disembarkation for foot passengers.

Twenty minutes later they were sitting in their hired car, having filled in the necessary forms and handed over a cheque to pay for it.

They had found the car and the man from the car hire firm waiting for them on the jetty, as they had been promised. Jim was now sitting in the driver's seat, and when the man had finished explaining to him the controls of the car and said good-bye to him, Jim drove off.

"Do you think you can find the right way through Stornoway?" said Susan. She now had the map in her hands ready, if necessary, to be the navigator for Jim.

"Oh, I expect so!" said Jim hopefully. "At any rate, Stornoway's not a very big town so it should be all right – so long as I can find the way to the Tolsta road."

As they drove through the streets of the town Jim found that the geography of the place was coming back into his mind without any difficulty. They picked up the Barvas road, and then came to the place in the outskirts of Stornoway where the Tolsta road branched off from it. About twenty minutes after that Jim and Susan, who were both keeping a careful look-out for it, spotted the "Glen Tolsta" signpost at exactly the same moment.

"There it is!" said Susan.

"Yes, that's our road," said Jim.

He turned the car off the main road to the right onto a tiny, single-track road, which did, however, have some passing places in it.

They now both remembered that this was the road down to Mr. MacAllan's cottage, down by the sea at the end of the road. The road lead them past a couple of other modern bungalows and the ruins of a deserted house and then, about half a mile from the place where they had left the Tolsta road, they saw Tolsta Cottage; and there was Mr. MacAllan himself, sitting on a low wall outside the house, smoking a pipe, and keeping a look-out for them.

Ian MacAllan stood up and waved a cheery hand to his visitors as he saw them arriving. Then he pointed to the wide sweep of gravel behind him which served as a parking and turning area for cars at the end of the road. Jim understood that he was being asked to leave the car there. He parked the hired car with the bonnet facing the low wall and the house at the bottom of the turning area. They stepped out of the car and shook Mr. MacAllan's hand.

"Aye, it's good to see ye!" said Ian MacAllan. "And ye're in good time!"

"Well, yes, I suppose we are," said Susan. "I think we said we thought we'd arrive here around six o' clock, but I see that it's only a quarter to six now."

Even before he had parked the car Jim was on the alert, his eyes keenly searching for any sign of Margaret MacAllan, Ian MacAllan's daughter; and this in spite of the fact that he was almost certain that she would not be there, and that, even if he should see her, he knew that he should, as far as possible, ignore her completely. He thought he could remember that Samantha had told them, when they had been planning their stay at Glen Tolsta Cottage, that Margaret was no longer working at the Lewis Hotel, where they had first met her. That, Jim thought, was only too likely as she had probably only been employed on a temporary basis; and now, he thought, she would probably be somewhere far away from home. Anyway, he told himself sharply, I shouldn't even *want* to see that girl again – I shouldn't even be thinking of looking out for her! But his eyes continued their search all the same.

"Nay, ye needn't bother," said Ian MacAllan. Jim had opened the back door of the car, meaning to pick up their rucksacks. "I'll bring yer luggage in afterwards Susan, having stepped out of the car, was standing and staring out over the sea as if she was spellbound and transfixed by the beauty of the view. In a moment Jim was at her side, also staring out across the bay.

"It's such a wonderful view," said Susan dreamily. "Don't you almost wish that we were staying here for the whole week, darling?"

"Well, I do, almost," said Jim. "This cottage really couldn't have been built in a better place for the view looking out over this bay. But our cottage at Tarbert should be just as good, I should think."

"Look, they've put out a table and four chairs on the sand down there," said Susan.

"Oh, splendid! It'll be lovely if they're going to ask us to sit down there presently," said Jim. He turned his head quickly, hearing the sound of the front door of the cottage opening, but it was only Mrs.

MacAllan coming out to greet them; there was still no sign of her daughter, Margaret. I mustn't ask about her, or mention her name, or even think about her, Jim told himself.

Mavis MacAllan invited her guests to come into the house.

"Yes, I thought that we could sit down there later on our little private beach, if you'd like to," she said.

"We'd love to!" said Susan, and Jim nodded his head to show his enthusiasm for the idea.

"But we can only sit there when the tide is at least half out, or lower," said Mavis MacAllan. "At high water this little cove of sand is nearly all under water."

"But low water this evening is at half past seven," said Ian MacAllan, "so we'll be all right there for a while."

"I thought that it would be a chance for us to sit outside for our supper as it's such a beautiful evening," said Mavis. She lead the way into the cottage, a modern two-storey house.

Inside the house Jim and Susan were shown into their room for the night. They were delighted to find that it was the same room at the front of the house, with an excellent view over the little cove and the wider bay beyond it, that they had occupied on their last visit there.

Half an hour later they were sitting at their places around the table on the sand of the little cove, eating their supper. Ian MacAllan had brought the meal down to them on a large tray; there were bowls of hot soup followed by a cold main course. While they were eating Jim and Susan were happily remembering their arrival by sea at the cove on their last visit to the cottage.

"I think it must have been just after the time of high water when we landed just here in the dinghy," said Susan.

"Was there any sand uncovered then?" asked Ian MacAllan.

"There was a little sand - very little - just around the place where the burn flows into the sea," said Susan. She turned her head to the right to look at the stream, the Allt Tolsta, which flowed underneath the car parking area in a pipe and then descended the steep bank down to the cove in a small waterfall. Once arrived on the tidal sand of the cove the fresh water spread out into a wider channel before being absorbed into the salt water of the sea.

"Did you see our house from well out in the bay?" asked Mavis MacAllan. "You were coming from Stornoway, I believe, so you would have to make a very long detour to sail around the Head?"

"We did see your house from quite a long way out in the bay," said Susan, remembering the voyage of the *Osprey* on that fine September afternoon. "It shows up well, you know, as it's white."

"But it was a long voyage, wasn't it, Sue?" said Jim. "At least, it seemed to take ages to sail right round the Head from Stornoway; and, of course, Sam and Roger, travelling here by road, got here long before us."

"It was lovely meeting them here in the Isle of Lewis," said Susan. "Gosh, I wish they could have come with us this time as well!"

The MacAllans glanced at each other for a second but did not say anything.

"It really was nice, meeting them here," agreed Jim. "And then, when we'd landed they took us for a picnic at a beach quite near here.

Do you remember it, Sue?"

"I do indeed. It was a lovely place where we went down a lot of steps in the cliff face to get down onto the beach; and it was close under that other headland, the one to the north of here,"

"Aye, that would be the Giordale Sands at North Tolsta, under the Tolsta Head," said Ian. "And ye met our daughter, Maggie, that time, I think? Was she na working in Stornoway at that time?"

Susan for a second glanced sharply at Jim, but he did not meet her gaze and looked away from her. She understood that he did not want to have to talk about Margaret.

"Yes," she said, "she was working as a barmaid in the Lewis Hotel, and we met her there, the four of us, when we were having lunch there."

"She's away now, studying in London," said Mavis.

"London!" said Susan in amazement. "But that's a long way from here! Is she at the University?"

"She is indeed. She's in her first year as an undergraduate at University College in the University of London."

"What's she reading?"

"Medicine. She's studying to become a doctor."

"Aye, five years of study in London to become a doctor," said Ian. "It's absurd when ye consider that we have our own guid Scottish universities – Edinburgh and Glasgow and other places where she could be studying medicine – but, no, our Maggie says she must be off to London to see what the big city is like!"

"But maybe she's right after all," said Mavis, "that London must be the best, after Oxford and Cambridge."

Jim was glad to hear that Margaret had gone away to London, and that therefore there was no chance that he would meet her accidentally.

But, in a way, I must admit that it's a disappointment to me that she's not here, he said to himself. And yet – how odd it is to think that we must have come very close to where she is now when we passed through Central London on our way up here!

CHAPTER SEVENTEEN

The next morning Jim and Susan took their leave of the MacAllans after breakfast as they set off to drive to Tarbert after stopping first in Stornoway to do some shopping. The day had dawned cloudless, and it certainly looked as if the sun would shine for more or less the whole of that day. Ian MacAllan, however, had told them that the spell of fine weather was forecast to come to an end in a day or two.

"Ye'd better make the most of today and tomorrow, then!" he told them. But ye should remember that tomorrow is the Sabbath, and ye'll find that everything is closed in Lewis and Harris on the Sabbath - everything except the Kirk."

"We're going to church tomorrow, Sue, aren't we?" said Jim.

"We might as well," said Susan. "I suppose we're sure to find the Church of Scotland at Tarbert?"

"Och, aye, ye'll be sure to find the Kirk there as Tarbert is the main village in Harris," said Ian MacAllan.

Jim and Susan arrived in Tarbert just after four o' clock, having stopped off for about two hours for a prolonged lunch picnic just off the main road. It was a delightful place that they had found (with the help of their map) where there were superb views ahead of them of the mountains of North Harris. It was a place, as Jim had said, like the bottom of a large round bowl, ringed around by rocky mountain peaks; in particular by the dark peak of Clisham, the highest peak in Harris.

They had seen that the road ahead to Tarbert zig-zagged its way up the flanks of those mountains towards a gap in the hills by Loch a Mhorgain, a gap as yet hidden behind the shoulder of another mountain, Tomnaval.

Jim had tried bathing his feet in the dark brackish water of a small burn which flowed sluggishly through the peat bog, but he had found it painfully cold, and had advised Susan not to try it.

They found their holiday cottage without any difficulty as they followed their written directions, which turned out to be precise and helpful.

"Gosh, what a lovely place!" said Jim wonderingly as he stepped out of the car.

"Yes, this view is simply superb, isn't it?" said Susan. "It could hardly be better. But shall we go in now to see what it's like inside?"

They found the front door key, as they had been instructed, under the dustbin. Susan fitted the key into the lock, turned it, and opened the door. They entered and found themselves in the kitchen.

There were not many rooms in the cottage so that it did not take long for them to explore it. They approved of everything they found there, and especially they were both delighted by the look of the main bedroom, which was on the first floor at the front of the house. The room had a double bed in it, and the view through the large window was (as the brochure had promised them) over Tarbert village and harbour and East Loch Tarbert.

"It's as good as the view from the MacAllans' cottage," said Jim, who was standing by the window, unable to tear himself away from the panoramic view.

"We really are lucky," said Susan, "and the bed is just wonderfully comfortable...! Do come and try it, darling, when you've done looking at the view." She had put down her bag beside the bed, flung off her shoes, turned back the quilt, and was lying very comfortably on the bed. A few seconds later Jim joined her there.

"We'd better ring up home after supper to check that all is well," said Susan a few minutes later.

"Oh, yes, we will," agreed Jim. "We promised that we'd do that when we got here."

An hour later, having eaten a simple supper in the living-room of the cottage, using some of the food they had bought in Stornoway, they approached the telephone. The telephone had no coinbox, but there was a book lying beside it in which all calls were meant to be entered. Susan picked up the receiver and dialled the Rhodes Castle number. Both of them, however, could hear the butler's voice, answering the telephone.

"Rhodes Castle!"

"Hello, Jack – Susan speaking."

"Oh, good evening, my Lady. You've arrived at your cottage at Tarbert safely, I hope?"

"Indeed we have. I hope all's well at the Castle, Jack?"

"Oh, yes, ma'am, all's well. Ailean Connor came to see me this morning to ask if she could possibly take a job with us."

"But who is Ailean Connor? I don't think I've heard that name before."

"She's the daughter of our Guide, Rachel Connor, ma'am, and she said she's very interested in gardening!"

"Oh, I see," said Susan. "Now that I come to think of it, I think Rachel did once mention her daughter's name to me when she said that Ailean was meaning to study botany or horticulture, and that she might be wanting to take a gardening job with us in the meantime. So did you tell her that she'd better come and have a word with me about it when we've come back?"

"Yes, my Lady, that's exactly what I did."

"Did you give her a provisional time for an interview?"

"Yes, ma'am. I told her to come back next Monday morning at nine o' clock if she wants to be interviewed for a job. I hope that's all right?"

"Yes, that should be perfectly all right, thank you, Jack. And there isn't anything else that you'd like to tell me about?"

"I don't believe there is, ma'am, but would you like to speak to Samantha now? She's just here now if you want to talk to her?"

"Oh, yes, Jack, I would; that would be a good idea."

"Very well, ma'am," said the butler. "If you would just hold the line for a moment I'll hand over the telephone to Samantha. Good-bye for now, my Lady."

"Good-bye, Jack, and see you soon!"

There was a pause of only a few seconds before Susan heard her maid's voice at the other end of the line.

"Hello, Sue! Are you and Jim getting on all right?"

"Splendidly, thank you!" said Susan. "We've had lovely weather so far, and all the stages of our journey here have gone very well, and now here we are in our holiday cottage, and we simply love it!" Susan and Samantha chatted together for a few minutes before Susan, mindful of the cost of the call, decided that it was time to ring off and say good-bye.

"Well, that's that," she said, "but it's good to know that all is well at home and that nothing's really happened except that Rachel's daughter, Ailean, wants to come and work for us, as you'll have gathered."

"Yes, I heard you and Jack talking about that," said Jim.

He decided at once that the wisest course for him would be to say as little as possible about Ailean Connor. Sue and I both know about my weakness where beautiful women are concerned, he reminded himself; and this Ailean surely *must* be a lovely young woman if she's Rachel's daughter! I'm going to have to be *very* careful, though, if she does come to work for us - I mustn't upset Sue again, as I once did very badly. However, from the very moment when he had first heard that Rachel Connor had a daughter he had been wondering what she would look like. Perhaps, though, she would not look much like her mother. She may take after her father in looks, he thought. He wondered for a moment what Mr. Connor looked like, but soon realized that he did not think he had ever seen him. Or perhaps she would look like a younger version of her beautiful mother. Oh, I do hope so! he said to himself, but a moment later he contradicted that thought as he reminded himself again that the less contact he had with attractive women, the better it would surely be for him.

While these thoughts were passing through his mind Jim was aware that he was, as it were, treading on dangerous ground. The real danger for him was, of course, immanent in the person of Rachel Connor, and he was well aware of it. He also reasoned that, whatever Ailean might look like, it was unlikely that she would turn his head in the same way as did the image of her mother. That image of Rachel Connor in all her classic beauty - the luscious sweep of her honey-blonde hair on the nape of her neck, the perfectly rounded outline of her chin (to say nothing of the well-rounded outlines of another part of her anatomy!) - these were features which could in a trice deliver him into a state of hysteria or madness. No, no! he said to himself very sharply, I must keep those images out of my mind! However, with a certain amount of conscious effort he was indeed succeeding in blocking out the "dangerous" images. Later that night, when he and Susan had retired to bed he was feeling rather pleased with himself. He thought, in fact, that it was very unlikely that any thoughts or images of Rachel would disturb his feelings of peacefulness and happiness. But he was wrong.

At some time in the small hours of that night a dream came to him; and it was indeed a very strange, and worrying, and even a really bizarre dream.

Jim found himself in a rather odd-looking room. At first he was not sure what it was about that room which made it look "wrong", but then his eyes quickly picked out those features of the room which seemed odd. The first of these was the high ceiling of the room. The walls, in fact, seemed to be so high that he could see no ceiling at all, and, for some reason, he did not want to look up in that direction. The second unusual feature was the pictures. The wall to his right, at which he was gazing, was so well covered by pictures – they were paintings of all shapes and sizes – that there was very little plain wall to be seen between the pictures. However, it was the lighting of that room, the third striking feature, which really caught his attention: he saw that the general effect was rather eerie – almost disturbing. It seemed to be night time. From somewhere behind him a powerful electric light was lighting up that wall of pictures to his right, but now he noticed a window high up in the wall ahead of him and, looking through the panes, he saw only black darkness. He glanced up a little higher, but the wall seemed to melt away into a penumbral gloom up there, and it was somehow disturbing to try to peer into that darkness so he lowered his gaze again – and immediately it came to rest on a woman sitting on a sofa.

The woman was sitting so still that for a second Jim wondered whether she was alive or a dummy. It was very odd that he had not noticed her before, or perhaps he had seen her, but without really noticing that she was there. Suddenly he saw that the woman was looking straight at him, and, for a moment smiling at him; and in that instant he recognized her. She was Claire Walker. However, he now noticed (why had he not noticed it before?) that she was almost naked. She was wearing nothing but a pair of white knickers. His first reaction to her nakedness was one of instant shock, but that, naturally enough, soon began to pass into excitement as his gaze moved downwards from her face until it became focused on a beautiful pair of well-rounded breasts.

"Don't do it!" said Claire suddenly.

"Oh, I'm so sorry!" said Jim in confusion, feeling that he was blushing heavily on being caught red-handed staring at her breasts. He turned his head hurriedly as he spoke.

"You mustn't stare at my breasts, Jim," said Claire. Her voice did not sound severe, as if she was scolding him, but only matter-of-fact. "I shall get dressed now."

"I won't look," said Jim meekly.

It seemed to take almost no time at all for Claire to put some clothes on. Then he heard her say, "You can look at me now, Jim."

He looked round and saw that she was now standing up and wearing a blue teeshirt and white trousers.

"Now listen carefully to what I have to tell you," she said. "This is important, Jim, and it concerns Rachel Connor. You will have to break your obsession with her."

"Oh, yes, I'm sure I ought to," he agreed.

"You *will* do it! I'm going to take you now to where Rachel is, and I'm going to tell you what you have to do when you see her – so listen carefully!"

"I am listening," said Jim.

"What you've got to do, as soon as you see her, is to go up to her and hit her – and make sure that you hit her hard enough to hurt her!"

"But I can't do that!" exclaimed Jim, appalled at the idea of using physical violence against Rachel Connor.

"You *will* do that! I didn't say, though, that you were to beat her up with so much violence that you would cause serious injuries. I said that you must hit her so that it hurts her a little – enough to make her strike you in return. Then, of course, she will be angry with you, and will never speak to you again. Come on now and follow me. There's no time to lose!"

Jim knew that he was powerless to do anything but to obey Claire's orders, but he found himself following her with a great sense of foreboding as she made for a door he had noticed before at the back of the room. The door seemed to open of its own accord as Claire came to it, and outside it he saw brilliant sunshine. They passed quickly through the doorway, and then Jim paused a moment and blinked his eyes once or twice in the sudden flood of light. It did not strike him (until afterwards when he had woken up) that there was anything odd or illogical about being in sunshine when only a minute earlier it had seemed to be night time. He glanced over his shoulder for a moment but was not really surprised to see no sign of that rather odd room, or indeed of any house or building. They were out of doors now in open grassy country, and Claire was running on ahead of him, so he also set off at a run to try to keep up with her.

It seemed to be only a second or two later when he caught sight of Rachel Connor. She was sitting on a grassy bank like the bank of a river, and at her feet there was a bed of rushes and yellow flags, and beyond that Jim could see water; there was a slow-flowing river meandering its way quietly through the meadows. Rachel (if it was Rachel) was sitting with her back to him, and for a moment he was not sure whether it really was her, but as he came nearer he recognized her beyond any doubt although she never turned her head to look round at him. It's Rachel all right! he said to himself – but how could I possibly hit such a lovely woman?

He looked round again for a second and saw that Claire had vanished. For a moment he was tempted to disobey her order and run away, but then, suddenly, his mood changed completely, and he felt a surge of inner strength arising within him. Suddenly what he had to do seemed easy. He wondered afterwards, when he was thinking over the contents of the dream, whether Claire had somehow remained invisibly present with him to ensure that he did as she had told him, but all that he was thinking at the time was, "now I'm going to hit Rachel!"

He came quickly up to her from behind and delivered a sharp smack to her right cheek. On the instant she turned her head, but she did not scream or shriek in surprise and pain; however, he saw a look of cold hatred in those greenish eyes which he had never seen before. But it only lasted, perhaps, for a fraction of a second. Then he felt a sudden sharp pain as he was struck on the back of his head by Rachel's hand and, at the same moment he felt himself falling; she had managed to catch him off balance and pull him down into the mud. Rachel, however, fell with him; he had somehow managed to pull her down with him (but he had no idea how he had done it).

Their struggle together on the ground was very brief. It seemed to Jim (afterwards) that they must have wrestled together for only a few seconds before Rachel rose again nimbly to her feet, but, as she did so, she gave him another sharp push so that he found himself lying on his face on the muddy bank. He picked himself up as quickly as he could from his prone position, knowing, as he did so, that Rachel must be running away from him as fast as she could. He stood up and looked around, but he could see no sign of anyone. Bother her for running away so quickly! he said to himself irritably. What was he to do? He knew that he was longing and needing to see her again, to see her *now* so that he could apologise for using physical violence against her - but how could he follow her if he did not know in which direction she had fled? He looked around again, saw no one, and began to walk, slowly, painfully, and aimlessly along a little path which lead along the river bank... and with that the dream came to an abrupt end.

The dream had ended, but Jim only became aware rather slowly that he was now awake, that it was some time in the night, and that he was lying in bed with Susan in the main bedroom of their holiday cottage in Tarbert. But what a wretched dream it had been! It seemed to him now almost unbearably sad that, having unwisely hit Rachel, he had been given no opportunity to apologize to her.

A little later, however, knowing that he was now thoroughly awake, another thought came to him.

I mustn't let Sue know what I've been dreaming about, he said to himself, but then he wondered whether she was asleep or awake, and whether, if she was awake, she might have heard anything that he might have said during his dream. The dim pre-dawn light in the bedroom made it quite light enough for him to see Susan where she was lying quite still on her side of the bed. It seemed to him that she was still fast asleep, which he thought was just as well.

The next time he awoke, however, his thoughts were immediately distracted in another direction. He woke to the realization that there was something wrong with Susan, and he felt a hot flash of alarm, almost of panic, pass through his body as he became aware of her obvious state of distress.

Jim knew that his mouth had gone dry as a result of the sudden shock he had received, so that at first it was rather difficult for him to speak.

"Sue, darling – what's happened?"

She was sitting up on her side of the bed with both hands clasped around her stomach, as if she were in great pain. He heard her moaning gently, but she did not seem to have heard his question at all.

"Darling, what's the matter – do tell me?"

Susan looked round at him with eyes which seemed out of focus. He saw that her face looked flushed.

"Darling... I feel dreadful!" she muttered.

"Oh, no!" Jim was now really dismayed and alarmed, and already he was wondering whether he ought to be telephoning for a doctor or an ambulance. He put an arm gently and lovingly around her shoulders. "But *how* do you feel, Sue, darling?" he continued.

Susan swallowed once or twice before answering him.

"I feel sick!" she said.

It was lucky, Jim thought, that the bathroom was next door to their bedroom so that Susan would not have to stagger very far to be sick. However, a quarter of an hour later, after a visit to the bathroom, things seemed to be looking more hopeful. Susan was lying on her back quietly, and was evidently feeling at least a little less uncomfortable, if not exactly better, while Jim was also lying there wide awake because of his anxiety.

"Jim, darling, I'll tell you what's the matter with me," she said presently "Darling, you needn't be alarmed – I'm pregnant!

"Well, yes, I must admit that I was really afraid for you, Sue, my darling. But... how can it have happened?"

"I don't know," said Susan. "It certainly *shouldn't* have happened, of course, as we've been most careful, haven't we, when we've been making love?"

"We have indeed!" agreed Jim.

"And I'm pretty sure that I've never forgotten to take one of my pills, so I really shouldn't be pregnant now. But there it is: I *am* pregnant, and we've just got to accept that fact."

"Of course! But it's wonderful news, really, to think that we're going to have a son or a daughter soon. Don't you think so, Sue, darling?"

"Indeed I do – I certainly think so!"

"Dad'll be thrilled when I tell him that you're expecting, and that he'll be a grandfather soon," said Jim. "And, of course, Carol and Victoria will be very pleased too!"

"And Mum and Dad at Soken Hall will be really delighted too when I tell them," said Susan. "But what do you think, darling? How shall we tell them? We're going to buy post cards tomorrow, of course, and write them, but perhaps for this news...?"

"Perhaps we'd better ring them up to tell them when we get back home?"

"Yes, I think that would be the best way to pass on this news," said Susan.

Jim asked whether she was feeling a little better, and she said, yes, she was although she still felt a little bit sick. Then Jim pointed out that it was Sunday morning, and they were on holiday, and that they could lie in bed for as long as they wanted to. He also suggested that presently, when he got up, he should bring her a cup of tea so that she could drink it in bed without getting up. This idea pleased Susan very much, but she added that she was sure that she was going to feel much better quite soon, so that there would be no need for them to alter their plan for that morning, which was that they would attend the service in the Kirk (having first found out the time of it).

He lay awake for a long time while he considered the implications of Susan's startling news. The shock of her unexpected illness, and his relief on discovering that her condition was not, after all, serious had made him, for the moment, forget about his dream altogether. Then suddenly he remembered it again. It had been a strange dream, he thought, even before it had turned really nasty. What could be the meaning of that strange room with a rather eerie, almost threatening atmosphere about it? It's certainly not any room in the house in Martin Lane where Claire lives, he thought – in fact it wasn't like any room I've ever seen anywhere.

Recalling the details of his dream, and trying to divine some meaning in them, he was becoming so fascinated that he had temporarily forgotten about Susan's condition. He gradually became drowsy and, without being aware of what was happening, he slipped once again into sleep.

Later that morning they both attended the Church of Scotland service in the Kirk.

When Susan had drunk the cup of tea that Jim had brought to her to drink in bed he had walked the short distance down into the village, heading for the Kirk (they had seen where it was when they had passed it the day before). He was going to look at the notice board outside the Kirk to find out the time of the morning service.

When he arrived there he learned that it was at the very convenient hour of eleven o' clock.

Good, he thought, that shouldn't be too early for Sue, if she feels well enough by then to come with me to the service.

At half past ten, after Jim had eaten a normal breakfast, and Susan a small one, she said that she was feeling much better, so they both set off to walk down to the Kirk. Jim had expected to find most of the service, except for the singing of the hymns, rather boring, and that was more or less what he did find. During the minister's long, rambling sermon he let his thoughts wander to such an extent that, if anyone had asked him afterwards what the minister had been talking about, he would have been at a loss for an answer. For most of the time he was thinking again about that dream and wondering whether it did indeed predict the end of his obsession with Rachel Well, he told himself, I suppose it'll be just as well if it does mean that! But perhaps it means that I'll fall in love with Ailean, although I don't actually remember seeing her in the dream? But - good heavens - if that were to happen I'd be no better off than I am now!

When the service was over they went to the Harris Hotel for lunch. However, it was Sunday, and they knew that almost everything in Tarbert, except the Kirk, was closed in deference to "keeping the Sabbath". Would the hotel be closed to non-residents? They found, however, that it was not closed, and that bar lunches were being served to non-residents. As they ate their lunch (Susan had said that she was now feeling hungry) Jim found that he could not altogether dismiss from his mind his worrying thoughts arising from his dream. Nor was he free from those thoughts for the whole of the rest of the holiday. He had, however, resolutely decided to say nothing about it to Susan so he kept all his worries to himself.

Chapter Eighteen

Jim and Susan's stay in their holiday cottage at Tarbert was over, but their holiday in Lewis and Harris was not yet quite over. It was a Saturday morning, and they had been asked to quit the cottage at least by ten o' clock in order that it might be made ready for its next occupants. Jim and Susan, however, were again planning to stay that night with the MacAllans in Glen Tolsta Cottage, but they had little more than forty miles to drive to get there, and all day to do it.

The weather had not exactly been kind to them during their stay at Tarbert. No one can sensibly count on having fine weather for a summer holiday anywhere in the British Isles, and that principle had certainly applied to Jim and Susan. From the Sunday onwards every day at Tarbert had seen the same sort of weather - it had been dull and cloudy and often wet - until the Saturday morning of their departure from Tarbert when, perversely, there had been brilliant sunshine in an almost cloudless sky. And, because the day was so beautiful and they had so much time in hand, they very sensibly decided to take a diversion to fill in the middle part of the day by sight-seeing and walking. With that idea in mind they had paid a visit to the little hamlet of Lemreway in the rugged south-eastern part of Lewis, and filled in several hours there, largely by quietly sunbathing.

It was about half past three in the afternoon when they once more set off in their hired car to drive back to Stornoway, en route to Glen Tolsta Cottage. The hired car, however, never arrived in Stornoway.

That day Jim had once again been worried about Susan's health, and this time her complaint did not seem to be morning sickness. That morning she had complained of a severe headache which had, however (luckily) passed, but it had left Jim feeling worried. There was surely something seriously wrong with Susan's health – and it was not simply the fact that she was pregnant. That morning, with Susan's health in mind, Jim had sensibly decided to do the driving, and had driven them from Tarbert to Lemreway. Now, however, Susan had taken over the driving, insisting that her headache had completely disappeared. Jim, however, strongly suspected that Susan was not all right, and his suspicions were justified. They had arrived at the beginning of the long, straggling village of Balallan which straddles the main road for more than a mile.

Then suddenly Susan's hands slipped from the steering wheel as her body slumped forwards.

Afterwards Jim could never remember whether Susan had cried out at that dreadful moment, just before she lost consciousness, or whether she had remained silent. There was, however, no time for him to cry out in alarm; it all happened too quickly. The car went out of control, veered sharply to the left, collided with a low garden wall, and turned over onto its side. For a second or two he was aware of a totally confused mixture of sensations, but he thought (afterwards) that it had been mainly a feeling of falling into darkness. Then he knew no more.

*

When Jim came to his senses he found that he was lying on a rather hard bed in a small white room. He could not see very much of the room because there was a white curtain drawn around the bed. Suddenly he became aware of a violent, throbbing pain in his left temple and around his ear. Cautiously he reached up with his left hand to touch the painful area. But what was this? There was a sticking plaster applied to the side of his head; he must have cut it somehow. But where was he? Was he in a hospital? What had happened? Slowly and painfully he raised himself up on his elbows so that he would be able to look around, and perhaps discover where he was, but for a moment or two bright spots seemed to swim around in his field of vision, confusing him, so that he could not focus his eyes on anything. Then the spots cleared away, and he found that he could see again normally. He saw a table beside the bed with a glass of water on it and a small electric gadget with a button to press, labelled, "CALL". Should he press that button? For a moment, however, he sat perfectly still while he listened carefully to all the sounds that he could hear. It was certainly very quiet in that room, but a few faint sounds of people talking somewhere outside the room came to his ears. He decided to press that button, and heard a loud buzzer sound somewhere as he did so.

There was no time to wonder whether or not he had done the right thing by pressing that button. Almost immediately, it seemed, he heard the sound of the door being opened. A hand appeared and drew back the curtain around the bed, and there was a tall, good-looking, middle-aged lady looking down at him.

The lady was wearing the blue uniform dress of a nursing Sister, and around her waist was a broad black belt, fastened at the front by an old-fashioned silver buckle. Jim found himself looking into a pair of bluish-grey eyes as the Sister spoke to him.

"How are you feeling now, Mr. Sandy?" Her voice was calmly reassuring, not sharp. Jim, however, felt tired and confused, and had no idea how to answer her.

"Oh...! I don't know," he muttered.

"Do you feel any pain in your head?"

"Yes, I do; it's very painful. It throbs." As he answered his left hand was touching the plaster on his temple, although he did not know it.

"You had quite a bad cut there on your temple," said the Sister, "but we've put some stitches in it and dressed it for you, and it should soon start to feel less painful. I'll give you something to take for that now."

"Where am I?" asked Jim rather feebly.

"In hospital," said the Sister. "You're in the A. and E. department of the Stornoway hospital, and I'm Sister Joan MacElroy, looking after you at present. You were brought in here this afternoon by ambulance, following a road accident."

"I can't remember that," said Jim.

"No, I dare say you can't. You and your wife were both unconscious when you were brought in here."

"My wife? But where is my wife now?" At the mention of his wife Jim suddenly felt agitated. He made an attempt to stand up, and was immediately aware that he felt giddy. Standing up was clearly going to present him with problems, but with a quick gesture of her hand Sister MacElroy stopped him. He sank back thankfully onto the bed.

"No!" she said. "You mustn't try to stand up yet. Now listen to me. Your wife is all right. We're looking after here in this department. We'll let you go and see her quite soon."

"But... but what's happened to her?"

"She has had a stroke. The doctor has examined her, and he confirmed that she has suffered a mild stroke, and we think that it must have occured immediately before your car crashed."

"A stroke? Oh, no...!"

"Now, don't alarm yourself, Mr. Sandy. This has not been a very serious stroke. We can assure you of that as we've taken an X-ray scan of her brain so as to find out exactly what has happened. And we gave you a scan too as you were unconscious, but in your case we found nothing worse than concussion - which will pass. But you really need not be too worried about your wife's condition, Mr. Sandy. The doctor said that she's not in a deep coma - he's expecting her to recover consciousness any time around now."

"Oh, that's good!" said Jim with relief. He thought for a moment and then asked another question. "But will she have to stay here for a long time?"

"It depends on what you mean by 'a long time'," said Sister MacElroy, who was now sitting down on the end of the bed while she was talking. "I should dsay that she's certain to be kept here in hospital for at least a week, but, of course, it's not for me to say how long she will need to stay here."

"A week! But that's going to be dreadful!"

"Well, a lot will depend on what the consultant says when he comes to see her. Mr. Drummond is our brain injuries and strokes consultant, but he won't be coming here again until Monday morning, as it's now Saturday evening."

"So we'll just have to wait?"

"I'm afraid so; and, of course, that may well mean that you will have to change all your plans. Do you live here, or are you on holiday here?"

"We were on holiday here," said Jim.

"I thought that perhaps you were. Have you come from England?"

"Yes, we live in Dorset."

"Ah, Dorset. So you've come a long way for your holiday, Mr. Sandy, and I'm really very sorry for you - it's such a shame that this should have happened to your young wife while you were away on holiday - but there you are, it has happened; and at least you can be sure that she is in safe hands while she's receiving treatment here."

"It's good to know that," said Jim. "But how did you know my name, Sister? I don't think I ever told you that I'm Mr. Sandy?"

"No, you didn't; and I hope you'll forgive us for finding that out in our own way. What I think happened was this: one of the ambulance crew, who picked you up out of your car at the roadside, discovered your name from a document which was in your wallet; and your wallet, apparently, was in the pocket of the jacket you were wearing. No, it's all right – "Jim was looking anxiously around the room as Sister MacElroy was speaking – "we have your wallet and jacket and other personal things stowed safely away here for you – you needn't worry about them!"

"Oh, thank you!" said Jim.

"Right, I think we've talked enough for now," said Sister MacElroy. "Would you like a cup of tea?"

"Oh, yes, please, I certainly would!"

"Very well, I shall ask Staff Nurse to bring you some tea, and we'll give you a tablet to take to relieve the pain at the same time."

Sister MacElroy stood up, smiled at him briefly, and walked briskly across the room to the door. She was about to disappear through the doorway when Jim thought of something else.

"Sister!"

"What is it?" This time Sister MacElroy's tone was not exactly irritated, but it was certainly brisker than before.

"I need to telephone," said Jim. "I must let them know at home that we won't be able to come back on Monday morning, as we'd planned to."

"Later!" said the Sister briefly. "We'll bring the telephone to you later, Mr. Sandy; but you ought to have a rest for an hour or so after you've had your tea. This time she gave him no time to answer, but turned again quickly and closed the door behind her.

Once Sister MacElroy had gone Jim tried to think about his situation, but he very soon found that, for one reason or another, he simply could not think coherently. He knew that he wanted to know what had happened to himself and to Susan (particularly to Susan), but nothing more than disconnected flashes of thoughts would come into his mind. It seemed impossible to think through any idea while he was feeling strangely tired, and was also thoroughly distracted by the pain which felt like a continuous thumping going through his head. Had Susan really had a stroke? Could he really believe that something so serious had happened to her? He was not sure that he could believe it, but he was sure that that was what the Sister had told him.

Then he remembered that she had said something about a car crash and an ambulance that had brought them to the hospital. A car crash?

But where had they been going in the car? How had an ambulance appeared from somewhere to bring them into this hospital? I really can't work out what's happened, he thought, and I don't really want to try to think – but I wish they'd let me see Sue!

His wish came true almost as soon as he had thought it. The door opened, and a young, fat-looking nurse bustled into the room, pushing a metal trolley on wheels.

"I've brought you a painkiller, Mr. Sandy," said the Staff Nurse.

"Sister says that you're to take it now." She took a small white tablet from a bottle on her trolley and handed it to Jim, and then handed him a small plastic mug with cold water in it to swallow the pill.

"Thank you," said Jim weakly. He swallowed the pill with one or two mouthfuls of water.

"And Sister said to tell you that your wife has regained consciousness. You can come and see her now if you'd like to."

"I certainly would like to!" said Jim.

"Very well, then, you can come with me now."

"Thank you... but I felt a bit giddy when I tried to get up before."

"Then just take your time," said the nurse. "Stand up as slowly as you like, and I'll help you."

Reassured, Jim took her advice and, with the nurse holding him firmly by one arm, raised himself up slowly until he was standing on the floor.

"How do you feel now?" asked the nurse. "Can you walk with me now?"

"Yes, I'm feeling better," said Jim. "The giddiness seems to be passing. I can walk with you - if it isn't too far?"

"No, we haven't far to go. Your wife is in the room just on the opposite side of the passage."

With an arm linked around the nurse's arm Jim tottered across the floor of the room and out into a passage outside. The nurse opened the door of another room exactly opposite to the door through which they had just come out. Jim saw another small room very similar to his own room, but then his eyes focused on a bed on which someone with short dark hair was lying. Was it really Susan?

Another door opened and Sister MacElroy came into the room

"Ah, there you are, Mr. Sandy," she said in a kindly voice. "Would you like to sit down on this chair beside your wife's bed? Do you feel that your giddiness is passing now?"

"Yes, it is passing, thank you," said Jim as he sat down thankfully in the chair beside the bed. He saw as he did so that Susan seemed to be asleep. At any rate, her eyes were closed and she looked peaceful, but it was clear that she was in no way aware that he was sitting close beside her.

Sister MacElroy drew up another chair and sat down beside Jim, but for a moment she turned round to speak to the Staff Nurse, who was standing just behind them.

"Thank you, Staff, you may go now; I'll look after Mr. Sandy while he's in here with his wife. And then you'll bring him a cup of tea to his room in about five minutes? He won't be staying here any longer than that."

"Yes, Sister," said the Staff Nurse.

"Yes, I can only let you stay here for a few minutes this time, Mr. Sandy, as your wife is under sedation," said Sister MacElroy.

"Under what?"

"The doctor has given her some medicine to make her sleepy because he doesn't want her to excite herself, or to be bothered by any ideas which might upset her; but it would be good for her to know that you're here. What's your first name, by the way, and your wife's first name?"

"I'm Jim, and my wife is Susan."

"Right!" Sister MacElroy now addressed the recumbent figure of Susan, lying in the bed. "Your husband, Jim, is here, Susan... Susan!"

Watching her carefully they saw Susan open her eyes, but her face was quite clear of expression. It was clear that she was not seeing them.

"You talk to her now, Jim," urged the Sister in a quiet voice.

"And you could take her by the hand - I think she should recognize you and respond."

It was a worrying moment for Jim, but he decided that he might as well trust the Sister. He leaned over the bed until his face was close to Susan's, and then, to his great delight, saw that she was watching him. Yes, the beginning of a smile was appearing on her face.

"Sue, darling, it's me, Jim! I'm here with you." He was speaking to his wife softly but urgently, and now he took her hand.

There was now no doubt about Susan's response; they both saw her smile broadly. Thank heavens! Jim was saying to himself with great relief. Sister MacElroy was looking over his shoulder, also watching carefully. Jim kissed Susan gently on the cheek.

"I love you, Sue, my darling!" he murmured. He stood where he was for a minute or two as if he was almost afraid that to release her from his close contact might plunge her back into unconsciousness, but he gradually loosened his grip on her hand.

Then he saw that her lips were moving as if she was speaking, or trying to speak to him. Susan's lips moved, but they could hear no sound coming from her mouth. Jim was suddenly worried again, and turned round quickly to find out what Sister MacElroy thought about it.

"Don't worry!" she said at once. "She will probably soon remember how to speak, but I expect that it would encourage her if you were to talk to her again."

Jim took hold of his wife's hand again and spoke her name softly, and then again a few seconds later a little more loudly. Susan had closed her eyes but, on hearing Jim's voice, she opened them again.

Then she found her voice.

"Jim?" Susan's voice was quiet, but distinct, and Jim was thrilled to hear her speak again.

"Yes, Sue darling?"

"Where am I?" She spoke slowly, her words slightly separated.

"In hospital. We're both in hospital while they're looking after us here."

"In hospital," repeated Susan quietly. She did not say any more.

He realized that she seemed perfectly content to know that she was in hospital, and did not want to talk at the moment.

"I think we'd better let her sleep for a while now," said Sister MacElroy. "Remember, Jim, that your wife is under sedation; she should be sleepy now." She signed to Jim to come with her.

Jim, however, when he had stood up again, took one last look at his wife, lying on that bed. "She looks very peaceful," he remarked.

"Yes, I think she is very peaceful," said the Sister. "I don't think that she is feeling any pain anywhere. We've examined her carefully, you know, but we found no injuries of any kind, internal or external, on her."

"So she's only suffered a stroke?" said Jim. "But that's bad enough, isn't it?"

"Yes, of course it is. Any stroke, even a mild one, is a serious medical event. But don't worry about it too much. I'm fairly sure that your wife's chances of recovery are quite good but, having said that, we don't know yet what the extent of any paralysis may be."

"Paralysis?"

"Yes, paralysis down one side of the body usually occurs following a stroke. Your wife had a small blood clot in the right-hand side of her brain, which may mean that the left-hand side of her body has been to some extent affected; but we can't assess that properly until she feels ready to start to try moving about."

"But when will that be?" asked Jim.

"Oh, quite soon, I should think," said the Sister. "Probably even by later this evening, or tomorrow. But I think that we can be reasonably optimistic about your wife's chances of regaining any lost mobility, Mr. Sandy. We have a good Physiotherapy Department in this hospital where we can help stroke patients to gradually regain the use of paralysed muscles."

"Well, that sounds quite promising, I suppose," said Jim doubtfully. He knew that he was being urged to feel optimistic about Susan's chances of making a good recovery, but he could not really believe that anything would cure her if it should turn out that she had been left severely paralysed by the stroke. And what are the chances of that anyway? he wondered gloomily as he returned to his bed, where he found a cup of tea waiting for him.

*

Jim was not expecting to see any visitors that evening, and he was certainly not expecting any pleasant surprises. His first visitor of that evening had been a police constable, who had been shown into his room by Sister MacElroy about an hour after he had left Susan's bedside. Later on, even before the constable had finished questioning him, a second visitor had been announced for him.

Lying on the bed, he had fallen into a pleasantly drowsy state – almost he had fallen asleep – when the policeman had been shown into his room. Immediately he had felt agitated and upset, but he need not have been worried. The constable, who had sat down on a chair at the bedside to talk to him, had immediately adopted a friendly tone, so that Jim had soon realized that he had come to see him only in order to try to help him. He had gathered that he was the regular constable resident at the Police House in Balallan village which, by pure luck, had been no more than twenty yards away from the site of their car crash. He had been the first person to arrive on the scene, he had explained, and had at once used his radio to call for the ambulance which had whisked them off to the hospital. Having asked Jim a number of preliminary questions – his name, his wife's name, their address, and so on – the policeman had asked Jim where they had been going when the car had crashed.

"We had been going to a house called Glen Tolsta Cottage," Jim had remembered. It's about eight miles the other side of Stornoway. We know the people who live there, you see, so we were going to stay there tonight and tomorrow night; and then we were going to go home to Dorset on Monday – but, of course, we won't be able to do that now."

The constable had then asked him whether he had yet been able to contact anyone by telephone to explain what had happened and to discuss the changes that would be necessary to their travel plans. Jim had told him that, yes, a telephone had been brought to him some time earlier, and he had rung up Mrs. MacAllan at Glen Tolsta Cottage to tell her what had happened. "I told her that Sue would have to stay in hospital for quite some time, so she certainly would not be coming to Glen Tolsta Cottage, but I said that I wasn't sure yet where I would be tonight. I told her that I would ring her up again later when I'd asked whether I'd be allowed to stay here tonight, or not."

The interview was concluded with the policeman asking questions about the car and the precise circumstances of the accident, but Jim told him that he could remember nothing whatever beyond the point where he had seen Susan's body suddenly slump forwards as she had let go of the steering wheel. The constable wrote in his notebook. The door opened, and Sister MacElroy's head appeared round the door.

"Excuse me, constable, but have you nearly finished interviewing Mr. Sandy?" she asked. "I have a lady here who wants to see him, but she will wait, of course, until you've finished with him."

"I have very nearly finished, Sister," said the constable. "If you would give us just two or three more minutes, please - no more than that - I'll have completed my questions."

He was as good as his word, and two minutes later the constable was putting away his notebook and pen in a pocket of his tunic. He stood up and smiled pleasantly.

"Well, that's it, Mr. Sandy; and thank you for your co-operation.

I'll be on my way now as you have another visitor waiting to see you, I believe. And may I wish you and your wife all the best, and a good recovery!"

"Oh, thank you!" said Jim, who had hardly been listening to what the constable had been saying. Who, he wondered, could this lady visitor possibly be who wanted to see him now?

He shook hands with the constable, who then left the room, closing the door behind him. There was, however, no time for him to go on wondering who his second visitor could possibly be. The door opened again, and in came Sister MacElroy.

"Here's another visitor for you, Mr. Sandy," she said with an enigmatic smile. "Come in, please, Mrs. Burton!"

"Samantha!" gasped Jim in amazement. He was so astonished to see the tall, good-looking, fair-haired lady who had followed the

Sister into his room that he almost fell backwards onto the bed, but managed to check himself.

"Hello, Jim!" said Samantha, smiling at him for a moment. She had come into the room looking very serious, without the slightest hint of a smile.

"However did you get here, Sam?"

"I'll tell you in a minute," said Samantha, "when we've talked about more important things. How are you, Jim; and how is poor Sue now?"

"I'm all right, really," said Jim. "So far as I know the only thing that's happened to me was that I had this bang on the side of my head - "he put a hand up to the sticking plaster on his temple" - which left me with concussion and then a nasty headache when I was conscious again. But poor Sue has had a stroke. I suppose you know that, Sam?"

"Yes, I know that. Aunt Mave told me what had happened after you'd rung her up."

"Your Aunt Mavis? I didn't know you were staying with her, Sam."

"No, but I wasn't staying with her until yesterday. It was yesterday evening when I arrived at Glen Tolsta Cottage."

"Just you, Sam?"

"Oh, yes, just me. Roger couldn't come because of his work. You see, Jim, the idea was that I was going to give you and Sue a nice little surprise this evening when you arrived at Glen Tolsta, and found me there. But then, about an hour ago, the telephone rang, and it was you ringing up from here to say that Sue had had a stroke, and would have to stay in hospital for quite a while. I felt so shocked when Aunt Mave told me about it that at first I could simply hardly believe it.

Then Aunt Mave said that we'd better come in the car straight away to the hospital to find out how bad Sue's condition is, so she brought me in - and here I am."

"Oh, yes... but where is your aunt now, Sam?"

"She's waiting for me in the big lounge by the main entrance because she said that they would only allow one visitor at a time to see Susan. So I left her there while I went round to the A. and E.

Department; and when I got there I asked at the desk where Lady Susan Sandy was, but the person behind the desk wasn't sure, so she said I'd better go to Sister MacElroy's office, and ask there, and she gave me directions to find the way there along various passages. Well, I found the office all right, and luckily Sister MacElroy was there, so I told her what I wanted. She said, was it Jim Sandy's wife, who'd had a stroke, that I was looking for? I said, Yes, it was; but then she said that she couldn't let me see her now because she was asleep and she didn't want her to be woken up. I gathered, though, that you'd been allowed to see her briefly, and that they don't think that her condition now is all that serious – which comforted me just a little, I suppose – but I wish I could have seen her all the same."

"I expect they'll let you see her tomorrow, Sam," said Jim.

"Oh, yes, I'm sure they will. They'll let us both come and visit her tomorrow. Sister said that, as tomorrow's Sunday, visiting time is the whole afternoon, starting from two o' clock, right up to eight o' clock. And Sue should have moved by then out of A. and E. into a ward somewhere else. We'll have to ask at the desk by the main entrance where to go when we arrive."

"So I ought to come with you to visit Sue tomorrow afternoon, Sam? But that means that I'd better be at Glen Tolsta Cottage tonight, as we'd originally planned?"

"Oh, yes, it does definitely mean that," said Samantha. "Aunt Mave is expecting you, so we're all going to go back to Glen Tolsta Cottage together when we leave here. You'd better have a word with Sister first, Jim, before we go, but I know it's going to be all right because I've already spoken to her about it. I gathered that they'll be glad enough, really, not to have to find a place for you here as there'll be no need for you to be kept in here any longer."

"Oh, I see. So I suppose we might as well go now, seeing that your aunt is waiting for us in that lounge?"

"Yes, I think we might as well go now. Do you feel all right to travel in the car now, Jim, or would you prefer to have a rest and wait a while?"

"No, I feel quite all right to travel now," said Jim. "My headache is really not bad at all now – it's almost gone."

"Right, we'd better go and find Sister, and ask her permission for you to come with me now. At least, you stay here, Jim, while I'll go and see whether I can find her."

Samantha was only out of the room for a minute or two before she returned with Sister MacElroy. Jim, meanwhile, was feeling too stunned by the latest turn of events to think coherently about anything. The totally unexpected appearance of Samantha on the scene had certainly been another shock to his system, but he had to admit to himself that at least it had been a pleasant shock. Yes, I'm really very glad that Sam's come, he said to himself. She's always so cool and calm and capable of dealing with just about anything!

The door opened, and in came Samantha with Sister MacElroy.

"Right, so you're off now, Mr. Sandy?" said the Sister. "But you'll be back tomorrow afternoon, I expect?"

"Yes, I'm going now, if I'm allowed to?" said Jim.

"Yes, it's perfectly all right for you to be discharged if you want to go now. How does your head feel now?"

"It feels much better, thank you, Sister."

"That's good! But if you come to visit your wife tomorrow you won't see me, by the way, as I have a day off work on Sundays. I'll be back here on Monday morning; but Mr. Drummond, the consultant, will be doing his round of the ward on Monday morning so he will, of course, examine your wife and make his prognosis; and then in the afternoon at visiting time I could tell you about it."

"Thank you, Sister... but you couldn't let me go in and see Sue now, quickly, just to say good-bye?"

But Sister MacElroy was shaking her head.

"No, I'm sorry, Mr. Sandy, but I'm not going to allow that as your wife is asleep now, and I think she should be allowed to sleep, while she is under sedation, for as long as she needs to, without being disturbed. But when she wakes up we'll certainly tell her that you'll be coming tomorrow afternoon. Is that all right?"

"Oh, that's all right," said Jim; but he said it doubtfully. What if Sue's condition were to worsen during the night? If that were to happen she might urgently need to see him, but he would not be there. However, it seemed as if the Sister had read his thoughts.

"But don't you be worried about your wife in the meantime, Mr. Sandy. The doctor said that her condition is stable, and that means that another stroke is most unlikely; but, of course, if anything untoward *did* happen we would contact you straight away. But to do that we would, of course, need to know the telephone number of the place where you're going to be staying."

"Oh, good heavens!" said Jim. "I haven't got a clue what it is!" He looked hopefully at Samantha.

"I can't remember either what the Glen Tolsta telephone number is," said Samantha. "But it doesn't matter. Aunt Mave will obviously know her own number, and we can ask her now when we go round to the main entrance."

"I'll come with you, if you like?" suggested Sister MacElroy helpfully.

With the Sister leading the way along various passages and down a flight of stairs they presently found themselves in the large lounge by the main entrance to the hospital. When they had found Mavis MacAllan, and Sister MacElroy had made a note of the telephone number of Glen Tolsta Cottage, and they had said good-bye to her, they went out into the car park outside the hospital buildings. Mavis MacAllan had already expressed her shock to Jim on hearing the news about Susan, but now, as she approached her car, she thought of something else.

"By the way, Jim, what happened to the car you were driving - or at least I think you said that Susan was driving it?"

"I don't know," said Jim. "The policeman I was talking to said that they've towed it away to the main police station in Stornoway, and that they're going to keep it there at least for the rest of the weekend. And he said that it looked as if they would consider it a write-off as the left-hand side of the bonnet has been badly smashed in."

"Oh, my goodness, but that sounds dreadful! And yet you say that Sue is quite uninjured?"

"Yes, she really is uninjured. It's quite remarkable, but there doesn't seem to be a cut or a bruise on her. I know that because they allowed me to see her - briefly."

"And have you seen her, Sam?"

"No, they wouldn't let me see her today. Sister said that she was asleep, and she must be allowed to sleep until she wakes up."

"Well, here we are, my dears," said Mavis MacAllan. They had come to the place where she had parked her car. "But, Jim, would it be a good idea, do you think, to call at the police station now, before we go home? I dare say you could do with some things taken out of your hired car?"

"Oh, yes, I do need some of my things out of that car," said Jim. "Thank you, Mrs. MacAllan. In fact, I might as well take out all of my baggage, and Sue's, as we won't be able to use the car any more, even if we wanted to."

Mrs. MacAllan drove her car round to the police station in the middle of the town and parked it in the yard behind the building.

"Oh, gosh!" said Jim when a police officer showed them the car which they had been driving earlier that afternoon.

"You *have* been lucky, really!" said Samantha as they inspected the front of the damaged car. The lights were smashed, the bumper was twisted, and the radiator was well dented; but all the damage, they saw, was to the nearside of the car only.

Jim knew well enough what Samantha meant, and had to agree with her; and he knew that Susan had been especially lucky as she had received no injuries. Yes, she has been lucky, he told himself, in spite of this dreadful thing that's happened to her, but I can only hope that she'll recover, and not be completely paralysed.

CHAPTER NINETEEN

"Your wife is in Physiotherapy now," said the nurse behind the desk, when Jim had explained that he had come to visit his wife, Lady Susan Sandy.

"Oh!" said Jim. "So we'd better wait here, or else come back here later today?"

"Oh, no," said the nurse. "It'll be quite all right for you to go and see her now - in fact, it would be a good thing for you to be with her now, Mr. Sandy, as it will perhaps give her some encouragement. Do you know the way to the Physiotherapy Room?"

"We've no idea where it is!"

"It's just along the corridor from here. If you'd like to follow me I'll take you there."

The nurse lead the way along the corridor, passing various doors to the right and the left, and then opened a pair of double doors at the end of the corridor. They entered a large room.

It was Monday afternoon, and soon after two o' clock. Jim and Samantha had arrived at the hospital, hoping to visit Susan. This time Mavis MacAllan was not with them. Samantha, reckoning on having to stay in Lewis for at least a week, had hired a car so that she and Jim could go to the hospital to visit Susan when they wanted to, without the necessity of having to ask Mavis MacAllan for a lift every time. They had asked at the reception desk by the main entrance where they would find Susan, and had been told the name of the ward where her bed was, and how to find the way there. They had followed their instructions, found the right ward, and had then asked again at the nurses' station where they might find Lady Sandy.

Sister MacElroy had risen to her feet immediately, a frown on her face, on hearing the double doors being opened, but when she saw who was entering the room the frown left her face.

"I've brought Mr. Sandy and Mrs. Burton, if you don't mind, Sister," said the nurse rather apologetically. "You said it would be all right to bring them in here if they came to visit Lady Sandy?"

"Yes, I did say that," said the Sister. "Thank you, Nurse!" Jim noticed that she was smiling at him. "Good afternoon, you two! Now, I was just explaining to your wife, Mr. Sandy, the principles and methods of the treatment we're going to use in here, and I'll just repeat it briefly for your benefit. Do, please, have a seat on the sofa, both of you."

"Thank you, Sister," said Samantha after waiting for a moment for Jim to speak first. She noticed that his face was looking very pale, and wondered what was the matter with him. I suppose he's feeling very shocked at seeing poor Sue looking so helpless, sitting in that wheelchair, she thought.

Jim was in a state of shock, but it was not because of Susan. He had received a nasty shock as soon as he had seen what the interior of that room was like. He saw that the wall opposite to the doors through which they had entered was almost completely covered by all sorts of pictures, large and small; and on the instant his memory went back to that upsetting dream. Yes, what he was now seeing could be nothing other than that strange room he had seen in his dream, the room with one wall covered with pictures. It's just as I remembered it, he thought, but the next moment he realized that his thoughts were becoming confused. No, he had dreamed of that room *before* he had ever seen it in waking life – and whatever could that mean? This was indeed a shocking turn of events! he thought.

He felt a hand on his shoulder and looked up to see that Sister MacElroy was looking carefully into his face.

"Do you feel all right, Mr. Sandy? You're looking rather shocked?" The Sister's voice was quiet, but calmly reassuring, and Jim found that he was feeling better. "That's right, you sit down there.

Would you like me to fetch you a glass of water?"

"Yes, please," said Jim weakly. He was indeed feeling somewhat light-headed from the shock of finding himself in the room of that dream, but he now realized that he was standing in front of the sofa.

He sank down onto it thankfully without another moment's delay.

Sister MacElroy was out of the room for less than a minute, but in that short time Jim's already shocked mind had been assaulted by yet another uncomfortable and worrying thought. He had just remembered how the ghost of John Dalmane had unexpectedly appeared one night in the Banqueting Hall of the Castle, and, in particular, how the ghost had seemed to pause a moment behind Susan's chair. Could that possibly have been a warning that she was to suffer a stroke? he now found himself wondering. But fortunately (perhaps) there was no time to worry about that now. The Sister had returned with a glass of water in her hand.

She handed it to Jim, who drank from it at once. He made an effort to sound as if he felt all right again.

"Thank you! I'm sorry about that, Sister, but I'm feeling much better now."

"It's all right; you needn't be sorry," said the Sister. "I understand. I know that it's come as a shock to you to see your wife looking so ill when you are accustomed to seeing her as a fit and healthy person, but you really needn't worry about her now. She's actually making good progress, although it may not seem like that to you. I must tell you that Mr. Drummond, the consultant, came in to see her this morning, and when he had examined her thoroughly he said that the prognosis was good."

"You mean, he was satisfied with her progress?"

"Yes, exactly so; and he said that we should be looking at sending her home in about a fortnight – if the course of physiotherapy goes well."

"A fortnight!" said Jim in horror.

"Oh, yes, it will need at least a fortnight until we are likely to see any tangible results from the course of intensive physiotherapy that we're beginning this afternoon." Sister MacElroy then went on to explain that Susan's stroke had paralysed the left-hand side of her body from the neck downwards although, luckily, she could still turn her head. Then she went on to explain that Mr. Drummond, having assessed the effects of the stroke, had concluded that these effects should in time, and with plenty of physiotherapy and determination be reversible; she should find that the use of muscles now paralysed would slowly come back to her. That, said Sister MacElroy, was precisely the goal they were aiming for. Then she turned to Susan, sitting quietly in her wheelchair beside the sofa, and addressed her directly.

"That's right, isn't it, Susan? You're going to do plenty of exercises while you're staying here with us so that you can get better, and learn how to start moving about again?"

"Oh, yes, Sister," said Susan quietly.

"I'm sorry that we've been ignoring you while we've been talking about you, but, you see, your husband, Jim, is here, and I've been explaining to him what Mr. Drummond said, and what it means."

"That's all right," said Susan. "I understand what you've been saying so far." She turned her head and saw that Jim was anxiously watching her, and a smile lit up her face.

Jim stood up and went over to the wheelchair to greet his wife.

"Sue, darling, it *is* good to see you!" he said tenderly as he bent down to kiss her.

"Oh, Jim, darling...!" murmured Susan, raising her right hand to touch her husband on the shoulder, while her left arm hung limp and motionless over the side of the wheelchair.

It was for Jim a moment of very mixed emotions as they kissed briefly. He felt a sudden great rush of love for Susan, heightened because of her enfeebled state, but at the same time other quite contrary thoughts and feelings were passing rapidly through him. In particular, the effects of the double shock he had so recently received were still reverberating through his mind and body. He returned to his seat on the sofa and saw that Sister MacElroy was smiling at him.

"That's good, Jim!" she said. That was very good... but now shall we get on with Susan's treatment? No, stay here!" Jim had made a move as if to stand up again, but the Sister stopped him with a wave of her hand. She went on to explain what the first stage of the treatment would be.

"We're beginning by looking at all these pictures that are on the wall; and in fact, Susan, you had just chosen your favourite picture before your husband came in, I think?"

"Yes, I think so," said Susan rather doubtfully.

"Oh, yes, you were telling me before how hard it was to make up your mind about choosing a favourite one."

"It is hard," said Susan. "There are two that I like almost equally, and it's hard to choose between them. I love that little painting of Adam and Eve and the Apple Tree - I suppose they are meant to be Adam and Eve?"

Would you care to point to it?"

Using her right hand, Susan pointed to the picture she had referred to. Sister MacElroy was watching her carefully.

"That one - the little picture just above and to the left of the very big one in the bottom row," said Susan.

"Yes, I believe they are Adam and Eve. And your other choice?"

"That would have to be the very big one – and I think that I would choose that one as my favourite if I had to narrow my choice down to one."

"For any particular reason?"

"I really love the atmosphere in that painting. The light in that sky is simply fascinating – the contrast between the pale blue sky and that swirling mass of dark clouds – I love it! But I can't quite make out what's going on in the foreground, although there seem to be some figures there? Perhaps my eyesight has been affected by the stroke?"

"I don't think it has," said Sister MacElroy. "Would you like me to move you a little nearer to that picture to have a closer look at it?"

"Oh, yes please, Sister, if you would."

Sister MacElroy pushed Susan's wheelchair closer to the picture that interested her so that she could study some small figures in the foreground. Jim and Samantha were also staring at that painting, but Jim was mainly preoccupied with trying to remember whether that particular picture, or for that matter any of the others, had appeared to him in that dream. Luckily I can't remember anything at all about any of the dream pictures! he thought.

"I can see now what's going on there," said Susan. "It's some sort of agricultural work: there's a cart there, and a cart–horse between the shafts, and some men busy doing something – probably they're gathering something?" She looked round towards Jim and Samantha on the sofa as if to ask what they thought about it.

"I think it's a really fascinating painting," said Samantha. Yes, I entirely agree with you, Sue; and I particularly like the bare trees in that wood: it must be a winter scene. But what do you think, Jim?"

"What?" said Jim, startled out of his reverie. "Sorry, I was thinking about something else. Yes, I love that picture too – I do really!"

"I like it so much that I'd like to be able to take it back home," said Susan. "It would look good hanging somewhere in the Castle - probably in the Hall, or on the main stairs - but it would have to be put into a nice gilded frame, of course. But do you know who painted it Sister?"

"Well, actually I've no idea who the arist was," said Sister MacElroy. looking up from a notebook in which she had been busily writing some notes. "I must confess that I'm not particularly interested myself in that sort of thing. But won't he have signed his name somewhere on the painting?" She came close up to the painting, beside Susan's wheelchair, and began to scan the bottom of it carefully.

The painting was a winter country scene, and it certainly was, as Susan had said, very atmospheric. Much of the middle ground of the picture was occupied by a wood on a gently sloping hillside, while in the foreground there were men gathering something with a cart and a cart-horse. To the left of this there was some water which looked like either the sea or a lake.

"There's a sort of smudge here which looks as if it might be someone's initials," said the Sister, pointing with a finger. "But I'll tell you what: I'll ask Matron about it when I next see her - and that should be later this evening."

"Is she interested in art?"

"She's *very* interested in art, Susan; but, as I said, it's not really my thing at all. She's sure to know more about it than I do." The Sister paused, and looked at her watch. "Yes, I thought so. I'm sorry, but I must be going now as I've work to see to in another department; but I'll ask Staff Nurse to come in to continue your physiotherapy."

"Oh, thank you, Sister," said Susan.

Sister MacElroy then went on to explain that the rest of the physiotherapy session would be given over to massage and some gentle exercises to encourage the unblocking of paralysed muscles. She explained that, as they had guessed, the initial part of the session, studying the pictures, was meant to encourage stroke patients to think and to talk and to stimulate their interest generally in things outside of themselves.

"And I must say it's gone extremely well- exceptionally well – and I'm sure you'll be pleased, Jim, to know that your wife's ability to speak normally is in no way impaired."

"Yes, of course. I'm feeling very pleased about that," said Jim.

"Ought we to leave now, Sister, as you're going?" asked Samantha. "We don't want to get in the way!"

"Oh, no, there's no need at all for you to leave now, unless you want to," said Sister MacElroy. "If you'd like to stay here until the end of the session I'm sure that you would continue to give Lady Sandy support and encouragement. But I must go now. I'll see you again tomorrow, or the next day, I expect?"

"Oh, yes - probably tomorrow!" said Samantha.

Sister MacElroy hurried out of the room and closed the double doors behind her.

"Well, are we going to stay until the end of this session?" said Jim, looking at Samantha.

"Oh, yes, I think we might as well stay," said Samantha, "as Sister thinks it would be a good thing for us to stay here. But what do you think, Sue?"

"I don't mind whether you stay, or not," said Susan unhelpfully.

"We'll stay here!" said Samantha decisively. We certainly will as we've come here to visit you, Sue. And don't worry, Jim, I'm sure the physiotherapy won't be too boring for us."

"Oh, well..." began Jim; but there was no time for him to say anything more as at that moment the doors opened again and the Staff Nurse, whom they had seen before, bustled into the room.

For the rest of the physiotherapy session Jim hardly spoke at all. He very quickly lost interest in what the nurse was doing with Susan as his shocked and worried mind wandered off into a private world of introspection. However, well before the time had come to say good-bye to Susan he had decided that he simply *must* talk with Samantha about that dream when they returned to Glen Tolsta. Yes, I'll tell her everything about it, he told himself, as I should think I'd go mad if I didn't!

At the end of the physiotherapy session walked back with Susan and the nurse to the ward where her bed was. The Staff Nurse pushed the wheelchair, and Jim went ahead to hold the door open for the passage of the wheelchair. Half a minute later they were back at her bedside.

"No, I'll lift her myself!" said the nurse when Jim asked whether he could help her.

In no time at all, it seemed, Susan was lifted out of the wheelchair and into the bed. Jim could not help marvelling at the nurse's strength.

"Visiting time's over now!" said the nurse, with a glance at her watch. "You can come back this evening if you like, at six o' clock, or else you could come back tomorrow at two o' clock for afternoon visiting."

"Come on, Jim," said Samantha, "we must leave now as they want to see the last of us for this time - we must keep to the rules! Good-bye for now, Sue! We'll see you again tomorrow."

"Good-bye, Sue, darling!" said Jim, bending down to give her a quick kiss.

"Sue seemed much more talkative today than she did yesterday, I thought," said Samantha as she walked with Jim down the passage leading away from the ward where Susan was.

"Yes, I thought so too," said Jim. "It's certainly encouraging to know that her powers of reasoning and speech are not affected."

"Talking and thinking about those pictures has helped her a lot.

I hope that Sister will remember to ask Matron about that big country scene that she particularly liked."

"I expect she'll remember," said Jim. And I certainly won't be forgetting about those pictures very soon either! he thought.

CHAPTER TWENTY

Jim had hardly said a word since he had climbed into the car but, as they left the outskirts of Stornoway behind them, he decided that it was the right time to mention the matter that was pressing on his mind.

"Sam," he said, "there's something I want to talk to you about, but I'd like you to keep it a secret; I don't want Sue to know anything about it."

"Oh, well," said Samantha, "I don't mind you sharing a secret with me so long as it's not something that Sue really ought to know about."

"No, it isn't anything like that; it really isn't. It's a dream that I had."

"A worrying dream?"

"Yes. There were some parts of it that were very worrying indeed."

"Oh, really? But when did this happen, Jim? Was it last night, or did it happen at some earlier time?"

"I can't remember now exactly when it happened, but it was while we were staying in our cottage in Tarbert. I think it was during the first night that we were there, and I'll tell you everything about it that I can remember, Sam."

"But *can* you really remember much of it now, Jim? ? It's over a week now since you dreamed it, if it was on your first night in

Tarbert, and I usually can't remember my dreams after about a minute or two after waking up – if I remember them at all, that is! But I suppose that this dream must have been very striking in some way?"

"It was – it was a very striking dream indeed – in fact, some of it was really bizarre." Jim paused a moment, his thoughts temporarily distracted by the sight of a beach of bright sand close to the road; they had passed the village of Tong and were now seeing the Coll Sands, glowing in the strong afternoon sunlight.

Samantha, driving the car, waited patiently for him to continue his narrative, but realized that he might need to pause to remember some of the dream details.

"You see, it was like this," continued Jim presently. "I saw a room, Sam; a big room and a rather strange room, and I was there in it, and in front of me there was a wall that was absolutely covered with pictures – just like the wall of that Physiotherapy Room where we've just been."

"Oh, really?"

"But don't you see, Sam? I saw that wall covered with pictures in my dream several days *before* I'd ever actually seen it – if it was the wall of the Physiotherapy room that I saw in my dream."

"Oh, good heavens, yes; I see what you mean, Jim! You're saying that you seemed to be seeing into the future in that dream?"

"Yes, it did really seem to be like that!"

"Well, that really is amazing, Jim, if it is as you say it is!"

Samantha was silent for a moment, considering the problem. "But are you sure about it?" she continued. "Can you remember what the rest of the room looked like in your dream?"

"Oh, gosh, I don't know whether I can!" said Jim. Now he was silent for a little while as he tried to recall more details of the strange room of his dream. "Well, I can remember a few more details about that dream room," he said, "but I dare say that you might be right all the same, Sam; it probably wasn't the same room

- I mean, the room in my dream probably wasn't the Physiotherapy Room, in spite of the pictures.

"Was there a sofa in your dream? We were sitting on a sofa when Sue was looking at those pictures."

"Yes, there was a sofa, but I wasn't sitting on it; and that reminds me, Sam: there was another strange twist in the dream at that point. I saw Claire Walker sitting on a sofa."

"Who?"

"She's our tenant at the house in Roehampton, but I don't think you've ever met her?"

"No, I haven't, but I know now who you mean. But do go on, Jim."

"Well, I saw Claire Walker sitting on this sofa, but the odd thing was - she was stark naked from the waist upwards! Yes, you may well smile, Sam!"

"Oh, was she, indeed? That sounds interesting!"

"Yes, it certainly was!"

"Well, Jim, I think the meaning of *that* part of your dream is clear enough to me!"

"Don't laugh at me, Sam! I'm just telling you everything that I can remember from the dream. I could have passed over that particular detail, you know."

"But you didn't! Anyway, I suppose you could say of that part of your dream that it was nothing more than a typical male fantasy? No doubt Roger has that kind of dream from time to time, but whether it's me naked that he sees then, or some other woman, I really don't know and, frankly, I wouldn't like to ask him about such things. They're best kept private, aren't they? But look here, Jim, I'm sorry, but we're getting away from your account of your dream. Was there more, or did it end with that delightful vision of Claire Walker with most of her clothes removed?"

"Oh, no, there was a good deal more of the dream after that. The next thing that happened was, I think, that Claire told me to follow her, so I followed her out of that room into the open air.

"What! Do you mean to say that Claire simply walked out just as she was- almost in the nude?"

"Oh, no!" said Jim, who was becoming almost irritated by Samantha's flippant tone and frequent interruptions to his narrative. She's not taking this seriously! he complained to himself. "She quickly put some clothes on before she went out," he continued aloud. "I was forgetting that bit. And then she told me that we were going to go out to find Rachel Connor, and that she was going to tell me what I had to do to break my obsession with her. You know about that, don't you, Sam?"

"Your crush on Rachel Connor? Oh, yes, Jim, I know about that.

But do go on." Samantha was now no longer smiling, and her tone sounded serious again.

Jim related the rest of his story, telling of how Claire had ordered him to strike Rachel, and of how he had done so, and of the sad consequences of hitting her.

Samantha remained silent for a little while after Jim had finished giving her his account of his dream.

"Well, Jim," she said presently, "it was an odd dream, certainly, and thank you so much for telling me about it; but, as for the meaning of it - or at least the meaning of the Rachel Connor part of it - I'm not at all sure. I'll tell you what: If you'll give me some time to think over what you've told me then perhaps we could talk about it again later?"

"That's fine!" said Jim. "I realize that you can't really think about that now while your concentrating on driving this car."

"That's right, Jim," said Samantha. A minute later, however, they reached the place where the small road which lead down to the cottage diverged from the main road. "Here we are," she said. "You know, it always surprises me how soon one seems to get here after leaving behind the last outskirts of Stornoway."

At Glen Tolsta Cottage they were greeted by Mavis MacAllan, who told them that she had just had a telephone call from Susan's mother, Lady Walton.

"She told me that a few minutes earlier she had rung up the hospital, and had been allowed to have a few minutes to chat with Susan herself which, of course, must have been a lovely thing for both of them."

"But it must have been just after we left the hospital when Lady Walton rang up?" said Jim. "Would you say that was about twenty minutes ago, Sam?"

"Yes, it must have been about twenty minutes ago when we left," said Samantha.

"Well, I gathered that what Lady Walton wanted to suggest was that Susan might like to go and stay with her for a week or two after she's discharged from hospital, and before she goes home to Rhodes Castle."

"That's a good idea!" said Samantha. "And was Sue keen to take up that offer?"

"Well, apparently she wasn't," said her aunt. "Susan seemed to be very doubtful about that idea, so I think that instead Lady Walton is now thinking of coming presently to Rhodes Castle... But let's go in and have some tea now. I'm sure that you two must be ready for some tea after your hospital visiting?"

"Thank you, Aunt Mave," said Samantha. "A cup of tea would be nice now!"

"Thank you!" said Jim.

They had been standing outside the house, but now Mavis MacAllan lead the way into her kitchen, where Jim was cheered up by seeing that several good things had already been laid on the kitchen table, which was covered by a white table cloth.

"Do take a seat at the table, my dears," said Mavis MacAllan kindly, "and we'll have tea as soon as the kettle has boiled."

The table was laid for three people; Ian MacAllan was not at home. Jim remembered that he had been told that he worked in a fishermens' co-operative (whatever that was) somewhere in the west of the island; no doubt he would return from his day's work there in the evening. Meanwhile, the sight of Mrs. MacAllan's home-made cake and sandwiches looked appetising, and made Jim feel hungry; but, all the same, he said very little while they were seated at the table, having their tea. There were many worrying thoughts weighing heavily on his mind. For one thing, he knew that he was upset and worried by the thought that time was again passing very slowly now that they had left Susan behind in the hospital. Yesterday was a dreadfully boring day, he thought – except for the time when we were visiting Sue. And this morning was almost as bad, and again this evening there'll be nothing to do – unless I go for a walk with Sam again – so I suppose that time will pass only very slowly. Then another thought struck him. But thank heavens I've got Sam staying here! If she wasn't here I don't know *how* i could pass the time, as I don't really know the MacAllans. Gosh, I hope that Sam doesn't decide that she has to return home before they discharge Sue from hospital!

*

Susan put down the book she was trying to read on the bed as a smile of pleasure and surprise lit up her face as she saw who was coming into the ward. Jim waved a cheery hand as soon as he saw her; and Susan, after a moment's delay to make sure that it really was Jim and Samantha that she was seeing, waved back to him.

"Well, well, what a surprise!" she said happily. "I thought you said that you weren't coming back until tomorrow?"

"Yes, we did say that, Sue," said Samantha, "but we've changed our minds. We thought we'd give you a surprise visit this evening. And here we are!"

"It's a lovely surprise!" said Susan, and Jim knew that she meant it.

"Sue, darling," he said, "Mrs. MacAllan told us that your Mum had rung up the hospital just after we'd gone, and that you'd been talking with her."

"Yes, that's right; i've had a word with um on the telephone," said Susan. "That's it, Sam, you can sit here." She indicated the chair that was positioned by her bedside table. "And you could get yourself a chair from somewhere in the ward, darling - I think there are plenty of them - and bring it over here."

"Well, it is nice to see you again!" said Susan when Jim had returned to the bedside with a chair. "And Mum's coming to stay with us in the Castle some time after I've been discharged and got back home myself. She actually wanted me to come to Soken Hall, but I said I thought it would be better this time if she came to us, and so we agreed on that."

"That's a good idea, Sue," said Samantha. "And I guess that Mr. Drummond would agree that that was a good idea too?"

"Well, when Mr. Drummond was talking with me this morning he asked where we lived, and I said we'd come from Rhodes Castle in Dorset. Then he asked how we'd come here, and how long it had taken, so I tried to remember how we'd made our journey up here, and I told him that it had been mostly by train, and that it had taken two or three days. Then he pointed out that he thought that it wouldn't be good for me to have to make another long slow journey like that in order to get back home. He suggested that we ought to speed up the travelling, and that the best way would be to fly from Stornoway Airport. He said that he knew there was a daily flight from Stornoway to Glasgow because he'd used it himself, and that we could probably change planes at Glasgow and fly on to London."

"We should have thought about that before," said Samantha. "By air would certainly be the best way to get you from here to London, if it can be arranged; and then taking the train for the rest of the journey. What do you think, Jim?"

"Yes, I agree with you, Sam, that we ought to fly from here - if we can get that arranged," said Jim. "So I think we'd better call at the airport tomorrow morning to see what we can find out."

They continued to chat for about another hour, mostly about Susan's medical condition, and the likely consequences it would make for future arrangements and plans; but when Jim suggested that they should leave before Susan became over tired Samantha readily agreed with him.

On their way back to Glen Tolsta Cottage their conversation soon turned again to the subject of Jim's dream

"I've been thinking over what you told me about that dream," said Samantha "and I think it's fairly clear to me now what it means - the part of the dream that concerned Rachel - assuming, that is, that it's right to interpret a meaning in it. Perhaps, though, it isn't? I should think that there are probably a good many dreams that people dream where there is no meaning at all to be deduced?"

"Oh, yes, I think that you're probably right there, Sam," said Jim. "But surely we could say that this dream must have a meaning? It was so unusual, and so vivid - and surely it was odd that I could still remember a good deal of it long after it was over?"

"Yes, I think there was a real meaning in this dream. I think it was telling you that you should be prepared to put up a fight against your infatuation with Rachel - you were physically fighting and struggling with her in the dream, weren't you?"

"Indeed I was."

"Well, Jim, I must say that I don't like that part of it. It seems like a warning to me. I think it could be your subconscious mind warning you that unless you are prepared to push Rachel right out of your life - even with some force, if necessary - you might even find yourself walking hand-in-hand with her at some time in the future. And that, you know, would mean that your marriage to Sue would be ruined!

Well... what do you think, Jim?"

"I'm afraid you're right, Sam," he said gloomily. "I've thought about it a lot too, and I've come to much the same sort of conclusion."

"Well, I'm no expert in this sort of thing. I dare say that Freud could have found out more meaning in your dream imagery than I could ever hope to find - especially in that bit about Claire!"

Jim, in spite of his worries, suddenly found that he was almost laughing at the reminder of his dream vision of the half-naked Claire Walker.

"Oh, Sam, don't tease me about that! I couldn't help it, you know."

"No, of course you couldn't; I realize that. But seriously, Jim, I think that your dream was warning you to expect serious trouble unless you can somehow manage to detach yourself emotionally from Rachel. But don't despair! I don't know what you can, or ought, to do about it, but I hope that you'll keep in touch with me; and I'll try to help and advise you, if I can."

"Do you really mean that, Sam?"

"Yes, of course I do. You can always come to talk with me any time you like, Jim, although I can't guarantee that I can always give you helpful advice - but I can try to do that."

"You're very kind to me, Sam!" said Jim.

CHAPTER TWENTY-ONE

The taxi bringing Jim and Susan from Sherborne station stopped outside the front door of Rhodes Castle. As it stopped they saw that Jack, the butler, and Samantha were coming out to greet them. Then, as if it was a well planned operation, they saw that more of the senior staff of the Castle were coming out to welcome them back home and to commiserate with Susan on being so suddenly struck down by a serious illness.

My goodness, Jack's made them all come out to welcome us back!" said Jim as Julia Garten, the Cook, came up to shake Susan's hand, and to say how pleased she was to see the mistress safely back at home. She was followed by Peter Ashcroft, the Head Gardener, and with him came a young woman with dark hair whom they had not seen before.

"Well, it's very nice to see everyone again here!" said Susan, when Jack had helped her to sit down in her wheelchair. "It was kind of you, Jack, to think of organizing a little welcoming party for me, and I appreciate the gesture; but, you know, I feel a little like Mr. Rochester in *Jane Eyre*, when he came back home and all his servants came out of the house to welcome him back."

Jack, the butler, laughed briefly.

"Ah, yes, m' Lady; I know what you mean!" he said; but Susan was doubtful as to whether he really knew the passage from Charlotte Bronte's novel to which she had referred.

The Head Gardener shook Susan's hand, and then the young woman with dark hair stepped boldly forward to introduce herself.

"Hello, my Lady, I'm Ailean Connor; and you've agreed that I can come to be interviewed for a gardening job under Mr. Ashcroft."

"Ah, so you're the daughter of our Guide, whom I've heard about via the butler. But I suppose your mother is busy at the moment?"

"Yes, I think she's busy conducting a tour of the Castle right now," said Ailean, "so she couldn't come out with us to welcome you."

"That's all right," said Susan. "And I'm sure you're welcome to come to work for us, Ailean, but, if you don't mind, we'll talk about that tomorrow, rather than now. Would you like to come along to the Estate Office at nine o' clock tomorrow morning so that Jim, or I, or both of us, can have a little chat with you?"

"Oh, yes, I'll do that; thank you, my Lady!" Ailean made a little curtsey to Susan but, before she left the group around her wheelchair to hurry after the Head Gardener (who was already stumping back towards his potting shed) she managed to catch Jim's eye, and to give him a meaningful look. Jim could not fail to notice the light that was shining in her dark eyes at that moment as she caught his eye, but nevertheless he felt unmoved by that unexpected moment of eye contact.

Up to the moment when Ailean Connor had introduced herself, Jim had had no room in his mind for any thoughts other than thoughts of Rachel. As the taxi had drawn nearer and nearer to the Castle he had felt the tension within him steadily increasing. He had remembered that returning to the Castle *could* mean that he was about to see Rachel again; but he could either be in for a big thrill or a real disappointment. By the time they had reached the Inner Lodge, and passed through the gateway to the Inner Drive, with the front door of the Castle all but in view, his state of tension had become almost unbearable. At the moment when Rachel's daughter, Ailean, appeared on the scene he was trying to reconcile himself to a grudging acceptance of his bitter disappointment. Rachel was definitely not there among the welcoming party. He was very disappointed, but at the same time he knew perfectly well that he ought to be feeling greatly pleased and relieved that Rachel was not there; he briefly remembered that dream again. As for Ailean: he had completely forgotten that she existed, and it came as a shock to him to be reminded of this fact.

His initial impression of Ailean was also something of a disappointment. He had assumed, since he had first heard about Ailean, that she would have fair or blonde hair like her mother, but the sight of her dark brown hair came as something of a shock to him. True, he saw before him an attractive girl – perhaps even a beautiful girl – but one who (at first glance, at least) did not seem to look at all like her beautiful mother. So she must have inherited more of her father's features than her mother's, he thought, as he noticed that she had very dark brown eyes, matching her hair. He also noticed in Ailean a figure that was quite different from her mother's. She had a tall, slim, athletic build and – what he noticed most – no sign of her mother's well rounded bust. He thought that she must be at least as tall as her mother, if not a little taller.

Jim was so lost in his thoughts that he had noticed that it was beginning to rain until he suddenly heard Susan's voice, saying, "Look here; I think we'd better go indoors now as it's just coming on to rain."

"Of course, my Lady," said Jack dutifully. "Now, when we come to the steps up to the front door would you like us to carry you up in your chair?"

"No, no!" said Susan. "I'm going to walk up those steps, using my two sticks. I've been practicing climbing stairs while I was in hospital, and I'm getting on quite well now!"

"I'm glad to hear it, m' Lady. So you'll be in your usual bedroom tonight, as you said you meant to be?"

"Yes, we're going to sleep there as usual. Good, that's the first step done all right!"

Susan was slowly ascending the flight of stone steps which lead up to the front door of the Castle, supporting herself on the two walking sticks which had been given to her, along with the wheelchair by the hospital. Jack was walking beside her, and Jim was coming along behind, and both of them were watching her carefully, ready to catch her if she looked like falling. The rain was no more than a drizzle, so that it was not seriously wetting them, but the sky looked dark and threatening.

Samantha had disappeared indoors with Cook, but now she reappeared in the doorway. In the end she had remained staying in Glen Tolsta Cottage almost until Susan was ready to be discharged from hospital, but she had travelled back to the Castle (by train) a few days before Jim and Susan had flown back to London.

"I'll bring that wheelchair in," she said. "We don't want it getting wet, and it looks as if it's going to pour down any minute now.

Anyway, tea's ready for us now in the Green Drawing Room."

"Thank you, Sam," said Susan.

Before he had come up the steps behind Susan, Jim had had time to look around and, in particular, to glance in the direction in which Ailean and the Head Gardener had gone; but there was sign of them.

Ailean will have to go home early today if it rains, he thought, unless Peter finds her something to do in the potting shed. He looked at his watch. It was just after four o' clock. I suppose she's reckoning to stay here until five o' clock, if it doesn't rain too heavily, he told himself, but of course she's free to go any time she wants to today as she isn't officially employed here yet. But tomorrow morning... I hope I won't have to talk to her on my own!

That look she gave me...! I hope that Sue will be with me in the Estate Office!

In the sitting-room of their house in Yetminster Rachel and Ailean Connor were having their supper. Ailean had just told her mother that she was going for the job interview at the Castle tomorrow morning at nine o' clock.

"So I'll come in with you, Mum, as you start work at nine o' clock."

"That's all right - but I should be careful with Jim, if I were you!" warned Rachel. "That is, if you find you're alone with him in the Estate Office. You know what I mean, don't you?"

"Oh, yes, Mum, I know exactly what you mean - I'll be careful!" said Ailean.

*

Jim was feeling decidedly nervous as he walked down the long corridor in the West Wing of the Castle towards the Estate Office. He was walking that way, rather than by his more usual short cut across the bailey, as it was raining heavily at that moment; but already the sky was brightening, and it looked as if the rain would soon stop. Peter will find some work for Ailean to do, no doubt, in spite of the ground being sodden because of all this heavy rain, he thought. He was wishing that Susan could have come with him to do this interview with Ailean, but he knew that her absence that morning was unavoidable. It was not as if Susan were acting unkindly or spitefully, knowing that he would be bound to be feeling somewhat nervous at the prospect of talking with that girl on his own. The fact of the matter was, she had reminded him, that she had an appointment to see the District Nurse that morning; the Nurse would be coming to the Castle some time between breakfast and lunch time, Susan had told him, so she would have to wait in her bedroom. Jim knew that the visit of the District Nurse was important for Susan as she would be bringing with her various pieces of equipment that Susan would need to keep up with her physiotherapy exercises.

He knew, of course, that it was essential that he should be in the Estate Office before Ailean should arrive there, but when he sat down at his desk the clock on the desk showed that it was only twenty-two minutes to nine. Bother! he thought. I know I'm not going to be able to concentrate on anything else while I'm waiting for that girl to appear, but I suppose I'll have to try! He reminded himself of the things he would have to say to her. "Darling, it's perfectly simple,"

Susan had said when he had protested that he wouldn't know what to say to her. "Just ask her to give you all her personal details, and especially details of all her qualifications, and write them down like we do for all job interviews. And then you could ask her what her ambitions are, and what she hopes to achieve by working for us."

There was a huge pile of envelopes on the in-tray on the desk, the mail which had accumulated during his long absence from the Estate Office. He knew before he started to open the envelopes that the great majority of them would contain correspondence of little or no interest to him, and that most of it would concern tenants' ground rents. It was very unlikely that there would be anything in that pile of mail of sufficient interest to take the edge off his growing feeling of apprehension and tension.

Luckily for Jim, Ailean turned up on the early side for her interview, being very keen not to be late. At seven minutes to nine came the expected knock on the door.

"Come in!" he said, at the same moment feeling his tension suddenly leaving him, like the snapping of an over-taut string.

Ailean Connor, wearing a bright green mackintosh with a green hood over her head, and dark green corduroy trousers, came into the room.

She gave Jim a half smile only for a second as their eyes met, but then she looked rather serious.

Jim had quickly reminded himself that it would be advisable to address her in a formal manner as "Miss Connor", and not to call her "Ailean". We don't know each other yet, he told himself.

"Good morning, Miss Connor," he said politely. "Do have a seat, please." He indicated a chair which he had drawn up for her so that she could sit at the desk, facing him. He was now feeling that his normal confidence in speaking to strangers had more or less returned to him.

"Good morning, Mr. Sandy, sir!" said Ailean Connor. She threw back the hood of her mackintosh, revealing a beautiful head of shoulder-length dark brown hair. My word! he thought. She really *is* beautiful – but she's not much like her mother!

"Would you like to take off your mackintosh?" he suggested.

"I think I'll keep it on, thank you."

"Just as you like, but I think that the rain has stopped now."

"Yes, the sun's coming out now, but I think there'll be more showers presently," said Ailean; "but I think it'll be fine enough to do some work outdoors."

"I gather that you're very keen to come to work in the gardens here?" said Jim.

"Yes indeed, sir, I am!"

"On a permanent basis? You're not just looking for a temporary job here, are you?"

"Oh, no, sir, I'm not looking for a temporary job; I'm hoping for a permanent position here. But if you could do that for me, sir, I might need to have a year or two off so that I could study botany at university; and then, hopefully, I could come back fully qualified."

"I see. Yes, I could certainly arrange that for you, Miss Connor. Oh, by the way, my wife sends you her apologies for not being here to talk with you this morning. She couldn't come, you see, as she has an appointment to see the District Nurse sometime this morning."

"Oh yes, that's all right, sir," said Ailean.

"You mentioned university, Miss Connor. Have you, in fact, got a place at a university?"

"Yes, sir, I've already been accepted at Imperial College, London, so I'll be starting there in September."

"To read horticulture?"

"To read horticulture and botany."

"I see. So, if I sign you onto our payroll now as one of our assistant gardeners you could work here until you start your studies at University in September. But then, I assume, you would like your position here to be kept for you so that you could come back to it when you've finished your studies and graduated? Is that right?"

"Well, sir," said Ailean, "if you could do that for me, that would be what I really want to do."

Jim paused for a moment before answering her. He knew, of course, that it was out of the question that he should disappoint Rachel Connor's daughter but, in any case, she was speaking to him so earnestly and seriously that he felt very touched; he would have had to grant her request anyway, irrespective of who she was. Up to that point in their conversation they had been avoiding direct eye contact; Jim had noticed that Ailean had been looking down all the time she had been speaking, almost as if she were afraid to look up at him. Suddenly he realized that she must be feeling at least as nervous as he had felt before she had entered the room, if not more so. Clearly he must try to put her at her ease.

"Yes, I can do that for you," he said quietly. He looked up quickly as he spoke and managed to catch her eye for a moment. They smiled at each other briefly, but then Ailean looked serious again.

"Oh, thank you so much, sir!" she said.

"All right, Miss Connor, I'm putting you onto our payroll to work here as an assistant gardener until you wish to leave us in September to start your studies at London University. But there will be vacations as well as term time, and perhaps you would like to return to your job here during some of the vacation time?"

"Oh, yes, I'm sure I should want to do that. Thank you very much, sir!"

"You seem to be very keen to pursue a career in gardening, Miss Connor? Have you any particular ambitions in mind in that field?"

"Well, sir - if you don't mind me saying this - I think I should like to stay here until, in the end, perhaps I might be promoted to the position of Head Gardener. You see, I think I'd enjoy taking some of the decisions myself about what's done in the gardens - in matters like choosing what plants ought to go in which beds, and things like that - always subject, of course, to Lady Sandy's approval, and to your's."

"Well, that sounds to me like a very worthy ambition. But, Miss Connor, I think that you should remember that there are likely to be others working in the gardens who could be eligible to be promoted before you."

"Oh, yes, I realize that, sir."

"Well then, it only remains for me to note down your personal details; so, if you don't mind, Miss Connor, I'll ask you a few more questions - your full name and address, your age, your health, your academic qualifications, and that sort of thing - and then I'll be able to let you go so that you can start work properly under Mr. Ashcroft."

"Yes, sir; that's fine by me!" said Ailean.

Jim proceeded to put his questions - the usual routine questions for any job interview - and to write down Ailean's answers in the spaces on the application form which he had in front of him on his desk. Then, when he had finished writing down her answers, he paused for a moment to look at what he had written down and, in particular, to read again through her list of "A" Level passes. There were five of them, all very good passes in science subjects: Biology, Botany, Mathematics, Physics, and Chemistry; and there were also six good "O" Level passes. It's pretty impressive! he thought. She's got five "A" Level passes in science subjects, and they're all excellent grades – she's obviously very brainy!

"Well, Miss Connor," he said, "your list of qualifications is really very good – excellent, in fact!"

"Oh, thank you, sir!" said Ailean, looking away from Jim so that he would not notice if she was blushing.

"I realize, though, that you'll probably need those qualifications and a university degree if you're thinking of going on to become a head gardener and to study horticulture seriously."

"That's just what I thought."

"By the way, Miss Connor – I hope you won't mind me asking you this – is your family descended from Irish ancestors? The name 'Connor' sounds rather Irish to me?"

"You're quite right, sir," said Ailean. "We do come from Ireland; at least, my father was Irish, but his surname was actually 'O' Connor' when I was born, but he changed it to just 'Connor' soon afterwards when we came to live in England."

"So you were born in Ireland?"

"I was born in Northern Ireland, actually – in Belfast, to be precise. But father has three brothers who all still live in Ireland. Uncle Ian lives at Toome in County Antrim in Northern Ireland, Uncle Michael lives at Buncrana in County Donegal, and Uncle Gerry lives in a remote spot beside the sea near Kilalla in County Mayo."

"Are Counties Donegal and Mayo in the Republic?" asked Jim, whose ideas about Irish geography were very vague.

"Yes, they are. County Donegal is in the north-west corner of Ireland, but County Mayo is way out in the west with an Atlantic coastline, and Uncle Gerry's house is in a remote spot beside the sea."

"It sounds like a lovely place! I suppose you've been there?"

"Oh, yes, sir, several times; and it really is a lovely place, as you say. You get a gorgeous view, looking out over Kilalla Bay from the bedrooms on the first floor... I love staying there!"

"I'm sure you do, Miss Connor," said Jim. But what you've been saying makes me think that Sue and I ought to think of going over to Ireland sometime."

"Oh, I'm sure you'd love it, sir, if you like Scotland! They say that parts of the West of Ireland look very like the Hebrides."

"Do they really? Well, Miss Connor -" (he glanced at the clock) "- it's nearly twenty past nine so I'd better let you get off to work now, or Mr. Ashcroft will be wondering why I've kept you here so long."

"All right, sir, but thank you *very* much for confirming that I've been given a job here! I'm sure I'll be very happy working here." Ailean stood up, preparing to leave the room.

"I hope so, Miss Connor," said Jim, "but I'll write to you in a few days time so that you can see the details of your contract with us in writing." He rose to his feet, shook her hand, and they said good-bye to each other. A moment later he was standing by the window, watching Ailean as she walked rapidly away along the path which lead around the north-western corner of the Castle.

When the green-clad figure of Ailean Connor had disappeared from his view Jim sat down again at his desk, but for several minutes he did nothing more while he remained lost in his thoughts. She seems to be very pleased with herself, he thought. He had noticed a certain subdued excitement in a peculiar light in her dark eyes while they had been talking, and this had seemed to be increasing towards the end of the interview. Could it really be that she had found that she was being strongly attracted to him, he wondered, or was it simply that she was feeling very pleased at having secured a long-term job at the Castle, doing the work that she enjoyed best? I wonder...? he thought. Then he began to wonder what had prompted him to mention Ireland to her. He had certainly never planned to enter into any unnecessary conversation with her, but... Well, there's been no harm done in asking her about her Irish ancestry, he told himself. It was just an idea that came to me on the spur of the moment; and anyway, I never mentioned her mother... and she didn't either. And I simply *mustn't* let myself think about Rachel! he told himself sharply.

He took an envelope from the pile on his in-tray and opened it. He took out a typed letter and looked at it, but found to his surprise that he was not really seeing it. Instead in his mind's eye he was seeing a delightful vision of a green-clad figure, a lovely young woman with very dark eyes and dark hair - Ailean Connor. Could it, just possibly, be that he was beginning to fall in love with her? I wonder...? he thought.

CHAPTER TWENTY-TWO

Two days later Jim opened an envelope and was profoundly shocked by the contents of the letter contained in it.

The day had begun just as nearly every day at Rhodes Castle began (unless they were taking their breakfast into the garden). Jim and Susan were quietly enjoying their breakfast in the Breakfast Room. Jim, having finished eating his toast, was reflecting on the fact that he had not seen Rachel since they had returned to the Castle. Well, that's a jolly good thing, really! he told himself, while he finished drinking his cup of coffee. Then he remembered that it was not due entirely to luck or chance that he had not seen her. He knew that she would always try to keep to the official timetable when conducting the guided tours of the Castle and grounds, while he - partly by accident, but sometimes by his own deliberate choice - had been avoiding being in those places where he might meet her on one of the tours - he had not forgotten the apparent warning in that strange dream.

Samantha came into the room with an envelope in her hand.

"There's just one letter this morning, and it's for you, Jim," she said. Items of mail which appeared to be personal were always brought directly to Jim or Susan by Jack or Samantha, whereas anything addressed to "The Manager" or "The Estate Office" was taken to the Estate Office.

For some strange reason Jim felt a peculiar flash of apprehension pass through him as Samantha spoke and handed the letter over to him.

"Thank you, Sam," he said. He managed to speak calmly enough in spite of the strange feeling which had suddenly arisen inside him. Don't be absurd! he told himself sharply. It's only a letter - it can't bite you - and if it is some bad news then you'll just have to read it and get over the shock!

He opened the envelope with slightly shaky fingers. He had glanced first at it to see if he could discover any clues there as to who had sent it, or what it was likely to contain, but he only saw that it was addressed to "J. Sandy, Esq." and that it had a Sherborne postmark. He glanced up quickly at Susan, sitting opposite to him at the table, before taking the letter out of the envelope, and saw that she was watching him closely; evidently she too had detected that some unusual tension, connected with that letter, was in the room.

"What is it, darling?" she said quietly. "I hope it's not bad news?" Jim was already taking out the letter, unfolding it, and beginning to read it as she spoke.

"My goodness!" he gasped. "No, it's not bad news, so that's all right, but it's jolly shocking to me all the same!" He paused, uncertain for a moment whether he ought to tell his wife more.

"Is it?" said Susan. "But do go on, darling, and tell me what it is - unless it's something private, of course."

"No, it isn't private. It's a letter from Roger Burton, but - well, what he's suggesting is just so amazing - so staggering - that I can hardly take it in!"

"Oh, I see," said Susan. She said this in such a calm, matter-of-fact tone that Jim, startled, looked up at her face and saw that she was smiling at him.

"Do you know something about this, darling?" he asked uncertainly.

"Maybe I do!" she said. "But, if it isn't private, perhaps you'd like to read it out to me?"

"Yes, I'll do that," said Jim, who was now feeling calmer, having realized that either Susan, or Samantha, or both of them together, had been the instigators of the proposal set out in the solicitor's letter.

This was the letter which Jim read aloud to Susan:-

Wednesday, 21ˢᵗ July 1965.

Dear Jim,

I am writing to put to you a proposal which may, at first, seem rather shocking, but which would, I think, be much to your advantage. It has been proposed that you should receive a Life Peerage when the next New Year's Honours List is published. The title which has been approved for you would be: "Baron Sandy of Rhodes Castle", and this would entitle you to style yourself "Lord Sandy of Rhodes Castle", or just "Lord Sandy" for short. I can tell you that the Lord Chancellor has signalled his approval to your ennoblement, and that, if you are agreeable with the idea, the Prime Minister would recommend to Her Majesty The Queen that your name be included in the next New Year's Honours List (which is published at the end of the year). I gather that there would be a short ceremony in the House of Lords for your Investiture and Swearing-In, and that this would probably take place early in the New Year on a date yet to be fixed. Your wife, no doubt, will be able to tell you more about that.

I said that this could be much to your advantage, bearing in mind that there may well be litigation pending concerning the possible right of inheritance of

Rhodes Castle. I do not wish to go into any technical details on the legal side of this matter in this letter; suffice it to say though that the title "Baron Sandy of Rhodes Castle" would undoubtedly strengthen your case to be considered the rightful Heir to Rhodes Castle in the event that the Earl and Countess of Saint Helens (Lord Richard and Lady Jane Dalmane) may start an action in the County Court.

That, briefly, is the position at the present time. If you wish to take up this offer for your ennoblement (and I would advise that you should do so) could you please make an appointment to see me in my office, not later than 31ˢᵗ August 1965, but preferably sooner (i.e. within the next week or two).

With best wishes,
Yours sincerely, Roger Burton.

"Well, that's it, but I can hardly take it in!" said Jim. "It's almost unbelievable!"

"Darling, I hope you'll forgive us for springing this surprise on you," said Susan seriously. "I hope you're not angry about it. It was meant to be a nice surprise for you!"

"Oh, it is - it *is*! And I'm not a bit angry about being taken by surprise like this, but it's just that..." He paused, uncertain of what exactly he wanted to say.

"That you can hardly take it in?" suggested Susan.

"Exactly! But it'll take me quite some time to get used to this idea, I expect. By the way, Sue - if you don't mind me asking - was it your idea, or was it Sam's?"

"Well, I don't think that it came from either of us originally," said Susan, after a moment's thought. "I believe it was Uncle Geoffrey who originally had this idea that perhaps at some time the title 'Baron Sandy' might be conferred on you. Darling, do you remember that evening, not so long ago, when Aunt Nora and Uncle Geoffrey were staying here with us, and we got onto talking about titles, and about you being the Heir to Rhodes Castle, and things like that?"

"Oh, yes, indeed I do," said Jim. "It was in the White Drawing Room when we were having drinks before dinner, wasn't it? And we were talking about Dick and Jane Dalmane, I think, and about whether the title 'Earl of Saint Helens' ought to pass on to him. But I think that perhaps Geoffrey Padgate did say something about a title for me some day. I can't remember now what he actually said, of course, but I think that perhaps he meant that I ought to have a title presently - because of being married to you."

"I think that was it, darling. Well, anyway, I thought about that idea quite a lot after that, and the more I thought about it, the more I thought that you really ought to have a title; so in the end I talked to Sam about it, and she said she'd tell Roger, so that perhaps he could do something about it to make it happen."

"And now, evidently, he has done something about it!" said Jim.

"In fact, it seems to me that he must have put in a lot of hard work on my behalf to get it all organized, so that it only remains, I suppose, for me to say 'Yes' to this Life Peerage and make an appointment with Roger to sign the necessary documents."

"So you think that you are going to accept this peerage?"

"Oh, yes, I'm pretty sure that I'll go ahead with this offer - it really would be stupid to turn it down as such a chance would never come again.

"I'm sure you're right about that, darling; and I can tell you that Uncle Geoffrey is very keen for you to accept it as well. He says that he'd love to be your sponsor in the Lords, and that means that he would accompany you in the rather quaint little ceremony that happens when a new peer is introduced in the House."

"Gosh! And all this is going to happen to me if I say 'Yes, I want to be Baron Sandy'... I can hardly believe it!"

"You will though presently, I expect, darling."

"Well, I suppose I'll get used to the idea presently." Jim paused a moment, and then chuckled as another thought came to him. "I wonder what Dad'll say, though, when he knows I'm going to become a Lord?"

"I dare say he won't believe you!"

"I'm pretty sure he won't believe me - well, not at first anyway."

"Are you going to ring up your Dad tonight, darling?"

"Oh, yes, I think I'd better do that tonight while this peerage business is in my mind. And maybe I'll ring up Mum as well. I'll pass on the news, but they won't believe me!"

A few minutes later, having finished their breakfast, they were leaving the Breakfast Room.

"Are you sure it's all right, darling, what we've done?" asked Susan as Jim pushed the wheelchair out into the Great Hall. "After all, we have taken a great liberty in plotting - I suppose you could say that - this Life Peerage behind your back?"

"Well, you made a very good job of keeping it secret!" said Jim. I had absolutely *no* idea that this was being planned until I had that letter in my hands this morning. But I don't want you to be at all worried by the secrecy side of it, Sue, darling. I honestly don't mind about that; in fact, I would say that I'm feeling really thrilled about it - but I'm still finding it hard to believe that this is really going to happen!"

*

That evening Jim rang up his father in Cockermouth to pass on his good news.

"You won't believe this!" he said, when he had told his father that he had received some very surprising news in the post that morning. "I'm going to become a Lord sometime in the New Year."

"What?"

"I've had a letter from Roger Burton, Sam's husband, the solicitor, telling me that I'm going to be offered a Life Peerage in the New Year's Honours List."

"What...! Are you pulling my leg, Jim?"

"Oh, no, Dad, it really is true that I'm being offered a Life Peerage. But I couldn't believe it myself at first - and I can hardly believe it even now!"

"Well, good heavens - you really *do* surprise me, Jim! But what, exactly, is the title you're being offered? Do you know that yet?"

"Yes, I'd become Baron Sandy of Rhodes Castle."

"Phew! Well, I never! You'd become Baron Sandy... You will be taking it up, I suppose?"

"Oh, yes, Dad, I'll be taking it up; I couldn't let a thing like this just pass me by!"

"Quite right, Son, quite right! And you're being given this honour, I suppose, simply because you married Susan Dalmane?"

"Yes, that's how it is. Well, no, I suppose that's not quite the whole story. You see, Dad, Roger, the solicitor, says that it may be very helpful if we have a legal case against Richard and Jane Dalmane, if I'm Baron Sandy of Rhodes Castle."

"Ah, yes, I see...! This dispute you told me about before as to who should inherit the Castle. Let's hope that it gets sorted out satisfactorily for you as soon as possible."

""Oh, yes, we certainly hope it will be. But you see, Dad, Dick Dalmane is now officially and legally the Earl of Saint Helens - or he will be, anyway, by the time I get my title - so I expect that that can only make matters more complicated. Anyway, Roger does say in his letter that when I become Baron Sandy of Rhodes Castle our case will be strengthened, because then I can be considered to be the rightful heir to Rhodes Castle. But we've no idea how it's all going to work out, so I think that all we can do is trust Roger Burton, and do whatever he advises us to do."

"That sounds like a good idea, Jim; I'm sure you can always trust a solicitor you know to do his best for you."

"Oh, he will do that, Dad; he certainly will. But how are you and Jackie getting on? And how are things going on at the mine?"

"Well, let's say that things are plodding on much as usual at Leadthwaite; but Jackie and I are keeping well enough, thank you. But there's really nothing more exciting that's happened in the mineral line to report to you about, Jim."

"You haven't found any more gold?"

"We haven't seen so much as another speck of gold since we had that surprising find in the Grains Gill - but it's not for lack of trying to find it!"

"You mean, you've been out looking for gold again?"

"Yes, Jackie and I have been back to that place on two or three occasions, and we've searched the river, and done a bit of panning, and found absolutely *nothing!*"

"Oh, how very disheartening, Dad!"

"Yes, I must say we are feeling rather disheartened and disillusioned by our failures; but, Jim, as Jackie said to me the other day, we do know that there *must* be a vein somewhere up there that has, or had, some gold in it. The only thing is, though, can we ever find it? You see, it's all very well finding little bits of alluvial gold in the river, but we're never going to make our fortune out of that sort of thing! Frankly, Jim, if we can't find a vein with a reasonable amount of gold in it, without having to spend a fortune first on securing the mining rights, and the cost of drilling boreholes to find it, then I'm afraid that we'll have to forget about the dream of becoming gold miners."

"Oh dear! That sounds very disappointing when you put it like that."

"Yes, I know it does," said Mr. Sandy. "But, as you said yourself, Jim, you never know how things are going to turn out, and we haven't quite given up yet on our hopes of finding gold in commercially viable quantities. I have, in fact, been talking to our solicitor quite recently about this."

"Getting advice?"

"Exactly. You see, Jim, the position is like this. I've written to the owners of the site, asking permission to carry out some trial borings for minerals on their land, but they've refused to give that permission in their reply. Mind you, I was careful to say nothing about gold when I wrote to them, so their refusal can have nothing to do with knowing that there might be a gold-bearing vein somewhere up there."

"I see," said Jim. "But did they give you any grounds for their refusal?"

"They said that it was on 'environmental grounds' - meaning that the drilling rigs and other works would look too unsightly on that unspoilt hillside; and I must say that I do have some sympathy with that view. However, that's where the solicitors and the legal advice come into the story. I think our only hope now is to persuade them, with a solicitor's letter if necessary, that we could carry out our work with a minimum of mess, and then clear up all the mess we do make when the job's completed. But once we get a solicitor involved in this we'll have to consider the question of expense carefully. We might end up having to pay a huge bill for legal expenses, and still not succeed in getting permission to do our work. So there it is, Jim: we seem to be perched on the horns of a dilemma, as you might say."

"Gosh, yes, I see, Dad; your negociations do seem to have reached a rather sticky point, don't they?"

"Yes, you certainly could call it a sticky point, but at least it's not what you'd call an impasse - or not yet. Well, Jim, very many thanks for giving us your most interesting news, but I'm going to pass the telephone over to Jackie now, as I think I've talked for long enough. She's just here beside me."

"Okay, Dad, I'll hang on. Good-bye for now!"

"It's Jim on the line with some very interesting news!" said Mr. Sandy as he handed the telephone over to his wife, Jackie.

After a moment's pause Jim heard Jackie's voice on the telephone.

"Hello, Jim, I was just busy in the kitchen when you rang up, but I can spare a few minutes now. You have some interesting news for us, I hear?"

"Hello, Jackie," he said, wondering whether, in fact, she had already managed to overhear the substance of his good news. "I have indeed had some rather startling news that came in a letter I had this morning. They're going to make me into a Lord. I'm going to receive a Life Peerage."

"Good heavens, Jim! That *is* startling news indeed!"

Jim noticed that her surprise sounded quite genuine, and that her reaction to his news was, in fact, much the same as his father's had been. He went on to tell her more about his forthcoming elevation to the peerage, but Jackie soon cut him short.

"I think you ought to be thinking about your telephone bill," she suggested, "so we'd better bring this call to an end now. But it is really wonderful news that you're going to become Baron Sandy of Rhodes Castle. Your father and I will be really proud of you, Jim!"

"Oh, well," said Jim rather awkwardly. "I... I haven't *done* anything, you know, to deserve this honour."

"But you *have* done something, Jim - you've married Susan, the Countess of Saint Helens! And that, you could say, was a pretty smart move!"

"Oh, look here, Jackie, we didn't get married with any ulterior motive in mind for me, like receiving an honour. We've married simply because we love each other!"

"Oh, yes, I'm sure you do; and I'm sorry, Jim, but I was only teasing you when I said that it was a smart move. All the same, I suppose it is because your wife is the Countess of Saint Helens that they're going to give you a Life Peerage?"

"Yes, you're right about that, Jackie, I should say. Well, good-bye, and good luck with your negociations for permission to make the boreholes to look for gold at Carrock!"

"Oh, thank you, Jim; but we'll let you know as soon as there are any significant developements on that front. Good-bye for now!"

"Good-bye, Jackie."

A minute later Jim was passing on his father's news to Susan.

"Do you remember those tiny bits of gold that Dad showed us?" he said.

"Oh, yes, I do indeed!" said Susan. "Has he found any more yet?"

"No, he hasn't." Jim then went on to explain that his father would probably have to engage his solicitor's help in order that they could then advance their plans for looking for veins of gold in the Carrock hillside.

"Well, that's an odd co-incidence, isn't it, that your Dad's dealing with his solicitor just when we're dealing with our's? But do you know, Jim, darling, I'd love to see this place where they found those little pieces of gold in the river. I hope you'll take me there sometime - if I ever recover enough to walk properly, that is."

"Oh, I expect you will, Sue," said Jim. But he knew in his heart that he did not really mean it.

When, a few hours later, he was trying to settle himself comfortably on his side of the bed he was still thinking over what Susan had said about wanting to see for herself the place where the gold had been found. There would be no difficulty in arranging to stay for a week or two at his father's house in Cockermouth so that they could visit the mining sites. But would Susan have recovered sufficiently from the paralysing effects of her stroke to make it a practical idea if they were to arrange it for some time next summer? Certainly her condition seemed to be improving at the moment: she had now recovered a little sensation and movement in her left arm and left leg. But perhaps, he thought, her improvement would only go so far, and no further. Perhaps she would always be partly paralysed down her left side. Perhaps she might even suffer another stroke? That was a dreadful thought but, as it had happened once, presumably it could happen again. And if it did what might happen to Susan then? Jim now began to wish heartily that he could turn off his distressing train of thought, but he found that he could not. It was a long time before he finally fell into an uneasy sleep.

CHAPTER TWENTY-THREE

As the weeks passed by, and summer passed into early autumn, Jim noticed that Susan was gradually changing. He noticed first the gradual changes to her moods and behaviour. The changes to her physical appearance due to her advancing pregnancy did not really become noticeable until October when, they reckoned, she was about five months pregnant. Although he told himself over and over again that her increasing lethargy and apathy were perfectly normal under the circumstances he still felt worried about her.

One day, when he was feeling more than usually worried about Susan, he decided to confide his worry in Samantha.

"Well, Jim, I'm pretty sure that you needn't be worried about it," she told him, "although admittedly I'm not speaking from first-hand experience, as Roger and I have decided that we don't want to start a family – or at least, not yet."

"I see," said Jim, wondering how old Samantha was. It was all very well, he thought, for her to say "not yet", seeing that she must surely now be well into her forties.

"Mind you," said Samantha, "I think that it's a pity that she's stopped doing her physiotherapy exercises. Perhaps she'll want to start them again after the baby is born, but in the meanwhile, Jim, we'll just have to keep an eye on her, and, if necessary, call the doctor. We'll have to do that sooner or later anyway, as the birth will have to be by caesarian, and that'll mean that she'll have to be in hospital for the birth."

"Yes, I know; but there shouldn't be any problem about that, Sam, because Sue seems to be quite agreeable to that idea herself."

"That's good," said Samantha. "Actually, Jim, I got the same impression myself when Sue and I were talking about the birth a few days ago. I reminded her that there's no maternity department at Sherborne, which means that she'll have to be prepared to travel quite some distance when the time comes to go into hospital. I suggested that she might choose to go to Yeovil or Bournemouth for the birth, but then Sue said that she thinks that she might as well go to London."

"London?"

"The Queen Mary Hospital at Roehampton, because it's so close to the house in Martin Lane."

"Oh, I see," said Jim. "Oh, what a good idea! So I'll be able to live with Claire when I'm not visiting Sue in the hospital."

"Yes, you'll be able to live with Claire Walker... but you'd better be careful about that, Jim!" Samantha suddenly broke off into a chuckle as she remembered what Jim had told her of the way Claire had appeared to him in his dream.

"Oh, Sam... *really*! Yes, of course I'll be careful. The sort of thing that happened in that dream definitely won't happen when I'm staying there as I expect I'll be mostly on my own, in my own room - when I'm not visiting Sue in the hospital."

"We'll have to hope that all goes well with Sue when she goes in to have the baby," said Samantha. "But I expect it will. That doctor seemed to be quite satisfied with Sue's general condition, I gathered, when he last called to see her."

"Yes, he said that everything seemed to be going on just as it should; and he did say that he thought there was no reason for me to be worried about her - but it's hard not to be!"

"I know what you mean," said Samantha.

"Well, Sam, I'd better be getting back to the Estate Office now to get on with some work there. Thank you for letting me talk with you, though. It's taken a weight off my mind!"

"That's all right, Jim; you know you can always come to talk with me confidentially at any time you like."

"Thanks very much, Sam."

Jim left Samantha's private sitting-room in the Burtons' second floor flat and made his way down the main staircase into the Great Hall. Then he set off down the long dark passage which lead, eventually, through the kitchen, and then, via another long passage to the Estate Office. He went by this circuitous route, rather than by the much shorter route straight across the bailey, as it was still raining heavily. It had been raining for most of the day, and now it was almost two o' clock, and still the sky looked heavy and thunderous, as if the rain had no idea of stopping its steady downpour for some hours to come. As he passed the door of the Green Drawing Room he was tempted for a moment to turn in there, but he went on; he had left Susan lying on the sofa in there, fast asleep after her lunch. It's a good idea, he told himself, that Sue's taken to having a rest after lunch... and I rather wish that I could too!

As he came into the Estate Office he suddenly remembered Ailean Connor, and wondered what she would be doing in the rain. Perhaps Peter Ashcroft would have to send her home early because of the inclement weather. He remembered that it had been just as wet on that morning, about six weeks ago, when she had come to see him about a possible job, and he had signed her on as one of the assistant gardeners. But it brightened up on that morning, he remembered, whereas it doesn't look as if we'll ever see any brightness today! But hadn't that been a memorable occasion for him as well as (no doubt) for Ailean? He had to admit to himself that it had, although, predictably, he had seen little of her since that morning.

The next day. which was a Friday, was quite different to the dark, wet, and dismal day which had preceded it. It dawned sunny and very pleasant, and although a little cloud came into the sky in the middle of the day, it had dispersed again by mid–afternoon. At tea time the sun was shining in a cloudless sky, the wind had dropped to practically nothing, and it felt comfortably warm out of doors.

"Let's have our tea on the balcony today," said Susan.

"Oh, yes, let's have it there!" agreed Jim happily. "It's a perfect afternoon to be sitting outside in the sun!"

Susan told Samantha that they would be taking their tea out onto the balcony, and invited her to join them, but she declined the offer, saying that she was too busy with other jobs. Samantha passed the word on to Jack, the butler, who presently carried a tea tray out onto the balcony above the front door of the Castle, where Susan and Jim were already sitting. They kept a garden table and chairs on the balcony throughout the summer and early autumn for the eating of outdoor meals, and had used the place on many occasions since they had returned from their Scottish holiday. But on this particular afternoon they had hardly begun their tea when Jim, looking up from the cake he was eating, suddenly noticed a figure on a bicycle coming up the inner drive towards the Castle.

"Look, there's someone coming on a bike," he said.

"So there is!" said Susan, glancing up in her turn.

The figure on the bicycle quickly came nearer, and they soon saw that the rider appeared to be a girl. They heard the scrunching of gravel under the wheels of the bicycle as it approached the front door, and then, just before she put a foot to the ground to stop, the rider glanced upwards and saw the watchers on the balcony.

"Why, it's Jack Wonstannley's daughter again!" said Jim, recognizing the girl at the same moment that she recognized him.

"It's Mary Wonstannley!" said Susan. "Hello, Mary!" She and Jim waved their hands cheerfully.

"Hello, Lady Sandy!" Mary Wonstannley shouted back. "I sure hope you don't mind me just turnin' up suddenly when you weren't expecting me, though?"

"Of course we don't mind a bit!" said Susan cheerfully. "Would you like to come up and join us here, Mary, seeing that you've come back here?"

"Oh, well, that would be very kind of you, Lady Sandy," said Mary Wonstannley.

"I'll run down now to show her the way up here," said Jim, who had already risen to his feet.

"All right," said Susan.

Once he was back inside the Castle Jim rushed down the main staircase with a sudden eagerness to welcome Mary Wonstannley which he would have found very difficult to explain. He knew that he was not, and never would be, attracted to Mary. At the same time he was wondering why she had returned to the Castle; he had never expected to see her again. In his hurry to get to the front door to welcome Mary he almost collided with Jack, the butler, in the Great Hall; he also was heading for the front door.

"Oh, sorry, Jack; I'll let her in!" he said quickly.

"Very good, sir!" said the butler curtly. "And one more cup and plate for tea?"

"That's right. Thank you, Jack!"

Jim opened the front door and saw Mary Wonstannley standing at the foot of the stone steps, having padlocked her bicycle and propped it up on the steps beside her.

"Do come in, Mary!" he said.

"Oh, thank you, sir," said Mary Wonstannley. "But I should tell you, sir, that I've come back because Dad has lost a book, and he figures that he must have left it here, so I said, Okay, Dad, I'll go back to the Castle and try to find it."

"Oh, I see. Well, we must look for that book; but first, would you like to come up to the balcony to have some tea with us?"

"Oh, sure I would! Yeah, I reckon I'm pretty thirsty so it would be great to have some tea, thank you!"

"Have you biked a long way today?"

"Yeah, I guess I have, really. I've come from Frome, and I reckon that would be around thirty-two miles; but I done more than that some days."

"Have you really? Well, if you'd like to follow me, I'll lead the way up to the balcony."

They went into the Hall, from where Jim lead the way up the main staircase and then through the front bedroom onto the balcony.

"Jack's bringing an extra plate and cup," he said as he drew up a third chair to the table.

"Good!" said Susan. Do have a seat, Mary, please."

"Thank you, ma'am!" said Mary Wonstannley, sitting down in the chair that Jim had pulled out for her. They usually kept four garden chairs on the balcony so there was room for four chairs around the circular table. Jim and Susan had already been sitting opposite to each other, so Jim had put the extra chair for Mary between the other two chairs so that she would be facing outwards over the balcony.

Jim sat down again, feeling decidedly uncomfortable because of the close presence of the young girl sitting to his right. She must surely still be a teenager, he thought, perhaps even younger than Ailean Connor. Even though he was definitely not attracted to her, Mary Wonstannley's very close presence was, in a way, exciting and disturbing for him; and the fact that she was now sitting between himself and his wife made him even more tense. He told himself quickly that he would have to be extremely careful about his behaviour while Mary was sitting so close to him; he resolved that, if possible, he would not look round at her at all, and that he would join in the conversation as little as possible. At the same time, however, he knew that it was very important that he should appear to Susan to be perfectly calm and normal – in fact, to be just as he would be if Mary were not there at all. Oh, heavens, I seem to be in an impossible situation! he thought desperately.

Luckily for him, Susan and Mary were doing all the talking. It was almost as if they were ignoring his presence at the table.

"Well, it's nice to see you again, Mary!" said Susan. "Have you had a good cycling trip?"

"Oh, yeah, it's been great, thank you, ma'am!" said Mary. "It's been fantastic! But as I was saying to your husband, it's because Dad left something of his here that I've come back. He's lost a book, and he reckons he must have left it here."

"Oh, well, we'll have a look for that after tea. Ah, here comes Jack."

The door behind them opened, and the butler came out onto the balcony, and set another cup and saucer and a plate of sandwiches in front of Mary Wonstannley.

"Thank you!" she said, smiling at the butler for a moment. Jack, however, remained looking as impassive as ever.

"If you'll be needing more tea presently, ma'am, just ring the bell for me, and I'll come and fill the pot for you," he said politely.

"Thank you, Jack; I'll do that," said Susan. A small brass bell had been brought up on the tray with the tea things.

The butler retired from the scene, and Susan began to question Mary Wonstannley about her cycling trip.

"So how far did you go before you had to turn back?"

"Well, ma'am, I reckon that Carlisle is about as far as I got to – though I did go just a little further north because I wanted to get into Scotland."

"Ah, so you didn't get right up to John O' Groats this time?"

"That's right, not this time I didn't, but I sure would like to ride right up there sometime! But, you see, there really weren't no time to go further than the Scottish border as I'm hoping to get back to the States before the end of this month. I'm going to start studying at college, you see, ma'am."

"Oh, I see. And what are you going to be studying, Mary?"

"I'm gonna be studying Modern Languages, ma'am, like I've been studying French and Spanish at High School, because I wanna be a teacher of languages myself."

"Well, that's a very worthy ambition, I'm sure," said Susan. "I wish you well in your studies, Mary."

"Oh, thank you, ma'am! But I figure that Spanish is a particularly good language for us North Americans to learn because they speak it over the border in Mexico and practically all over Latin America - except in Brazil."

"Ah, yes, I see. So I expect you have quite a sizeable minority of the population in California who speak Spanish as well as English?"

"Yeah, that's exactly how it is, ma'am; and especially so near the border with Mexico."

Presently the conversation returned to the subject of Mary's cycling tour of England.

"So are you going to be heading back for London when you leave here?" asked Susan.

"Yeah, that's right. I'll be heading for Heathrow Airport when I leave Yetminster tomorrow morning."

"Yetminster?"

"I'm reckoning on going to Yetminster when I leave here later this afternoon, so that maybe I can stay at that pub in the village where Dad and Phil Oakley stayed - 'Ye Olde' something - I've forgotten its name."

"Would you like to stay the night here, Mary?"

Mary Wonstannley looked at Susan in amazement, but her eyes were sparkling with excitement.

"Gosh...! Do you really mean that, ma'am?"

"Of course I do!" said Susan. "You'd be very welcome to stay the night here if you'd like to."

"You bet I'd like to! Oh, ma'am, but that would be simply great to stay at Rhodes Castle! Oh, thank you very much, ma'am!"

At this point Jim, who had not said a word during all the conversation with Mary. looked up and, against his will and better judgement, met her gaze for a moment and then quickly looked away from her again. Until that moment he had been careful to look only either down at his cup and plate, or out over the view of the gardens from the balcony. He now suddenly felt that there was something very touching about this young girl's obvious excitement at the prospect of spending a night at the Castle; but still he did not say anything.

"I wonder what your Dad will say when he hears that you've spent a night here?" Susan was saying.

"Oh, I figure he won't be too pleased when I tell him!" said Mary.

"You think he'll feel a little jealous of you?"

"Yeah, I reckon he will feel like that; but then I reckon he should be mighty pleased if I can find his book and return it to him."

"What's the title of the book?" asked Jim, surprising himself by suddenly finding a convenient place to enter into the conversation.

"It's called, 'Tales from the Haunted Houses of England'," said Mary Wonstannley, "and he says that if he can't get it back he'll have lost it for ever as it's out of print in the States, so he can't buy it again at a bookshop."

"I think I've seen it in the Tower Library," said Jim. "Is it a hard-backed green book, Mary?"

"Yeah, that's exactly what Dad said it was. Gosh, it'll be great if we can find it there!"

"We'll go down there right after we've finished tea," said Susan.

Just then they all looked round towards the drive as the sound of a motor vehicle being driven fairly fast up the inner drive came to their ears.

"It's the minibus," said Jim.

"Ah, so I guess it's one of the Guided Tours, like the one we were on?" said Mary.

"Yes, that's what it is," said Susan.

While Susan and Mary had been chatting Jim had remembered that the three-thirty guided tour would be going on somewhere out there, and that it would probably come up to the Castle while they were having their tea on the balcony. This, in its turn, had reminded him that he would almost certainly see Rachel Connor, the Guide (if he wanted to see her) when she stepped out of the Castle minibus to gather the tourists around her before bringing them into the Castle. But I mustn't look at her when she arrives, he had told himself firmly. I mustn't see her at all

– I must look the other way when the minibus arrives.

"I think they're a little late today, aren't they, darling?" said Susan, glancing at her watch.

"Yes," said Jim, quickly looking at his watch in his turn.

"They're supposed to arrive here from the Visitor Centre at half past four, but it's nearly twenty to five now." He hoped that the tone of his voice did not betray his feeling of rising agitation, but he already knew that the temptation to look down when the bus had stopped, and see Rachel Connor, was going to be far too strong for him to have any hope of resisting it.

The minibus stopped by the steps leading up to the front door, just below the place where they were sitting. Jim found that he could hardly breathe. Would Rachel be the first person to appear out of the minibus, or would she let the passengers disembark before her? Luckily for him his time of unbearable tension only lasted for a second or two.

The door of the minibus opened, and Rachel Connor stepped smartly down onto the ground; then the watchers saw her turn at once to assist any of the tourists who needed assistance to step safely down the two steps from the bus to the ground. It was obvious that the Guide was concentrating carefully on her job, and was quite unaware that she was being watched from above.

"So the new Guide is doing the job now on her own, I guess?" said Mary Wonstannley, looking round at Susan.

"Oh, yes," said Susan. "Mrs. Grookes, who was, I think, still acting as the Guide on the day when your father and Doctor Oakley came on the tour, has left us now, and Mrs. Connor has taken over as our new Guide; and she's managing extremely well from what I hear. But you haven't actually been on one of the guided tours yourself, have you, Mary?"

"Oh, no, ma'am; I arrived too late to join that tour the others were on. But perhaps tomorrow morning? What time does the first tour of the day go off?"

"It starts at ten o' clock in the morning, and finishes at twelve."

"Oh, well, I figure I might as well join that tour as there's really no need for me to leave all that early, I guess."

Jim had heard nothing of this conversation as the whole of his attention was concentrated on watching Rachel Connor. He saw her go back into the bus for a moment to check that everyone had come out. Then he saw her come out again to address her assembled flock of tourists.

"Now before we go into the Castle I'd like to tell you a little bit about what we can see from here. This side of the Castle is the south facade..."

Jim listened happily to the Guide's voice as she began to speak, using much the same words as he had often used himself at this point in the tour. Although in his days as the Guide the tours had not penetrated inside the Castle they had always come up to the front door to look at the magnificent south facade, and to have its main features pointed out for the tourists. To his ears Rachel Connor's voice had a rather musical quality and was unique; it was soft and resonant, and to hear her speaking always added an extra thrill to the excitement which exuded from her.

However, the visual aspect was disappointing for him as, naturally enough, he could only see the top of Rachel's head properly from his vantage point above her. Then he saw that she had finished speaking and that she was leading the visitors into the Castle. She's been rather brief this time, he thought, but of course she must be thinking of catching up with her schedule. Released from his spell of enchantment, he remembered that Mary Wonstannley and his wife were there with him on the balcony. He looked up and saw that they were deep in conversation, and apparently ignoring his presence, just as he had been ignoring their's for the last few minutes.

"So you're not into ghosts and that sort of thing?" Susan was saying.

"Oh, no, ma'am," said Mary. "I figure that sort of thing just doesn't interest me, although Dad's mad keen on ghosts and haunted houses and such."

"Well then, shall we go and look for that book now, if you've finished eating, Mary? Or would you like another sandwich? Or some more tea?"

"I've eaten enough, thank you, ma'am, but I'll have a little more tea, please."

"You don't mind drinking this China tea? I expect it's not what you're used to?"

"Oh sure, it's great, ma'am!" said Mary enthusiastically. "You're right, though; I haven't drunk it before!"

Susan poured some more tea from the teapot into Mary's cup, but then paused a moment, the teapot still in her hand, as she caught Jim's eye.

Jim had been bracing himself to hear some sarcastic remark, knowing that Susan was well aware that he had just been staring at Rachel. However, she simply fixed him for a second or two with a silent look before she offered him some more tea in such an ordinary voice that he was not sure whether he was being accused of paying excessive attention to Rachel, or not.

"Some more tea for you, darling?"

"Oh, yes please, Sue, darling!" he said gratefully. "I'd like another cup, please."

Some ten minutes later, having finished their tea, they came indoors again to look for Jack Wonstannley's missing book. Jim had just said, "I think I know where it is. If no one's moved it since I last saw it, it should still be lying on the desk." He was very much hoping that they were not about to meet Rachel and her party of tourists again. With Sue around, once is quite enough for this afternoon! he told himself firmly. He looked at his watch again, and reckoned that he should be safe in that respect; the touring party should by now have descended the stairs and would probably be in either the Ball Room or the Banqueting Hall. They came to the top of the main staircase, and Jim was relieved to see that the way was clear; the touring party must have already gone down ahead of them.

They found Jack Wonstannley's book without any difficulty. Mary Wonstannley unzipped a side pocket of her blue rucksack and stuffed the book into it.

"Dad'll be pleased about this when I tell him!" she said.

"Would you like to ring home from here tonight, Mary, to tell him you've found it?" said Susan.

"Oh, sure, ma'am, that'd be great to do that, if you don't mind!"

"That'll be quite all right," said Susan; "and I'll ask my maid to get one of our spare rooms ready for you tonight. But what would you like to do now, Mary? I suppose, if you're going to join the first guided tour tomorrow morning, you won't really want to be shown around the place now?"

"Well, ma'am, I reckon I'll get on my bike again now, and have a bit of a ride round about here, and then come back... about what time would you like me to be back here, ma'am?"

"Oh, shall we say about seven o' clock as we usually have our dinner around half past seven? In any case, I don't suppose you'd want to be out and about on your bike any later than that at this time of the year. Of course, you may want to come back earlier – we don't mind!"

"Oh, right, ma'am, thank you very much, but I guess the sun sets soon after seven o' clock, so I reckon I'd best be back by that time, or sooner."

Mary Wonstannley set off again on her bicycle, but this time she left behind her rather bulky blue rucksack. Jim had lent her a local map which showed all the small roads which were suitable for cyclists in that part of Dorset. They asked Samantha to prepare a small spare bedroom for their visitor, so she took the blue rucksack up to the little room which had once been Jim's bedroom in the days when he had been the Guide, and made up the bed in there.

*

At dinner time with Mary Wonstannley sitting at the table and eating with them, the conversation soon turned naturally enough to the subject of ghosts and, in particular, to the ghosts of Rhodes Castle.

"Dad told me that they got no ghosts on film that time they was working in the Tower Library, but they actually saw two ghosts there," said Mary. "He told me that the last time I rang him up, but I figure he wasn't too disappointed really."

"I know," said Susan. "He wrote me a very nice letter and told me how they'd failed to capture the ghosts on film, but he said that they had captured something else at that critical moment. If I remember rightly I think he said that one of their instruments had captured what they called 'fluctuations' in the electro-magnetic field. That was it, wasn't it, darling?" Susan was now looking across the table to where Jim was sitting.

"Yes, I think that was it," said Jim. "And there was a graph enclosed with his letter to show how their machine had actually recorded those fluctuations. Do you know how those gadgets were supposed to work, Mary?"

"Oh, no, sir - I haven't a clue how they work!" said Mary. "But, yeah, he told me about that too, and he said that he and Phil are mighty pleased with those results!"

"How's he getting on with the book he's planning to write?" asked Susan. "Has he started to write it yet?"

"Oh, yes, ma'am, he has indeed; he's got the first chapter finished, and now he's well under way with a second chapter. It's not going to be a long book, he says, but he's going to put into it everything he knows about the ghosts of this place. Actually a great deal of it will be based on information which he's received from *his* Dad - my Grandad. You see Grandad actually lived and worked here for quite a long time, so he got to find out a lot about the Castle and the ghosts."

"Oh, yes, we've heard about your grandfather working here as valet to the Earl of Saint Helens - my late husband's father," said Susan.

"But is your grandfather still alive, Mary?"

"Oh, yeah, sure he is; and I reckon he's in fine form considering that he's well into his eighties! But we haven't seen him for some time as he lives in New York, and he don't come over West to see us nowadays. But he's sent Dad a great deal of stuff which is coming in useful for his book: diaries and letters and papers, and such."

"I see. Well, I hope the book will be a great success; and we'll look forward to selling copies of it here when it gets published."

"Yes, a book about the Rhodes Castle ghosts should be a best seller in the shop at the Visitor Centre," agreed Jim.

"Well, we must pass on our best wishes to your Dad in this endeavour of his," said Susan. "So will you give your Dad that message from me, Mary, when you next speak to him?"

"Oh, sure, ma'am; yeah I'll give him that message," said Mary.

*

The next morning Mary Wonstannley was with Susan and Jim in the Breakfast Room, but Jim somehow hardly noticed her presence. Soon after breakfast was over Mary rode down to the Visitor Centre on her bicycle to be ready for the start of the ten o' clock guided tour, but by the time she left the Castle Jim had already gone off to do a morning's work in the Estate Office. It was a Saturday morning, which meant that the office was open only from nine o' clock to mid-day.

The morning guided tour also ended at mid-day, and at about ten minutes past twelve Mary Wonstannley returned to the Castle to pick up her rucksack and to say good-bye to her host and hostess. As the weather was fine Jim had gone straight up to the balcony to join Susan there to wait for Mary Wonstannley to appear once again on her bicycle.

They came down to the Hall as soon as they caught sight of her coming up the drive, and found that Samantha was already standing by the open front door with the well-filled blue rucksack.

"Shall I give it to her?" asked Jim.

"If you like, Jim," said Samantha.

Jim put the heavy rucksack down on the ground just as the bicycle pulled up beside him.

"Oh, thank you, sir!" said Mary as she propped up her bicycle against the steps.

"Are you setting off now, Mary?" asked Susan.

"Yeah, right now I'm on my way," said Mary as she quickly fastened her rucksack into its place on the luggage grid of her bicycle. "I wonna get as far along the road as I can today, as I'm aiming to get to Heathrow on Monday morning, if I can."

"Well, good luck to you, Mary," said Susan cheerfully. "And you'll remember to give your Dad my message, won't you?"

"I'll remember," said Mary. "Well, good-bye, ma'am, and many thanks to you for letting me stay the night here. It's been great staying here!"

"It was very nice of you to call in here on your way back," said Susan. "We've really enjoyed having this opportunity to talk with you."

Mary Wonstannley glanced at her watch.

"I must go now," she said. "Good-bye, ma'am! Good-bye, Jim!" She shook hands with each of them, and then, without another second's delay, quickly mounted her bicycle and rode away. As she went she briefly raised an arm to wave a final farewell.

"Good-bye, Mary!" shouted Jim and Susan, waving their hands towards the rapidly disappearing cyclist. But Mary Wonstannley, her head down, was riding hard, and they were not sure whether she had heard them. They watched until the bicycle disappeared from their view by the Inner Lodge, having passed through the white gate.

"She definitely takes after her father, doesn't she?" said Susan wonderingly. She was leaning on her walking stick and still staring down the drive, as Jim also was doing.

"You mean, in being so energetic?" he said.

"Yes. I can hardly believe that she's been all the way up to Carlisle and the Scottish border on that bicycle in the few months since we first saw her!"

"I can hardly believe it either, but she obviously just loves biking."

I wonder whether we'll see her again sometime? mused Jim as they went back into the Hall. I thought before that I'd never see her again – but I was wrong!

CHAPTER TWENTY-FOUR

Some two weeks after the departure of Mary Wonstannley an air mail letter with an American stamp was delivered to Rhodes Castle. Jim and Susan found it lying on the table in the Servants' Common Room when they came in there to have their lunch with Samantha.

"A letter from America!" said Jim as soon as he saw the envelope.

"It'll be a thank-you letter from Mary Wonstannley, no doubt," said Susan as she sat down at her place at the table.

"It's adressed to 'Lady Sandy and Mr. J. Sandy'," said Jim, picking up the envelope, "so it must be meant for both of us. Do you want to read it first, Sue?"

"All right, I'll read it aloud; it'll be interesting to hear how Mary's been getting on since she left us."

Jim handed over the envelope, but at that moment the door from the kitchen opened, and Samantha put her head round the door.

"Ah, here you are now! Lunch is going to be ready in about five minutes."

"All right, Sam, we're in no hurry," said Susan.

"Was this letter the whole of today's post?" asked Jim.

"Yes, it was," said Samantha. "It came pretty late today, too – about ten o' clock." On most days the post came early enough in the morning to be opened while they were eating their breakfast.

"Well, thank you for putting it here for us," said Susan; "and five minutes will just give us time to read through this letter before you bring in the lunch."

Samantha disappeared back into the kitchen, closing the door behind her.

This was the letter which Susan read aloud:-

145 Presidio Avenue,
San Francisco,
CALIFORNIA.

Dear Lady Sandy and Jim,

This is to tell you that I've gotten safely back home and to say, Thank you very much for the night I stayed with you in the Castle.

I reckon I really enjoyed my time staying in the Castle, and when I told Dad about it I figure he was really envious of me!

(I knew he would be!)

My bike ride back to London was pretty good, and I did get to Heathrow on Monday morning like I'd hoped to, but when I tried to book a flight they said I'd have to wait until Wednesday morning because of my bike. That's no matter, I said, so I spent the rest of that Monday and Tuesday touring around London, seeing things, which was great! Then I got the Wednesday morning flight back to New York where I had to change planes, and then I got another flight back to San Francisco. I rang up Dad from the airport to say, Hi, Dad, I'm back, and so I got back home.

I remembered to pass on your message; in fact the first thing I said to Dad when I met him was that you had sent him your best wishes for the writing of his book. Well, ma'am,

I can tell you that he was mighty pleased to get that message! He says that the writing is going well and he's really looking forward to the days when you'll be selling copies of his book in the shop in your Visitor Centre.

Well, I figure that's all I have to tell you except to say that I hope I can see you again some day, and next time I want to see Scotland. I figure that if I could start my bike ride somewhere near the Scottish border (perhaps from where I got to this time) then maybe I could get right up to John O' Groats. I reckon that would be a really good bike ride.

Right, I must close now.

With Best Wishes, Yours sincerely,
Mary Wonstannley.

"Well, that's that," said Susan. I'm glad she had such a good time on her travels and got safely back home, but it does sound as if we could be seeing her again sometime, doesn't it?"

"It does," said Jim, "but I suppose that we should have guessed that she'd want to do a cycling tour of Scotland when she told us she'd got as far as the border."

"Yes, she really wanted to go further, and would have gone further if she'd had more time. But she said that she wanted to be back at home in time for the start of term at her new college, and she must have managed that."

The door from the kitchen opened again, and Samantha came in carrying a tray on which there was a dish with something hot and steaming in it and three hot plates.

"Here we are - it's macaroni cheese today," she said.

"Oh, good!" said Jim happily. "I think that's my favourite lunch time dish!"

Samantha set the tray down on the table and then, using an oven glove, put the hot dish on the mat laid in front of Susan's place. Then she put the hot plates in front of Susan.

"Was it a letter from Mary Wonstannley?" she asked.

"Yes, it was," said Susan, "and she's talking of coming back again sometime to tour Scotland on her bicycle, and to come and see us again."

"I'm not surprised," said Samantha. "She seems such an energetic person. In fact, she takes after her father in that way, doesn't she?"

Jim noticed that Samantha had expressed very much the same opinion about Mary Wonstannley as Susan had expressed before, when Mary had left them. Well, she *does* take after her father, he thought.

*

It was on Christmas Day that Susan announced that she would shortly be moving to London for the birth of her baby in the Queen Mary Hospital in Roehampton. She and Jim were sitting in the White Drawing Room of Rhodes Castle with Lord and Lady Walton, waiting for the Christmas Dinner to be served. Susan's parents had arrived at the Castle to stay over the Christmas period on the evening of the twenty-third of December (which had been a Thursday), and they were planning to return to Soken Hall on the following Tuesday.

"Well, I must say, I think that's a very sensible idea," said Lady Walton, Susan's mother. "Of course you must be somewhere close to the hospital of your choice when the time comes for you to go in for the birth. It wouldn't do at all for you to be a hundred or so miles away from London when the time comes."

"Indeed it wouldn't," said Lord Walton. "But when you say you'll shortly be moving to the house in Roehampton, Sue, have you, in fact, got a particular date in mind?"

"Well, not really, as it depends on what Claire and John are doing at the moment," said Susan. "Obviously we'll need to give them a few days warning that we're intending to move in there for a while, but I think that we were vaguely thinking of going there next Thursday - if Claire agrees to that."

Jim was not surprised or upset that Susan had chosen to reveal to her parents their plans to move to Roehampton before the New Year, and to stay there until the baby was born. Or at least we'll have to stay there until Sue and the child are out of hospital, and well and strong enough to make the journey back home, he told himself.

He was not particularly looking forward to the imminent move as it would inevitably lead to a certain amount of disruption to the usual routine of his day's work. However, the idea was that he would carry on the essential work of the Estate Office from his room in the house in Roehampton, with the post being forwarded to him by Jack, the butler, from the Castle. But was this idea going to work, or was it not? Would Jack know which items of mail were important enough to be forwarded, and which ones could be left to accumulate on the in-tray of the Estate Office desk? Jim had often wondered how it was going to work out but, he thought, clearly they must give it a try as he might have to be away from the Castle for well over a month, and obviously the work of the Estate Office could not be allowed to grind to a full stop for such a long period of time.

There was also going to be another consequence of a long absence from the Castle which was causing him some uneasiness: he would not be able to see Rachel while they were living in London.

Thinking about this, he had told himself that it was going to be a really good thing that there could be no chance of any accidental meetings with Rachel Connor while he was away. However, he could not convince himself that he was going to be a happier man on that score. It's all very well, he said to himself, to argue that it'll be better for me to be well and truly separated from her for a while. It's all very well to say that, but the truth is that I don't see much of Rachel nowadays anyway - in fact, I very rarely come across her; and when we do meet it's usually no more than a momentary "Hello!" exchanged between us...

"Would you like some more sherry, sir?"

Jim was startled to hear the voice of the butler beside him; he had not realized that he had sunk quite deeply into a reverie. He glanced down at his empty sherry glass for a second, and then looked up and saw that Jack was there with the sherry decanter in his hand.

"Oh, yes - just half a glass, please," he said. "Thank you, Jack."

The butler filled his glass and then returned the decanter to the side table which he used when the gentry were sitting in the White Drawing Room. Then he left the room. Jim knew that he would be going to the kitchen so that, when the dinner was ready to be served he would come in again to announce that fact. He's a really good and conscientious servant! thought Jim.

*

Later that evening when they were all seated in their places in the Dining-Room for dinner, the conversation turned to the interesting question of who, exactly, should be considered to be the rightful heir to Rhodes Castle. Lady Walton had just pointed out that it had been a brilliant idea on the part of their solicitor to think of making Jim into a Baron so that he would then become the unquestionable heir to the Castle.

"Actually, Mum, I beieve the idea originally came from Uncle Geoffrey," said Susan.

"Well, whoever it came from it was a really brilliant idea!" said Lady Walton.

"It was an absolute master-stroke, if you ask me!" said Lord Walton enthusiastically. "And that reminds me, Jim: I think our congratulations are in order for your forthcoming elevation to the Peerage!" He took his wine glass in his right hand and raised it as if to propose a toast. "Here's to the true Heir to Rhodes Castle! Welcome to the Peerage, Jim!"

CHAPTER TWENTY-FIVE

Julia Sandy was born on the second of February at five minutes to ten in the morning. That evening Claire Walker answered a telephone call from the Queen Mary's Hospital in Roehampton at around five o'clock. She gathered that it was a staff nurse calling from the hospital's Maternity Unit, and that she was wanting to talk with Mr. Sandy.

"Yes, I'll get him for you," said Claire, "but can I tell him that you have some good news for him?" She could tell from the tone of the nurse's voice that the call was not going to bring some bad news.

"Yes, you can tell him that," said the nurse. "You can tell him that he now has a daughter, and that the child and her mother are both doing fine!"

"Oh, that is splendid news!" said Claire happily. "Now if you would hold the line, please, I'll just get Mr. Sandy to speak to you."

Jim was already standing beside the armchair where Claire had answered the telephone. His heart had missed a beat on hearing the telephone ring, and then for a few seconds, as Claire answered the telephone, his hands had gripped the back of the armchair rigidly. Would it be the dreadful news that he had been fearing all day – or would it not? And then suddenly he could tell from what Claire was saying that the news from the hospital was good news; Susan had not, after all, died under the anaesthetic, as he had feared must have happened. He felt most of his tension leave his body immediately as his hands released their tight grip on the armchair.

"Here you are, Jim," said Claire, smiling at him and handing over the telephone to him. "You have a baby daughter now, as I expect you've gathered, and she's doing fine, and so is Sue."

"Thank heavens for that!" he said as he took the telephone from Claire's hand. He now almost felt like breaking into laughter, so great was his sense of relief, but he managed with an effort to speak in what he judged would be a calm and reasonable voice.

"Hello! Jim Sandy speaking."

He was told that his wife had given birth that morning to a baby girl by caesarian section, that the operation had gone through without complications, and that they were both now out of theatre and resting in a recovery ward of the Maternity Unit. Then the staff nurse told him that, if he wanted to, he could now come to visit his wife and daughter.

"Oh, good, I'll certainly do that," said Jim. "But am I allowed to bring a friend with me if I come this evening?"

"Yes, by all means you can do that," said the nurse.

"Thank you!" said Jim. "We'll be along shortly." He hung up the receiver and handed the telephone back to Claire, who replaced it on the table beside her armchair. Then he looked round at her rather sheepishly. "I hope you didn't mind me asking if I could bring you as well?" he said.

"Of course I don't mind!" said Claire decisively. "You did right, Jim - I certainly want to come along to see Sue and the baby."

"That's good!" said Jim, returning to his armchair. He sat down again.

"But we don't want to go immediately as I expect you'd like to finish your tea first?" They were both looking at a piece of cake on Jim's plate which he had not yet touched, and at a partly drunk cup of tea.

"Oh, thank you, Claire!" said Jim, now smiling happily. He ate his slice of cake with relish, but then thought that he had better explain why he had not wanted to eat it earlier.

"Actually, Claire, I was feeling really, really nervous while we were waiting for that call from the hospital, and I think that made me not want to eat anything. I hope you don't mind?"

"Oh, no, I quite understand," said Claire. "But you're feeling much better now that you know that it's good news, aren't you?"

"Oh, yes, I certainly am!" He drank the rest of his tea and then looked up again expectantly, but was surprised to see a rather serious look on Claire's face.

"Jim," she said, "I hope you won't mind me saying this, but were you, perhaps, half expecting some dreadful news when the hospital rang up? Have I read your thoughts correctly?"

"Yes, you have," said Jim seriously. "I was dreading that when the call came it might be to say that Sue had died."

"Oh, Jim, I am most awfully sorry! It was my fault for putting that sort of ideas into your head yesterday when I was telling you about how I nearly died in childbirth. I shouldn't have said anything about that, especially at a time like this. It must have been most upsetting for you to have to think about that with Sue just gone into hospital to have the baby. Oh, I really am very sorry, Jim, that I said what I said then."

"Oh, it's all right, Claire, I... I don't really mind about it now," said Jim awkwardly. He knew that he was now feeling deeply embarrassed as he had never intended to force this woman (who, whether he liked it or not seemed to be becoming a part of his life) into making a grovelling apology to him.

"You can forgive me for upsetting you so badly?"

"Oh, yes, I most definitely can! Anyway, I'm feeling happy again now, so I don't want to think about it any more."

"Of course," said Claire. "The news from the hospital is really wonderful, isn't it? I can hardly take it in!"

"And I can't either!"

"Well, Jim –" Claire broke off for a moment as she looked at her watch "– It's eight minutes past five now, and I'm longing to go along to the hospital to visit Sue, and you must be too; but I think, if you don't mind, that we ought to wait until John comes home from work so that I can tell him where we're off to before we go. Is that all right with you?"

"Oh, yes, that's quite all right with me," said Jim, knowing that he did not really mean it, and hoping that Claire would not be able to read his thoughts again, as it seemed she had been able to do a little earlier. Gosh, I hope her husband doesn't decide to come with us! he said to himself. His presence would just spoil the feeling of this evening completely!

*

Jim was getting used to the routine of life in the house in Martin Lane, and by the end of January he was almost beginning to think of it as home. Jim and Susan kept in regular touch with Jack and Samantha at the Castle by telephone, and so knew that everything was going on there as it should.

On most days Jim did not see very much of either John or Claire Walker except at breakfast time and at dinner time in the evenings. A corner of their spare bedroom had been transformed into a temporary Estate Office, and Jim would usually sit at the desk there. typing letters and attending to other business matters from after breakfast until lunch time, although, when the weather was fine, he liked to take a mid-morning break from his office work by going for a walk by himself around Putney Heath. Then after lunch he would usually have another session of office work. Claire had lent him a typewriter, and so he was able to proceed with his work almost as if he were back at home in the Estate Office in the Castle.

Susan, in contrast to Jim's rather solitary existence, usually spent much of each day at that time in the company of her friend, Claire. On most mornings they would load Susan's wheelchair into the back of Claire's car, and then Claire would drive into Central London, where they would spend a happy time shopping, chatting, and having a mid-morning coffee in a restaurant. Sometimes, when the sun was shining and it felt warm enough to walk out of doors, they would go into one of the Royal Parks (usually St. James's Park, Claire's favourite, and of which Susan was also very fond). Susan would climb out of her wheelchair and walk about a little, supported by her walking stick, while Claire would urge her not to try to walk too far, and not to overtire herself.

In those January days, which were the eighth month of Susan's pregnancy, Claire felt that it was her duty while she was with Susan to keep a close eye on her and to ensure, as far as possible, that nothing untoward (from a medical point of view) occurred while they were out together.

"You must let me know, Sue, if you feel any unusual pain down there," said Claire one day, looking down at Susan's prominent bump as they walked in St. James's Park, "so that we can call the doctor right away and get you rushed into the hospital, if he thinks it necessary."

"You're quite right, Claire," said Susan seriously. "Yes, I promise you I will let you know right away if I think anything unusual is going on down there; or, if you're not about, I'll tell Jim, or John, so that they can call the doctor. I certainly don't want to try to go into labour as my own doctor said that that might even kill me."

"And then, maybe, the child would be born dead as well," said Claire. "No, we mustn't let anything like that have a chance of happening. We must err on the side of caution, Sue, and get you into hospital sooner, rather than later."

A week later, when Claire called her doctor to come to see Susan, he concurred with Claire's opinion that it was better to err on the side of caution.

"I'm going to have you admitted to the Queen Mary's Hospital right away, Lady Sandy," he said when he had examined her carefully. "Not that I think that anything more is going to happen to you today, but it is getting near your time, and I agree that we'd better err on the side of caution. You'll be in safe hands, Lady Sandy, in the hospital."

"Yes, but when do you think the baby will be born, doctor – or, at least, when do you think they'll decide to deliver it by caesarian? Tomorrow, perhaps? Or in a few days time?" Susan, who was lying comfortably in the bed with her head propped up on several pillows, smiled hopefully at the doctor.

"Well, of course, it's very hard to say exactly when it'll be," said the doctor thoughtfully. "But, if you press me... I think I'd say it will probably be the day after tomorrow, rather than tomorrow. But you never know..."

"I see," said Susan.

"Now, if I could use your telephone, please, Mrs. Walker," said the doctor, "I'm going to call an ambulance so that we can have Lady Sandy admitted to hospital."

"But do we really need an ambulance?" said Claire. "The hospital is so near. I could easily take Lady Sandy there in my car, you know?"

"Well, it's kind of you to offer to do that, Mrs. Walker, but I really think that it would be better, on this occasion, for Lady Sandy to be carried into hospital lying down comfortably on a stretcher. But I think that it would be a good thing if you and Mr. Sandy could go with Lady Sandy in the ambulance so that you can see her comfortably settled into her hospital bed."

"Oh, yes, we'll come too, won't we, Jim?" said Claire.

"Yes, we'll come," said Jim.

"Now, if you'll just come with me, doctor," said Claire, "I'll show you where the telephone is."

Claire, who had been sitting on a chair at the head of Susan's bed, rose to her feet. Doctor Digby, her family doctor, who had been sitting on the side of the bed beside his patient, then got up to follow her out of the bedroom.

"Mind your head, doctor!" Claire reminded him when she came to the doorway. Doctor Digby was a very tall man. He stooped and followed her through the doorway.

Jim remained sitting where he was. He was sitting on a stool on the other side of the bed to the side where Claire had been sitting, looking rather glum and very worried.

"Darling, I'm sure there's no need for you to look so worried," said Susan when the other two had left the room. "I'm perfectly sure that everything's going to be all right with me while I'm in the hospital."

"Oh, I hope so, Sue, darling!" he said anxiously.

"And anyway, you and Claire are coming with me now. You mustn't stay there too long, but I expect there'll be forms to fill in for my admittance, so they'll probably need you to be there anyway to answer questions. And I expect Claire will probably come in her car so you'll be able to go back in the car."

A minute or two later Dr. Digby, stooping again as he came through the doorway, followed by Claire, came back into the bedroom.

"It's all arranged for you, Lady Sandy," he said. "They're going to send an ambulance, which should be here in about a quarter of an hour, to pick you up. So you'll be all right, and I must be on my way now, Lady Sandy." He came over to the bed to shake Susan's hand.

"Good-bye, doctor, and thank you so much for coming to see me," said Susan, shaking the doctor's extended right hand heartily.

"It's been a pleasure, my Lady!" said Dr. Digby, smiling broadly.

"And may I wish you the best of luck, Lady Sandy. Good-bye!"

Everyone in the room was now smiling as the doctor, with a final friendly wave of his hand, left the room with Claire.

"What a nice man that doctor is!" said Susan happily as soon as he was out of her sight.

"Yes, isn't he?" agreed Jim, knowing that Susan had been impressed by his gallant but courteous behaviour.

"Now, darling, we'll just have time when Claire comes back to get a few things packed that I'll need before that ambulance comes."

Claire returned to the bedroom within a minute of leaving it, having briefly and quickly seen off Dr. Digby, and thanked him, from her front door. She went straight over to a cupboard door, opened it, and took out a small suitcase from a shelf inside the cupboard.

"My goodness, Claire, you have got things well organized!" said Susan admiringly.

"Will this be big enough?" said Claire, holding up the suitcase for Susan to see it. "It's a bit smaller, I think, than your own suitcase."

"It'll be fine," said Susan. "I'm not going to bring very much with me into hospital."

"And if you want any more you can just let us know, and we'll bring it."

They packed Susan's personal belongings into the suitcase, and then it was arranged that Jim would travel with Susan in the ambulance, while Claire would follow behind it in her car.

*

It was about an hour and a quarter later when Jim and Claire left the hospital to drive back along Roehampton Lane to Martin Lane.

"Well, that's that," said Claire as she drove her car out of the hospital grounds and onto the main road. "I think Sue seems comfortable enough where she is now."

"I think she seems to be almost happy now that she's in hospital," said Jim.

"Yes, because she knows that there will always be plenty of well trained, professional staff on hand, day and night, ready to help her when anything happens."

For a moment Jim pondered the truth of what Claire had just said but, now that he was alone with her, he found that it was hard to continue to think about Susan. Sue will be all right now, he told himself, but I'll be alone with Claire a good deal of the time for the next few days, I expect, so I'm bound to think about her. Well then, what do I think about Claire? Do I still find that I'm not being attracted to her? Or is that situation gradually changing, or will it change now that Claire and I are going to be on our own at her house for a few days? Ought I to admit to myself that she is, in a way, a damned attractive woman?

He was just beginning to think that the answer to that last question must surely be, "Yes, I ought to admit it", when he realized that the short journey back from the hospital was already over. Claire was about to turn off Roehampton Lane at the junction of Martin Lane.

"Here we are, back at home!" said Claire cheerfully.

"Oh, yes," said Jim rather doubtfully. He suddenly found that he was wondering what he ought to do for the rest of the morning.

It seemed, however, that Claire was thinking along much the same lines as himself. As she unlocked her front door she suddenly turned to Jim with, he thought, a rather naughty, flirtatious smile on her face.

That smile, however, vanished almost as soon as it had appeared.

"What shall we do now?" she said as she came into the hall, followed by Jim. "It's only half past ten, you know, so it's still quite early really. But perhaps we'd better go into the kitchen first to have a cup of coffee, don't you think?"

"Oh, yes, I think that's a good idea," agreed Jim willingly enough.

As he followed Claire down the rather narrow, dark passage which lead from the hall towards the kitchen he suddenly had the feeling that, now that he no longer had Susan's company, Claire was going to adopt a rather motherly attitude towards him. Or had that momentary flirtatious glance she had given him been an indication that other desires were in her mind? Does she mean to seduce me? he wondered briefly. But there was no time to wonder as they had reached the kitchen, and Claire was speaking again.

"This doesn't seem at all like a Monday morning, does it?"

"No, I can hardly beieve that it is Monday morning," said Jim. "I think it's because we're not doing the things we'd usually be doing on a Monday morning."

"Yes, that must be it," said Claire. As she had been talking she had been switching on her electric kettle, and getting out two cups, and putting them on the table. "That's right, Jim, just leave it anywhere you like." Now that they were indoors Jim had taken off his anorak, and now Claire was beginning to unbutton the long black coat she had been wearing out of doors and in the hospital. "It's nice and warm in here, isn't it?" As she spoke Claire took a coat hanger off a hook on the back of a door (the back door, leading out to the garden) and hung up her coat on it. Jim had already put his anorak over the back of a chair. He could hardly prevent himself from gasping audibly with pleasure and excitement as he saw again the outfit which Claire was wearing under her coat. Oh, good heavens, she *does* look sexy in that tight-fitting red jersey! he thought. It was, of course, not the first time that morning that he had seen Claire wearing that red jersey; she had been wearing it at breakfast time and afterwards when they had been sitting with the doctor beside Susan in the bedroom, but somehow he had not really noticed it then. She *must* be thinking of seducing me! he thought happily.

Jim was seeing a new Claire that morning, a Claire whom he had never seen before. Even when they had been staying in the house with her last summer, and he had seen her on more than one occasion wearing a tight-fitting top, emphasising the magnificent outlines of her very shapely breasts, he had not thought that she was acting in any way provocatively. Now, however, it was quite different. He was quite sure that she was deliberately trying to create an atmosphere of mounting excitement and tension; and she was certainly succeeding in that aim, although he wished he knew what thoughts were going through her mind.

Just what was she intending to do with him, he wondered, now that the two of them found themselves alone in the house together?

"Can I help you?" he asked uneasily. He was still standing up, not wanting to sit down while Claire was on her feet.

"No, it's all right, Jim; do sit down, please," she said, giving him another quick, meaningful smile. "I'll be sitting down myself in a minute or two when we've got the coffee made, and then we'll be able to talk."

About what? he wondered. "Oh, yes!" he said aloud, trying not to look directly at the exciting outlines of her bust under the red jumper. And then, quite unexpectedly, that strange dream of Claire and Rachel came again into his mind; but now, of course, he was only interested in the part of the dream in which he had seen Claire in a partially naked state.

He had, in fact, remembered that dream on a number of occasions since they had moved to Roehampton in the days just before the New Year. However, although he had occasionally remembered it, he had never let the memory perturb him in any way. He had simply let the thought of the dream pass into his mind, and then pass out again, while knowing that to be reminded of it did not mean that he was beginning to find that Claire was attractive to him. He had been quite certain, until that morning, that he still did not think of Claire as an attractive woman.

This morning, however, he was just as certain that that situation had now changed. And then an idea occurred to him as he sat down at the kitchen table. I wonder, he thought... whether I ought to tell her about that dream? At that moment, however, Claire came over to the kitchen table, carrying two cups full of coffee, one of which she set in front of Jim. Then she put a jug of milk and a plate of biscuits on the table and, having sat down, pushed the biscuits towards Jim.

"Do, please, help yourself," she said kindly.

"Thank you, Claire," said Jim politely, taking a biscuit. No, he said to himself, now is *not* the time to tell her about that dream, but perhaps I'll get a chance to tell her later on – if she starts a conversation that could lead us into that sort of discussion.

A moment later, when she had drunk a mouthful of her coffee, Claire asked him a question.

"Tell me, Jim, how did you first come to meet Sue? I've often wondered how you two first met each other?"

"Well, I first met Sue quite by chance one day at the railway station in Cockermouth, which was where I was living at the time," said Jim.

"Oh, good heavens, at Cockermouth!" exclaimed Claire in obvious surprise. "But was that quite some time ago?"

"Oh, yes, I suppose it was. It was, I think, in the summer of 1959 – nearly seven years ago – when I was working in the police at Cockermouth."

"Oh, were you really? I say, Jim, you don't mind me asking these rather personal questions, do you? I don't want to be nosey, but – well, it's just that you and I don't seem ever to have had a chance before now to have a chat together, have we?"

"Yes, that's quite true," said Jim thoughtfully. No, I don't mind at all talking about these things. In fact, to tell you the truth, I think I really enjoy reliving my wonderful memories, like my memories of that day when I first met Sue. Can I tell you more about it?"

"Please do, Jim," said Claire.

So Jim began to tell Claire about the events of that momentous day as he remembered them, but he decided straight away that he would not be too honest about revealing his reasons for leaving the Cockermouth police. There's no need to let her know that I was, in a way, running away from the police on that day, he thought quickly. I'll just give her the gist of it briefly. He told Claire that early on that June morning Lord and Lady Dalmane had come to Cockermouth station to catch a train to Carlisle, and then catch the "Royal Scot" to London.

When you say, 'Lord Dalmane', Jim, I take it you mean Sue's first husband, John Dalmane?" said Claire.

"Yes," said Jim. "I do mean him, but what happened was that he got arrested by the Cockermouth police, and thsat meant that he missed the train that Sue and I travelled on. You see, there was a murder hunt going on at Cockermouth at that time, and we had a picture of our Wanted Man printed on posters; it was one of those 'photo-fit' pictures. But you see, Claire, the thing was that, unfortunately for him. Lord Dalmane happened to look extremely similar to the man in that picture."

"Oh, my goodness! So the police made a mistake and arrested the wrong man?"

"That's exactly what happened. You see, Claire, it was like this..." Jim told her that, in order to fill in some time while waiting for his train, Lord Dalmane had decided to take a walk along the railway line with a friend of his, Mr. Beck, an engine driver; but they had been spotted by a sharp-eyed constable, and this had lead to Lord Dalmane's arrest. Then he told Claire of how he and Mr. Beck had hurried back to the station, and of how, when he arrived there, he set eyes on Lady Dalmane for the very first time and instantly fell in love with her.

"It really was love at first sight, you know, when we met each other on that station platform, and I've been in love with Sue ever since. But at first she wasn't very keen on me because I was part of the Cockermouth police force which had just arrested her husband, causing him to miss his train. I explained that I was leaving the police and travelling to London to look for a new job, but Sue wasn't much impressed by me saying that."

"Yes, I can quite understand that," said Claire. "No doubt she would have been very concerned about the sudden disappearance of her husband just when she'd been expecting to travel in the train with him."

"That's just how she said she was feeling at that time," said Jim, "so, of course, she was decidedly cool towards me - at first - until I did something which, I suppose, was really rather a stupid thing to do - although I didn't think so at the time - but it turned out in the end that it was a very lucky thing that I did it. You see, Claire, I was sitting in front of her in the train, but I was longing to peep at her, although I didn't want to keep turning my head to get glimpses of her.

But then I discovered a way of looking at her without turning round. Do you see the stone in this ring, Claire?" He held up the little finger of his left hand, on which was his signet ring with a polished carnelian stone in it, and Claire nodded her head. "I found that I could see a reflection of her in my ring stone, and so I began to look at her in that way, never thinking that she would realize what I was doing."

"But she caught you in the act, peeping at her furtively?"

"She did indeed!"

"My goodness, Jim! But surely that was a very foolish thing to do, considering that you hardly knew her at all at that time?"

"Well, at the time I didn't think it was foolish," said Jim, "although Sue did scold me a little, and she did tell me that I'd done a foolish thing. But then, Claire, an astonishing thing happened - well, I thought it astonishing - she told me that she wanted to have a private talk with me. She asked me to try to find an empty compartment when I got into the 'Royal Scot' at Carlisle so that she'd be able to come along and join me there for a private talk. Well, of course, I felt thrilled and very excited when I heard that, but I couldn't imagine just what she could be wanting to talk about. Well, I found my empty compartment, and Sue came and joined me in it. And do you know what it was, Claire, that she'd come to tell me? She said that if I'd like to come with her to Rhodes Castle she could offer me the job of Guide of Rhodes Castle, which would mean that I'd be able to live-in there. So, of course, I said at once that I'd love to come with her and become the Guide of Rhodes Castle. So that's how I first came to live with Sue."

"Well, just fancy that!" said Claire. "Do you know, it sounds as if you were extremely lucky that day? I think you could say that you had quite a series of lucky co-incidences."

"Oh yes, indeed!" agreed Jim. "In fact, I've often called that day my Lucky Day!"

"Yes, it really was that, wasn't it? But I don't think I've ever had a Lucky Day to compare with that! I think my younger days, when I was a student, were really rather dull, on the whole."

"But surely you must have had some good times?" said Jim, not wanting to believe her too literally.

"Oh, yes - but who hasn't?" Claire shrugged her shoulders, and then tossed down the last drops of her cup of coffee. "At any rate, Jim, I remember that I once did something rather naughty in my student days, which I could tell you about - if you like?"

"Oh, please do, Claire! That sounds interesting!" Jim felt a sudden surge of returning excitement on hearing Claire's mention of "doing something rather naughty".

Claire's smile broadened for a moment, almost as if she was going to break into laughter; but she did not laugh.

"Well, I don't know whether you would call it interesting, or not," she said, "but, Jim, this is something I've never told Sue about – and I don't think that you ought to tell her either." Now, suddenly, her tone sounded serious.

"No, of course I won't, if you think I shouldn't," said Jim, equally seriously.

"Then I'll tell you," said Claire after a little thoughtful pause. Suddenly she was smiling again as she continued. "You see, Jim, it was like this: when I was a student at college I had a boyfriend for a time- this was before I met John, my husband – and this boyfriend had a father who was the editor of a men's magazine, or what, I believe, is sometimes called a 'top shelf' magazine. I'm sure you know the kind of thing that I mean, but I'm not going to ask whether you ever look at such things yourself." She paused a moment, and gave Jim a rather searching look.

"Yes, I know what you mean," he said quietly, hoping that he was not blushing. He did not dare to say any more, but now he was becoming distinctly excited as he began to guess what was coming next in Claire's story.

"Well, one day," she continued, "he came to me with the suggestion that I should make an appointment to come to his father's studio to be photographed for his magazine; but I, at first, was absolutely shocked by the idea of doing that because, of course, I knew that it would mean taking off most or all of my clothes to be photographed naked. So I said, No, I couldn't possibly do it, and I think that on that occasion we left it like that. But he wasn't going to give up. Several times after that he tried to persuade me to change my mind. He kept saying things like, 'You have such a *fantastic* figure, Claire, that you really ought to let people see what your breasts really look like'. So in the end I found that I had to agree with him and, rather reluctantly, agreed to the photo session.

So, to cut a long story short, that was that: a set of pictures was published in the magazine of me wearing very little or, in some of them, stark naked; but as for whether they caused a stir, or not – well it's not for me to comment on that, Jim."

Jim had been listening in fascinated astonishment to the unfolding of Claire's story of her photo-shoot, but now, as she paused, he hardly knew what, if anything, to say in response. And then suddenly he remembered his dream again, and realized with something of a shock that the part of his dream in which he had seen Claire naked from the waist upwards must have had a prophetic element to it. But that makes it like the room with the wall covered with pictures that I saw in that dream, he thought – at least it will be, I suppose, if she's going to undress for me now to show me those breasts!

His gaze had not been focused on anything in particular while these thoughts had been rapidly passing through his mind, but now he looked up at Claire, and was not surprised to find that he could focus his attention nowhere except on those magnificent curves which were stretching the front of her jersey. He decided that the moment had come to tell Claire that he had dreamed about her.

"Thank you for telling me about your photo-shoot, Claire," he said rather awkwardly, "but it's reminded me of a dream I had about you."

"Oh, has it? But when did you dream about me, Jim?"

"I believe it was some time last summer." Jim suddenly found himself trying to remember when he had dreamed that dream.

"So it wasn't a recent dream, while you've been staying here?"

"No, it wasn't," said Jim. "It was... er... I think it was while we were away on holiday in Scotland that I had this dream. Anyway, let me tell you about it, Claire, and then you'll understand why I've been reminded about it."

"Okay!"

Jim began to relate his account of that strange dream, but he decided, as he went along, that he would concentrate most of his detail on the part which had featured Claire sitting in that room with a wall of pictures, and sketch over the second part of the dream, which mainly concerned Rachel, very briefly.

"So now you'll understand, Claire, how it was that I was reminded of that dream when you told me that you'd been photographed naked," he concluded, when he had told her how the dream had ended.

"Yes, indeed I understand," said Claire. "But *really*, Jim... what a very *naughty* dream to tell me about!"

"Oh, well... er..." Jim stammered awkwardly into silence. He was now feeling so confused and embarrassed that, for the moment, he had no idea what he ought to say to Claire. I shouldn't have told her about that dream! he told himself angrily. Even after what she told me, I shouldn't have done it. Now feeling rather miserable, he looked down towards his feet and waired for her to make some further remark.

"Don't worry about it, Jim," he heard her say, now in a quite different voice. "I don't mind!"

"Are you sure?" he said, looking up at her hopefully. "Oh, Claire, I am so sorry that I, er... dreamed about you like that. And then I shouldn't have told you about it."

"Nonsense!" said Claire. "You can't help what you dream about any more than I can, or than anyone can. And you were quite right to tell me about it, Jim – definitely quite right!"

"Oh, well, it is kind of you to say that, Claire!" He had now slipped easily back into his former mood of happiness and excitement, as he had seen that Claire was smiling at him. She wasn't really scolding me at all, he told himself with relief. Once again his gaze was becoming fixed on the pleasing curves of Claire's bust, and once again he felt that he was unable to do anything about it.

"But, Jim, after what I've been telling you, and you've told me, I don't think we can do anything less than to let you have a quick look to see what I've really got in there, under my red jersey!"

"Oh, Claire...!" Jim found that he was suddenly so breathless with excitement that he could say no more.

"But first we'd better have those curtains pulled," said Claire, jumping quickly to her feet. In a moment she had pulled the curtains across the windows on the side of the room which faced the street.

Within the next few seconds the red jersey had been pulled off over her head, and then, just as rapidly, she pulled off the white vest she was wearing underneath it. Then, smiling, she paused a moment in her undressing and turned to face Jim with her breasts now covered only by a rather skimpy white brassiere.

"Now, you must tell me, Jim, if I look like the way you saw me in your dream!" she said playfully. The next moment the brassiere had been unfastened and flung on the floor with the other discarded garments.

Jim gasped, but found himself quite speechless, and all but paralysed with amazement and excitement at the sight of the beautiful woman standing before him, naked from the waist upwards, her long blonde hair hanging loosely over her shoulders. As his gaze re-focused itself on the curves of her breasts, now exposed for him in all their beauty and symmetry, he quickly became aware that they did indeed look like the breasts he had seen in his dream. Only the real thing is even better, of course! he thought happily.

Claire, however, did not allow him more than a few seconds to stare at her. Suddenly she came up to stand close beside him, and then, before he knew what was happening, she flung her arms around his neck and kissed him warmly on the cheek. Then she released him.

"Well," she said in a quiet voice, "what did you think?"

But Jim did not answer her. For a moment he thought he was going to faint as his eyes lost their focus and he felt suddenly dizzy. He staggered backwards a step or two and collapsed into his chair.

"Are you all right?" said Claire. She had picked up her brassiere, and was about to put it on again, but now she paused, looking at him carefully.

"Yes, I'm all right," he answered her; and indeed the moment of faintness and giddiness had passed as soon as he had sat down again. "Oh, Claire, that was - *wonderful!*

"Well, I hope it wasn't just a bit too exciting for you!" said Claire as she hastily pulled the cups of her bra over her breasts and fastened the clip to hold the garment in its place.

"No, of course it wasn't!" said Jim almost indignantly. "You look absolutely *fantastic*, Claire, with nothing on up there!"

"Oh, yes, but - how did you think my breasts compare with what you saw in your dream?" Claire was finishing her dressing while she was speaking, pulling on her vest and red jersey again.

"Well, really, from what I can remember of the dream - and of course I can't *really* remember what I saw then - I'd say that what I've just seen was remarkably like what I saw in my dream."

"Was it really?"

"Yes, I'd say it was," said Jim. "But the real thing, if you know what I mean, was, well, more exciting to look at. I hope you don't mind me saying that."

"No, of course I don't!" said Claire. "But do you know, Jim, I'm thinking now that really I've gone too far in what I've just done; that I've been very naughty, and that perhaps I owe you a sincere apology for behaving in a way that you may have found rather offensive."

"Oh, no, no, Claire; please don't even think of apologising for taking off your clothes for me. I've just found it a *wonderful* experience, and I really can't thank you enough for it." He had just been wondering whether Claire had seriously meant what she had just said about her "very naughty" behaviour, or whether it had been more of a tongue-in-cheek remark, not meant to be taken seriously; but her expression at that moment defied his scrutiny.

"Well, it's kind of you to say that," said Claire, and now she was smiling at him again. She glanced at her watch. "Look here, Jim, it's almost eleven o' clock, so perhaps it's time we were thinking of other things?

"You mean, like getting some work done?"

"Yes, that's what I was thinking. Were you reckoning on getting some of your Estate Office work done this morning?"

"Well, yes, really I was thinking that that was what I ought to be doing, until... well, until we got busy doing something else!"

Claire laughed, but a moment later she sounded serious again.

"All right, Jim, I'm going to let you get on with your office work now, but I only hope that I haven't over-excited you so much that you won't be able to concentrate on it!"

*

Ten minutes later Jim was sitting at the desk in the spare bedroom with a piece of typing paper inserted in the typewriter in front of him, but the letter he had hoped to type seemed to have ground to a full stop with only the address and the date typed at the top of it. Damn it, she has over- excited me! he thought. Now I can think of nothing but those gorgeous, fantastic breasts! Just then, however, another thought came unexpectedly into his mind. I told her about that dream, he thought, but I never told her that part of it came true afterwards. I didn't tell her about the Physiotherapy Room in the Stornoway Hospital, with its wall well covered with pictures - just like the wall I'd already seen in my dream. I suppose I could have told her that it seemed that dreaming about that room was like seeing into the future - but I dare say it was a good thing I didn't. If I'd told her that I'd seen into the future in that dream she might well have decided not to take off her clothes. She might well have concluded that taking off her clothes to show me her breasts would have amounted to making the future "come true" - and I expect it would have been very upsetting for her to contemplate that sort of thing.

It was a very sobreing thought.

CHAPTER TWENTY-SIX

"Oh, Sue, she's lovely!" exclaimed Claire in delight, looking down at the baby girl lying in her cot.

"She's got dark eyes - they're just like your's, Sue!" said Jim happily.

"Yes, so they tell me," said Susan dreamily, opening her own eyes for a moment and smiling at Jim and Claire, who were bending over the infant's cot, which was beside Susan's hospital bed.

"I think that Sue must be still feeling the effects of the anaesthetic," whispered Claire to Jim privately as they saw Susan's eyes close again. "Either that, or she must be under sedation."

"Yes, I expect so," said Jim quietly. "She seems to be very sleepy anyway."

"But just think, Jim - you're a father now! You're the father of this tiny little girl."

"I know," said Jim, staring in wonder at the tiny creature lying in the cot. "Yes, I know it, but I can't really believe it. I can't really believe that this is my daughter, Julia."

"She is very tiny, isn't she? But look, Jim, she has black hair like her mother. I think she may well grow up to look very like Sue."

"That'll be wonderful if she does!" said Jim. He glanced at his wife for a moment, but her eyes were closed and she seemed to be asleep. "Sue's asleep again. I wonder whether we ought to go now, Claire, as we can't talk to Sue if she needs to sleep now?"

"Well, perhaps we'd better go in a minute or two," said Claire, "so we can come again tomorrow morning for a proper visit; I expect Sue will be feeling much better by then, and properly awake and able to talk with us."

"Oh, I hope so!"

"She should be. Ah, here comes a nurse, so perhaps... Ought we to go now?"

"No, it's quite all right to stay here if you want to," said the nurse.

"Well, thank you," said Claire, "but, all the same, I think that perhaps we will go now as we can't talk with Sue - Lady Sandy - while she's asleep."

"Just as you please," said the nurse. "I'll be back in a few minutes to feed the baby, and if you want to stay to watch that you're welcome to."

"Do you mean, you're going to bottle-feed her?" asked Claire.

"Yes, that's what we're doing today as Lady Sandy isn't ready to breast-feed her yet."

Jim and Claire said good-bye to Susan, but received no answer; she was obviously asleep, and the baby was also quiet in her cot. They asked the nurse to tell Susan, when she woke up, that they would return in the morning (visiting in the Maternity Unit was allowed at any time of the day), and then they left the ward together.

"What a tiny baby your daughter is, Jim!" said Claire as they walked along a corridor towards the exit. "Do you know, if she'd been any smaller, I expect they would have had to keep her in an incubator; but then she's not all that premature, is she?"

"Well, no," said Jim. "I suppose she isn't. We reckoned, actually, that the full nine months would have taken us to about the middle of this month, but today is only the second."

"Yes, February the second is a very good day to have a birthday because it's Candlemas today."

"Oh, yes, so it is!" said Jim. He remembered that Susan had often reminded him that the second of February was the Feast of Candlemas; and this, in its turn, reminded him that Claire, like Susan, seemed to be a regular worshipper on Sundays.

"No doubt you'll be having Julia baptised presently?" said Claire. "You are quite sure that her name is Julia, aren't you?"

"Oh, yes, we're absolutely sure about that. Her full name is Julia Mary Sandy, but she's going to be called Julia."

"It's a nice name – a very nice name!"

"Yes, we both think so; but I'm really rather glad that she's a girl as we still hadn't decided on a name for a boy, although we'd narrowed down the choice to either Tony or Tim – but now we won't have to make that decision anyway."

They came out of the hospital, but continued to chat as they drove back to the house in Martin Lane.

*

"Do you know, Sue," said Jim, "that when the hospital rang us up yesterday evening at about five o' clock I thought it must be to give us some dreadful news. I thought that they were going to tell us that you'd died."

"Good heavens!" said Susan. "What ever made you think that?"

"Oh, well..." Jim suddenly looked and sounded flustered, and wished that he had not told his wife what he had been thinking. "I just thought that it was possible that the hospital might have bad news for us."

"It was my fault," confessed Claire. "I think I must have put that idea into Jim's head when we were having our supper on the evening of the day you went into hospital. We were talking about the pain and difficulties and dangers of giving birth naturally, and I related the story of how I nearly died from a haemorrage after Rose was born. I know that upset you quite a lot, Jim; and I was really sorry afterwards that I'd told you about it."

"It's all right now, Claire," said Jim quickly. "You needn't worry about that any more."

"All right, Jim, and thank you for saying that," said Claire. "We won't worry about it any more."

It was ten o' clock in the morning, and Jim and Claire had come back the next morning, as they had said that they would, to visit Susan and Julia. They had found Susan sitting up in bed, and looking quite alert and cheerful while she was breast-feeding the baby.

"To change the subject: It's good to see that you're looking so much better this morning, Sue!" continued Claire. "I see they've taken that drip out of your arm. Does that mean that you're able to eat and drink normally again now?" When they had visited Susan on the previous evening they had noticed that she had been attached to a drip to give her food and fluid intravenously.

"Yes, I'm feeling much better this morning," said Susan, "and, in fact, I've had a good breakfast! And, as you can see, Julia is having a good breakfast too!" Susan was sitting up with one breast partly exposed, and Julia was sucking it greedily.

"Yes, it's good to see that!" said Claire.

"It's great!" agreed Jim. "But does Julia cry much, Sue? We haven't heard her crying yet."

"She was crying just before you came in," said Susan, "but it must have been just to tell me that she needed feeding. She quietened down as soon as I gave her my breast."

They chatted together for a while until presently, when Susan felt that the baby had had enough milk, they laid her (with Claire's help) back in her cot. Then Claire asked a question which had also been on Jim's mind.

"Has anything been said yet, Sue, about when you and Julia are likely to come out of hospital?"

"Well, nothing definite has been said yet about our coming out," said Susan, "except that they've told me that we'll definitely be staying here over this weekend. A doctor saw me this morning, and she said that everything is still going on all right by Monday morning, they might let us come home on Tuesday or Wednesday."

"And then you're coming back to stay with us for a while?" said Claire.

"Oh, yes, I think we'll have to, if you don't mind. You see, it's quite a long journey to go back to Rhodes Castle."

"But of course you should come back to stay with us in Roehampton for a while after your discharge from Hospital," said Claire. "You'll be more than welcome!"

"It's kind of you to say that, Claire, but we must remember that you and John are coming to stay with us at Rhodes Castle towards the end of this month,"

"Yes, and we're very much looking forward to that!"

"Well then, it would make sense, I think, for us all to travel down to the Castle together when we want to - when we feel ready to go - but we've got to bear in mind the date of Jim's ceremony in the House of Lords."

"And what's the date for that?"

"The twenty-fourth of this month, which I believe is a Thursday; and today's a Thursday so it must be three weeks from today."

"H'm," said Claire. "In that case don't you think, Sue, that it would be best for you and Jim and Julia to stay at our house until after that ceremony is over? But what do you think, Jim? After all, it's *your* ceremony we're talking about!"

"Oh, well..." said Jim, suddenly startled out of a daydream when he had not expected to be spoken to. "Well, I think that's a good idea as it would save us a trip down to Dorset, and then having to come back to London, and then having to go down to Dorset again."

"And I agree with you, darling," said Susan. "Claire's quite right. It would be best to stay in London until you've been formally introduced as Baron Sandy of Rhodes Castle, and then we could all go down to the Castle together.

So that seems to be settled, thought Jim. For several minutes he had hardly heard the conversation between Claire and Susan while his gaze had been wandering around the large hospital ward. It's rather odd that Sue didn't choose to be in a private ward when they offered her that, he thought, but I suppose she thought she'd feel lonely and isolated in a private ward. Then he found that he was thinking again about his forthcoming Introduction Ceremony in the House of Lords. I wonder whether I shall feel dreadfully nervous when it comes to the time for it? he asked himself. But, after all, surely there won't be any need to be nervous as we'll be rehearsing it all the evening before, and Geoffrey Padgate will be my sponsor... Oh, my goodness! We'll have to change the arrangements if we're going to stay in Roehampton until after it's over.

"Sue?" he said.

"What's that, darling?"

"We've invited the Padgates to come to Rhodes Castle two days before my ceremony in the Lords. You remember that?"

"Oh, yes, darling, I remember that we've made that arrangement, and that they've accepted our invitation. But why did you mention it?"

"Well, because it won't work if we're going to stay here in Roehampton until some time after February the twenty-fourth!"

"Oh, gosh, yes, I see what you mean!" said Susan. "Either we will have to go back home before they arrive, or we'll just have to put them off, I suppose."

"Don't worry about it," said Claire quickly. "Surely the easiest way to deal with that problem, Sue, would be to ask your aunt and uncle to come to stay with us in Martin Lane, instead of staying at Rhodes Castle?"

"But surely, Claire, that would be putting you to a lot of extra trouble?" said Susan.

"Nonsense!" said Claire. "Of course it wouldn't! I can assure you, Sue, that we'd be delighted to have your aunt and uncle to stay here in Roehampton, so as to save you an unnecessary journey down to Dorset, and back again. You know we've got that second spare room?

Well, let's offer it to them!"

"Oh, Claire, it really is good of you to say that! I think that idea may well save the situation for us."

"Well, you could put it to them," said Claire. "I think it's worth a try, if you know what I mean."

"It is worth a try," said Susan. "Jim, darling, I think that perhaps - if Claire doesn't mind you using her telephone - you could give Uncle Geoffrey a ring tonight, and explain our situation to him, and pass on Claire's invitation; and then we'll find out what they want to do."

"Of course Jim may use our telephone for that," said Claire.

"Right, I'll do that," said Jim. "I'll tell you what, Sue: I could ring them up *before* we come to visit you this evening, and then, if I get an answer from them, I can come and tell you what it is."

*

The moment he saw her, Jim told Susan that the new arrangement would be fine. He had spoken to Nora Padgate on the telephone, he told her, and then to Geoffrey Padgate, and they had both understood the situation, and they both thought that it would be an excellent idea to stay at a house in London, rather than at Rhodes Castle.

"And did it sound as if they were disappointed not to be coming to the Castle?" asked Susan.

"Your Aunt didn't sound in the least disappointed," said Jim, "and neither did your Uncle when I spoke to him. He said it would make it much easier for them, and easier for us too."

"That's fine!" said Susan.

CHAPTER TWENTY-SEVEN

Ten days after she had been admitted to Queen Mary's Hospital Susan was discharged on the Wednesday of the next week (the ninth of February). Claire came in her car at one o' clock to bring Susan and Julia back to the house in Martin Lane. Luckily it was not particularly cold for a February day, but Julia was nevertheless well wrapped up to protect her from the chilling effect of the external air on the short car journey along Roehampton Lane. Jim pushed his wife and daughter along the hospital corridors in Susan's wheelchair (with Julia cradled in her mother's arms); then he pushed them through the exit doors and through the car park to the place where Claire had parked her car.

Finally he took Julia in his own arms during the delicate business of transferring Susan from the wheelchair to the front passenger seat of the car, knowing that Susan was likely to be both slower and weaker in her movements following ten days of confinement in hospital.

"Hush, Ju!" said Jim soothingly (he hoped it was a soothing voice) as he rocked his tiny daughter in his arms. The child was crying, but the crying soon stopped.

"You're doing fine, darling!" said Susan encouragingly as she settled herself in the front passenger seat.

"That's it, Jim!" said Claire. "You seem to have found the right touch for Julia!"

"I'll take her back now," said Susan.

Jim handed over his precious little bundle, which was now more or less quiet again, and took his place on the back seat of the car. I can still hardly believe that I'm Julia's father! he thought wonderingly.

Luckily, however, they were going to get quite a lot of help in looking after Julia because of Susan's disability. It had been arranged by the staff at the hospital that a nurse would visit the house twice each day in order to give Susan a little rest from maternal duties.

They were expecting the first visit that afternoon at around four o'clock, and the nurse would, if necessary, stay with them for an hour or two on each visit.

*

On the morning of the day when they were expecting the Padgates to arrive a letter came for Jim and Susan which looked quite innocent and unremarkable, but which, they guessed, contained unpleasant news even before they had opened the envelope. Jim, having finished his breakfast, had left the table in the part of the kitchen which they used as a dining-room, meaning to go upstairs but, as he came to the end of the dark passage, he glanced down the hall and saw that a small pile of mail had been pushed through the letter-box. Something prompted him to delay going up the stairs, and instead to go immediately to check whether any post had come that morning for him and Susan. He quickly found that there was one envelope addressed to "Lady Sandy and Mr. J. Sandy", and that the other four envelopes were all items of mail for Mr. or Mrs. Walker. The next moment, however, as he looked at the envelope addressed to Susan and himself, he felt something like a flash of fear stab through him as he noticed the postmark on the envelope: it was from nearby London S.W. 14. He also saw that, like all the post they had received at Martin Lane, it had been sent first to Rhodes Castle, and then forwarded on from there.

Already he was hurrying back along the passage towards the kitchen, the letter in his hand, and the rest of the post left lying where it had fallen on the carpet in the hall. Now he was looking decidedly worried as he re-entered the kitchen where Susan and Claire were still sitting and chatting at the breakfast table.

"What's up, Jim?" said Claire, glancing up at him as he came into the room. "You're looking very worried?"

"I think we've got a letter here from Dick and Jane Dalmane," said Jim, "and I think that you'd better look at it first, Sue."

"All right," said Susan as Jim handed the letter over to her. "But what makes you think it's from them?"

"It's the postmark," said Jim. "Look, it's from London S.W.14."

"So it is! And that, I think, means it's from East Sheen?" Susan was now looking at Claire for an answer.

"Yes, East Sheen is S.W.14," said Claire, who, of course, knew all that part of south-west London very well. "Or it could be Mortlake."

"You must be right, Jim, darling," said Susan. "It must be a letter from those Dalmanes, and, of course, it may well be bad news – or it may not – so we'd better open it right away and find out what it is." She was still holding the envelope, unopened, in her right hand, but now she paused, and seemed to be listening intently. There followed a second or two of tense silence.

"Julia'll be all right upstairs now," said Claire, guessing that Susan had thought that she had heard the baby crying. "Remember, Sue, that she's got the nurse with her – and we're all longing to know what's in that letter! You don't mind letting me know as well, do you?"

"Oh, no, not a bit, seeing that you know all about our quarrel with the Dalmanes. Right – here goes!"

As quickly as she could, Susan opened the envelope. However, as she pulled out the letter and took a first glance at it, she suddenly drew in her breath sharply.

"Oh, good heavens! What cheek! I really can hardly believe this!"

"What is it?" asked Jim, trying to see the letter that Susan was holding.

"Why, they've headed the letter as if they were already in residence in Rhodes Castle as their seat! Look, they've used a printed heading which says, 'From the Earl of Saint Helens, Rhodes Castle, Sherborne, Dorset'. Then they've added, in ordinary writing, 'Temporary Address: 4 Archers Road, LONDON SW14'." Susan held up the letter for a moment for the other two to see it.

"*Temporary* address indeed!" said Jim bitterly.

"It's the height of impertinence!" said Claire.

"It jolly well is!" agreed Susan. "Anyway, I might as well read it all out."

She began to read the letter aloud.

My dear Susan and Jim,

You may remember that when you came to stay a night with us in May of last year we agreed that we would be moving into the Castle in February of this year. In other words, we would be in residence in our seat now if we had not, at your request, delayed that move.

More recently we were very concerned and sorry to hear about your illness, Susan, and we would like to take this opportunity to extend to you our best wishes for a full recovery. We realize that, having suffered a stroke, the circumstances of your life must be considerably more difficult than they were before, and therefore we have thought it only right and fair to extend our deadline again for moving in to the Castle in oder that you may have more time to find yourselves a new home. With this in mind, we are therefore writing this to inform you that we shall be moving into Rhodes Castle on the first of July of next year; i.e. 1ˢᵗ July 1967. We would like to tell you that this is our final decision on this matter; we are not minded to move the date again to further delay our move to our seat, Rhodes Castle.

We hope that you will not be unduly inconvenienced by our decision.

Yours sincerely,
Richard and Jane Saint Helens.

Susan put the letter down on the table and looked up at the shocked faces of the other two.

"So that's it?" said Jim.

"That's it," said Susan, "and it *is* the height of impertinence - all of it! You're quite right, Claire!"

"Well, they do at least send you their best wishes for your recovery," said Claire.

"I don't believe they really mean it," said Susan.

"I bet they don't!" said Jim.

Susan picked up the letter again and began to re-read parts of it.

"'We agreed that we would be moving into the Castle in February of this year.' No, we didn't. *We* never agreed to that, did we?"

"That's right, Sue, we didn't," said Jim. "If I remember rightly, it was an entirely arbitrary decision on their part.

"'We have thought it only right and fair to extend our deadline again'," continued Susan, reading again from the letter. "*Generous,* aren't they, to extend their deadline? But as for saying, 'We hope that you will not be unduly inconvenienced by our decision': that is simply ridiculous! How could we not be inconvenienced by their decision to move into the Castle when we haven't invited them?"

"How indeed?" agreed Jim. "I think the whole tone of the letter is pompous and nasty!"

"It is indeed that," said Susan. "It really is upsetting to read through a letter like that." She paused a moment, and noticed that Claire was looking very thoughtful. "But what do you think, Claire?"

"What do I think?" said Claire. "Well, for a start, I certainly agree with everything that's just been said about it being a rude, pompous, and nasty letter; but I have, actually, just had another thought about it. Do you think, Sue, that they know that Jim is about to become Baron Sandy of Rhodes Castle? You haven't told them that yet, have you?"

"Well, no, I don't believe we have; at least I haven't. Darling, you haven't rung them up to tell them about that, have you?"

"Oh, no, I haven't!" said Jim. "I haven't spoken to them at all since that night we spent at their home."

"Well then," said Claire, "it's probably safe to assume that they know nothing about Jim's forthcoming elevation to the Lords; at any rate, there doesn't seem to be anything in that letter to suggest that they are aware of it. And if they were aware that Jim is about to become Baron Sandy of Rhodes Castle, they surely wouldn't be talking quite so confidently about moving into their seat, Rhodes Castle, in July of next year?"

"Why, Claire, that's brilliant!" exclaimed Susan joyfully. "Why didn't we think of it before? Of course that's what we must do: we must let them know straight away that Jim is very shortly to become Baron Sandy of Rhodes Castle."

"I could ring them up tonight to tell them about it," said Jim, "if that's all right with you, Claire?"

"Yes, of course you may do that," said Claire. "But don't you think that it might be even better to wait until Thursday evening when you will actually *be* Lord Sandy?"

"Why, yes, you're right again, Claire!" said Jim happily. "I'll ring them up after we've come back here, following the ceremony in the Lords, and I'll really shock them by saying, 'This is Baron Sandy of Rhodes Castle speaking' – but I bet they won't believe me – not at first anyway!"

"But I shouldn't pin all your hopes on that approach, if I were you," warned Claire.

"That's just what I was going to say," said Susan. "The use of shock tactics against them in this way may work – or it may not. We can only give it a try.

"We will!" said Jim decisively. "I'll ring them up on Thursday evening."

"Fine!" said Susan.

*

Jim doffed his hat carefully, and bowed to the Lord Chancellor for the last time. The ceremony was over, and he was now Baron Sandy of Rhodes Castle, although he could not yet quite believe in this fact.

Never mind, he told himself, the idea of being Lord Sandy will, I suppose, gradually sink into my subconscious; and anyway the main thing is that I've got through it all right, without making any serious gaffes! Then Jim saw that the Lord Chancellor was smiling at him for a moment, and he found himself happily smiling back. The next moment, however, having made a slight gesture with his hand to indicate that he was to follow him, the Lord Chancellor began to walk out of the chamber, followed by his sponsor, Lord Padgate. Jim immediately fell into line and followed them, remembering how they had rehearsed this procedure for leaving the Chamber of the Lords at the end of the ceremony. Jim walked sobrely along a few steps behind Lord Padgate, but as he walked he allowed himself one quick glance up to the Gallery, where the others were sitting, watching them. Yes, there they were: Susan, sitting in the middle of the group, with Nora Padgate to her right, and Claire Walker to her left; he was glad that none of the three ladies had moved from her seat since they had arrived there about half an hour earlier, but now he noticed for the first time that they were all smiling at him. Good, he told himself, they reckon I've managed it all right! It was the first time he had glanced up there since the beginning of the ceremony.

Lord Padgate passed through the main doors of the Chamber, the doors at the opposite end of the Chamber to the dais on which stood the ornate gilded thrones, one for the Sovereign, and one for the Sovereign's consort. Jim followed him through the doors but, once in the lobby outside the Lords Chamber, Lord Padgate paused and turned to face Jim, a smile on his face.

"Well, well, my Lord," he said – "that's that! But what did you think of it Lord Sandy? I bet you're glad it's over, though!"

"Well, er, yes, I suppose I am – in a way!" said Jim, aware that he was feeling rather dazed by the whole business. I don't really know *how* i'm feeling right now! he told himself.

Lord Padgate laughed.

"That's right, my Lord!" he chuckled. "Well, I don't know about you, Jim, but I could do with a cup of tea and a little sustenance after that, and I dare say you could too! Shall we head for the restaurant?"

"Yes, that's a good idea, if you'll lead the way," said Jim. "Anyway, we said we'd meet the ladies in there."

"So we did, so we'll do that. But you'll soon get used to the geography of this place, Jim."

Geoffrey Padgate was leading the way along a passage but, just before they came to the door of the Lords' Restaurant, they spotted the three ladies coming towards them from another direction, and saw Nora Padgate wave a hand cheerfully. Claire, her head down, was busily pushing Susan along the passage in her wheelchair. A moment later, however, she looked up and saw that Lord Padgate and Jim had reached the door of the restaurant, and that Geoffrey was holding the door open for the wheelchair to be pushed through it.

A few minutes later they were all sitting round one of many empty tables in the restaurant, waiting to be served. The place at that time (it was almost twenty minutes past three) was almost empty.

"Well, darling," said Susan, when Jim had sat down in the chair to her right which the others had left for him, "we thought that it all went extremely well, but I expect that you're feeling very pleased that you've got that over now?"

"Oh, yes, I think I am pleased that it's over and that it's gone all right," said Jim, "but, you know, I really don't think that I *feel* like Lord Sandy yet!"

"Oh, you will quite soon, darling, when you've got used to the idea... Ah, here comes the waiter to take our order. Shall I just order afternoon tea for all of us?"

"They had returned to the house in Martin Lane at just after half past four after a rather slow journey home via the King's Road, the route that Claire had chosen, but Susan had not felt unduly worried by the delays due to traffic congestion; and she was wise enough not to think of blaming Claire for her choice of route. It might have been just as bad - or even worse - if we'd gone the other way, she told herself sensibly. And, anyway, I needn't be worried about Julia; that nurse is very capable, and she's bound to be all right being looked after by her. However, when Claire had turned her car into Martin Lane to park it outside her house, Susan had said, "I'd better go up to see Julia right away!"

"It's all right, Sue," Claire had said. "I'll tell you what: I'll run up the stairs now and look in on Julia and the nurse, but then, if there's anything amiss, I'll come down to tell you right away; but otherwise, if she's quiet, I'll stay upstairs and change."

"I don't think my maternal instincts can be very good!" complained Susan when Claire had disappeared up the stairs, but Jim knew that she was saying it in a half-joking way.

"What do you mean, Sue, darling?" he asked quietly.

"Why, if my maternal instincts had been stronger, as I'm sure they should be, I'd have been worried stiff about my baby all the time that we've been away, and I wouldn't have let Claire go up to our bedroom first to see if Julia was all right. I'd have gone straight up myself.

But it must be all right, or Claire would have come down by now to tell me."

"I'm sure that you needn't be worried, Susan," said Nora, her aunt. "We haven't heard a sound from upstairs since we returned."

*

Jim had remembered the telephone call that he had to make to Dick Dalmane. I'd better ring him up now – if I can! he told himself. He dialled the number and, when the butler had answered the telephone, presently found himself talking to Dick.

"Oh, hello, I'm Jim Sandy, my Lord" he began. "But as from today I'm Baron Sandy of Rhodes Castle..."

"WHAT? Do you mean to tell me that they've just made you into a life peer? Or are you pulling my leg?

"Oh no, sir, I'm not pulling your leg – that's the honest truth!"

"Damn! Blast it...!"

Jim, startled for a moment to hear Dick Dalmane swearing, took the telephone receiver away from his ear for a moment and glanced round at Susan. However, he saw that she was clearly amused by what she had heard; she was smiling at him happily. He felt encouraged, and put the telephone back to his ear to continue the conversation.

"I beg your pardon, sir?" he ventured.

He heard Dick Dalmane sigh out a heavy breath of frustration.

"I am sorry... Lord Sandy. I do apologize for my language. But you do understand, I suppose, what that title of your's implies? To put it bluntly, you've scuppered my chances! Frankly, it is quite obvious that the title 'Baron Sandy of Rhodes Castle' conveys to *you* the heirdom of the Castle - my rightful seat as the Earl of Saint Helens - and I've no doubt that you'll be very pleased that it is so!"

Jim now felt that he was suddenly at a loss for words; he simply did not know what he ought to say next. It certainly sounded as if the Earl was conceding complete defeat over the matter of inheriting the Castle, but, surprisingly, Jim now felt almost sorry for him.

"Well, sir, I'm... er... sorry that..." he began, but Dick Dalmane interrupted him.

"Just a minute, Jim. I must have a word with my wife. Would you hold the line, please?"

As he continued to hold the telephone to his ear Jim now tried to picture the scene in the sitting-room of the Dalmanes' house. Jane Dalmane had, no doubt, been somewhere close to her husband all the time during the call, and now Jim found that he could easily overhear the conversation between husband and wife.

"What's the matter, darling? Are we not going to be able to move into the Castle after all because Jim Sandy's been given a new title so that he inherits it, rather than you?"

"That's exactly how it is, my dear," said Dick Dalmane.

"Oh, Dick, darling, how horrible! What a disgusting trick to play on us - to turn us out of our rightful inheritance in such a way!"

"That's exactly how I feel about it, Jane, darling; but I don't think I can do anything about it."

Jim took the telephone away from his ear for a moment when he saw that Susan wanted to say something to him.

"Is he telling Jane now what you've just told him?" Susan was speaking very quietly, in little more than a whisper.

"Yes, she must have overheard most of what I was telling him," said Jim, equally quietly. "Do you want to have a word with them now, Sue?"

"Not just yet, but I will have a word with Dick when you've finished talking to him.

Jim put the telephone back to his ear again, and again he heard Jane Dalmane's voice.

"So tell him, darling, that we're not going to be moving in, but that we are *not* going to give up our right to consider Rhodes Castle as our rightful seat."

"I'll tell him that now," said Dick Dalmane. "Are you still there, Lord Sandy?"

"Yes, I'm here," said Jim.

"I concede defeat, Lord Sandy, in the matter of our moving into the Castle. We won't be moving in after all. You have out-manoevered me, sir, in your very smart move of having yourself made Baron Sandy of Rhodes Castle, but - I must emphasise this - we are most certainly not giving up our right to call Rhodes Castle our seat. After all, it has been the seat of every one of the Earls of Saint Helens before me, as you well know, and it is, and will remain my seat. Have I made my position quite clear to you, Lord Sandy?"

"That's quite clear, Lord Dalmane."

"Very well, that's all there is to say about it. No, there is one more thing that I should say, isn't there?" The Earl made a slight pause before continuing, and Jim felt a sudden flash of apprehension as he wondered what was coming next, but he need not have worried. "I must congratulate you, Jim, on your elevation to the Lords!"

"Oh, thank you very much, sir!"

"Well, it would be churlish of me not to say that, wouldn't it - in spite of the fact that your wonderfully conceived plan has quite frustrated our hopes? But never mind that now. Welcome to the Noble Lords, Jim! No doubt we'll meet from time to time in the Chamber?"

"No doubt we will," said Jim.

"So I'll say good-bye for now."

"Oh, just a minute, Lord Dalmane, sir; my wife said that she'd like to have a word with you before we ring off." Feeling rather pleased with himself for the way that his talk with Lord Dalmane had gone, Jim handed the telephone over to Susan.

"Hello, Dick!" said Susan when she had taken the telephone.

"Hello, Susan. You'll have gathered, no doubt, that because of Jim's new title, which we had no idea about, we cannot possibly move into our seat, Rhodes Castle? No doubt you're very pleased about that?"

"Yes, of course we're pleased, and we're sorry if this news has come as a shock to you; but what I wanted to tell you was that we thought that the way you headed your letter, as if you were already resident in your seat, Rhodes Castle, was, to put it bluntly, a quite unnecessary piece of rudeness to us."

"Oh, come off it, Susan - you can't really mean that!"

"But we do mean it, don't we, darling?" Susan looked round at Jim, who nodded to her to show his agreement. "But never mind; don't let's think about that any more. You know, Dick, we really do appreciate your generosity in deciding to allow us to remain residents in our own home without the threat of eviction hanging over our heads!"

"Yes, we do!" added Jim, so that Dick Dalmane would be able to hear him.

"Don't mention it, Susan," he said.

"Oh, but I thought that I would just mention it!" said Susan.

They exchanged a few more pleasantries and then said good-bye to each other. Susan passed the telephone receiver back to Jim, who hung it up. Then they looked at each other happily for a moment before Susan suddenly flung both her arms up in an expansive gesture of triumphant relief.

"Darling, we've won! I can hardly believe that he's backed down - but he has!"

"Yes, we've squashed him!" said Jim. They embraced and kissed each other urgently for a moment, and then Susan rose to her feet.

"Come on, we must go and tell the others," she said.

CHAPTER TWENTY-EIGHT

"We're just coming up to the turn to the right for the Castle," said Susan, who was sitting in the front passenger seat beside Claire who was driving her own car. "There it is, where you see that finger-post, pointing to the right."

"I see it," said Claire, putting on her right-turn indicator and slowing the car down.

"It's a new signpost, actually, that they only put up last autumn," said Jim. "We asked the Council to put it up because of all the tourists we get."

"And I suppose this little house here must be a lodge of the Castle?" said John Walker, who was sitting beside Jim on the back seat.

"My word, what impressive gates you have!"

"Yes, that's the lodge called South Lodge," said Jim. "We've got a few other lodges, which you'll see presently."

"I say, what a gorgeous avenue of trees this drive is!" said Claire enthusiastically. "And there's the Castle in the distance!" The car was sweeping through the outer drive gates as she spoke.

"Here's home, Julia!" said Susan, holding up her baby for a moment as if to show her the distant Great Tower of the Castle. "This is where you're going to live." Julia, however, did not seem to be interested in anything but snuggling back in her mother's arms.

"I think she's getting sleepy now," said Claire.

"Yes, she is," agreed Susan.

*

They had left the house in Martin Lane, Roehampton, at half past nine in the morning, and had made an unhurried journey down to Dorset with a number of stops, mainly for the benefit of Susan and Julia. Then they had stopped to eat a lunch picnic on the Downs at White Sheet Hill, Claire having turned off the A30 main road where a sign pointed to the left to Middle Down (about eight miles short of Shaftesbury).

*

As they drove up the outer drive to the Castle Jim was once again thinking about Rachel Connor. Several times that day during the journey Jim had remembered that as they were now going back home, they were also going back to Rachel, or at least to situations where there might be a chance of meeting her. He was aware that his relatively long absence from the Castle of almost nine weeks had certainly had an effect on his feelings about Rachel: the fire of his passion for her had dimmed down a lot, and it had receded into the background of his thoughts and feelings. Now, however, he was returning to Rhodes Castle, and he wondered whether he would soon find himself once again trapped in the agonising ecstasies of an obsessive love which could never be properly satisfied. This thought, in its turn, had made him wonder whether his life would be sweeter and better if he could never see Rachel again. I almost wish that she would decide to leave us, so that I would never see her again, he said to himself rather sadly. Yes, my life really has been much more peaceful in London with her well out of the way; but now I'll see her again - perhaps any moment now - and then, perhaps, I'll find myself falling hopelessly in love with her once again. He looked at his watch and saw that the time was five minutes past two, and then looked quickly ahead again at the road. He could see that they were quickly approaching the Inner Lodge and the Visitor Centre. He knew that the second guided tour of the day would, if it was running to schedule, be somewhere near the Servants' Graveyard; and that meant that at any moment now he might catch sight of Rachel and her tour party.

He was startled out of his daydreams when John Walker spoke, asking him a question.

"I suppose those buildings over there are what you call your Visitor Centre?"

"Yes, and that little house is called the Inner Lodge," said Jim.

"But am I allowed to drive on through these gates?" asked Claire, putting her foot on the brake pedal of her car.

"Oh, yes, drive on!" said Susan. "Take no notice of that 'PRIVATE' sign; it's only there to stop our visitors driving their cars into this private inner part of our drive."

"Oh, look, those people here must be one of your guided tours?" said Claire, looking ahead to where they saw a large number of people walking, mostly in single file, down a narrow footpath and then out onto the drive.

"Just a minute!" said Susan. "Do you mind pulling up here for a moment, Claire, so that I can have a quick word with our Guide?"

Jim's heart had missed a beat when he had caught sight of the line of tourists coming out from the Servants' Graveyard. For a second or two his eyes searched desperately for Rachel, but then, as the car slowed down to stop, he saw her. There she was: the short and rather plump figure of Rachel Connor as seen from behind, with her unmistakable sweep of honey-blonde hair hanging lusciously on her shoulders - so different from Claire's longer and rather untidy blonde hair.

Susan wound down her window and waved an arm to attract the Guide's attention.

"Hello there, Rachel!"

"Oh, hello, Lady Sandy!" said Rachel Connor, recognizing her at the same moment. The car had stopped, and the next moment Rachel was standing by the front passenger window, looking in. For a second or two she looked straight at Jim, sitting behind Claire on the back seat, and gave him a hint of a smile, but then, almost instantly, her gaze shifted back to Susan and Julia. "It's good to see you again, ma'am," she continued politely, "and I see you have the newest member of your family here too! A girl?"

"Yes, this is Julia," said Susan. "And these other two are our tenants in our house in Roehampton, Claire and John Walker - and, of course, you know my husband, Jim. Well, Rachel, how are things going with you?"

"Splendidly, thank you, my Lady. We've been having very good numbers of people on the guided tours these last few days; and this afternoon I've actually got twenty-four people on this tour, which I think could well be a record number for a February day."

"Yes, it could well be!"

"But, if you don't mind, Lady Sandy, I'd better be moving my party on and staying with them. I don't want any of them to wander off and get lost while I'm talking with you."

"Quite right, Mrs. Connor! I won't keep you back. Good-bye!"

"Good-bye, Lady Sandy."

As the car moved on again up the drive Jim could not resist the temptation to turn his head to have one more look at Rachel. Ah, she's looking as lovely as ever! he thought.

Jim was not to know that he would not see her again for several years, so there was no thought in his mind to spoil his happiness at that moment. The fact that she had smiled at him, even though it had only been a half-smile and had only lasted for a second or two, meant a great deal to him.

"There's Ailean!" said Susan suddenly.

"She's your Guide's daughter, isn't she?" said Claire.

"That's it!" said Susan.

Jim had turned his head when Susan had called out, 'There's Ailean!', but somehow he hardly noticed the dark haired girl who was on her knees in a flowerbed, no doubt doing some weeding. Having just seen Rachel he could take little interest in Ailean. Susan, however, waved a hand cheerfully to her; and Ailean, who had turned her head to see who was in the car, waved back to them.

When they came to the Castle they saw that the massive outer wooden front door was firmly shut.

There seems to be no one about here to welcome us," said Susan as Claire parked her car beside the stone steps that lead up to the front door. "But, of course, it doesn't matter as they had no idea what time of day we were likely to arrive back here."

It was at this point that Jim managed to detach himself sufficiently from his daydreams to realize that it was up to him, and no one else, to take the lead in welcoming the visitors and Susan and Julia into the Castle. He sprang to his feet, opened the car door, and stepped out.

"Come along in, everybody!" he said. "The door won't be locked, so welcome to Rhodes Castle!" He opened the driver's door for Claire to step out as if he were a chauffeur. Goodness, he thought, I must have sounded rather as if I was the Guide, saying, "Welcome to Rhodes Castle!"

"Thank you, Jim," said Claire. "I say, I haven't parked in anyone else's parking space, have I?" She was looking at the only other car standing outside the Castle, a small green car, parked on the other side of the steps.

"No, it's fine to park here," said Jim. "That little green car there belongs to Rachel Connor, our Guide; but no one else is likely to want to park here now."

As he hurried up the stone steps to open the front door Jim was feeling much as he had often felt after meeting Rachel Connor. He had to admit to himself that it had been ass exciting as ever, and the fact that he had managed to mention her name aloud had sent an extra thrill through his body. He opened the outer front door of the Castle, and then the inner door, and then turned to help Susan to step out of the car, using her walking stick. He opened the car door and then held it steady while Susan found her balance as she stood up.

"Don't wait for me, you two," she said. John and Claire Walker were politely waiting for her at the top of the steps. "I can only move slowly. You take them in, Jim, darling, and Julia, if you can."

"Yes, I'll take Julia," said Jim.

"My word, it's rather dark in here, isn't it?" said John when he had followed his wife into the Great Hall.

"Yes, but look at those flags and banners up there!" said Claire.

"It certainly does look like a castle in here! Ah, someone's coming!"

Steps were heard drawing rapidly nearer on the long passage from the kitchen. A moment later Jack, the butler, appeared in the Hall.

"Oh, there you are; but I'm so sorry, my Lady, that I wasn't at the front door to welcome you when you arrived."

"Don't you worry about that, Jack," said Susan, who was coming through the inner front door while Jim held it open for her. "You didn't know what time we'd be coming because we never told you. Is all well here?"

"Yes, my Lady, all is well here, and you'll be pleased to know that the Nanny has arrived here this morning to look after the child.

And good afternoon to you, my Lord!" Smiling, Jack made a little bow to Jim, moving his head only.

"Thank you, Jack!" said Jim, smiling broadly in his turn. "I say, it's a good thing that your Nanny is here, isn't it, Ju?" He was holding and gently rocking the baby in his arms, but Julia continued to cry.

At that moment they heard a door being opened somewhere near the top of the stairs, and then a voice called out, "Just coming!" They all looked hopefully up the main staircase, and a moment later two women appeared on the landing: one was Samantha, and the other was the nanny whom Susan and Jim had engaged to look after the baby, a middle-aged lady smartly dressed in a blue nurse's uniform dress, and with a little white hat on her head.

"Hello, Sue!" said Samantha as she hurried down the stairs with the Nanny to join the others. "This is Mrs. Middleton, who's come to be Julia's Nanny. Mrs. Middleton, this is Lord Sandy and Lady Sandy, and their guests are Mr. and Mrs. Walker. And this is Julia, being rather noisy at the moment in Lord Sandy's arms!"

"Pleased to meet you, Lady Sandy," said Mrs. Middleton, dropping a little curtsey to her. "Pleased to meet you, Lord Sandy, sir." Again she curtsied. "Would you like me to take the baby now, perhaps - if that's all right with you, ma'am?"

"Oh, please do!" said Susan, almost as if she wanted to be rid of a burden that she could not cope with.

"Yes, that's a good idea," agreed Jim as he thankfully handed over the infant to the nanny.

"Now, Claire - but where is she?" said Susan, turning round, but for a moment not seeing John and Claire Walker by her side.

"Thank you, Jack!" said Jim, smiling broadly in his turn. "I say, it's a good thing that your Nanny is here, isn't it, Ju?" He was holding and gently rocking the baby in his arms, but Julia continued to cry.

Rachel Connor had a problem on her mind, and knew that she would have to have a private talk with Susan about it. It was the day after Jim and Susan had returned to the Castle from London, and when she had finished conducting the last guided tour of the day, she stepped into her car, where it was parked at the Visitor Centre to drive back to the Castle. It was a quarter to six in the evening when she returned to the front door of the Castle and walked in there. She was not sure whether she would be able to find Susan at that time, or what she would be doing if she did find her, but, of course, she could ask someone, if necessary, whether she could speak to Susan.

In the Great Hall she paused to listen. There seemed to be no one about the place, but from somewhere upstairs came the sound of the baby crying. She was just wondering whether to go upstairs to knock on Susan's bedroom door when she heard the sound of a door being closed somewhere in the long passage which lead to the kitchen. She immediately decided to walk in that direction instead.

Jack, the butler, had been sitting at his little desk in the butler's pantry (he used the room as a sort of private office), but had heard someone come into the Hall, and had decided that he ought to go and see who it was. He opened his door and saw Rachel Connor coming towards him along the passage.

"Oh, hello, Jack; I'm glad to see you!" she said as soon as she saw him.

"Hello, Mrs. Connor?" said the butler, wondering what she could possibly want him for.

"Jack, I need to find Susan as I've something urgent to talk about with her. Do you know where she is now?"

"I believe her Ladyship is in the Study at the moment, so, if you like, I'll just ask her whether she could have a word with you now."

"Oh, thank you, Jack," said Rachel Connor. She had, in fact, just walked past the closed door of the Study, but Jack knocked on the door, and heard Susan's, "Come in!" He entered the room, and Susan looked up from the letter she was writing.

"What is it, Jack?" she said.

"I'm sorry to interrupt you when you're busy, my Lady, but Mrs.

Connor is here, and she says she needs to talk to you urgently."

"Right, ask her to come in then."

Rachel Connor knocked lightly on the Study door, entered the room, and saw that Susan was looking at her gravely.

"Hello, Rachel," she said. "Is there some problem you wanted to talk to me about?"

"Well, yes, I suppose it is a problem," said Rachel.

"Do sit down, please," said Susan. "Look here, why not draw up one of the chairs to the desk so that we can talk more easily?"

Rachel Connor drew up a chair so that she could sit down at the desk, facing Susan.

"I'd better come to the point straight away," she said. "I'm really sorry to have to tell you this, my Lady, but I think that I'll probably have to give you my notice and leave the Castle very soon."

"Oh, no!" Susan looked and sounded genuinely shocked. "But why, Rachel? Are you not happy working here with us?"

"I'm very, *very* happy working here with you, ma'am, and it's really distressing to think that I'll have to leave you, but, you see, it's like this. My husband had a letter yesterday from the Managing Director of the company he works for, offering him promotion to a much better job within the company; in fact, they would like him to join the board of directors and to work at the company's head office. My husband told me about this last night when he came home and, of course, he's very keen to accept this offer; but you see, Lady Sandy, that would mean we'd have to leave our home here and move, so that I would have to give up my very good job here - which I really don't want to do."

"I see," said Susan. "Naturally you don't want to move from here if you don't really have to. But where is the company's head office? Where would you be moving to?"

"Well, it's in Ireland, actually, Lady Sandy - it's at Bantry in County Cork."

"Good heavens!" exclaimed Susan. "In Ireland! Oh dear, oh dear, Rachel! So we really would lose you if your husband accepts this promotion, as then, of course, you would have to go with him?"

"That's just how it is, Lady Sandy."

"Well, Rachel, I really am very sorry for you - I really do feel for you. You did quite right to come and tell me about it, but I *do* wish That I could do something that would help you - but, frankly, I don't think there's anything I could do to keep you here if your husband wants you to go to Ireland with him."

"Oh, he does, Lady Sandy, he certainly does. Mind you, he does say that he hasn't made up his mind yet - he's going to think it over carefully first - but I think that it's already quite certain that he will accept this promotion."

"But when would all this happen, Rachel? Quite soon?"

"Oh, yes, it's going to be very soon, worse luck. They're giving him just three weeks to make up his mind, and then, if they haven't heard from him by the twenty-first of this month, they'll assume that he's turning down their offer. But if he does accept the offer they'd like him to start work in his new position as a director of the company at the beginning of May."

"The beginning of May! But, good heavens, that's not giving you very much time to find a new home over in Ireland, is it? You'll presumably want to consult an estate agent, and then perhaps you'll want to go and inspect various properties before deciding to buy one? Or perhaps you'll be thinking of rented accomodation, at least for a start?"

"No, actually we won't be needing either to rent or to buy a house as the company owns a few houses in that part of Ireland, and they're offering us one of those to live in - rent free!"

"My goodness, Rachel, your husband must be saying that this offer, with a free house thrown in for good measure, is just too good to be passed over?"

"Yes," said Rachel, "that's exactly what he is saying; and, of course, he's really putting me under great pressure to agree with him, although he doesn't see it that way – naturally! And there's another thing. My husband was born in Bantry, so to go back to work there would be just like coming back home for him. I'm almost certain that he will accept this offer."

"Oh, Rachel... I am sorry for you as I'm afraid that you will have to be leaving us. Anyway, I suppose that you could give us one month's notice of your departure? I imagine that you wouldn't be going over to Ireland until some time after Easter?"

"Yes, that's correct, Lady Sandy. I believe that Easter Day falls on the tenth of April this year, so I imagine that we'll be making the move to County Cork sometime around the eighteenth or nineteenth of April. Mind you, there is one consolation about it: the country round about Bantry is simply gorgeous! We had a holiday there a few years ago, and, do you know, Lady Sandy, I really fell in love with that place, in a way. I suppose that going to live over there *would* be the fulfillment of a dream – if only I didn't have to give up my job here, which I really love doing."

"Ah, yes, you can't have it both ways, can you?" said Susan. She was silent for a moment, but then continued. "By the way, what does Ailean think about it? You'll have told her, no doubt?"

"Oh yes," said Rachel. "I told Ailean about this last night, and I think that she was really shocked, but then she said that she wouldn't think of leaving her job here for anything; she'll stay for just as long as you want her to stay, Lady Sandy. She said that she'd come and visit us occasionally for holidays if we go there – as I expect we will – but she definitely doesn't want to come with us to live over there."

The two women talked for a little longer, but then, remembering the time, Rachel Connor said that she ought to be on her way home.

"Then don't let me keep you, Rachel," said Susan. "Actually, I'm waiting for Jim to come back home – they should be back by now."

"To come back? But is he not at home this afternoon?"

"No, he's taken our guests, the Walkers, out touring this afternoon as he knows all the small roads and villages around here very well. I declined to go with him as I thought I was rather tired after lunch; Claire and I were out shopping in Sherborne for most of this morning. But I would have thought that they would have returned home by now - it's nearly five to six. Anyway, when Jim does come in I'll pass on to him what you've just told me, but - between ourselves, Rachel - I think he'll be devastated by the news that you're thinking of leaving us!" Susan caught Rachel's eye, and looked meaningly at her, and then both women smiled. They both knew that the other one also knew about Jim's heavy infatuation.

"Poor Jim!" said Rachel. "It'll come as a heavy blow to him!"

"Yes, I think so too!" said Susan.

Susan was just thinking of leaving the Study when, gazing idly through the windows, she saw Claire's red car coming up the drive to park outside the Castle. Jim was coming home with the Walkers, and Susan suddenly knew that she was afraid; it was going to be anything but easy to break Rachel's news to Jim, but she knew that it would have to be done somehow.

Some ten minutes had passed since Rachel had left the Castle, but Susan had very soon given up trying to finish the letter she was trying to write (which was a letter to the Becks to tell them about Julia). It's no good, she said to herself, I just can't concentrate on writing now that Rachel has broken this devastating news to me. I'll have to finish the letter tomorrow. I *must* tell Jim about Rachel when he comes in - I told her that I'd do that - but how can I possibly do it without upsetting him really badly? And if the news was upsetting for me, it's going to be far, far worse for Jim, my poor darling. So is there any way I could break the news gently, as it were? Or perhaps I could let him know about it without actually having to tell him myself, in the first instance? Yes, that's an idea: perhaps I could tell it first to Sam, and ask her to pass the message on to Jim...? But, no, that wouldn't do at all. It wouldn't be fair to make Sam do something that I certainly ought to do myself, something that I ought not to funk just because the thought of telling Jim the news myself really frightens me. What will his reaction be when I tell him that Rachel will, very probably, soon be leaving us, and that (very probably) he won't be able to see her again? And what will my reaction be to his reaction? I mustn't let this develope into a nasty jealous row between us - no, whatever happens, that must not happen. Yes, I know that he's in love with Rachel, but we've managed somehow for a long time to 'co-exist', as it were, within that mutual knowledge, and I surely want that state of affairs to continue, don't I - at least until his love for Rachel dies a natural death. Oh dear, oh dear, this is going to be awfully difficult...!

Claire parked her car by the steps to the front door. Susan, watching the car, saw Claire and Jim wave their hands to her from within the car as it stopped; Jim was sitting in the front passenger seat beside Claire as he had been acting as navigator for her. And at that very moment the germ of an idea took root in her mind. Maybe it wasn't going to be quite so difficult after all - provided that she had John and Claire's help.

She had already stood up to look out through the window, but now, with the aid of her walking stick, Susan began to stump across the room towards the door. A vaguely formed plan was beginning to shape itself in her mind. Of course I really ought to talk with Jim privately when I tell him about Rachel, she told herself, but I won't do that; I'll just let it slip out in the course of conversation with all of them. That should be a lot easier for me than if I had to tell him privately.

They met in the Hall as Susan had hoped they would. Jim had just come in through the front door, and was holding it open for Claire and John to follow him in.

"Hello, Sue, darling!" he called out cheerfully.

"Oh, hello, darling!" said Susan. "It's good that you're back now. Have you had a good trip?" Of course I can't go and dampen his spirits right away with Rachel's news, she told herself quickly.

"It's been splendid!" said Jim.

"Yes, we've had a lovely afternoon, thank you," said Claire.

"We've been to all sorts of interesting places, and we had our tea at a cafe."

"Where did you manage to find a cafe?" asked Susan. "You didn't go back to Sherborne, did you?"

"No, we had our tea in Yeovil, actually," said Claire, "but Jim took us there on a lovely round–about route on little country roads."

"We were actually in Somerset, apparently, for part of our route," said John. "We were taken along a very pretty road that runs along beside a reservoir."

"That was the Sutton Bingham Reservoir," said Jim. "We went to Yetminster first, then Netherton and Closworth, and then on to Halstock; and after that we took the road that runs by the reservoir, and came into Yeovil via North Coker."

"And after tea we came back to Yetminster again to complete our round, and we came through a village called Bradford Abbas," said Claire. "I can remember that name! And tomorrow we'd like to go to Cerne Abbas to see the famous Giant - but we hope you'll come with us tomorrow, Sue?"

"Oh, yes, I expect I could come with you tomorrow," said Susan. "The Giant of Cerne Abbas is certainly something well worth seeing. But shall we go and sit down now? We might as well be comfortable while we're talking."

A little later, when they were finding themselves seats in the Green Drawing Room, Claire said, "Well, how's your afternoon been, Sue? I suppose you've spent some time upstairs with Julia?"

"I did indeed," said Susan. "In fact, soon after you'd gone out at three o' clock I sent Mrs. Middleton off to take a break for a couple of hours while I sat in with Julia; so I think we're getting to know each other better now, as you might say. And then Mrs. Middleton came back, but Julia was asleep, so I went downstairs to the Study to write a letter, until I was interrupted by a knock on the door." She paused a moment to summon up her courage. Come on! she said to herself sharply. *Now's* the moment to tell him – you can't funk it now!

"Oh, yes?" said Claire, wondering why Susan had paused suddenly in her account of what had been happening at the Castle. "Someone wanted to talk to you?"

"Yes, it was Rachel," said Susan, "and she'd actually come to give me some rather distressing news." She paused for a second to take a quick glance at Jim's face, and saw that he was now watching her with an anxious look on his face. She continued quickly. "She'd come to tell me that she'd probably have to give her notice and leave us very soon."

"Oh... no!" gasped Jim quietly. Susan, watching him carefully, saw his face suddenly turn pale, but she understood that he was bravely trying to control his reaction of shock to her news.

"Oh dear, what a shame to be losing your Guide!" remarked John politely.

"Yes, it is a shame," said Claire. "That really is distressing news for you, Sue, as you've told me that she's an excellent person in that job."

"She certainly is!" said Susan.

"But why is she going to leave us?" asked Jim. "She must have given you a reason for saying that?"

"It's because her husband is going to change his job. Well, he's not exactly going to change it, but they offered him a promotion, and it means that they're going to have to leave this area."

"When?"

"Probably towards the end of April, Rachel said, so that he can take up his new position as a company director from the beginning of May."

"Oh... the end of April!" He said nothing more, and Susan knew that he was struggling to keep his emotions under control in front of her and the Walkers.

"Did they tell you where they would have to move to?" asked Claire.

"Yes, the Head Office of the company he works for is in Ireland, apparently – it's at Bantry in County Cork, Rachel said – so that's where they would be moving to; and, of course, that's a pretty long way from here so we wouldn't be seeing Rachel any more after they've moved – if they do move. Apparently they haven't come to a final decision yet, but Rachel did say that she thinks that it's pretty well certain that they will move to Ireland." Again Susan glanced at Jim, but she saw that he was keeping a grim-faced silence. My poor darling! she thought. He's trying to put a brave face on his feelings, but I suppose I shouldn't have broken this news to him in front of Claire and John.

Jim was really more stunned and shocked by the news of Rachel's probable imminent departure than he realized at that time. However, he knew that the most important thing was, as Susan had rightly guessed, to put a brave face on it. He told himself firmly that Susan must not be allowed to know that he was extremely shocked and distressed at the prospect of losing Rachel Connor's company for ever. As for the presence of John and Claire Walker at that time: that was a matter of no consequence to him. Such was his state of inner turmoil, counter-balanced by his frantic desire to disguise his obvious manifestations of shock, so that he would appear to Susan to be taking the news calmly, that he was hardly even aware that John and Claire were there with him in the Green Drawing Room.

It was not long after they had finished their dinner, and had returned to sit in the Green Drawing Room, that Susan announced to her guests that she wanted to retire to her bedroom to take an early night.

"So I hope you'll excuse me, Claire, if I say good-night to you and John now, and leave you," she said.

"That's quite all right with us, Sue," said Claire at once.

"What about you, Jim, darling?" said Susan, looking at him meaningfully.

"Oh, well, I think I might as well come with you now, Sue," he said, taking the hint, and knowing that Susan was longing for a chance to talk with him privately. "So I hope you won't mind excusing me too, Claire - although I don't really think that I ought to leave you two on your own in here."

"No, no, you run along with Susan!" said Claire firmly. "We don't at all mind sitting here on our own, do we, John?"

"Absolutely not!" said John. "We'll be perfectly happy on our own here, Jim."

"It was clear to Jim that the Walkers understood that he needed to go with his wife for the purpose of private discussion. He opened the door into the passage for her, and said good-night to John and Claire.

"Darling, it's good of you to say that."

"But I mean it, Sue, darling: I assure you that I really do mean that I'm going to feel very glad about getting rid of Rachel, as it were - getting her right out of my life. And, do you know, I was thinking much the same sort of thoughts in the car when we were motoring back home from London the other day."

"But how could you have been thinking about being glad to be rid of Rachel the other day, when she only broke this news to me this evening?"

"No, what I meant, Sue, darling, was simply that I was thinking that it would be a good thing if I could hear that Rachel was thinking of leaving us. And now, really rather incredibly, it seems that that wish is going to come true."

"Well, yes it does," said Susan. "But it does seem to me to be a rather wierd coincidence that Rachel should tell us today that she's planning to leave us soon, when you were thinking only a few days ago that it would be good if she were to go?"

"Yes, I know it may seem wierd, Sue, but... well, there it is! I know I'm going to be very upset about this, but I really do think that, underneath all my other feelings, I'm going to be very glad that this is happening, because, Sue, darling, I don't want to be in love with *anyone* - except you!" Jim suddenly realized that he was smiling again as he saw Susan's eyes sparkling at him, but, just as they came together in a close embrace they heard a familiar sound coming from somewhere upstairs.

"Julia!" said Susan. "We'd better go up and see what's going on there. It's high time that I went to see Ju anyway!"

"Yes, and I'm coming too," said Jim.

He was beginning to feel extremely fond of his little daughter, so now he was feeling almost happy as they climbed the stairs together and headed for the nursery. He knew, however, that the sense of relief he was feeling was only temporary, that his other emotions of shock and gloom would soon re-establish themselves, but at the moment such thoughts did not seem to matter at all. Tonight will probably be pure hell for me, he thought sadly, as the full implications of losing Rachel really sink into my mind... but I don't want to think about that now!

About half an hour later Jim and Susan were lying in bed together and talking. Jim had just switched off the bedside light, but neither of them felt ready to settle down for the night.

"Do you know, darling," said Susan, "that I nearly didn't give you that message from Rachel? I found it really hard, actually, to say what I had to say."

"Oh, Sue, I am sorry about that!" said Jim.

"But, darling, you needn't be sorry about it. After all, you didn't know about it until I told you."

"No, that's true; but as soon as you did tell me I guessed that it had been a real struggle for you."

"Yes, it really was!"

"But I expect it made it a little easier to tell because of John and Claire being there in the Drawing Room at the time?"

"That's exactly what I felt," said Susan. "It was a little easier to tell you because they were there. And it was good of you, darling, not to mind about that. But I know that you're feeling very upset, so I'm hoping that you'll be able to put it all out of your mind for now so that you'll be able to get off to sleep soon."

"Oh, I hope I can do that!" said Jim. But I don't think I've got much chance of dismissing all this from my mind and getting to sleep, he said to himself.

His surmise turned out to be more or less correct. He tried his best to make himself feel comfortable and relaxed, but he soon found that his situation was just as he had feared it would be; the turmoil in his mind had affected his whole body so that he did not feel in the least bit sleepy or relaxed. Eventually, however, mental exhaustion finally saved him as he fell into a light and fitful sleep.

Chapter Twenty-nine

It was Sunday morning, and the Walkers were getting ready to leave Rhodes Castle to return home to London. Now that she was about to go, Jim felt a sudden and quite unexpected wave of sadness come over him at the thought that he would not be seeing Claire again (probably) for quite a long while. But that depends on when we decide to go up to London for my maiden speech in the Lords, he reminded himself - unless Sue decides to go sooner for any reason.

"We've had an absolutely *lovely* time staying here," said Claire, "and it makes me feel really sad to think that we've got to leave you now to go back to London."

So Claire says that she feels sad too at having to leave us, thought Jim. But, after all, we've been with Claire and John all the time since the end of last year, and that's really quite a long time.

"Yes, it's been wonderful staying here," agreed John, "and we've enjoyed every minute of it - especially the trips that you organized for us, Jim."

"Oh well," said Jim, "they were nice, weren't they?"

"Especially the one to see the Giant at Cerne Abbas!" said Claire. "We've seen pictures of him, of course, but it was amazing to see the real thing!"

"It certainly was!" agreed John.

The time had finally arrived for the Walkers to say their final good-byes and to leave the Castle.

"Well, good-bye, Susan," said Claire, "and thank you again for giving us such a wonderful time, staying here." She embraced and kissed Susan, and then continued. "And just let us know the next time you want to come up to London, and we'll get things ready for you. Just one day's notice should be quite sufficient for us."

"But are you sure?" asked Susan.

"Oh, yes, quite sure," said Claire. "After all, you should remember that it's really your house, and so you should come whenever you want to."

"Well, that's very kind of you, Claire."

Claire turned to Jim, whose heart was already beating more quickly in anticipation of a possible kiss. While John was shaking Susan's hand, and thanking her politely for his stay at the Castle, Jim offered Claire his right hand to shake.

"Good-bye, Jim, and thank you again for guiding us on our tours around here, and for giving us a lovely time generally - and it won't be long, I expect, until we meet again!" Claire was smiling broadly as she leaned forwards and kissed Jim lightly on the cheek.

"Good-bye, Claire!" he managed to say, feeling that he wanted to go on to say more, but suddenly finding himself at a loss for words.

For a moment he was bewitched, held enthralled in a magical spell which had lifted him out of the dimensions of the real world. Then reality intervened, and he looked round anxiously at Susan's face, expecting to see there obvious signs of her displeasure at that kiss, but, to his surprise, she seemed not to have noticed that anything out of the ordinary had just happened.

Two minutes later he and Susan were watching Claire's car as it was driven away down the drive. They saw both Claire and John wave their arms through the car windows in a final gesture of farewell. They waved back to them, and then, a moment later, the car disappeared from their view beyond the white gate of the inner drive.

Jim and Susan remained standing where they were, each silently lost in their own thoughts. Then Susan spoke.

"It'll seem odd without them around the place, won't it?"

"Yes, it will," agreed Jim. "It's because they've been with us for a long time, Sue, that we've got used to them being a part of our life. We stayed with them in London for a long time, and now they've stayed here for the best part of a week."

"Yes, that's what it is. "Well, darling, we'd better be going in again; it's about time to be getting ready for church."

"Are you going to be reading this morning, Sue?"

"Yes," said Susan. "I'm reading the Epistle."

"Is it a well-known passage that you have to read?"

I wouldn't say that it is, but it's the passage set for today, the Second Sunday in Lent. And remember, darling, that you're reading the lessons at Mattins next Sunday morning!"

"Oh, gosh, so I am!" said Jim. He was by now quite well used to reading lessons in church on Sundays, but he still managed to feel qualms of nervousness every time he approached the lectern to read aloud.

*

The next morning Jim found that all thoughts of Claire had been wiped clean away from his mind as he woke from a very disturbing dream about Rachel Connor. However, although he woke to find disturbingly clear and beautiful images of Rachel floating tantalisingly in his mind's eye, he soon discovered that he could recall nothing from the action of the dream, which had so recently ended. But perhaps it's just as well that I can't remember now what actually happened in my dream, he thought, but I'm almost sure that it was another dream about her going away to Ireland so that I would never see her again – as usual!

*

Jim did not see Rachel on the day when the Connors left their home in Yetminster to set off for their new home in Ireland. When Susan explained to him what had happened he felt very upset and even a little angry that Rachel had not found an opportunity to say good-bye to him, but his feeling of resentment was somewhat assuaged when Susan told him that Rachel had left a note for him.

It was a Monday morning (the eighteenth of April), and Jim had set off at five minutes to nine in the car to drive to Sherborne as he had an appointment there with his dentist at half past nine. At around a quarter past nine Susan was in the kitchen, discussing the day's menu with her Cook, when there came a knock on the kitchen door.

"Come in!" said Susan. "Oh, good heavens, it's you, Rachel! I thought that it was tomorrow you were going to call in here before you set off?"

"It was going to be tomorrow, Lady Sandy," said Rachel, "but we've had to make a last minute alteration to our travelling plans, and that means we're setting off for Ireland this morning, instead of tomorrow morning, as we'd originally planned."

"So what's happened to make you change your mind about your departure day, if you don't mind me asking?"

"Well, it's just this, Lady Sandy," said Rachel. "I rang my Mum, who lives in Bristol, last night, to say good-bye and to tell her that we were setting off on Tuesday morning, so that we'd be reaching our new house in Bantry some time on Wednesday afternoon. I told her that that was our plan, but she wasn't at all satisfied with it. She said she really must see me to say good-bye in person before we leave for Ireland."

"Yes, I can quite understand that," said Susan.

"Yes; but I told her that we could probably come back over to England quite soon to pay her a visit, but she said that would not do at all. She *must* see me before we go away, she said; so you see, Lady Sandy, that really has left us with only one option: we've got to start from here one day earlier, and that means today – in about an hour from now, in fact."

"So you're setting off for Bristol this morning to go to say good-bye to your mother, and then you're going to moter on to – where do you cross from to reach Ireland?"

"From Fishguard, Lady Sandy, on a car ferry that'll take us over to Rosslare in County Wexford. But we're going to stay at my Mum's house tonight, and then moter on through South Wales tomorrow. You see we've already booked to cross to Ireland on Tuesday night's ferry from Fishguard, so we want to time the journey so that we can arrive there some time towards tomorrow evening. But it would be no use thinking that we could do all that journey in one day from here because of having to travel via Bristol as it's going to add a lot of extra miles to the journey – and, frankly, it's nowhere near the original route we'd planned to follow."

"Yes, I can understand that," said Susan. "Going via Bristol from here to South Wales must be a considerable diversion?"

"Oh, yes, I think so, Lady Sandy. "I'm no expert on maps, but I think that my husband's original plan was to head for Bath, and then Stroud, and then Gloucester. He said that we'd have to get to Gloucester because it's the lowest place where you can cross the Severn, so we'll still have to cross the river there tomorrow, and then head west through South Wales."

"I see," said Susan, although, in fact, she could not properly understand what Rachel was telling her without reference to a map. "I expect Jim would have chosen that way to get to Gloucester - the shortest way" But is it the shortest way via Bath and Stroud? she wondered.

"By the way, where is Jim?" asked Rachel. "I must see him to say good-bye."

"Oh dear!" said Susan. "But I'm afraid you can't do that now, Rachel - he's not here!"

"Not here? But where is he?"

"He had a dental appointment this morning, so he's gone in to Sherborne. You see, we both thought that it was tomorrow that you'd be leaving, so he was planning to see you tomorrow morning before you left for Ireland."

"Yes, but when was his appointment? Perhaps, if it was nine o' clock, I could just wait for him, although I did promise my husband that I'd be back home by a quarter to ten at the latest."

"But his appointment is for half past nine. I'm sorry, Rachel, but I'm afraid that the very earliest that I can expect him back would be about a quarter past ten, so it looks as if you'll have to miss seeing him.

Rachel Connor was silent for a moment as she considered the problem. Then she spoke again.

"But I think he'll be dreadfully disappointed, Lady Sandy, if I just disappear without having seen him to say good-bye. You know what I mean, I think?" She was looking Susan in the eye carefully as she said this.

"Oh, yes, I know what you mean, Rachel! said Susan. "He's heavily infatuated with you so, if he can't see you before you go, he's bound to be very disappointed. But - I'll tell you what - you could leave a message for him? I could lend you a pen and paper to write a message."

"Yes, that's a good idea! I'd better do that as I can't possibly wait until he gets back from Sherborne."

Susan took Rachel Connor into the Servants' Common Room (which was next door to the kitchen), opened a drawer in the dresser, and took out a notepad and a ballpoint pen, which she offered to Rachel. Then, while Rachel sat down at the table to write her message to Jim, Susan returned to the kitchen to continue her discussion with Cook. A few minutes later, the message written, Rachel returned to the kitchen.

"Well, that's it," she said. "I've left it on the table in there."

"I'll see that Jim reads it as soon as he comes in," said Susan.

"So are you off now, Rachel?"

"Well, I think that perhaps I might wait here for a few more minutes – just in case Jim appears."

"You're very welcome to stay here if you want to," said Susan, "but –" (she looked at her watch) "– I don't think that there's any chance of Jim being back for a while yet; it isn't even half past nine yet, so he won't have started his appointment."

"Ah, yes, you're right, Lady Sandy"

"But it's the thought of your daughter, Ailean, that worries me.

Is she really going to be all right, do you think, living all by herself in your house at Yetminster? That is the plan, isn't it?"

"Yes, Lady Samdy, that is indeed the plan, and Ailean has assured me that she's perfectly happy with it. You know, when we said Good-bye this morning when Ailean set off to come here to work, I half expected her to have second thoughts about it, and to be begging to be allowed to come with us to Ireland; but, no, she says that she'll be perfectly happy to go on living in our old house in Yetminster."

"Well, I call that really brave of her to take that attitude," said Susan, "but I hope that she understands what she is letting herself in for? But, you know, I'd be more than happy for her to come and live-in with Jim and I here in the Castle, where we could keep an eye on her."

"It's very kind of you to say that," said Rachel. "Now I did, in fact, take the liberty of telling her that if she finds the loneliness of living on her too much to bear she should move in to the Castle. I know that I really shouldn't have said that without first consulting you about it, Lady Sandy, so I hope you'll forgive me for that."

"You did quite right to say that, Rachel - quite right! As I said, I'd be more than happy for her to be living here if and when she wants to. But do you think she'll manage to do everything that needs to be done on her own? We could easily help her with some of her jobs - like buying her food, and cooking, and housework, and so on - if she finds that she could do with a little help."

"That would be good, Lady Sandy, if you could do that. It would put my mind at ease to know that you're going to look after her in my absence."

"Very well, then, I'll make a point of going round to Yetminster to see her when I can, and I think I could probably lend her my maid, Samantha, once or twice a week to do some housework for her; I'm sure that Sam would agree to that if I give her some time off work here to compensate for it."

The two women continued to talk for a few more minutes, but then Rachel Connor looked at her watch again.

"It's almost half past nine now," she said. "I'll have to be off in a minute or two."

"Don't let me keep you," said Susan, but even as she said it she knew that she was very much wanting to keep Rachel there, chatting with her. Oh dear, she thought, I don't want to let her go at all! This parting is going to be almost as painful for me, in a way, as it will be for Jim... "Ah, here comes Sam!" At that moment the door from the Common Room opened, and Samantha entered the kitchen.

"Oh, sorry; you're busy, Sue!" she said at once, turning to leave the room again.

"Stop!" said Susan quickly. "Don't go, Sam, unless you're very busy with something right now. You're just the very person I need to see now.

"All right!" said Samantha.

"Come and sit down here with us for a minute or two, Sam," said Susan. "Rachel's come to tell me that she has to leave us now to set off for their new home in Ireland, but first we just need to ask one favour of you."

"What can I do for you, then?" asked Samantha as she drew up a third wooden chair beside the other two chairs on which Susan and Rachel were already sitting.

A few words from Susan put Samantha in possession of the relevant facts.

"Yes, of course I'll do that for you," said Samantha. "I'll be delighted to give Ailean any help that she needs whenever she wants it."

"Oh, thank you so much, Samantha!" said Rachel, rising to her feet. "It's going to take a load off my mind to know that Ailean is going to get help in looking after her house. "But I must be going now!" She began to walk towards the door leading to the long passage to the Hall. Susan and Samantha had already risen to their feet to follow her.

"Oh dear, I *do* wish that you didn't have to go!" said Susan. "I didn't know that I was going to be so affected by this farewell, but I really will miss you, you know!"

"Oh, don't go on so, Lady Sandy - please don't!" said Rachel. "It'll make me feel even more upset than I already am; but it really is dreadful to think that I'm leaving here, and not coming back."

"We'll come and see you off anyway, Rachel," said Samantha.

"Yes, we'll certainly do that"!" said Susan.

They were walking slowly along the passage towards the Great Hall and the front door. When Samantha opened the front door (the inner door - the outer front door was already open) Susan was surprised for a moment to see a large black car standing out there instead of the small green car which she was used to seeing as Rachel's car. They saw that the back seat of the car was already piled so high with boxes and all sorts of things that it looked as if there would be little room left for any more baggage.

"Oh, I see that you've had to come here in your husband's car this morning," said Susan. "But, of course, when I think of it, you've got to leave your little green car behind now as you couldn't possibly take two cars with you over to Ireland."

"Yes, that's it, Lady Sandy," said Rachel, "but luckily I didn't have to sell my little green car. I've given it to Ailean as she's learning to drive now."

"Oh, that's good, Rachel! Is she having proper lessons now?"

"Not yet, but she soon will be. At the moment she's in the early stages of learning with her friend, who's two years older than her, and has recently passed the test."

"Is that a boyfriend?" asked Susan.

"No, but I rather wish it was!" said Rachel. "No, this is a girl, an old school friend of Ailean's, who also happens to live in Yetminster

- perhaps rather luckily! But I'd like to think of her finding herself a steady boyfriend, and settling down, and getting married presently."

"That must be every mother's wish for her daughter, Rachel. But we'll certainly do our bit here to keep her company when she's not working - she must come to share our meals as often as she needs to - and I'll ask her to come and have supper with us tonight, if she'd like to do that."

"That would be lovely for her, Lady Sandy," said Rachel. She looked again at her watch. "Oh, good heavens, it's gone twenty-five to ten! Quick! I must go!" She had been standing beside the car, but now she opened the driver's door and sat down in the driving seat.

"Good-bye, Rachel, and all the very best to you!" said Susan, quickly bending down and leaning forwards to shake the hand of her former Guide, and to give her a light kiss on the cheek.

"Good-bye and good luck, Mrs. Connor!" said Samantha, shaking Rachel's hand in her turn. "I hope we haven't made you late?"

"I'll be all right for time," said Rachel. "Good-bye, Lady Sandy, and thank you for saying you're going to look after Ailean. Good-bye, Samantha!"

The engine of the car was already running. Now Rachel released her handbrake, slipped it into first gear, and drove rapidly away, waving an arm for a moment through her partly opened window.

Susan and Samantha waved their hands and watched until the car disappeared from their sight.

"It's a pity she had to leave in such a hurry at the end," said Susan thoughtfully. "I felt that it was rather undignified for a farewell - didn't you, Sam?"

"Yes, I thought so too," said Samantha. "Mind you, it wasn't her fault that she had to be in a hurry, was it? But it's a very poor day to be travelling, isn't it? It's almost raining now." Both women looked up for a moment at the heavy grey sky of rain clouds, hanging over them menacingly.

"I think I can feel a few spots of rain in the air now," said Susan, "and it's pretty cool too standing out here. Let's get back indoors, Sam, before the rain comes on properly."

They turned and climbed the stone steps up to the front door.

"I hope Rachel didn't see Ailean anywhere in the gardens as she was driving away," said Samantha as she held the door open for Susan to pass through the doorway into the Hall.

"Oh, yes, to be hoped that she didn't!" said Susan. "She'll have said good-bye to Ailean once already this morning, and it would only be upsetting for both of them to have to do it again."

"But Jim will be *very* disappointed when he finds out what's happened," said Samantha. "I think you'd better tell him right away when he comes in that Rachel has had to leave for Ireland one day earlier than she'd planned. Or perhaps... you'd like me to break that news to him?"

"That's very sweet of you to offer to do that, Sam," said Susan, who had now sat down temporarily in the chair nearest to the front door, "but I really think that I ought to do that. Oh, I know he'll be angry, probably, when I tell him that Rachel's gone, and that he's missed his last chance of seeing her again; but, after all, it wasn't Rachel's fault that she had to leave us - I'd better remind him of that - and she has left that message for him - and that should cheer him up when I tell him about it."

*

Sod that Mr. Connor for taking Rachel away from me this morning so that I couldn't see her to say good-bye! said Jim to himself angrily as he stumped down the passage towards the door of the Common Room. It really is too bad that this should happen. And sod him for accepting this new job in Ireland, which means taking her away from me here! It's all his fault that this has happened, and I *hate* him for it! Ah...! There's Rachel's message to me on the table.

He had seen the message, a folded sheet of paper, lying on the table the moment he had entered the Common Room. He took the message, unfolded it, and began to read;

Dear Jim,

I am so sorry that I wasn't able to see you this morning to say good-bye, and that there wasn't time to let you know about our last minute change of plan. By the time you read this we'll either be on our way to Bristol, on the first leg of our journey to Ireland or, if not actually on our way, we'll be doing our final packing up at Yetminster. I hope you'll forgive me for not seeing you this morning, as I'd meant to, but there was really *nothing* I could do about it. We should reach Bantry on Wednesday evening, and then we'll send you a post card to let you know we've got there.

Well, Jim, although this is to say good-bye I don't want it to be a final farewell. I shall miss you and Susan and everyone at the Castle very much, but I do hope that you and Susan will come and visit us presently in our new home when we've had time to get settled in properly. You really must come, Jim: I'm looking forward to seeing you again.

With Best Wishes,
Rachel Connor.

And I'm certainly looking forward to seeing you again, Rachel! thought Jim. Or am I... really? Surely things will be better now between me and Sue with Rachel out of the way? Hadn't I been wishing before now that Rachel would disappear out of my life? And now that very thing has actually happened: she's gone!

As he had been reading through Rachel's message to him Jim had felt that his mood of bitterness was gradually changing. His feeling of simmering anger towards Rachel's husband was still in his mind, but the impact of Rachel's words was causing that anger to become buried in the back of his mind underneath some very different feelings, chiefly of pleasant surprise. He was, in fact, surprised that Rachel had written a message to him at all. In their brief meetings in and around the Castle he had always felt that she had never responded to him, when he had greeted her, with anything more than cold indifference. Yes, she had certainly been very much aware of his intense crush on her, but, apart from an occasional very brief smile, she had, he felt, never given the slightest encouragement to his love for her. Now, however, as he slowly and thoughtfully read through her message, and then re-read parts of it, it was, he thought, almost as if she was saying, "I love you, Jim!" "I shall miss you and Susan" he read. I shall miss *you*, Jim! Was that really what she was wanting to say to him – or was it not?

Then, suddenly, an idea came into his mind which turned his thoughts into a completely unexpected direction. He now found that he was remembering a train journey he had made some years ago on a beautiful April evening. In his mind's eye he saw before him Mr. Ruddock sitting in the driver's seat of the cab of a two-car diesel multiple-unit train, and there beside him was his guard, Tim Blencow, chatting with him. Then he found that he was seeing again the burning colours of a beautiful sunset through the windscreen of the cab. For a moment Jim was mystified, and even a little shocked by the appearance of these images from the day of his return home to Cockermouth, following his dismissal as the Guide of Rhodes Castle. How on earth could his brain have jumped so suddenly from thoughts of Rachel Connor to poignant images of a well remembered train journey?

Jim had by now forgotten that he had not meant to remain in the Servants' Common Room. His intention had been simply to go in there to find Rachel's message, to have a quick glance through it, and then to return at once to Susan who was sitting in the Green Drawing Room. But now, having read Rachel's message and started to think about it, why was he suddenly confronted with vivid memories of something that had happened a number of years before? It was a really bizzare turn of events, he thought, but something, surely, must have triggered it? But what was it? He now knew that he needed to find out what stimulus had been the trigger which had recalled those memories so vividly.

He closed his eyes, and now deliberately tried to recall more of the details of the final stages of that long train journey back to Cockermouth, but he soon realized that this approach to the problem was counter-productive. No, that doesn't work, he thought. He picked up Rachel's message and began to read through it again. "By the time you read this we'll either be on our way to Bristol..." he read; but at this point he abruptly stopped reading and gasped aloud as a sudden light seemed to shine in his brain. Yes, that's it! he told himself triumphantly. The problem's solved! It was just those words "by the time you read this" that suddenly reminded me of that train journey. I remember it well now. Sue had given me a letter in a sealed envelope which I wasn't meant to read until I was nearly back at Cockermouth, so I read it while I was sitting in Mr. Ruddock's train. And I believe that Sue had written those very same words in her letter to me: "By the time you read this you'll either be back at home, or perhaps you'll be sitting in a train somewhere near Cockermouth". I can't remember Sue's exact words, of course, but I'm sure she started a sentence with "By the time you read this..."

At that moment, however, Jim's happy train of thought was distracted as he heard the sound of footsteps and the tap of a walking stick in the passage outside the room. The door opened, and Susan came into the room. Jim looked up quickly, a smile on his face.

"Hello, Sue!" he said.

"Oh, darling, are you all right?" she asked anxiously. "Was it very upsetting, what Rachel wrote for you?"

"Oh, no, Sue, darling, it wasn't upsetting at all – honestly it wasn't!" As he spoke Jim, having stood up, was pulling out a chair from the table for Susan to sit down on.

"Thank you, darling," she said. "So is it all right?"

"It is all right about that," said Jim. "I'm sorry if you've been worried because I didn't come back to the Drawing Room when I'd said that I would, but I'd simply forgotten all about it. You see, that message set me thinking when I'd read it."

"What did it say?"

"She just said that she was really very sorry she'd had to leave without seeing me to say good-bye, and then she said that she'd miss both of us very much; and she wants us to come and visit them in their new home."

"We will, won't we, darling?" said Susan. "Yes, of course we must do that. Rachel told me that the country and the view around their new home is simply gorgeous!"

"I don't want to see her again!" said Jim dramatically. As he spoke the words with a careful deliberateness he was watching Susan's face carefully for her reaction, and, as he had expected, he saw at once a look of incredulity appear on her face.

"Do you really mean that, darling?" she said after a little pause.

"I think that I do. But you're surprised to hear me say that?"

"I am surprised!"

"Well, at any rate, Sue, let me put it this way: I honestly don't think that I'll mind from now on whether I see Rachel again, or not. That's what I was thinking about when you came in here just now."

"Oh, was it?"

"Well, Sue, darling, when I'd read Rachel's message there was something in it that reminded me of you, and reminded me that you're *far* more important to me than any other woman – including Rachel. There's one sentence in it which reminded me of a particular day, and then that reminded me of how much I love you. But look here, darling, I think that we should go back to the Drawing Room now as it's more comfortable sitting in there, and then I'd like to tell you all about it."

"That's a good idea!" said Susan.

As they were walking back along the passage towards the Green Drawing Room Jim said: "I don't mean, though, that I don't want to come with you to Ireland to visit the Connors in their new home. I'm sure you're right, Sue, that it would be lovely to go to Bantry to see what the country is like thereabouts. I suppose Rachel was speaking from personal experience when she told you about the gorgeous views around there?"

"Yes, she's been there before. Her husband is an Irishman, remember."

"Oh, yes, so he is. Yes, let's go there. It'll be something to look forward to - but *not* so that I can see Rachel!"

"Well, at any rate, Sue, let me put it this way: I honestly don't think that I'll mind from now on whether I see Rachel again, or not. That's what I was thinking about when you came in here just now."

"Oh, was it?"

"Well, Sue, darling, when I'd read Rachel's message there was something in it that reminded me of you, and reminded me that you're *far* more important to me than any other woman - including Rachel. There's one sentence in it which reminded me of a particular day, and then that reminded me of how much I love you. But look here, darling, I think that we should go back to the Drawing Room now as it's more comfortable sitting in there, and then I'd like to tell you all about it."

"That's a good idea!" said Susan.

As they were walking back along the passage towards the Green Drawing Room Jim said: "I don't mean, though, that I don't want to come with you to Ireland to visit the Connors in their new home. I'm sure you're right, Sue, that it would be lovely to go to Bantry to see what the country is like thereabouts. I suppose Rachel was speaking from personal experience when she told you about the gorgeous views around there?"

"Yes, she's been there before. Her husband is an Irishman, remember."

"Oh, yes, so he is. Yes, let's go there. It'll be something to look forward to - but *not* so that I can see Rachel!"

"Well, at any rate, Sue, let me put it this way: I honestly don't think that I'll mind from now on whether I see Rachel again, or not. That's what I was thinking about when you came in here just now."

"Oh, was it?"

"Well, Sue, darling, when I'd read Rachel's message there was something in it that reminded me of you, and reminded me that you're *far* more important to me than any other woman – including Rachel. There's one sentence in it which reminded me of a particular day, and then that reminded me of how much I love you. But look here, darling, I think that we should go back to the Drawing Room now as it's more comfortable sitting in there, and then I'd like to tell you all about it."

"That's a good idea!" said Susan.

As they were walking back along the passage towards the Green Drawing Room Jim said: "I don't mean, though, that I don't want to come with you to Ireland to visit the Connors in their new home. I'm sure you're right, Sue, that it would be lovely to go to Bantry to see what the country is like thereabouts. I suppose Rachel was speaking from personal experience when she told you about the gorgeous views around there?"

"Yes, she's been there before. Her husband is an Irishman, remember."

"Oh, yes, so he is. Yes, let's go there. It'll be something to look forward to – but *not* so that I can see Rachel!"

CHAPTER THIRTY

A fortnight after Rachel Connor had left for Ireland a post card and a small parcel were delivered to Rhodes Castle. Jim and Susan were in the Breakfast Room, and Mrs. Middleton and Julia were upstairs in the Nursery, when Jack, the butler, brought in the post to the Breakfast Room and handed it over to Susan.

"Oh, good, we've got a post card from Rachel at last!" she said, seeing the Irish stamp on the post card. "And what's this other thing?" Susan put the post card down on the table while she picked up a rectangular package containing something which was wrapped in brown paper. "Could be a book to judge by the shape and size of the thing?" she continued. "But I know what it is. Look, it's got an air mail sticker on it, and the stamps have got 'U.S. Postage' on them. It's from Jack Wonstannley!"

"It'll be his book about our ghosts," said Jim. "But shall we look at Rachel's card first, Sue?"

"You can have a first look at it now, darling, while I'm opening this parcel." Susan handed over the colour post card to Jim.

"I say," he said, "it *does* look like a nice place!" He was looking at the picture on the front of the card, which showed a very pleasant vista of rolling green fields stretching down a hillside to the blue water of a bay of the sea where there appeared to be a well wooded island not far out in the bay. He read the title printed on the bottom of the card before turning it over to read Rachel's message:

"View of Whiddy Island and Bantry Bay from near the summit of Mullaghneesha".

"Yes, doesn't it?" said Susan, who was busily cutting through the tape on the parcel with a spare knife from the breakfast table. "Are you going to read out Rachel's message, darling?"

"Yes, I'll read it aloud," said Jim.

Susan put the parcel down on the table so that she could listen properly while Jim read aloud the message that Rachel Connor had written on the back of her postcard.

"We arrived in Bantry as we'd planned on the Wednesday evening after we'd left Dorset. Our new house is lovely, and our views are simply fantastic! You can't actually see it in the picture on this card, but it's in a hollow on the side of the hill, looking down over the sea. We've had some very hectic days of settling in, of course, so there hasn't been any time yet for sight-seeing.

With Best Wishes, Rachel and Patrick Connor. P.S. Thank you for looking after Ailean and giving her supper at the Castle."

"Is that it?" said Susan.

"That's all," said Jim, "and you can see that Rachel didn't have any room left on the card to write any more, even if she'd wanted to."

"Ailean must have rung them up in their new house - or perhaps they rang her - but I'm glad to know that they know that Ailean's getting on all right."

Jim and Susan had, in fact, invited Ailean to have supper with them at the Castle on four occasions since her parents had left; and once they had gone to Ailean's house for supper in Yetminster.

Susan ripped the paper off the parcel to reveal a letter and a slim, dark blue hard-backed book, which was protected by a paper dust cover on which they saw a picture of the familiar sight of the south-east facade and the Great Tower of Rhodes Castle.

"That's nice, isn't it?" she said, looking at it admiringly.

"'The Ghosts of Rhodes Castle, by Jack Wonstannley and Dr. Philip Oakley'," read Jim from the dust-jacket of the book. "But I thought that we were going to have this book in a paperback version that we can sell in the shop? This hardback book would probably be too expensive for most of our visitors?"

"Yes, I think that is the idea that we're to have the book in paperback," said Susan. "I think that Jack has just sent us this one book in hardback so that we can see what it's like, and read it first ourselves - if we want to. He probably tells us that in his letter, which I'll open in a moment. And I hope he's telling us too that a first print-run of the paperback version will be delivered to us soon."

She picked up the enclosed letter, unfolded it, and began to read it.

"Yes. 'A consignment of one hundred paperback volumes will be delivered to your address within the next few weeks', he says. Good! We should, hopefully, be able to start selling the books at a profit."

"At a profit?" said Jim. "But do we know what they're going to sell for?"

"Yes, he says they're going to be priced at two shillings and sixpence each." Susan had already opened the book at the title page as she had been speaking. Jim got up out of his chair and stood just behind Susan (who was still sitting at her place at the breakfast table) so that he could look at the book over her shoulder.

"There's a Table of Contents," said Susan, who had turned over the title page. "Look, he's called Chapter One, 'Historical Outline'."

"So he has! He's obviously done a lot of work researching this." Susan turned over a few more pages.

"Oh, look, there's Beryl Buxton's grave!" said Jim suddenly.

"Yes, that must be a picture that Jack took the first time he was here," said Susan.

"I'm sure it is; and, if I remembrer rightly, he took two pictures in the Servants' Graveyard while I was doing that guided tour: one to show Beryl's grave in close-up, and one to show where it was in the whole of the graveyard."

"And this must be the close-up one, showing her name, her real name, Sarah Buxton, on it."

They were looking at an illustration in the book showing in close-up detail a rather plain gravestone. The title under the illustration read: "THE GRAVE OF SARAH (BERYL) BUXTON IN THE SERVANTS' GRAVEYARD".

"How well I remember that day!" said Jim chuckling at the thought. "You know, I thought at the time that that American man - we didn't know his name then - was being really tiresome, the way he was continually interrupting me, and going on about Beryl Buxton and her grave. He seemed to have an obsessive interest in her."

"But I don't think that we knew at the time that he was planning to write a book about her and about our other ghosts. It's all right, Sam, you can come in and clear the things off the table now; we finished breakfast ages ago, but we've got detained in here with some rather interesting post." Samantha had come into the Breakfast Room, but she seemed to be on the point of leaving it again when she saw that Susan and Jim were still there.

"We've had a post card from Rachel Connor, and Jack Wonstannley has sent us his book about the ghosts here in the Castle," said Jim.

"Oh, really?" said Samantha.

"Come in and have a look, Sam," said Susan. "Give yourself a minute or two off work to look at Rachel's card and to read her message."

"May I really?"

"Of course you may; it's not private." Susan handed the post card over to her maid, who pulled out a chair to sit down at the table.

"It looks really delightful, I must say!" said Samantha. She turned the card over to read the message on the other side. "Well, I'm sure they're going to enjoy living there," she continued, having read the card. "But, all the same, it was very clear that Rachel didn't want to move away from here. It was a shame that she had to go." She glanced quickly into Jim's face as she said this, but was rather surprised to see no response there.

"Yes, we thought so too," said Susan.

"And so that's the book about the Rhodes Castle ghosts?"

"Do you want to have a look at it now?"

"Oh, not now, Sue, if you don't mind, thank you; I'd rather be getting on with the jobs that need doing. But - I'll tell you what - perhaps I might have a quick look at that book at coffee time at eleven o' clock, if I could join you then?"

"Oh, please do, Sam!" said Susan. "That would be lovely. But I think that we ought to go out-of-doors for our coffee time today as it's such a lovely day, and looks like staying that way. What do you think, Jim, darling?"

"I think it would be a lovely thing to have our morning coffee in the garden somewhere," said Jim. "Were you thinking of the Private Lawn, Sue, or the summer-house?"

"I certainly was! It's just the morning to be out there and to relax and enjoy the cherry blossom!"

It was arranged that Samantha would bring the coffee tray out to the Private Lawn and join them for coffee there at around eleven o' clock.

"Oh dear!" said Jim. "It sounds as if one of the gardeners is mowing the Private Lawn just when we want to sit there." He and Susan, holding each other's hands, were ambling slowly along the path which lead to the little footbridge over the Rhodes Brook and the Private Lawn beyond it. "We may have to go somewhere else, Sue?"

"Oh, but let's just go and have a look at the lawn," said Susan.

"He may have nearly finished mowing it, you know, and then we could sit there in peace. Or perhaps, if we were to sit inside the summer-house with the door shut, if he isn't nearly finished we wouldn't really be bothered by the sound of the engine."

"Maybe," said Jim, but he said it doubtfully.

They walked on and then, just as they came to the bridge, the noise of the engine stopped abruptly.

"Good!" said Susan. "It sounds as if he's finished."

"He may be just emptying the grass bin?" said Jim. He glanced up for a moment at the huge old cherry tree. There was no time now to stop to admire the white cherry blossom seen floating against the blue of the sky behind it, but nostalgic old memories flashed through his mind for a moment, and then were gone. What mattered now was to find out whether it was going to be possible to sit peacefully on that lawn, or not.

They were still holding each other's hands as they walked on up the narrow, twisting path which lead through a gap in the screening bushes to the Private Lawn.

"Oh, it's Ailean!" said Susan suddenly as they came out onto the beautifully short new-mown grass of the Private Lawn.

"So it is!" said Jim.

Ailean Connor had at that moment just come out from behind the wooden summer-house; she was pushing a metal wheelbarrow with high sides which the gardeners used for collecting the grass cuttings when mowing.

On the lawn, near the summer-house, stood a small motor mower (not the large machine with a seat; this would have been unsuitable for use on a small lawn of irregular shape such as the Private Lawn was). Ailean was wearing a standard issue green gardener's teeshirt and blue jeans, while on her head, by way of a sunhat, was a white cotton peaked cap. All the gardeners at Rhodes Castle were given green teeshirts to wear as a sort of uniform while at work in the grounds; they were emblazoned on the chest with the legend: RHODES CASTLE in red letters, with the Dalmane coat of arms enclosed within a small circle above it.

Ailean waved a hand cheerfully as soon as she saw Susan and Jim approaching.

"Hello, Lady Sandy!" she called out. "I'll go now if you want to sit here."

"Oh, no, don't do that!" said Susan. "I can see that you've very nearly finished mowing this lawn so you'd better finish it first. Jim and I are going to sit out here, but we'll be going into the summer-house first to get out the deck chairs."

"Well, it shouldn't take me more than two or three minutes to finish this mowing," said Ailean.

"And then come and join us here for a coffee break, Ailean!"

"May I really? I'm not supposed to have another break until lunch time, you know."

"Don't worry about that, Ailean; just tell Mr. Ashcroft, when you see him, that I asked you to come and sit with us while we have coffee here. Oh, and you'd better go first, when you've finished the mowing, to the kitchen to get yourself an extra cup, or to get Samantha to bring you one if you find her there."

"Oh, thank you very much!" said Ailean.

Jim and Susan went into the summer-house, while Ailean Connor re-started the engine of her mowing machine. There were only a few short strips of grass near the middle of the lawn still left to be mown, and three minutes later she had the job completed. Jim and Susan, meanwhile, had brought out five deck chairs and a round wooden table from the room in the summer-house, and had set them down on a part of the lawn which was already mown. In addition to Ailean they were expecting Mrs. Middleton and Julia to join them on the lawn, as well as Samantha. Susan had gone upstairs after she had left the Breakfast Room to see the baby and her nanny, and had invited Mrs. Middleton to join them (if it was still warm and sunny) on the Private Lawn for eleven o' clock coffee. Julia, of course, would be coming out in her perambulator.

Ailean pushed the mowing machine to the edge of the lawn and left it there.

"I'll put it away later," she said. I just need to go and wash my hands now, and then I'll go to the kitchen, and then I'll be back here."

Ailean disappeared rapidly by another path which lead into the surrounding bushes. Jim knew that she was going to visit the new outdoor toilet which had been installed in a clearing in the bushes, a facility which was intended mainly for the gardeners.

It must be rather awkward for Ailean, he thought, being the only female member of the gardening staff. No doubt the men are used to disappearing into the bushes when they need to have a pee – but Ailean would hardly dare to do that!

Jim looked at his watch.

"We've got here rather early," he said. "It's only eight minutes to eleven now."

"Well, that's good, isn't it?" said Susan. "It means that we can have a few minutes on our own here before any of the others come. They probably won't come punctually for eleven o' clock anyway."

"And we don't really want them to do that," said Jim.

They sank back into their deck chairs to enjoy the warmth of the sunshine, the songs of the birds, and the quiet peacefulness of the private garden. They were not expecting Ailean to reappear at any moment; another new path, with a new footbridge over the brook, had been made to connect the new outdoor toilet with the main part of the gardens, and no doubt Ailean would go by that way to reach the kitchen when she left the toilets.

Jim closed his eyes, the better to enjoy the peacefulness of the Private Lawn, and to let thoughts come to him as they would. Ailean looks like a fairy, an Irish fairy, wearing that green top, he thought. It suits her so well... and, yes, I've got to admit that she is a damnably attractive girl anyway! That intense look in her sparkling brown eyes! That sly smile she always gives me when we meet! Oh, good heavens, I'd better look out - surely I don't want to fall in love with *her*! But I mustn't, I mustn't!

Or is it already too late? No, *surely* I'm not falling in love with her... or, at least, not yet! Dear me, it was bad enough being in love with Rachel, and I still *am* in love with Rachel, but that love is going to fade away slowly with time as my memories of her fade away. That love already is fading away, but it would be a dreadful thing, surely, to replace Rachel with Ailean - the daughter instead of her mother. No, but there's a different factor in the relationship this time, isn't there? I'm almost sure that Ailean is in love with me! And it's not just because of my title either; I'm pretty sure that she's been attracted to me ever since the first time that we met each other in the Estate Office. And she was wearing that bright green mackintosh! Dark hair, dark eyes, and wearing a green top... yes, she is like a little fairy... and she's *very* attractive! Yes, that's all very well - but what am I going to do about it?

At this point in his daydream Jim's train of thought was suddenly broken as Susan spoke.

"Are you remembering that other time when we were out here, and it was like this?"

"Oh, yes!" he said, opening his eyes with a jerk. "Well, *no*, not really," he added, realizing that he was not sure to which time Susan was referring.

"Darling - what do you mean?"

Jim suddenly laughed as he realized that what he had just said did not make sense.